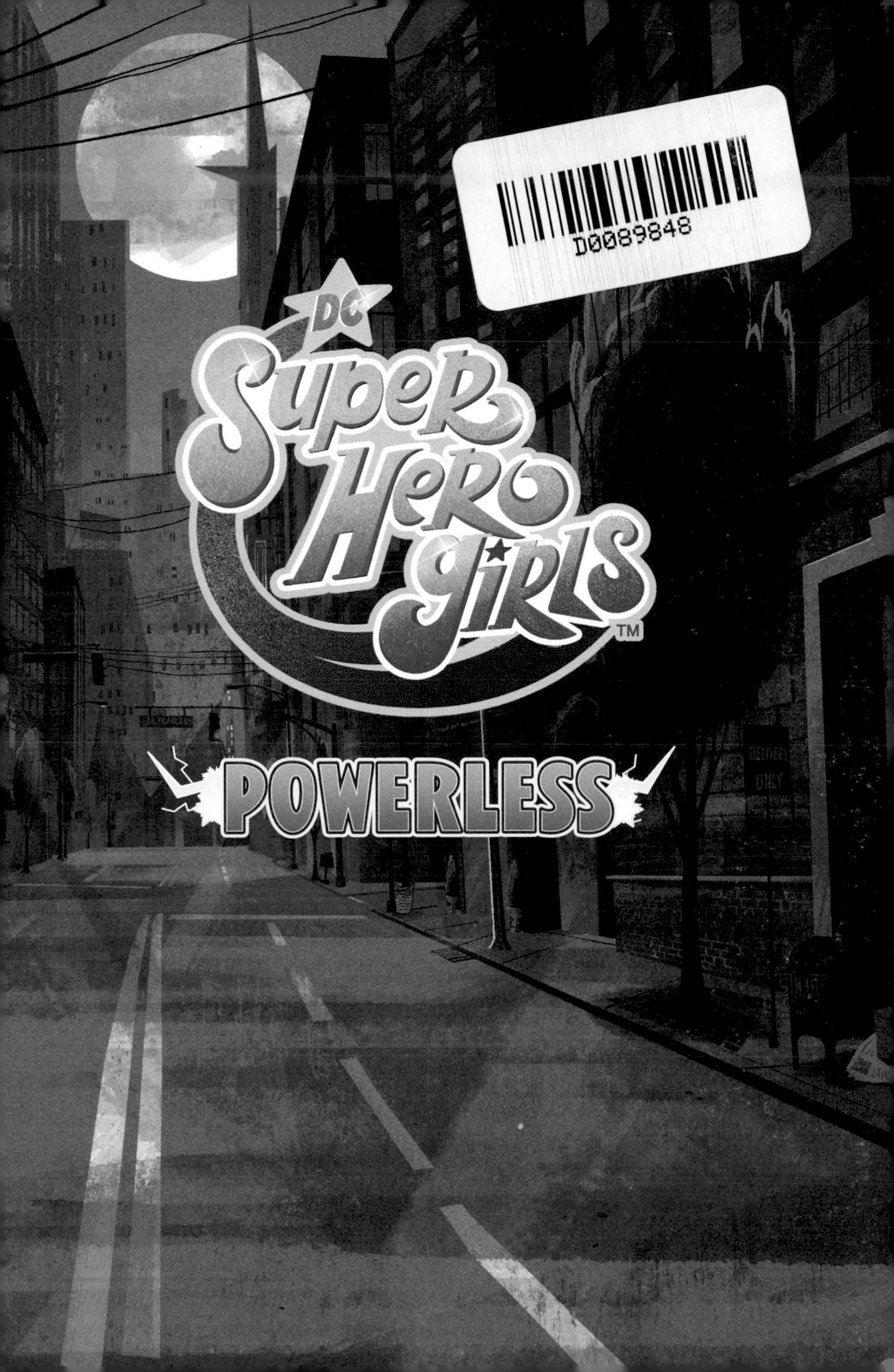
DC
Super Hero Girls™
POWERLESS
DELIVERY ONLY

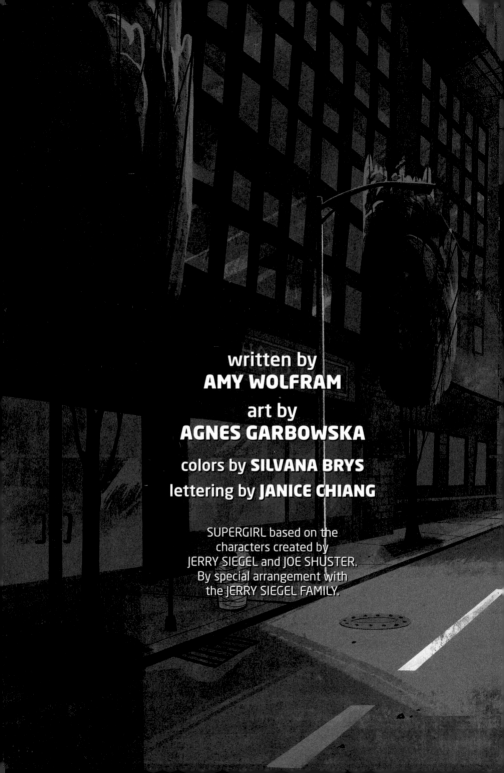

written by
AMY WOLFRAM

art by
AGNES GARBOWSKA

colors by **SILVANA BRYS**
lettering by **JANICE CHIANG**

SUPERGIRL based on the
characters created by
JERRY SIEGEL and JOE SHUSTER.
By special arrangement with
the JERRY SIEGEL FAMILY.

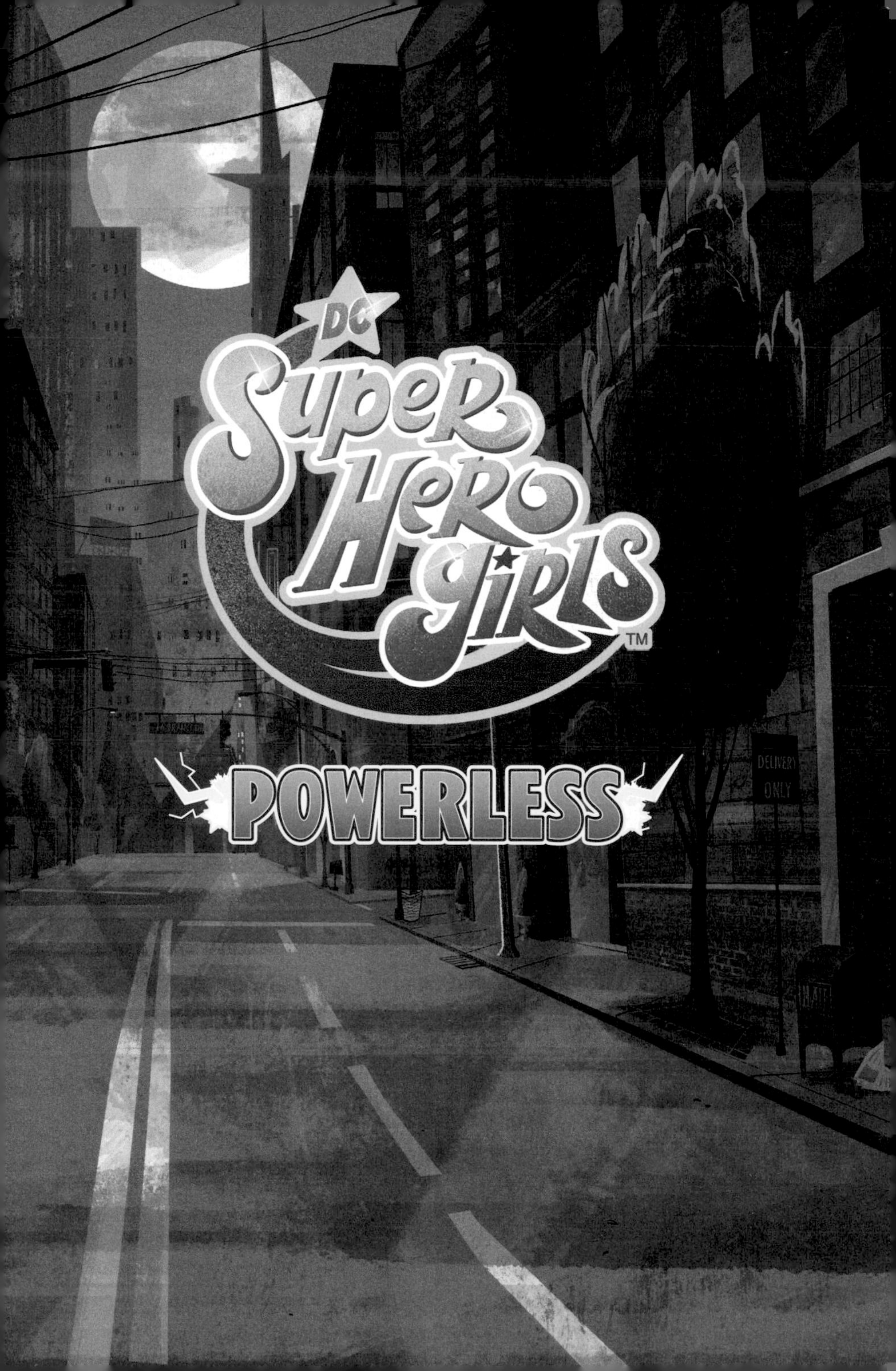
DC
Super Hero Girls™
POWERLESS
DELIVERY ONLY

KRISTY QUINN Editor
STEVE COOK Design Director - Books
AMIE BROCKWAY-METCALF Publication Design

BOB HARRAS Senior VP - Editor-in-Chief, DC Comics
MICHELE R. WELLS VP & Executive Editor, Young Reader

DAN DiDIO Publisher
JIM LEE Publisher & Chief Creative Officer
BOBBIE CHASE VP - New Publishing Initiatives & Talent Development
DON FALLETTI VP - Manufacturing Operations & Workflow Management
LAWRENCE GANEM VP - Talent Services
ALISON GILL Senior VP - Manufacturing & Operations
HANK KANALZ Senior VP - Publishing Strategy & Support Services
DAN MIRON VP - Publishing Operations
NICK J. NAPOLITANO VP - Manufacturing Administration & Design
NANCY SPEARS VP - Sales

PEFC Certified

This product is from
sustainably managed
forests and controlled
sources

PEFC
PEFC/29-31-337   www.pefc.org

DC SUPER HERO GIRLS:
POWERLESS

Published by DC Comics.
Copyright © 2020 DC Comics. All
Rights Reserved. All characters,
their distinctive likenesses, and
related elements featured in this
publication are trademarks of DC
Comics. DC logo is a trademark
of DC Comics. The stories, characters, and incidents featured
in this publication are entirely
fictional. DC Comics does not read
or accept unsolicited submissions
of ideas, stories, or artwork.

DC - a WarnerMedia Company.

DC Comics, 2900 West Alameda
Ave., Burbank, CA 91505
Printed at LSC Communications,
Crawfordsville, IN, USA.
2/7/2020. First Printing.

ISBN: 978-1-4012-9361-1

Library of Congress Cataloging-in-Publication Data

Names: Wolfram, Amy, writer. | Garbowska, Agnes, illustrator. | Brys,
   Silvana, colourist. | Chiang, Janice, letterer.
Title: DC super hero girls : powerless / written by Amy Wolfram ;
   illustrated by Agnes Garbowska ; colored by Silvana Brys ; lettered by
   Janice Chiang.
Other titles: Powerless
Description: Burbank, CA : DC Zoom, [2020] | Series: DC super hero girls |
   "Supergirl based on the characters created by Jerry Siegel and Joe
   Shuster. By special arrangement with the Jerry Siegel family." |
   Audience: Ages 8-12 | Audience: Grades 4-6 | Summary: When the electric
   grid and Gotham's cloud computing technology get knocked out on the same
   night, the Metropolis High Hamsters must figure out how to deal with the
   city's loss of power.
Identifiers: LCCN 2019049056 (print) | LCCN 2019049057 (ebook) | ISBN
   9781401293611 (trade paperback) | ISBN 9781779503688 (ebook)
Subjects: LCSH: Graphic novels. | CYAC: Graphic novels. |
   Superheroes--Fiction. | Electric power failures--Fiction.
Classification: LCC PZ7.7.W6 D35 2020 (print) | LCC PZ7.7.W6 (ebook) |
   DDC 741.5/973--dc23
LC record available at https://lccn.loc.gov/2019049056
LC ebook record available at http://lccn.loc.gov/2019049057

TABLE OF CONTENTS

chapter one
LINKED IN

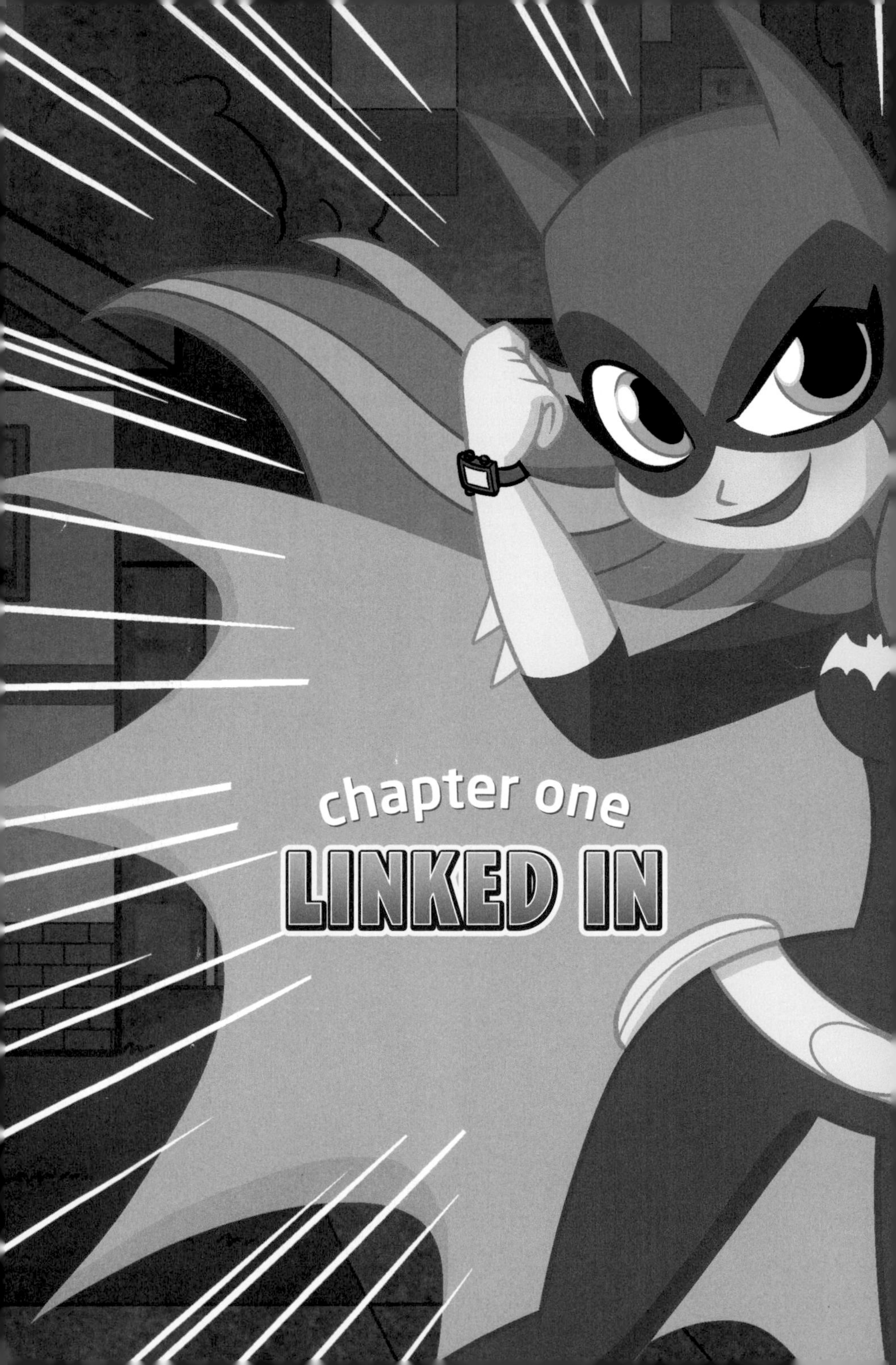

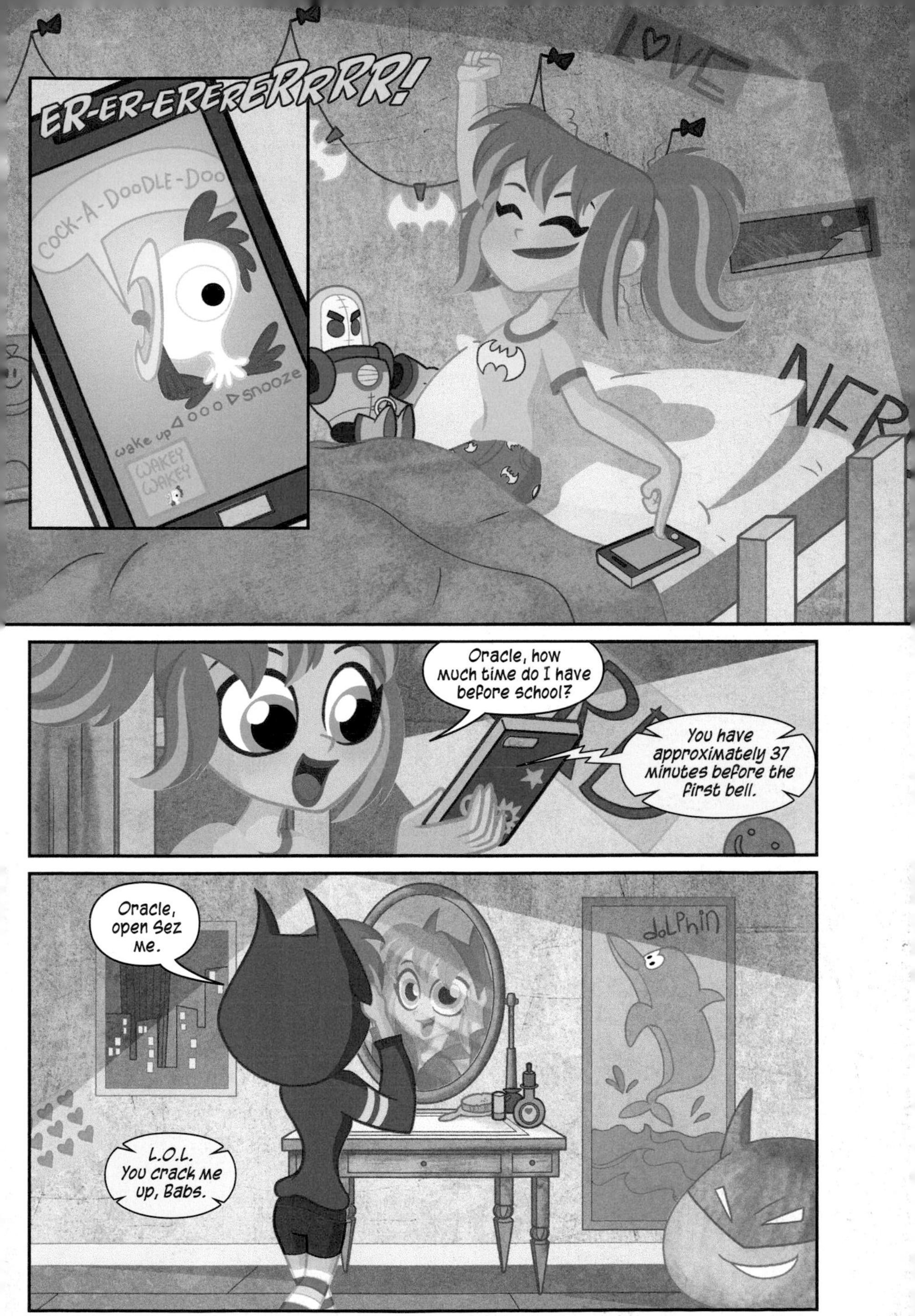
ER-ER-ERERERRRRR!
COCK-A-DOODLE-DOO
wake up
snooze
WAKEY WAKEY
LOVE
NER
Oracle, how much time do I have before school?
You have approximately 37 minutes before the first bell.
Oracle, open Sez me.
dolphin
L.O.L. You crack me up, Babs.

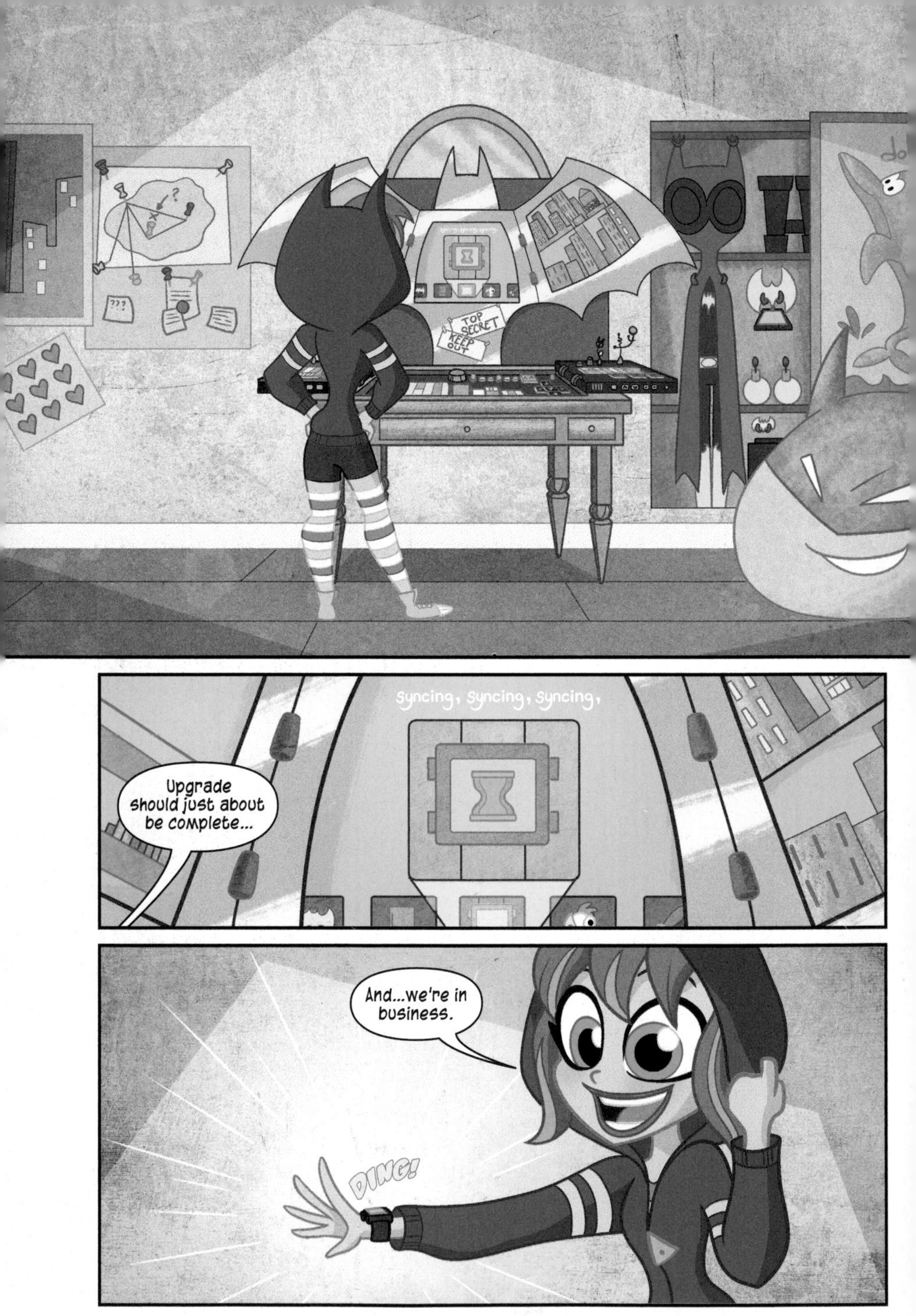
TOP SECRET
KEEP OUT
syncing, syncing, syncing,
Upgrade should just about be complete...
And...we're in business.
DING!

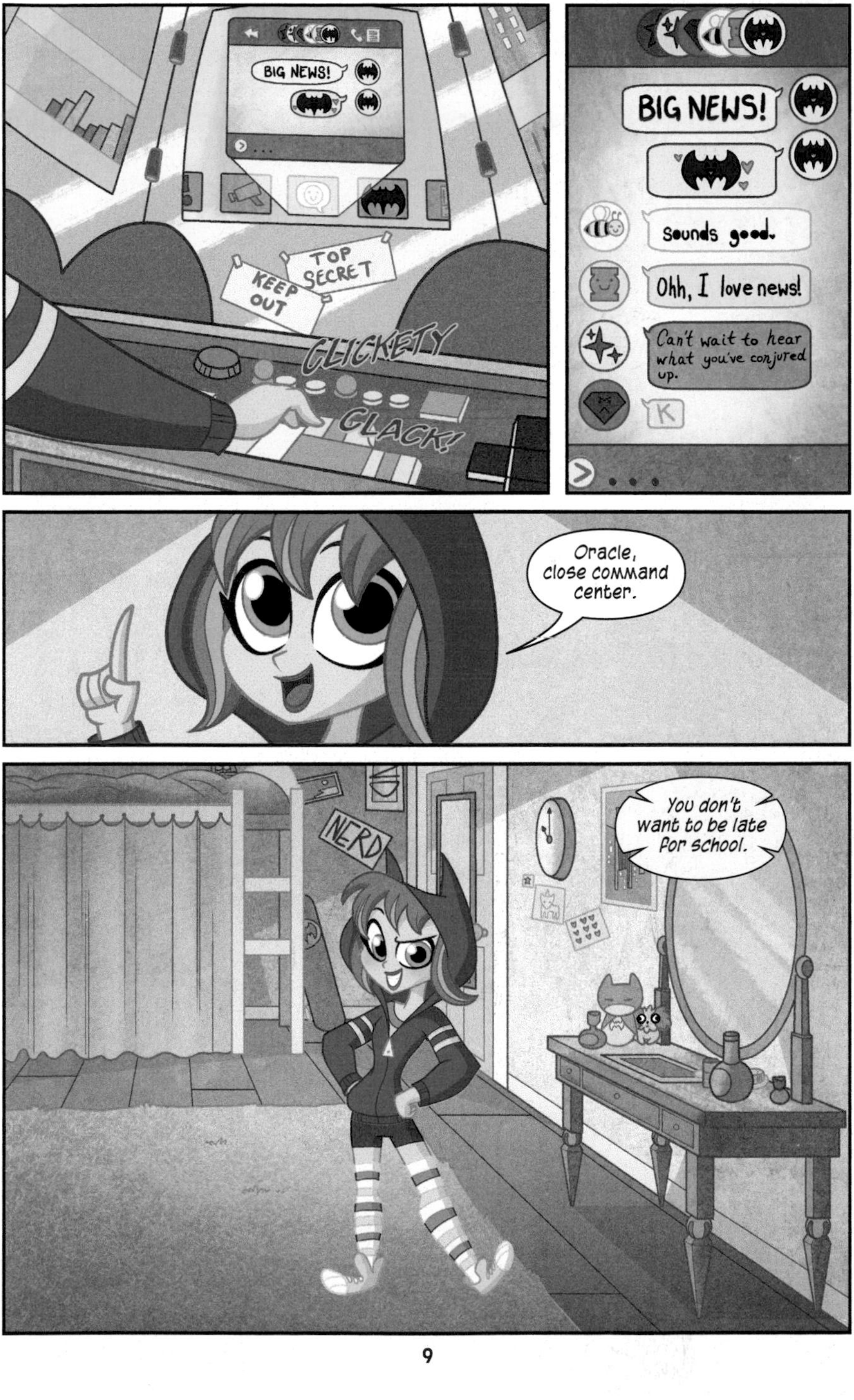
BIG NEWS!
TOP SECRET
KEEP OUT
CLICKETY
CLACK!
BIG NEWS!
sounds good.
Ohh, I love news!
Can't wait to hear what you've conjured up.
K
Oracle, close command center.
NERD
You don't want to be late for school.

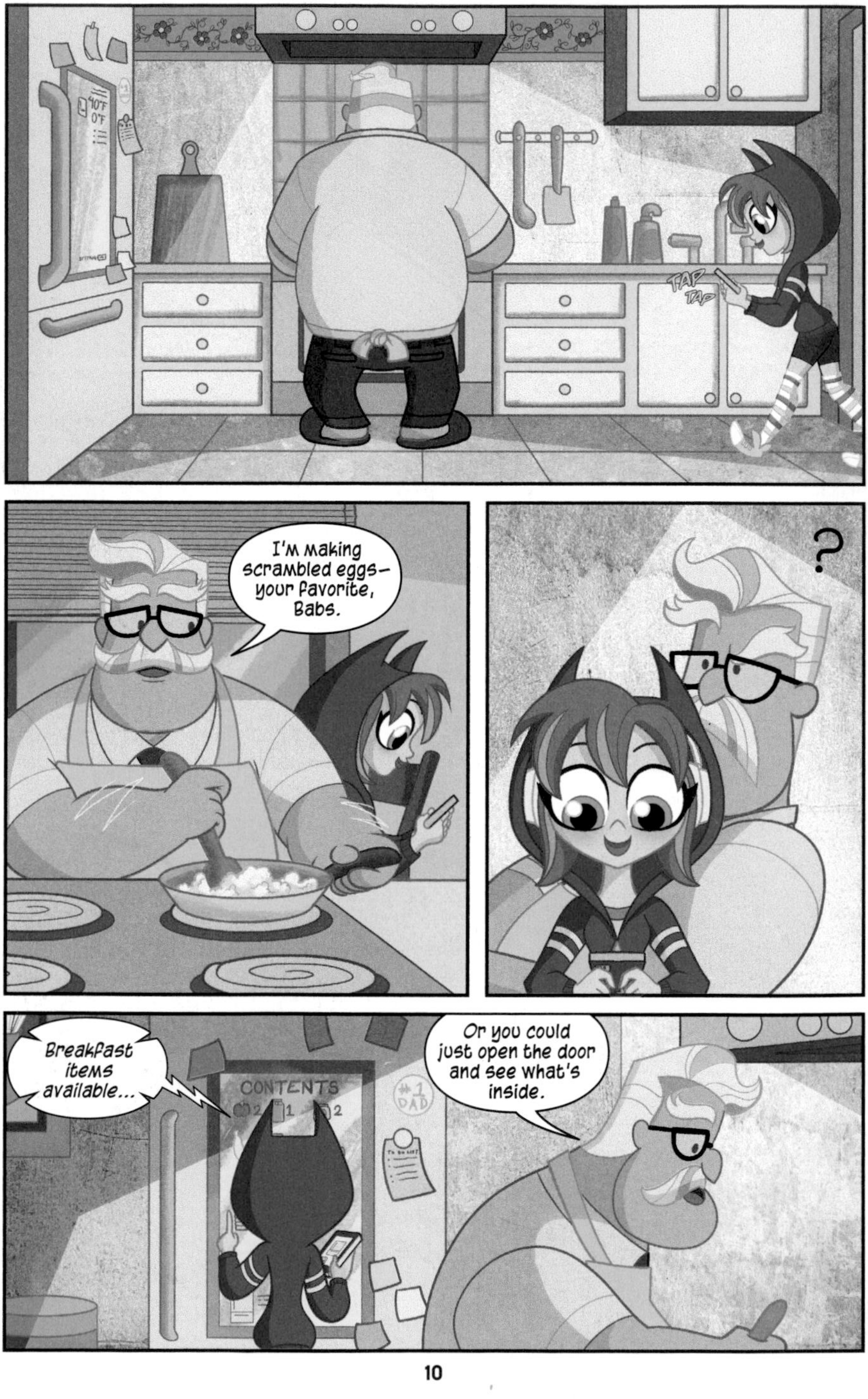
40°F
0°F
TAP
TAP
I'm making scrambled eggs—your favorite, Babs.
?
Breakfast items available...
CONTENTS
#1 DAD
Or you could just open the door and see what's inside.

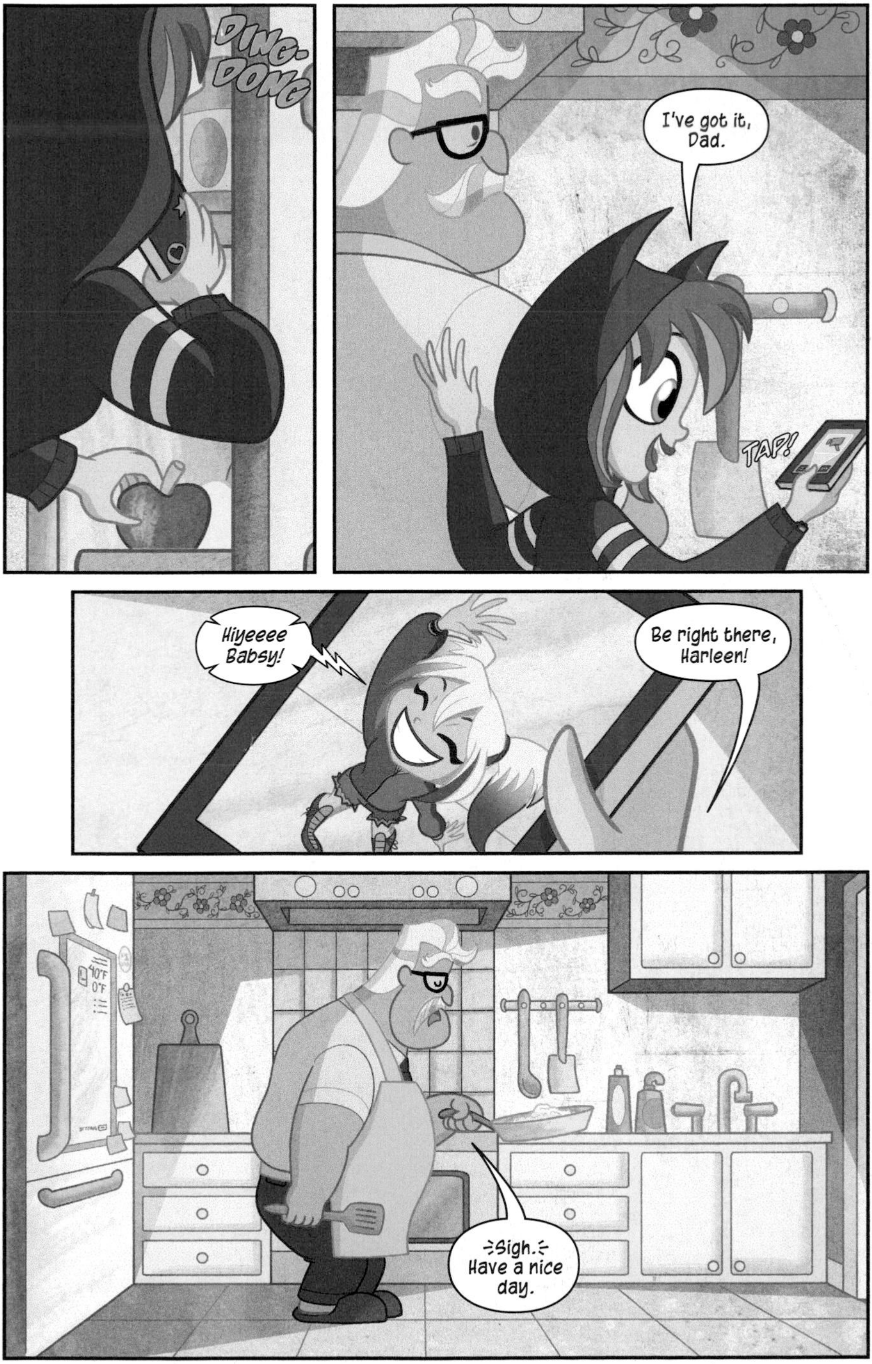
DING-DONG
I've got it, Dad.
TAP!
Hiyeeee Babsy!
Be right there, Harleen!
Sigh. Have a nice day.

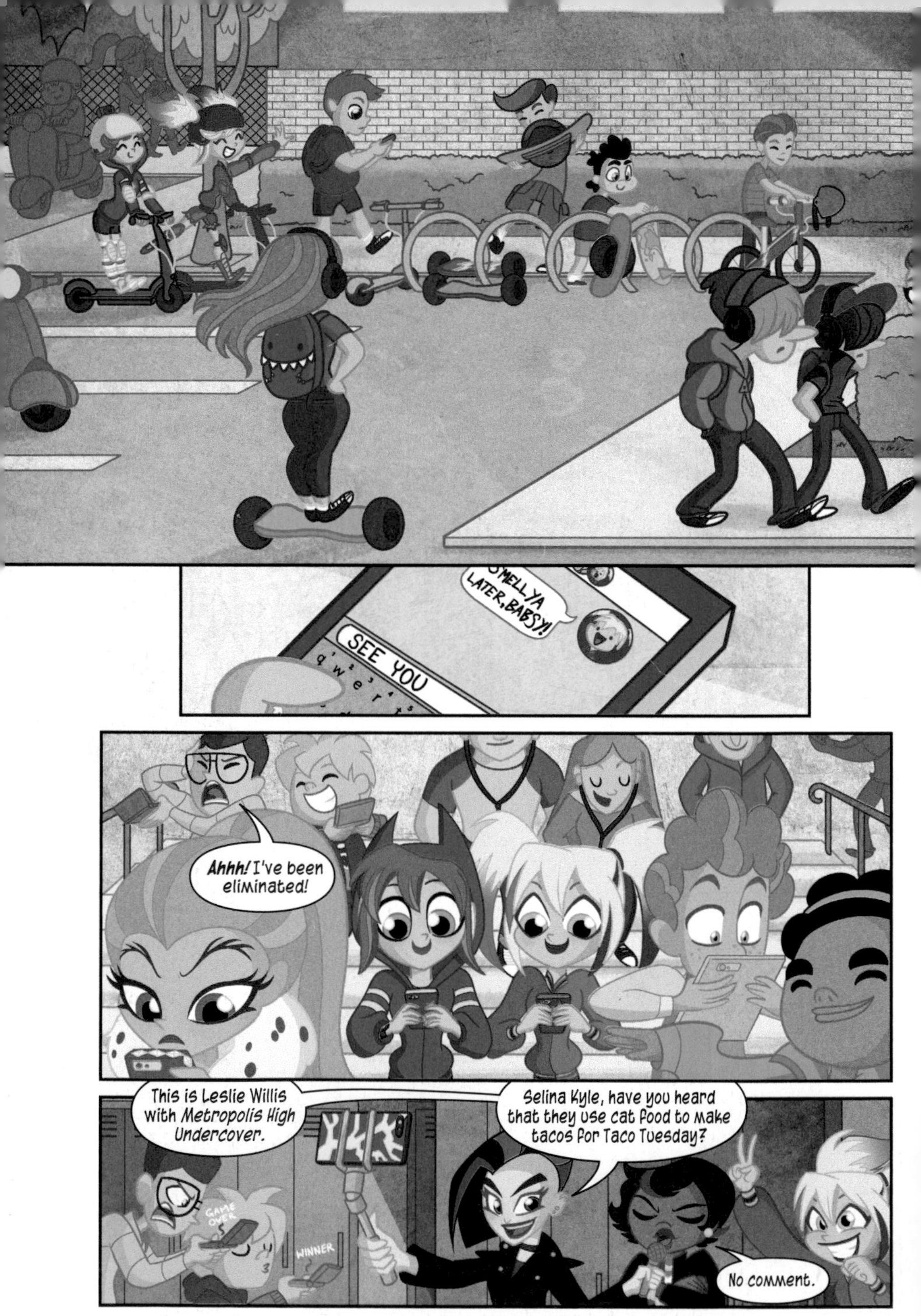
SMELL YA LATER, BABSY!
SEE YOU
Ahhh! I've been eliminated!
This is Leslie Willis with Metropolis High Undercover.
Selina Kyle, have you heard that they use cat food to make tacos for Taco Tuesday?
GAME OVER
WINNER
No comment.

Okay, Hamsters, we're *live* in the cafeteria. Miss Betty, what is the secret ingredient in these tacos?

TODAY'S SPECIALS
MYSTERY SPAGHETTI

FRIES
•POUTINE
•CHILI
CHEESE
•CHILLY

Just swipe your card and go!

You hear that, fellow students? What are they hiding?!

FRIES
•POUTINE
•CHILI
CHEESE

Karen, Zee, what do you think the Bat-news is from Babs?

SWIPE

KOMBU

Jessica.

...uh, I meant *Babs*-news about something that is totally not related to superheroes whatsoever.

FRIES

MYSTERY SPAGHETTI

Good save.

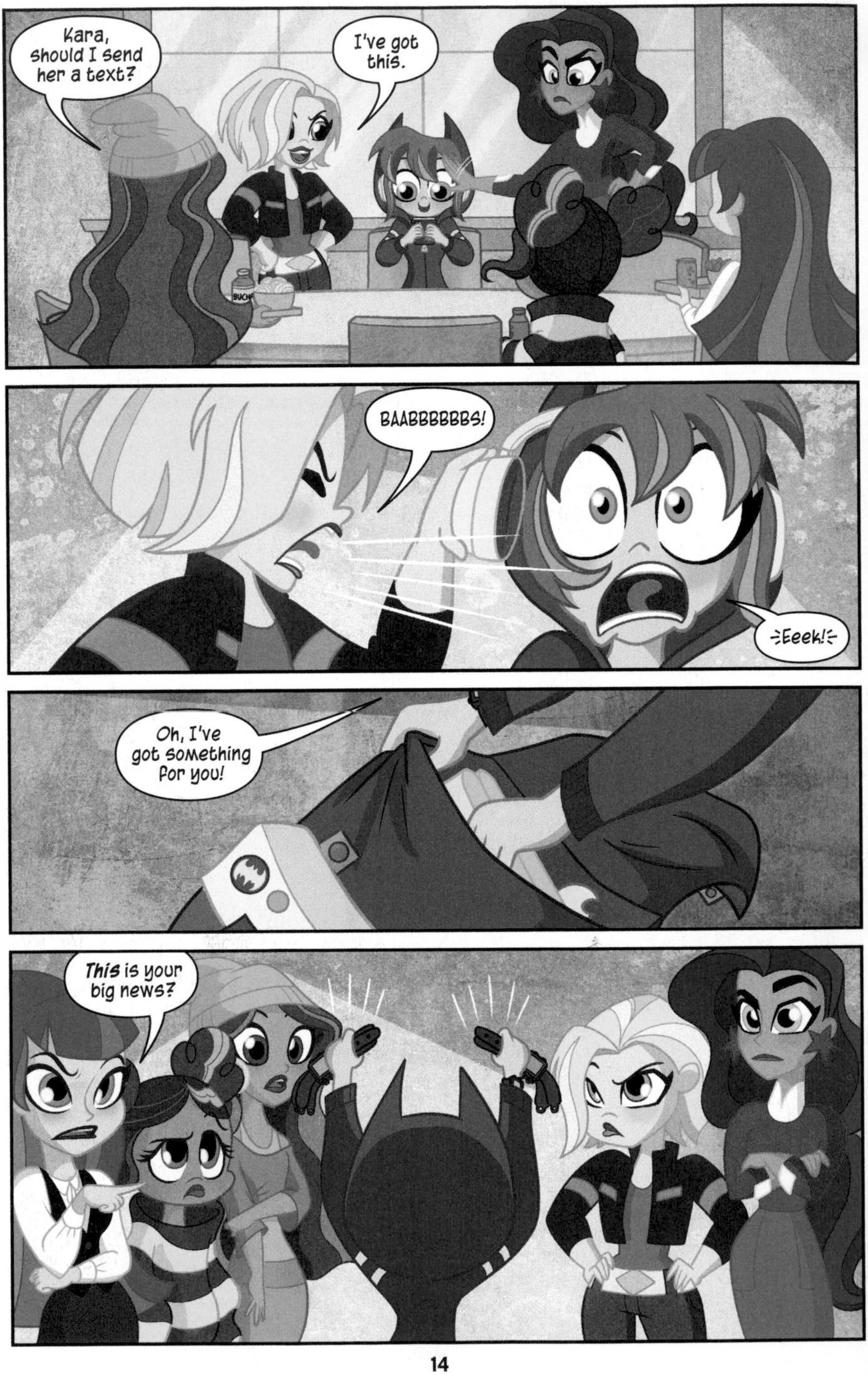

Kara, should I send her a text?
I've got this.
BAABBBBBBS!
Eeek!
Oh, I've got something for you!
This is your big news?

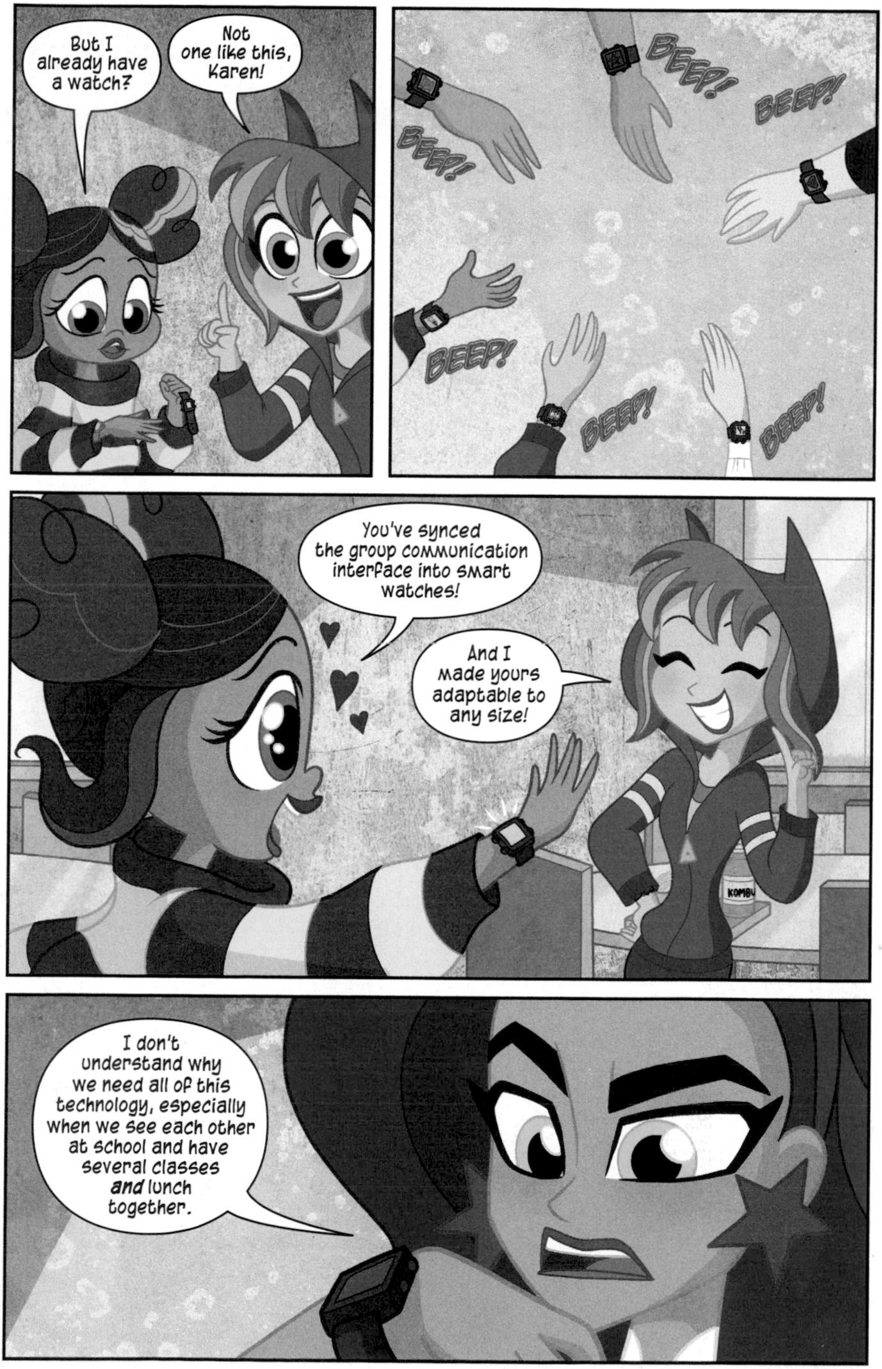

But I already have a watch?
Not one like this, Karen!
BEEP!
BEEP!
BEEP!
BEEP!
BEEP!
BEEP!
BEEP!
You've synced the group communication interface into smart watches!
And I made yours adaptable to any size!
KOMBU
I don't understand why we need all of this technology, especially when we see each other at school and have several classes *and* lunch together.

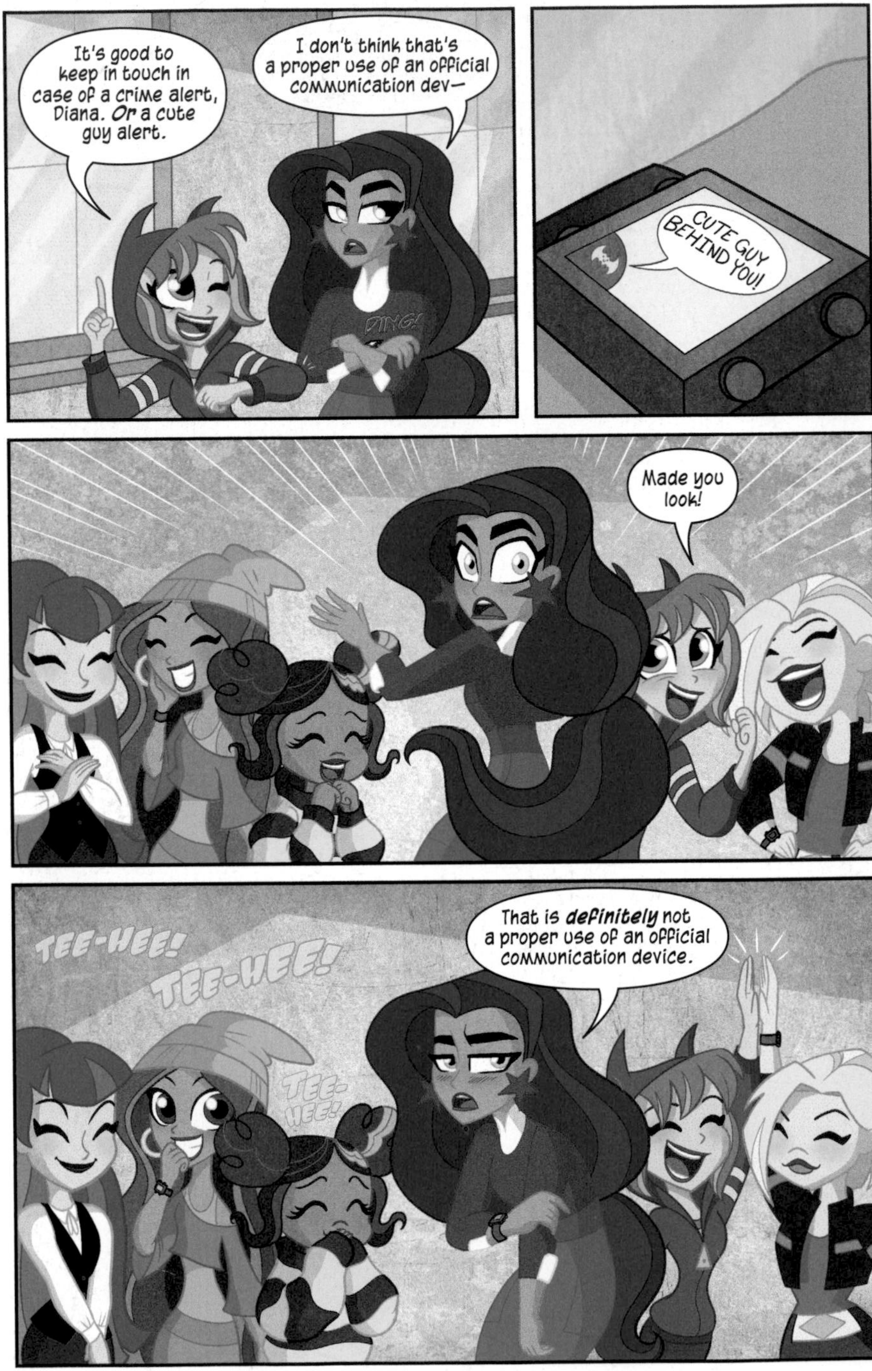

It's good to keep in touch in case of a crime alert, Diana. *Or* a cute guy alert.
I don't think that's a proper use of an official communication dev—
DING!
CUTE GUY BEHIND YOU!
Made you look!
TEE-HEE!
TEE-HEE!
TEE-HEE!
That is ***definitely*** not a proper use of an official communication device.

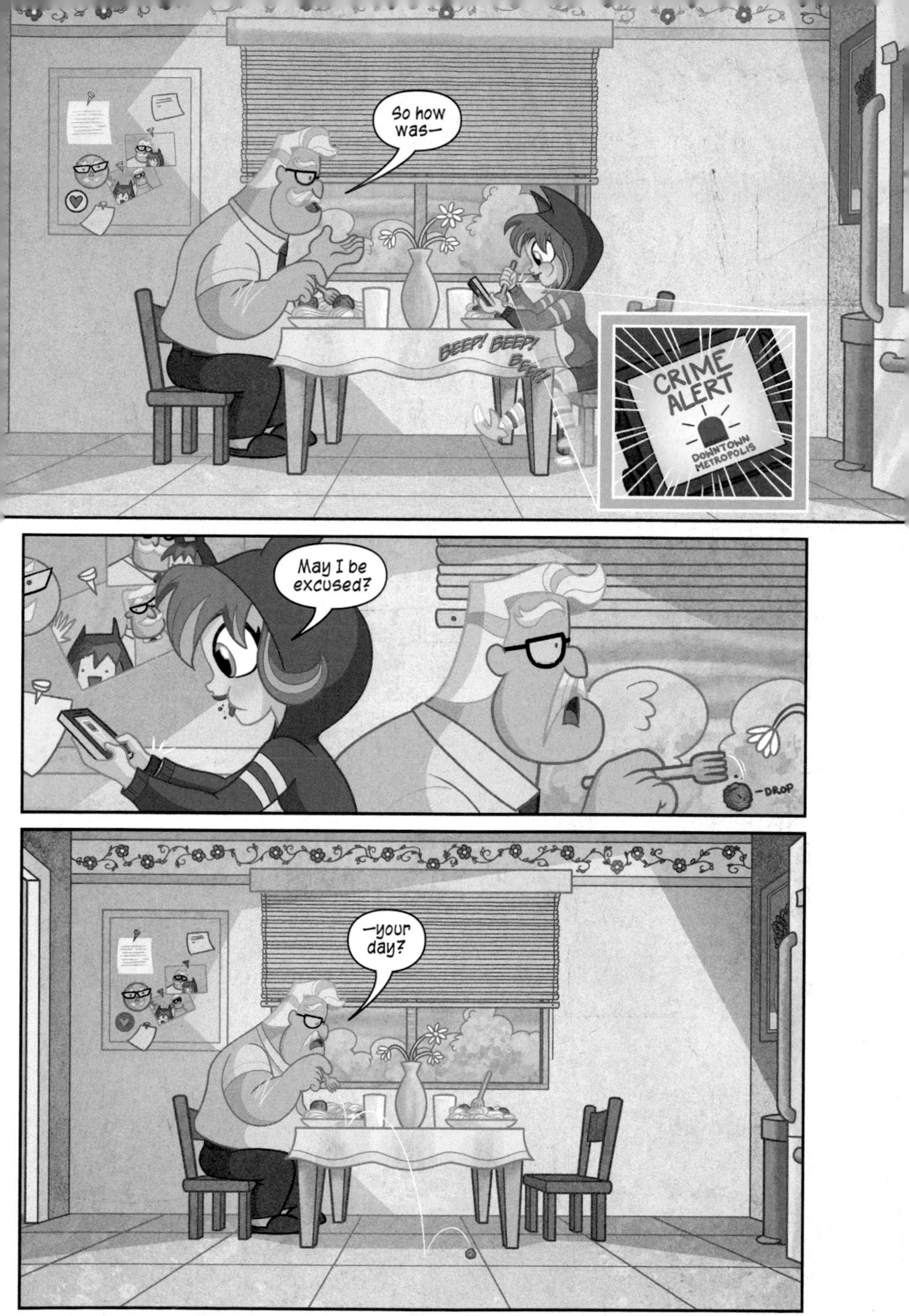
So how was—
BEEP! BEEP! BEEP!
CRIME ALERT
DOWNTOWN METROPOLIS
May I be excused?
-DROP
—your day?

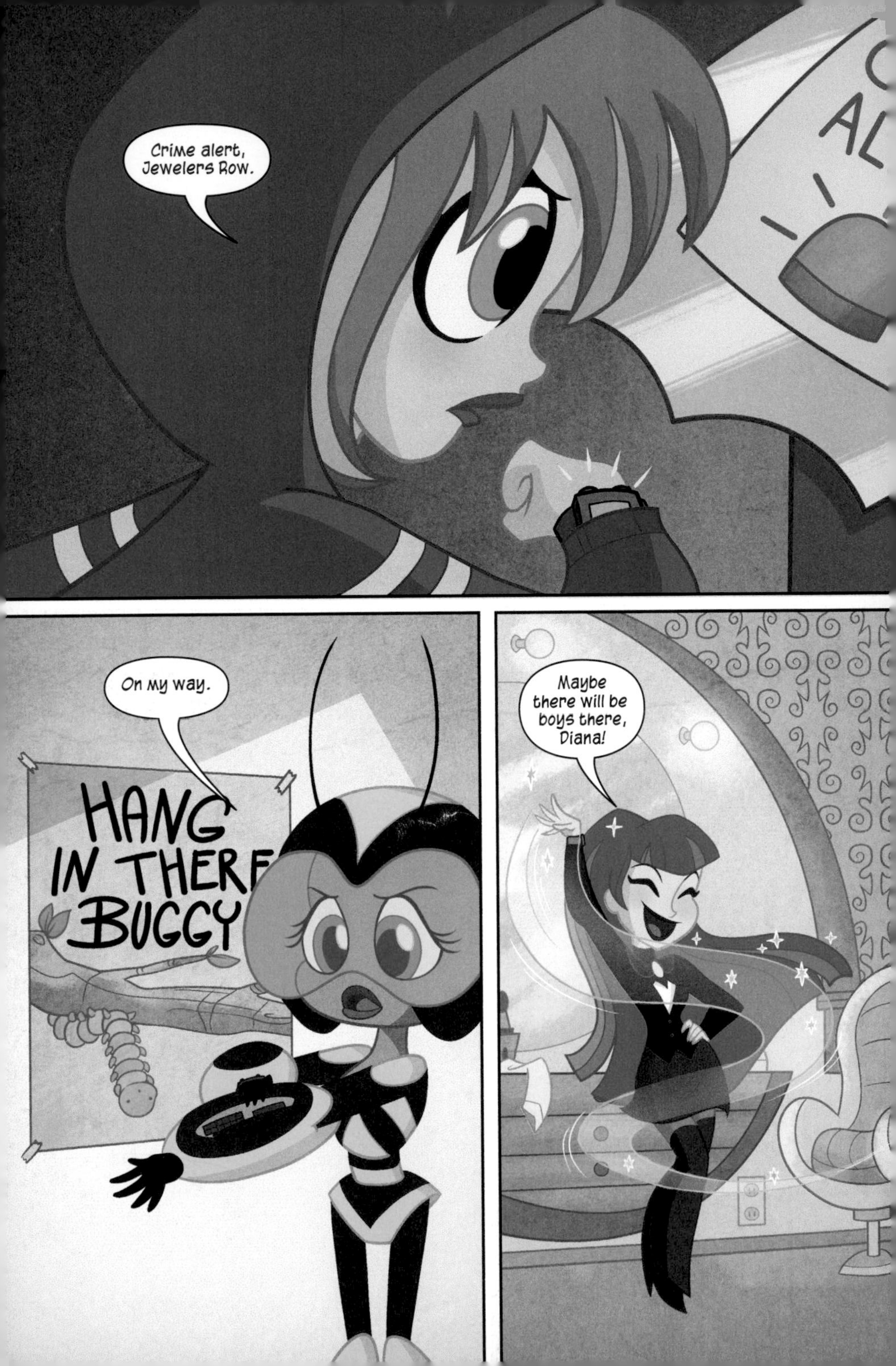
Crime alert, Jewelers Row.
On my way.
HANG IN THERE BUGGY
Maybe there will be boys there, Diana!

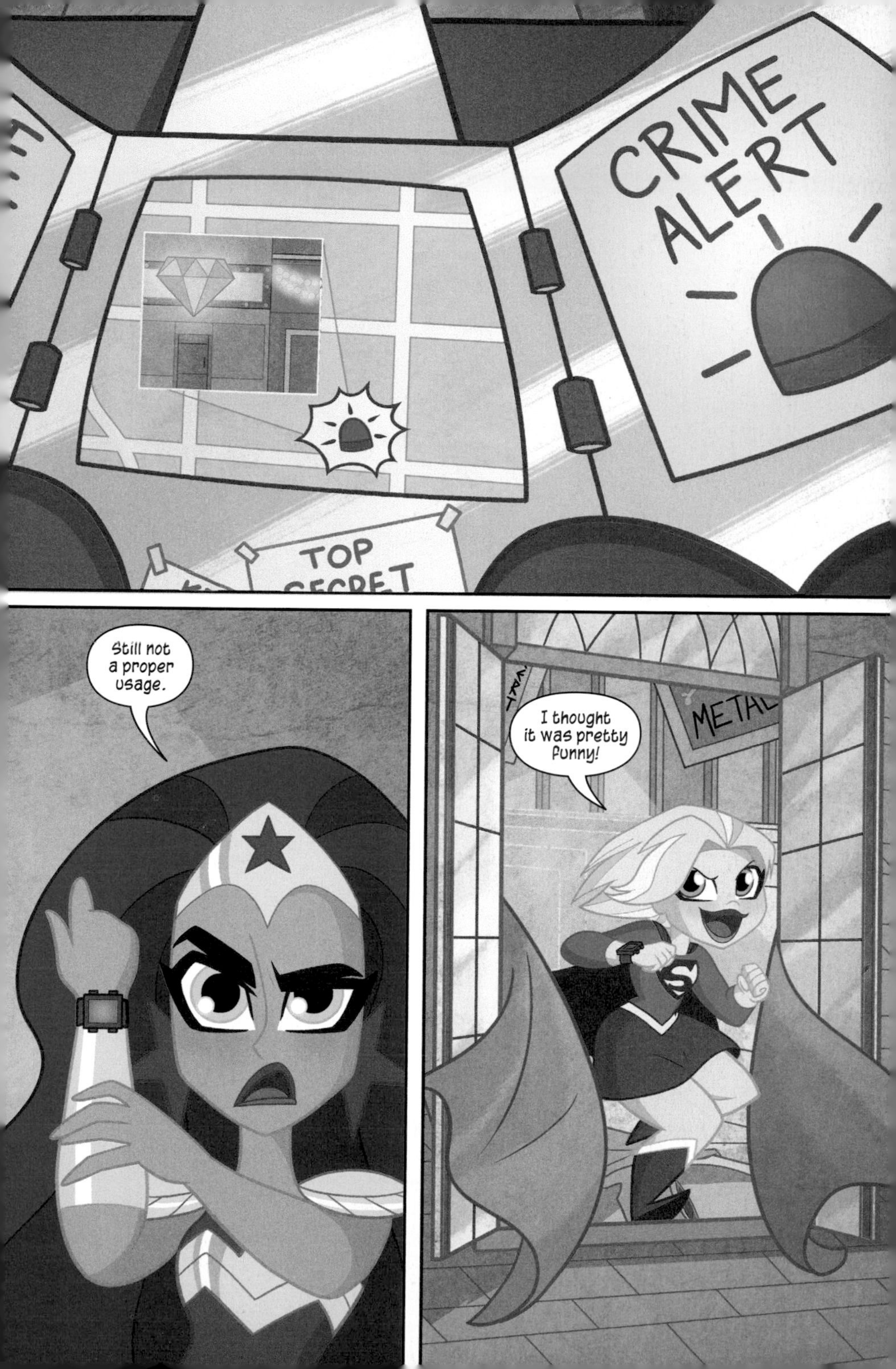
CRIME
ALERT
TOP
SECRET
Still not a proper usage.
METAL
I thought it was pretty funny!

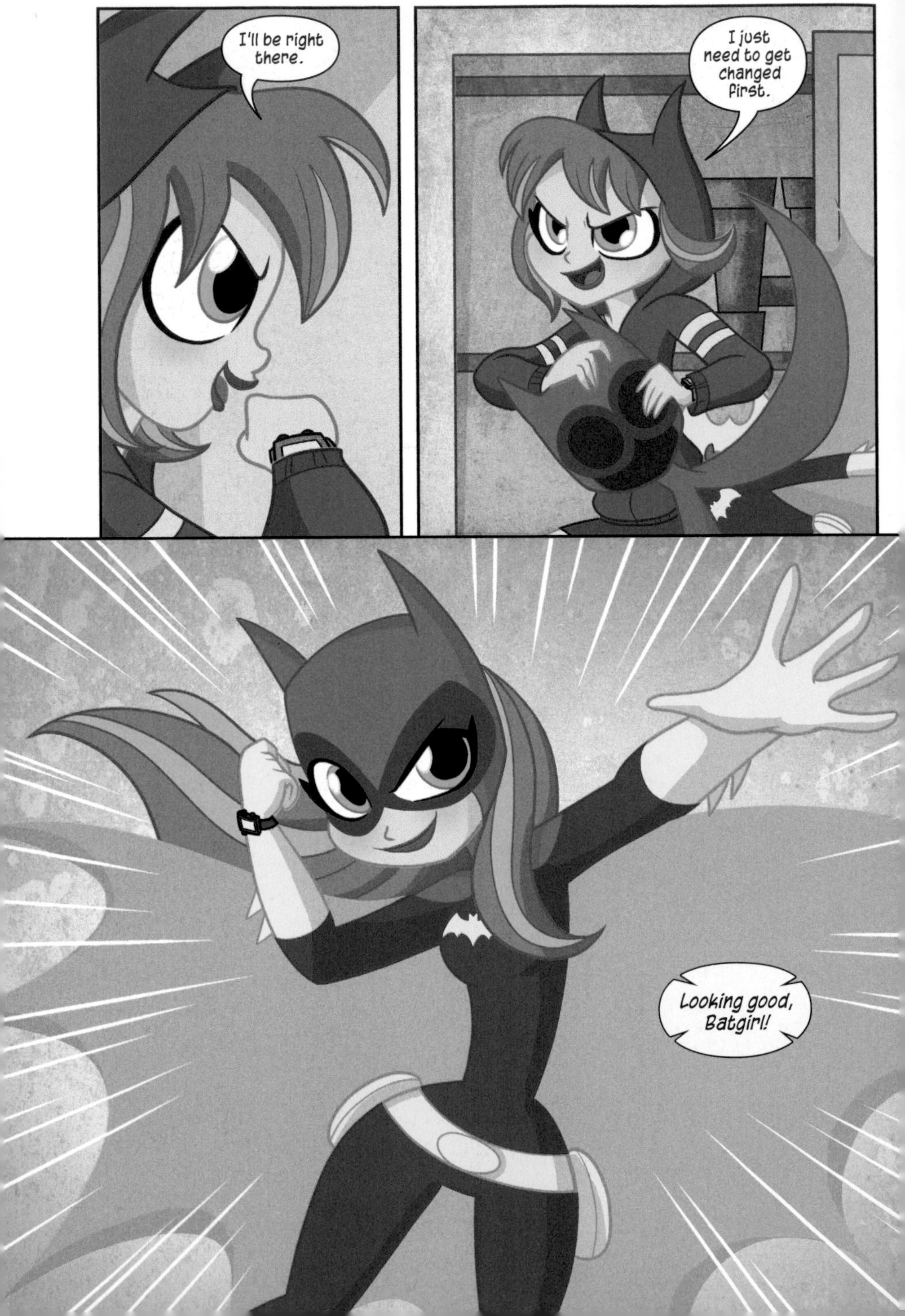
I'll be right there.
I just need to get changed first.
Looking good, Batgirl!

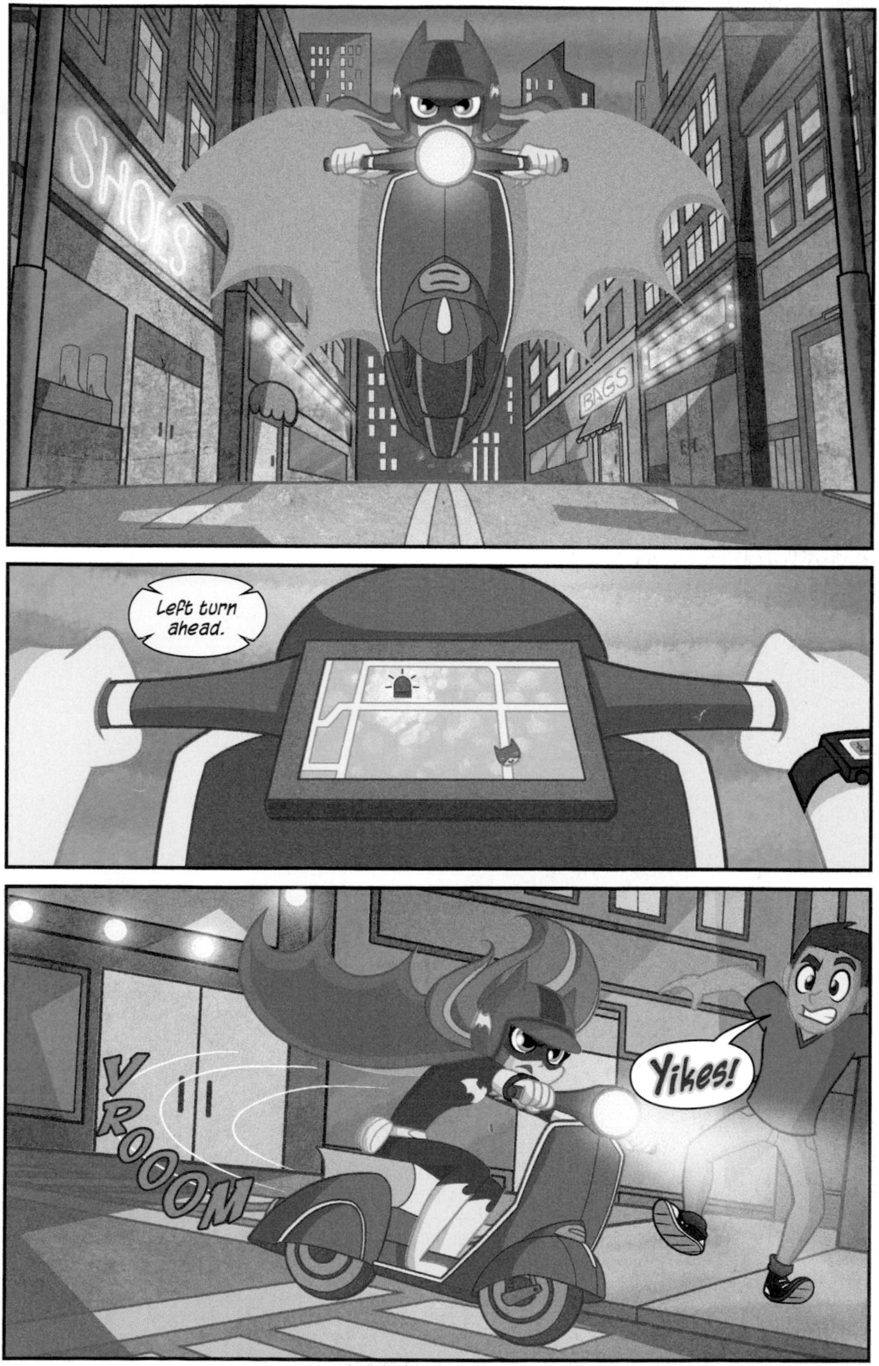
SHOES
BAGS
Left turn ahead.
VROOOM
Yikes!

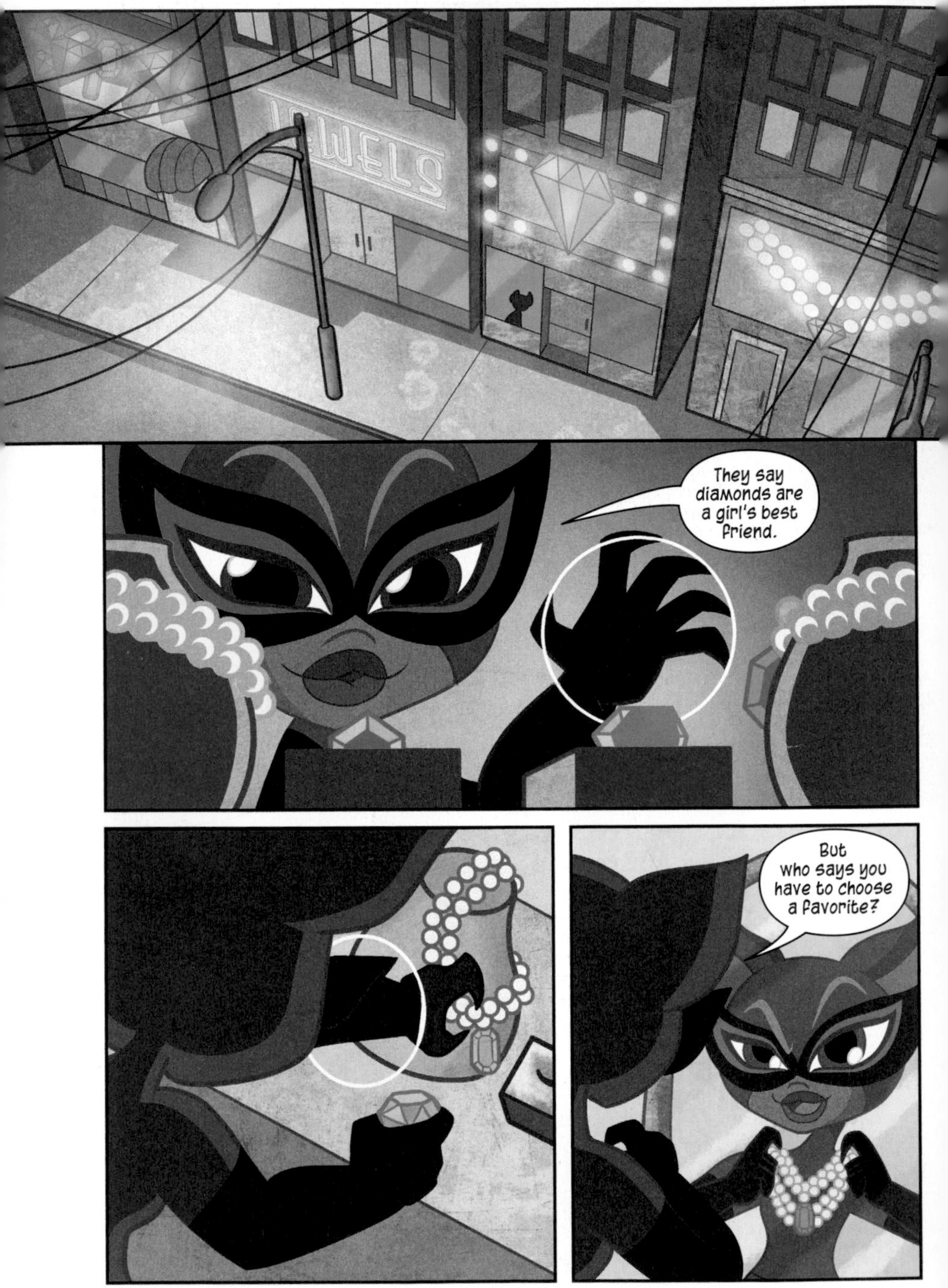
JEWELS
They say diamonds are a girl's best friend.
But who says you have to choose a favorite?

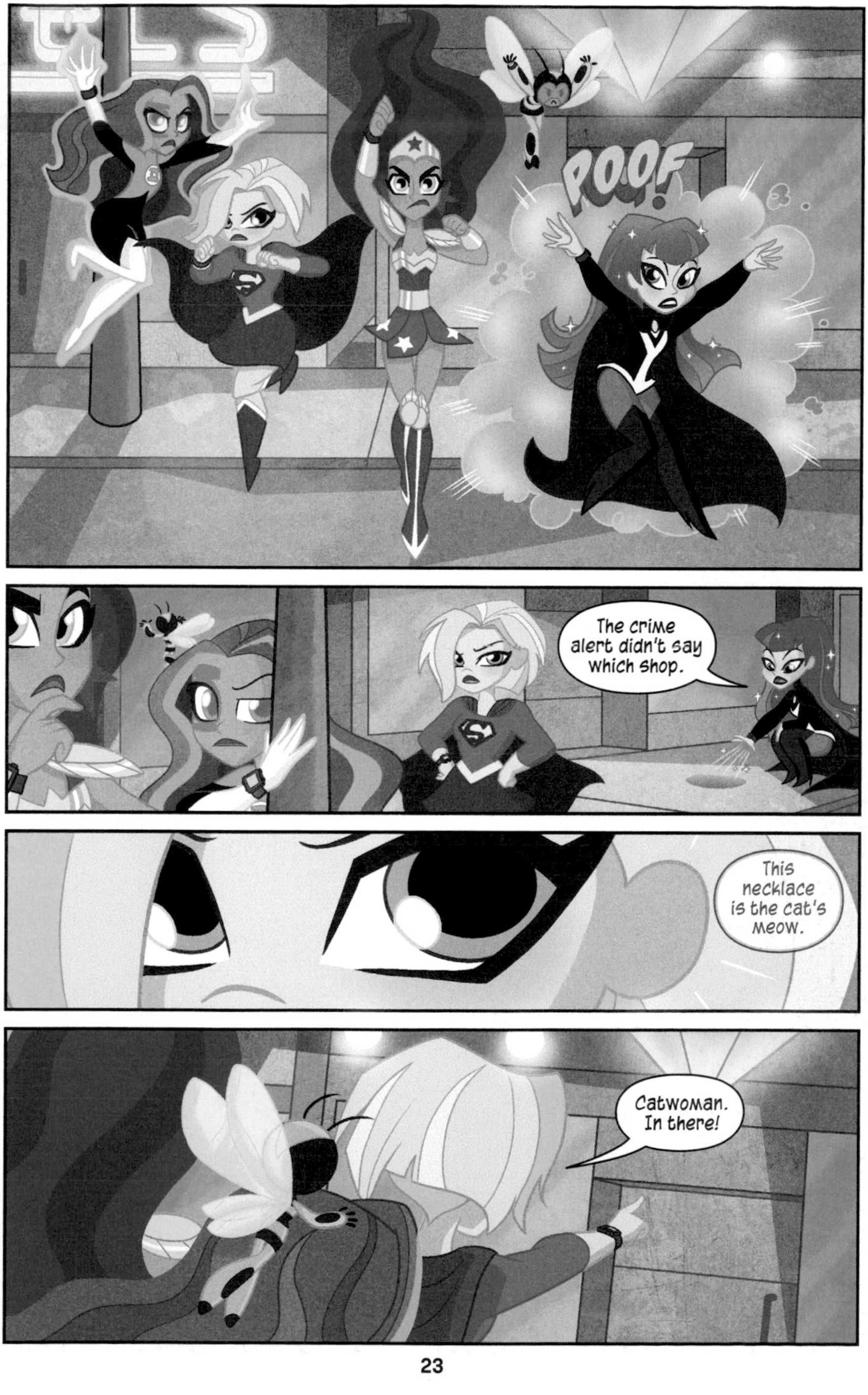
POOF!
The crime alert didn't say which shop.
This necklace is the cat's meow.
Catwoman. In there!

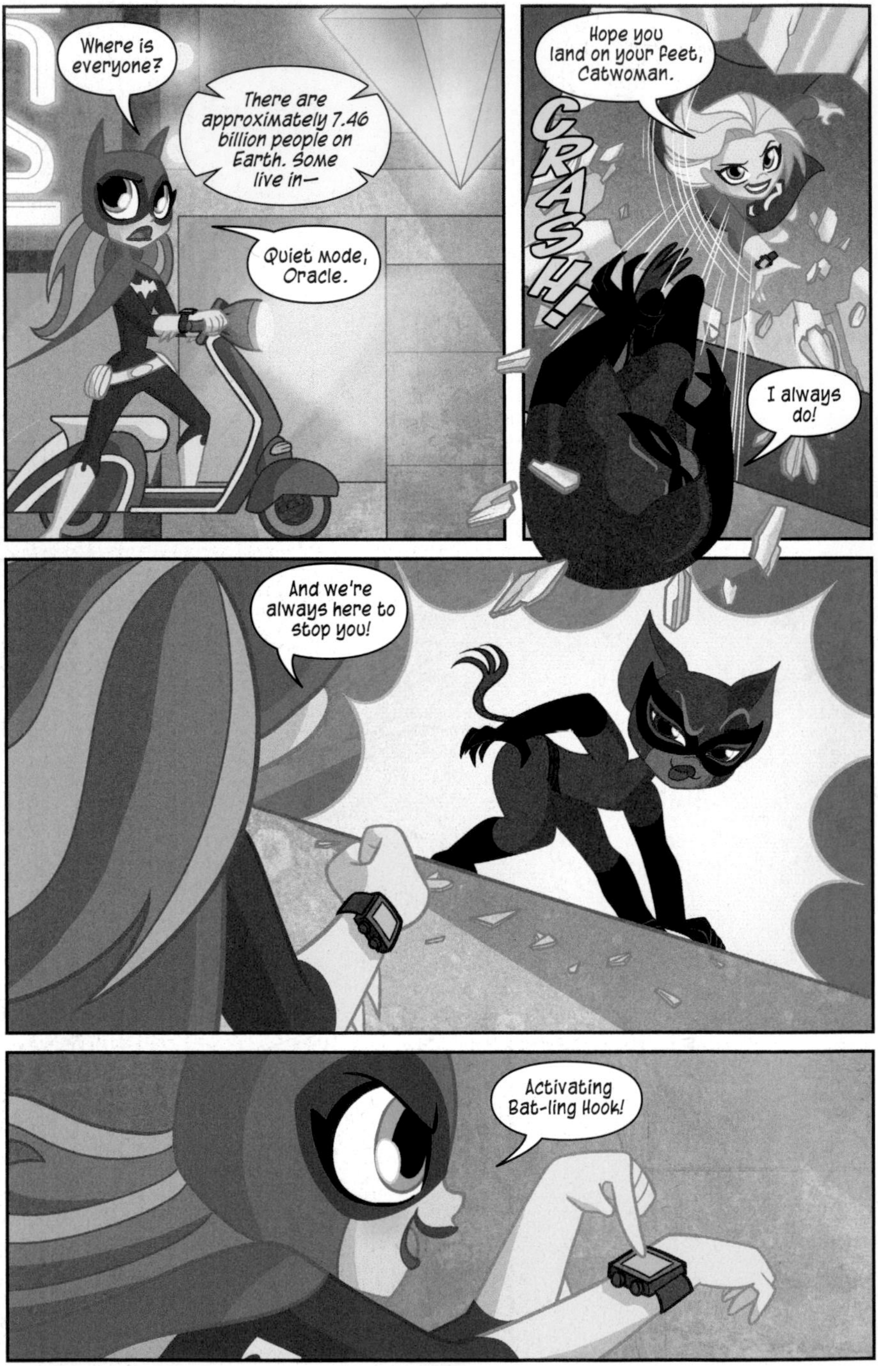
Where is everyone?
There are approximately 7.46 billion people on Earth. Some live in—
Quiet mode, Oracle.
Hope you land on your feet, Catwoman.
CRASH!
I always do!
And we're always here to stop you!
Activating Bat-ling Hook!

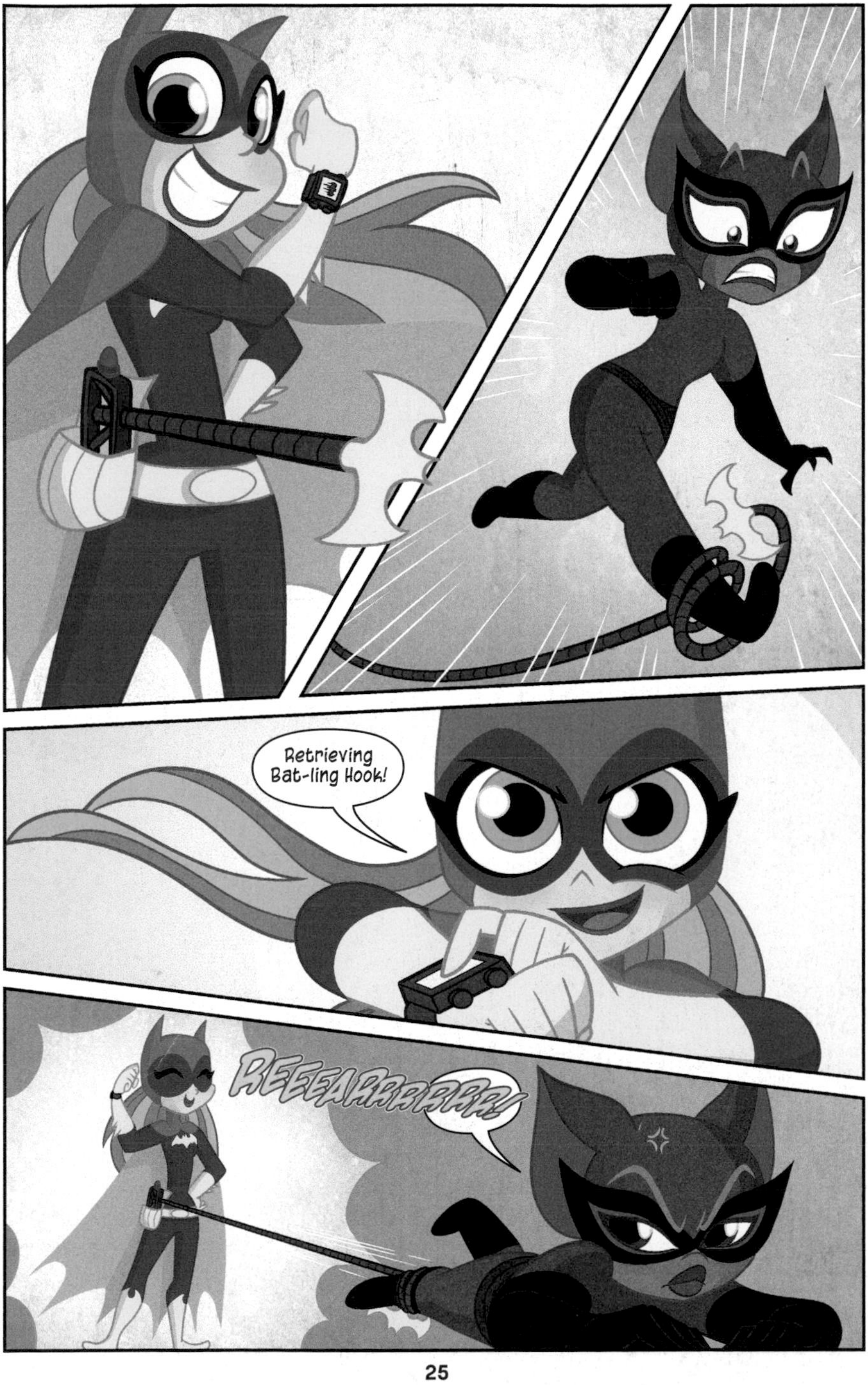
Retrieving Bat-ling Hook!
REEEARRRRRRR!

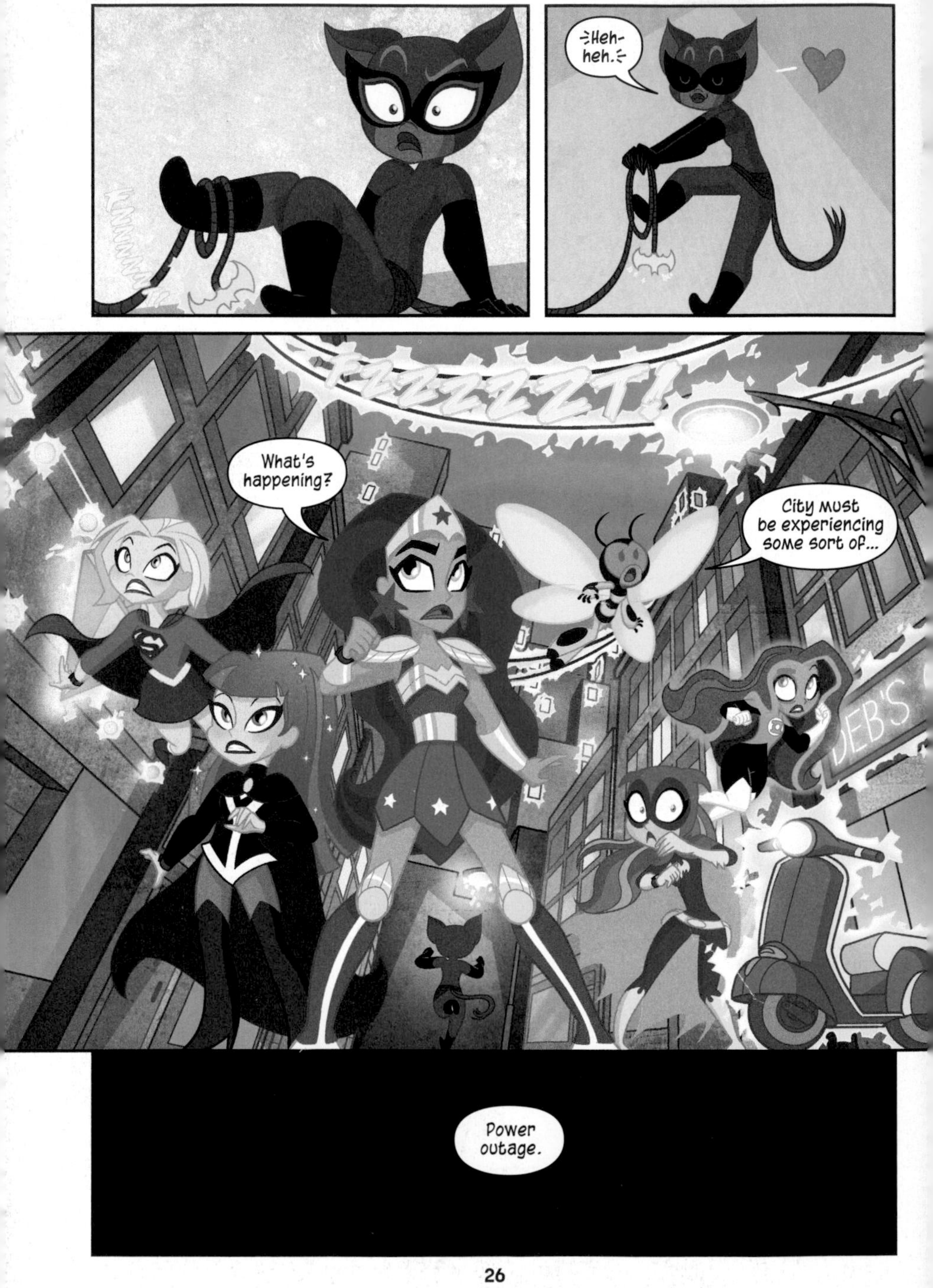
Heh-
heh.
FZZZZZT!
What's happening?
City must be experiencing some sort of...
DEB'S
Power outage.

chapter two
BLACKOUT

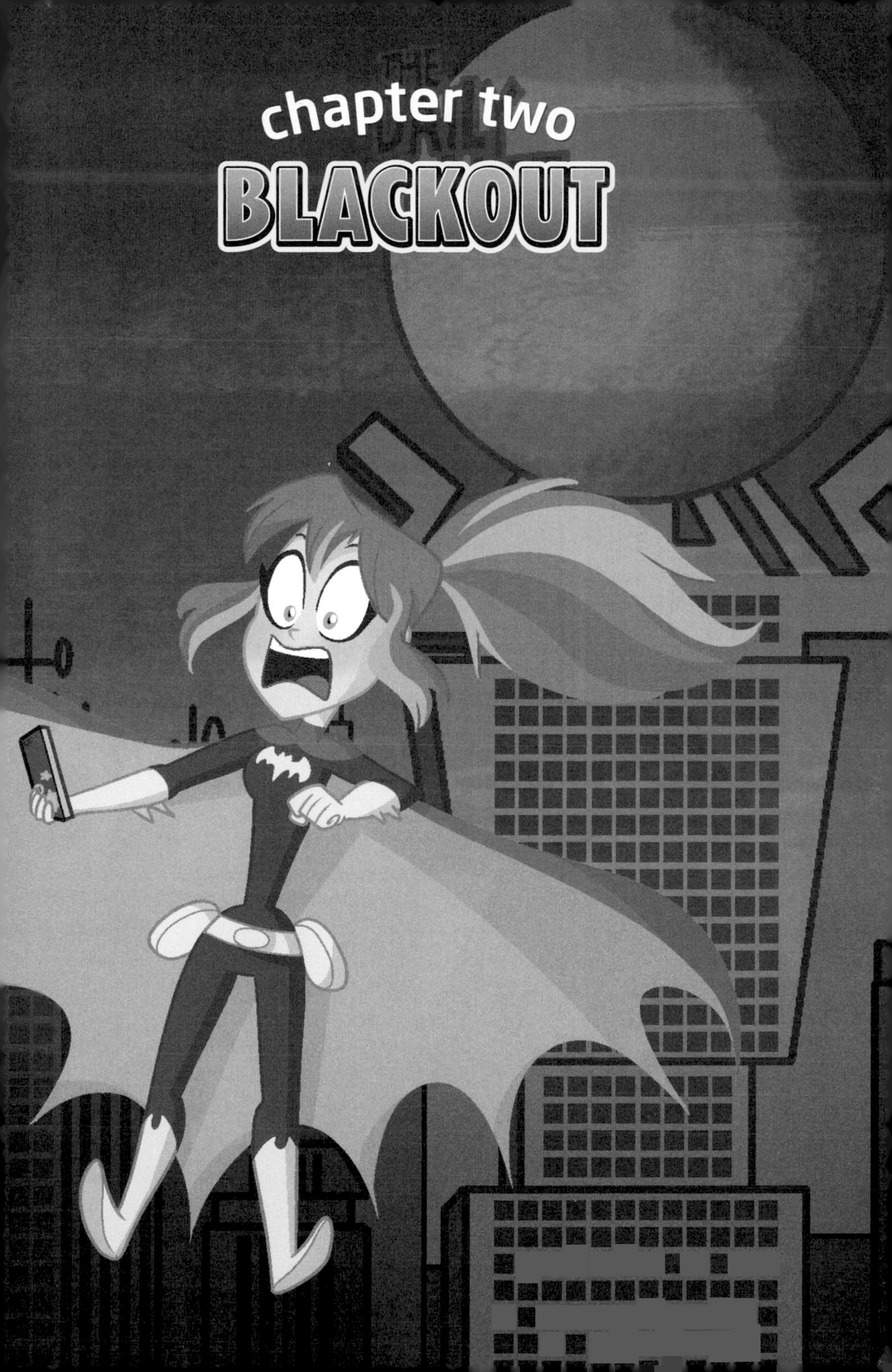

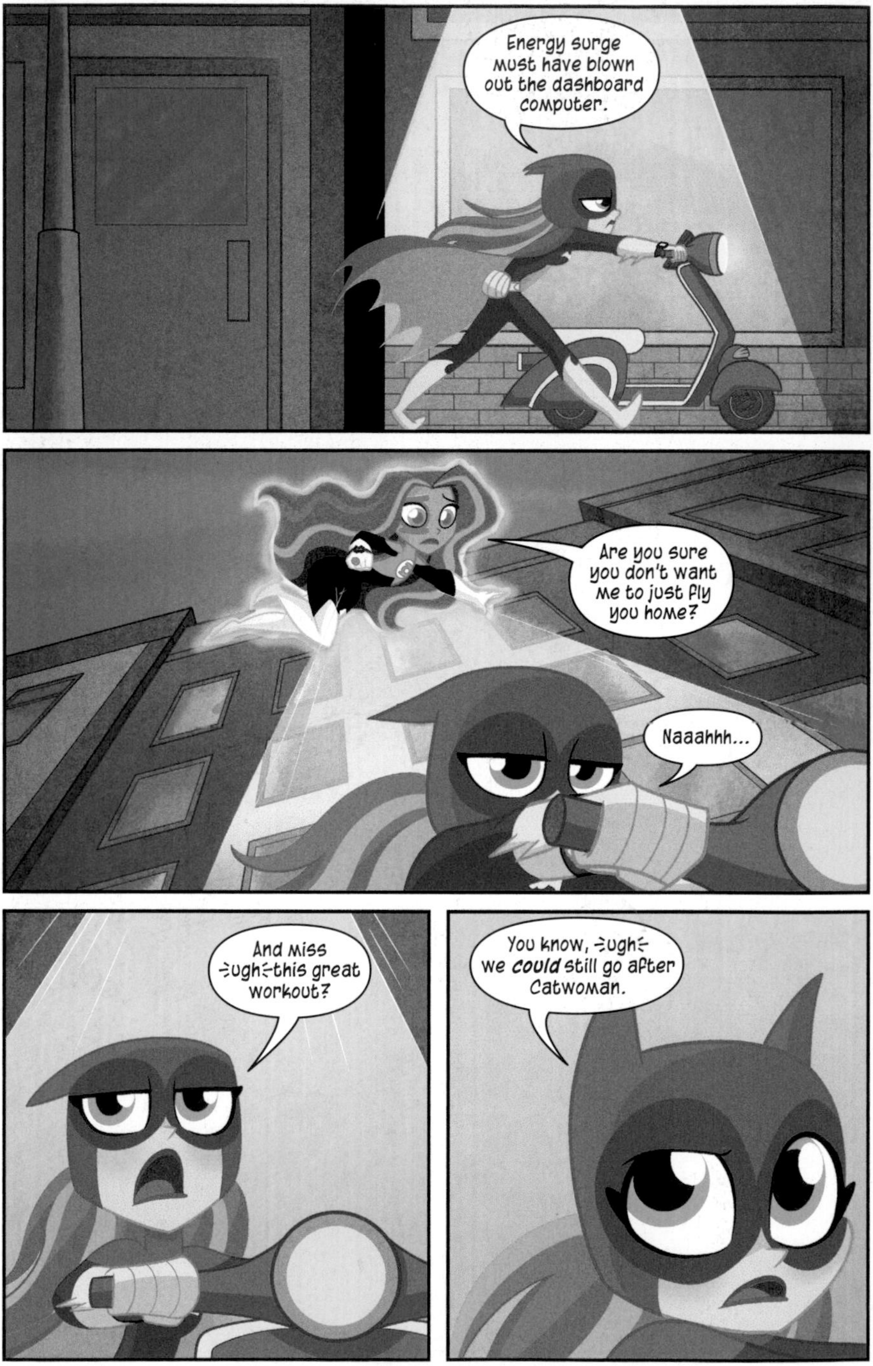
Energy surge must have blown out the dashboard computer.
Are you sure you don't want me to just fly you home?
Naaahhh...
And miss =ugh= this great workout?
You know, =ugh= we ***could*** still go after Catwoman.

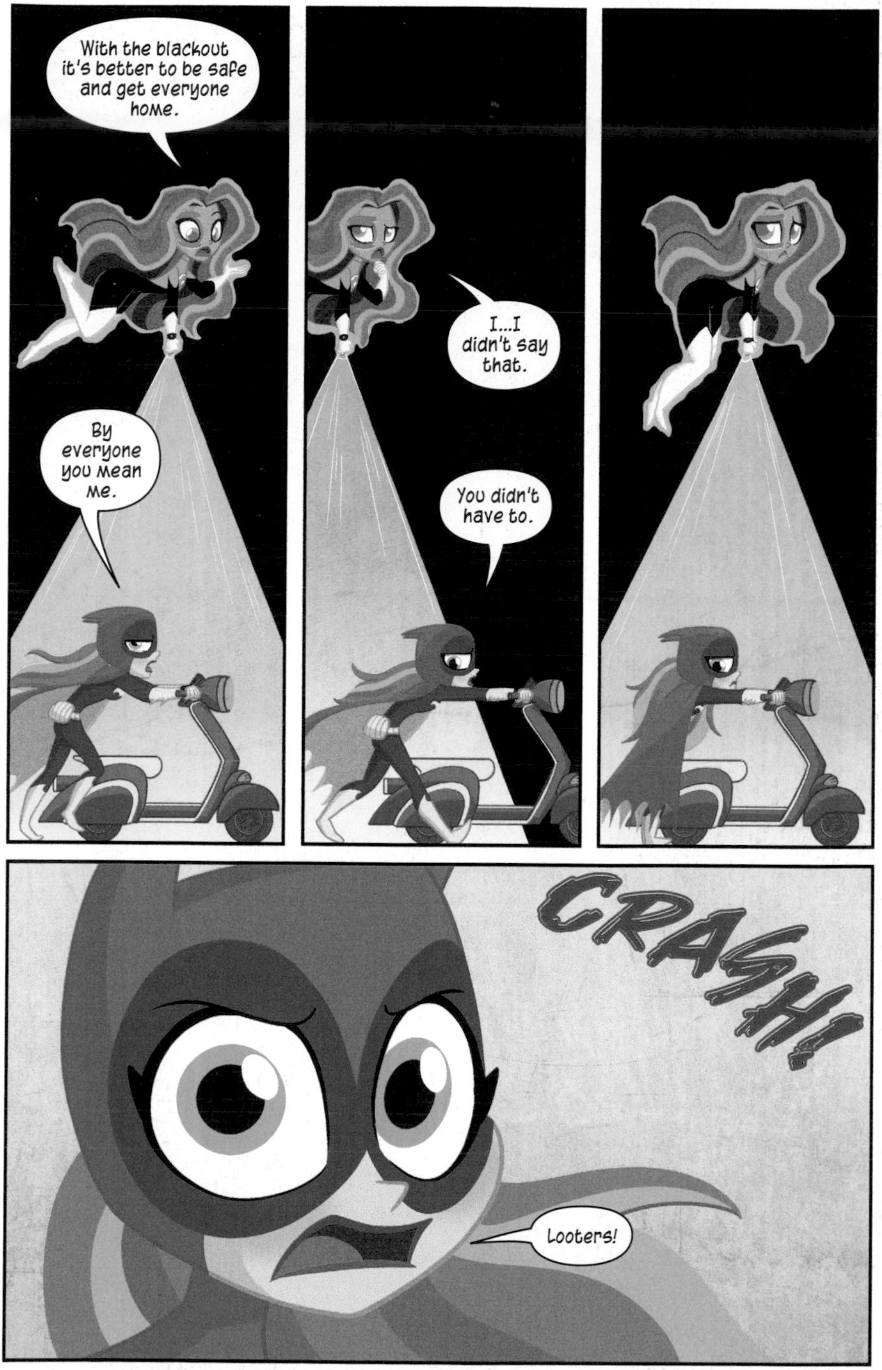

With the blackout it's better to be safe and get everyone home.
By everyone you mean me.
I...I didn't say that.
You didn't have to.
CRASH!
Looters!

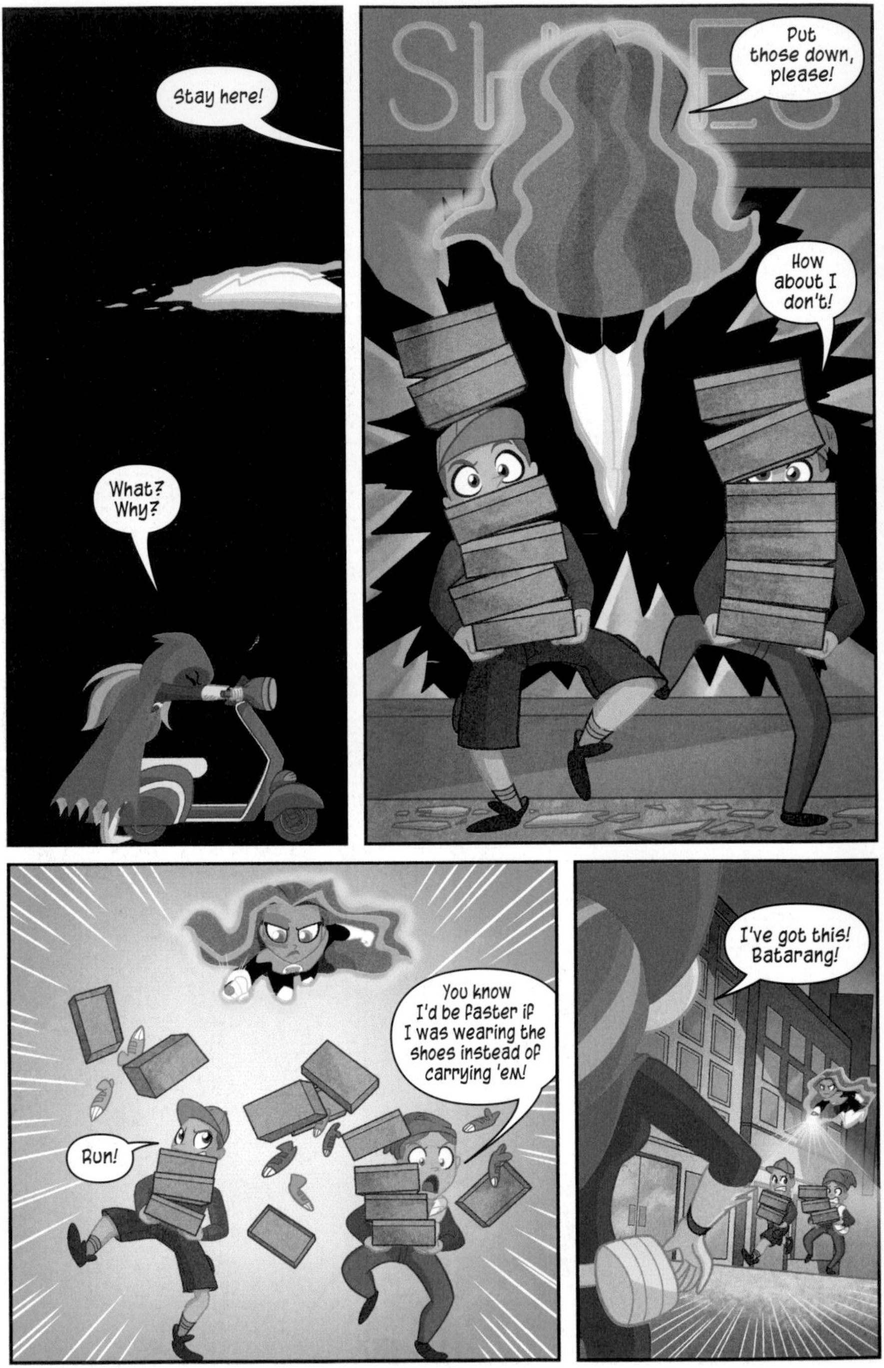
Stay here!
What? Why?
Put those down, please!
How about I don't!
You know I'd be faster if I was wearing the shoes instead of carrying 'em!
Run!
I've got this! Batarang!

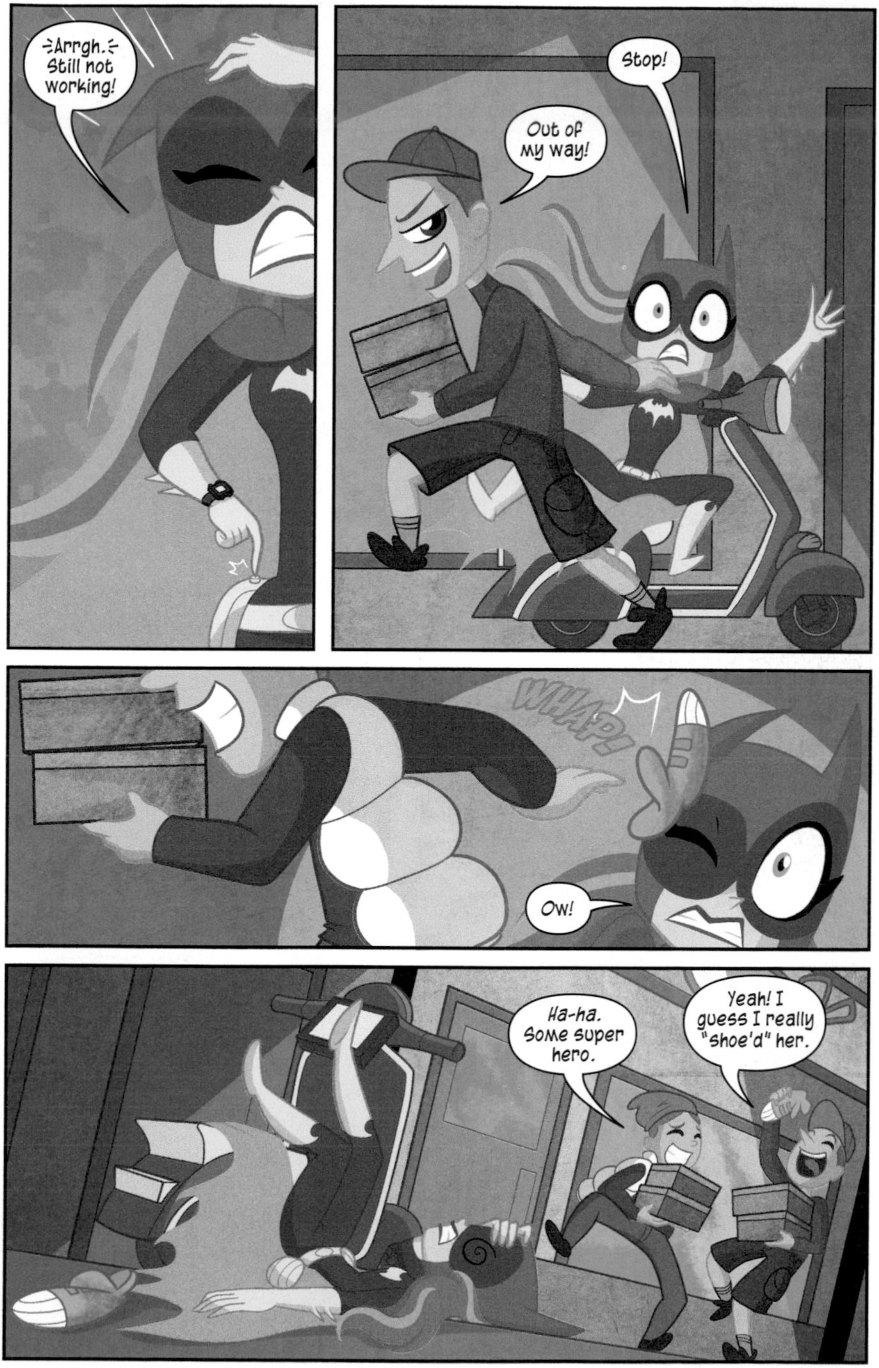
Arrgh. Still not working!
Out of my way!
Stop!
WHAP!
Ow!
Ha-ha. Some super hero.
Yeah! I guess I really "shoe'd" her.

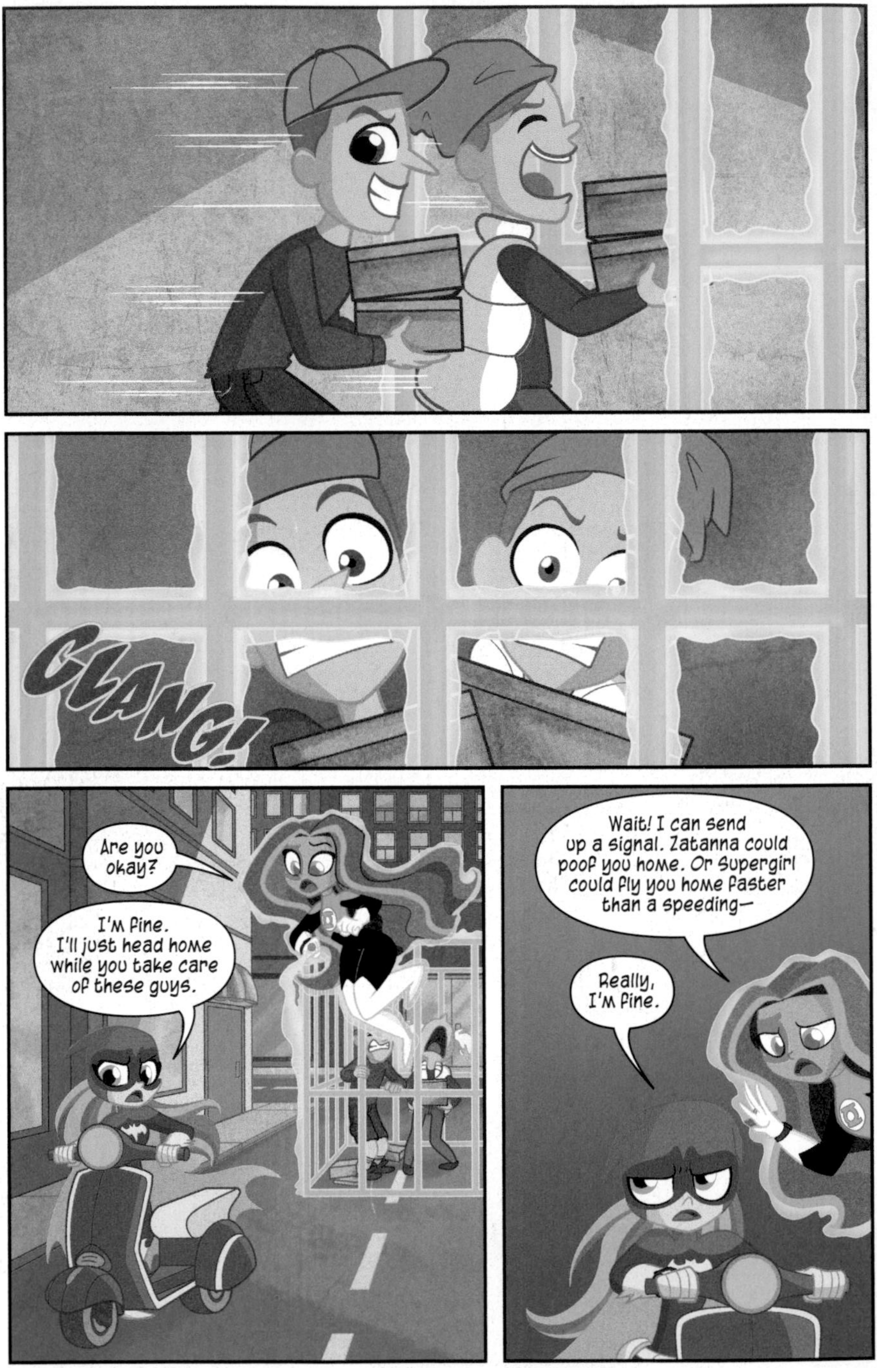
CLANG!
Are you okay?
I'm fine. I'll just head home while you take care of these guys.
Wait! I can send up a signal. Zatanna could poof you home. Or Supergirl could fly you home faster than a speeding—
Really, I'm fine.

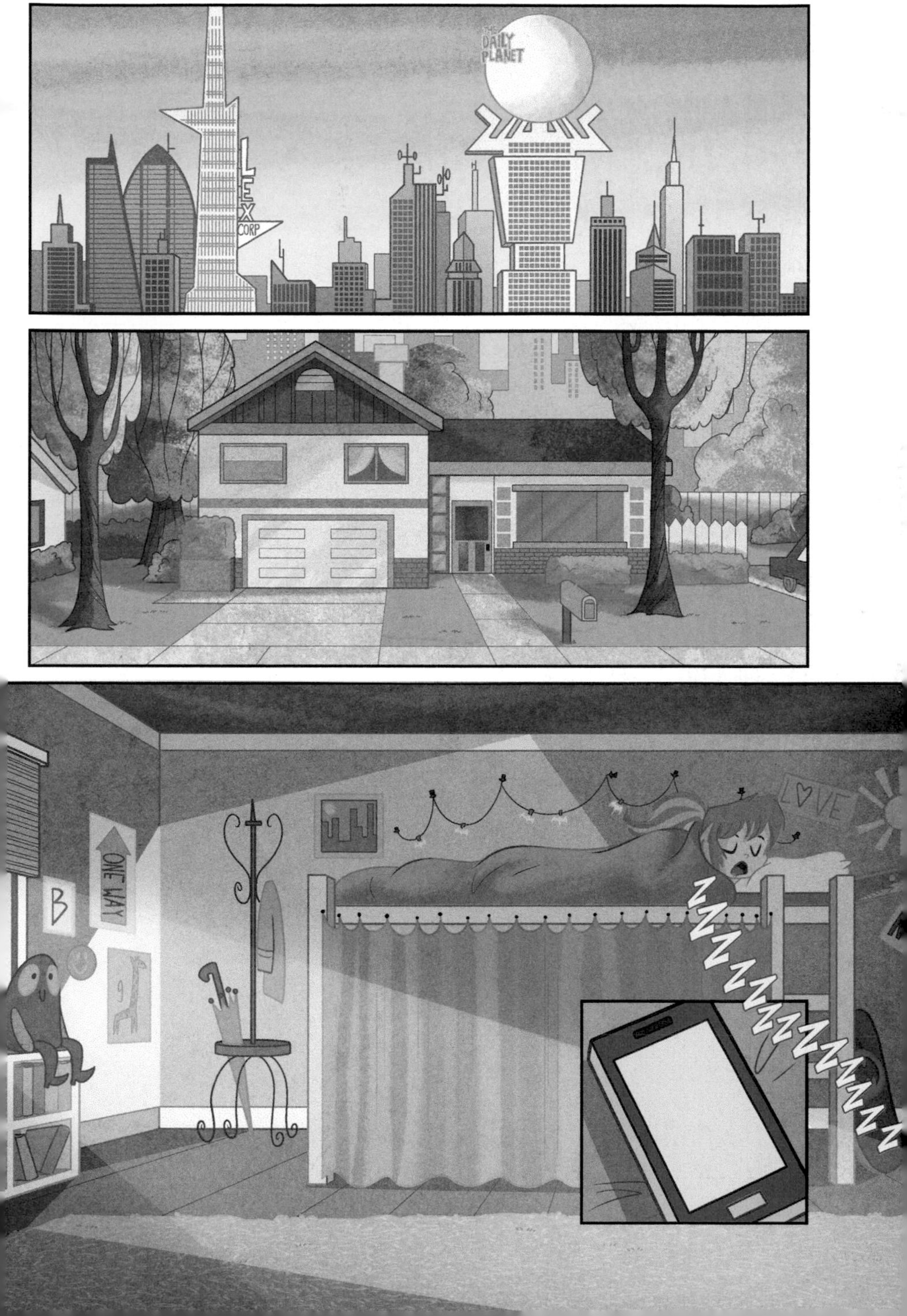
THE DAILY PLANET
LEX CORP
ONE WAY
B
LOVE
ZZZZZZZZZZZZZ

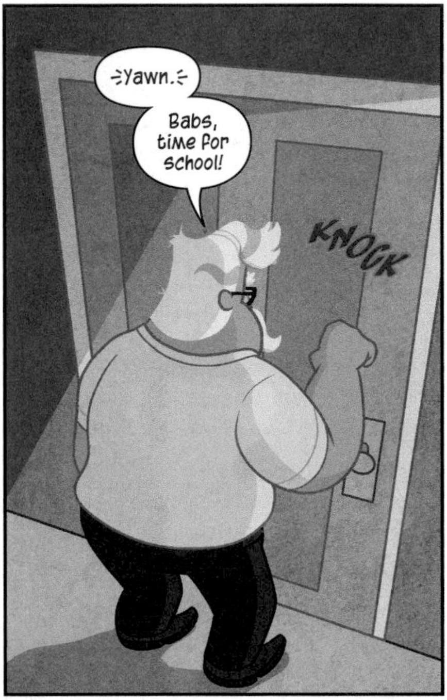
-Yawn.-
Babs, time for school!
KNOCK

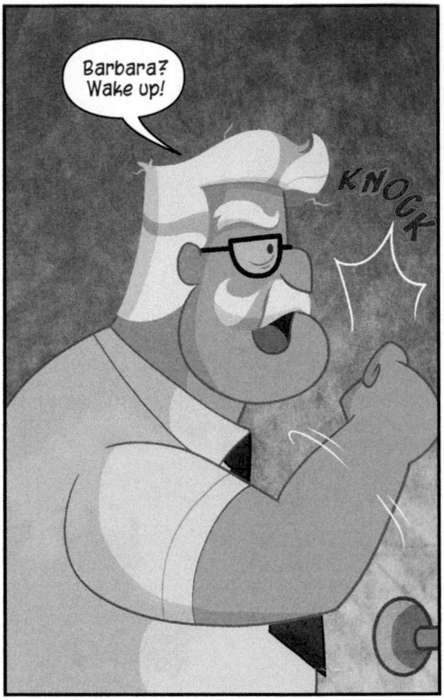
Barbara? Wake up!
KNOCK

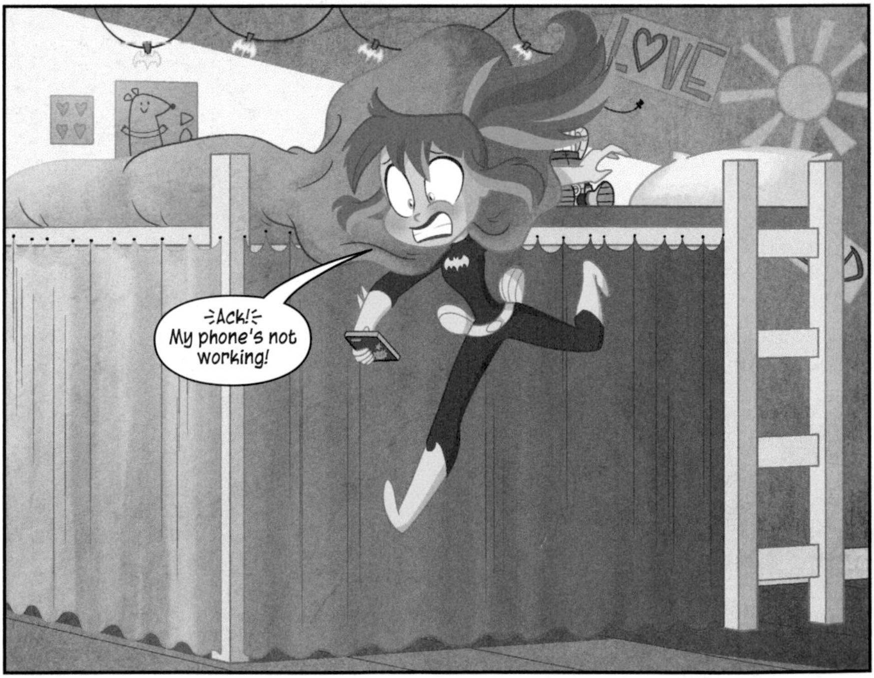
LOVE
-Ack!- My phone's not working!

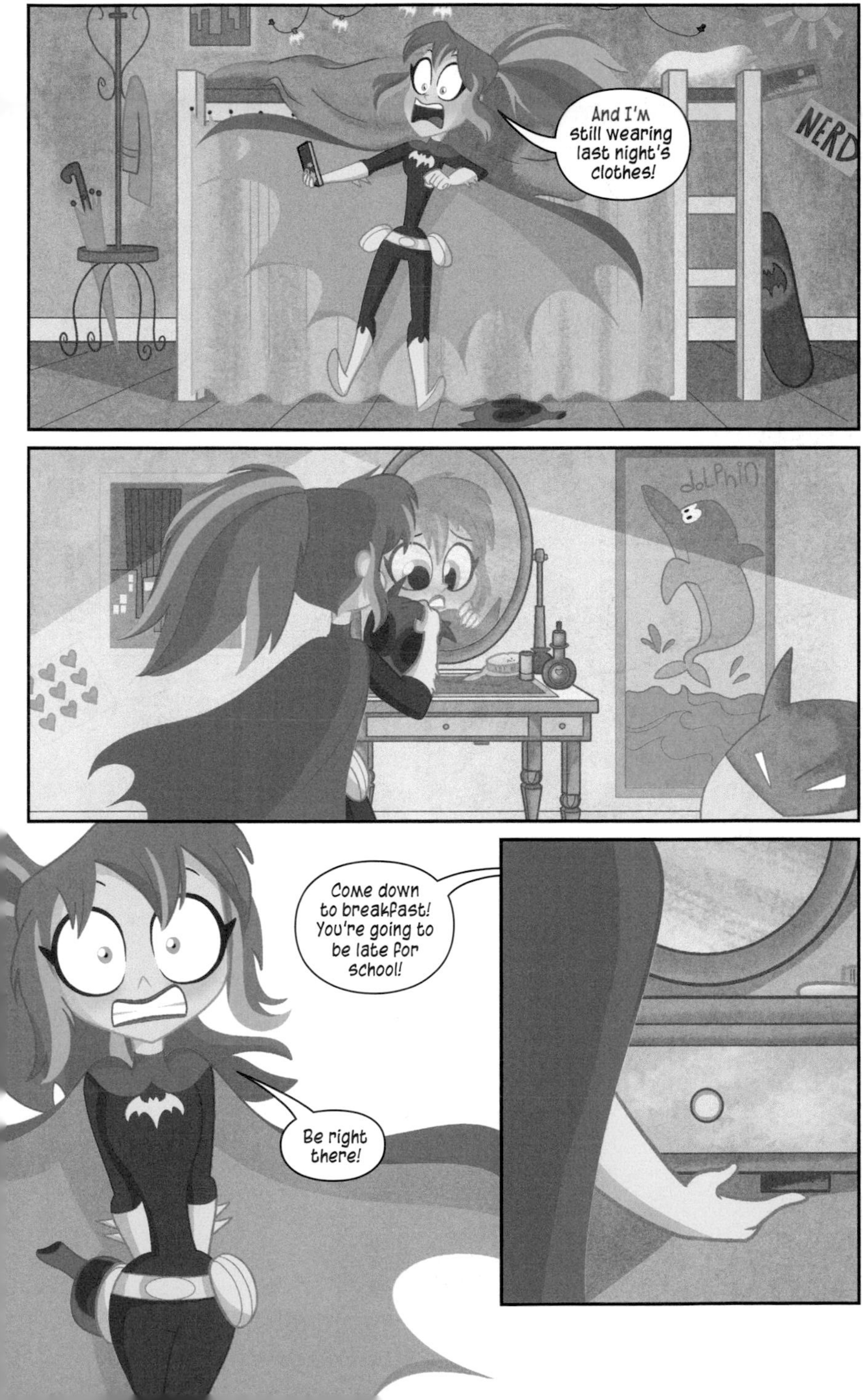
NERD
And I'M still wearing last night's clothes!
dolphin
Come down to breakfast! You're going to be late for school!
Be right there!

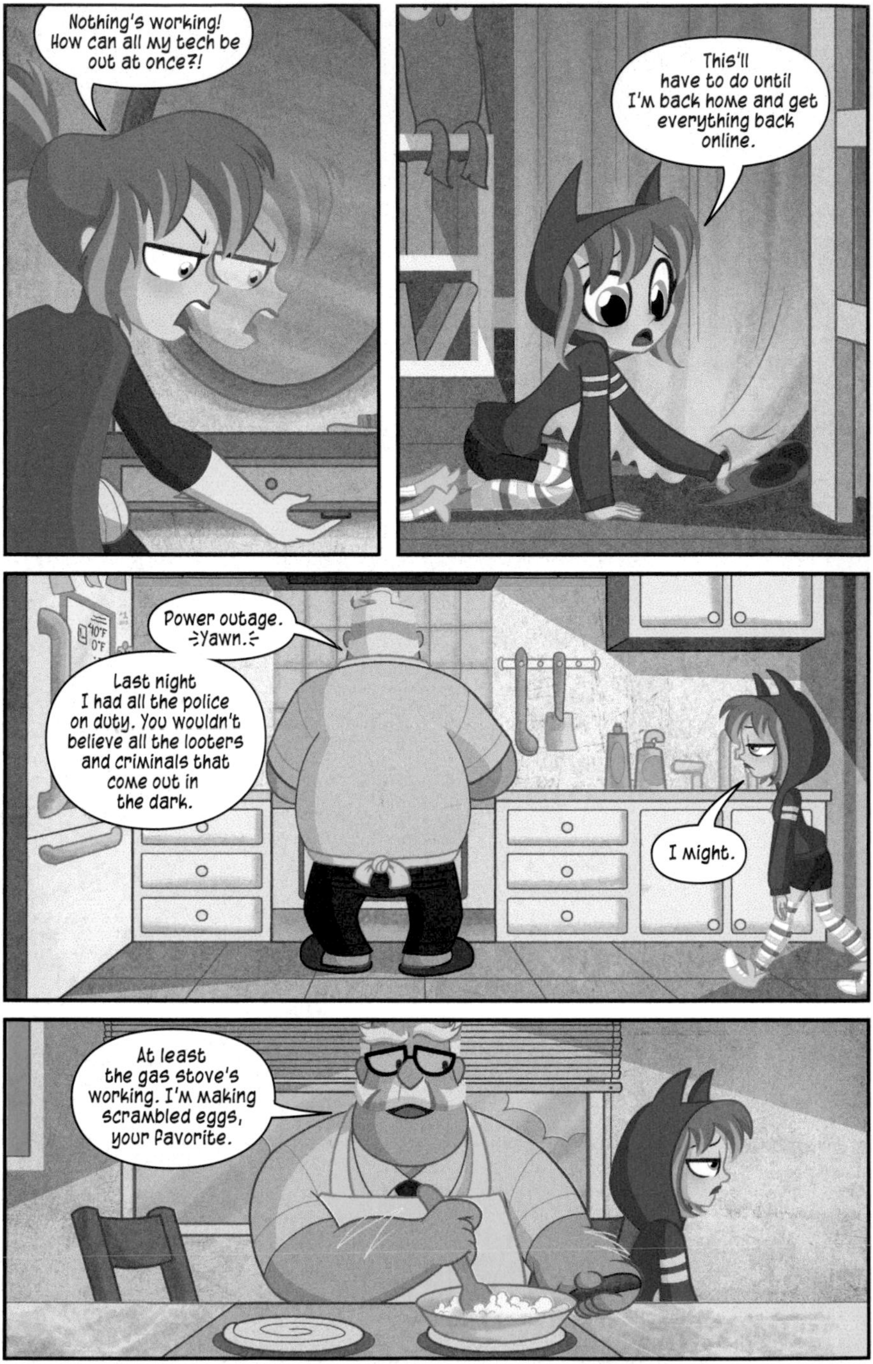
Nothing's working! How can all my tech be out at once?!
This'll have to do until I'm back home and get everything back online.
Power outage. ⋞Yawn.⋟
Last night I had all the police on duty. You wouldn't believe all the looters and criminals that come out in the dark.
I might.
At least the gas stove's working. I'm making scrambled eggs, your favorite.

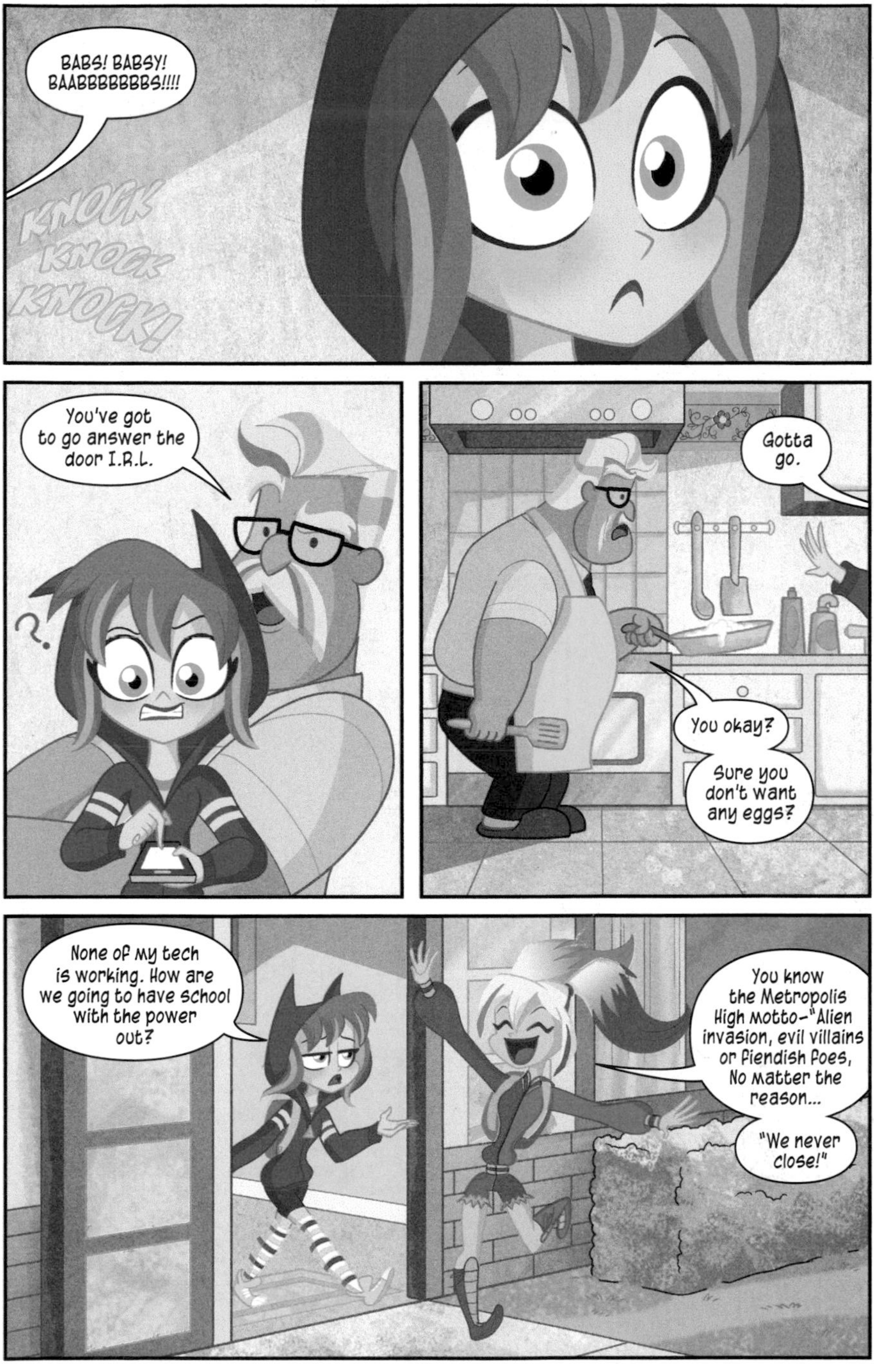
BABS! BABSY! BAABBBBBBBS!!!!
KNOCK KNOCK KNOCK!
You've got to go answer the door I.R.L.
Gotta go.
You okay?
Sure you don't want any eggs?
None of my tech is working. How are we going to have school with the power out?
You know the Metropolis High motto—"Alien invasion, evil villains or fiendish foes, No matter the reason...
"We never close!"

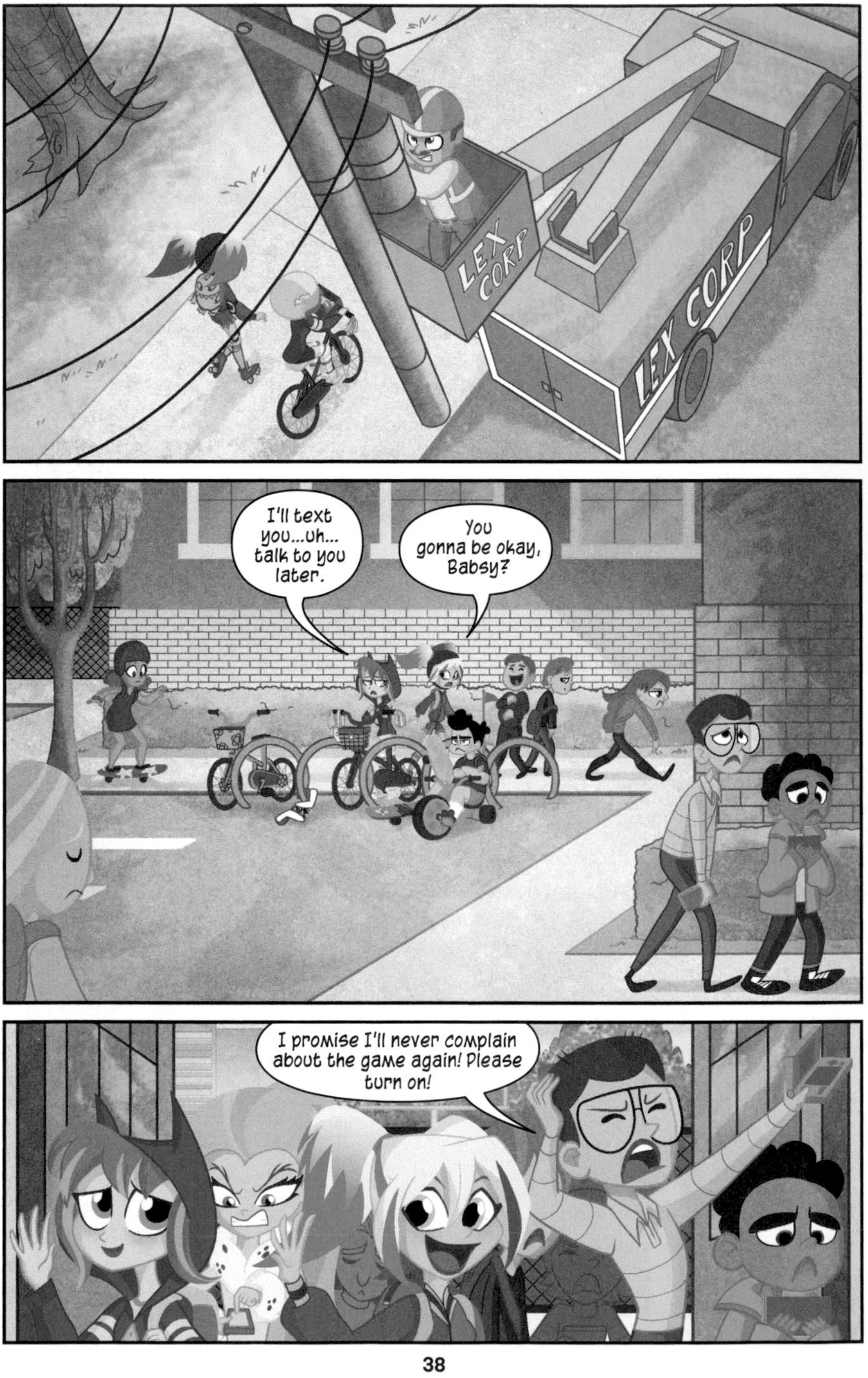
LEX CORP
LEX CORP
I'll text you...uh... talk to you later.
You gonna be okay, Babsy?
I promise I'll never complain about the game again! Please turn on!

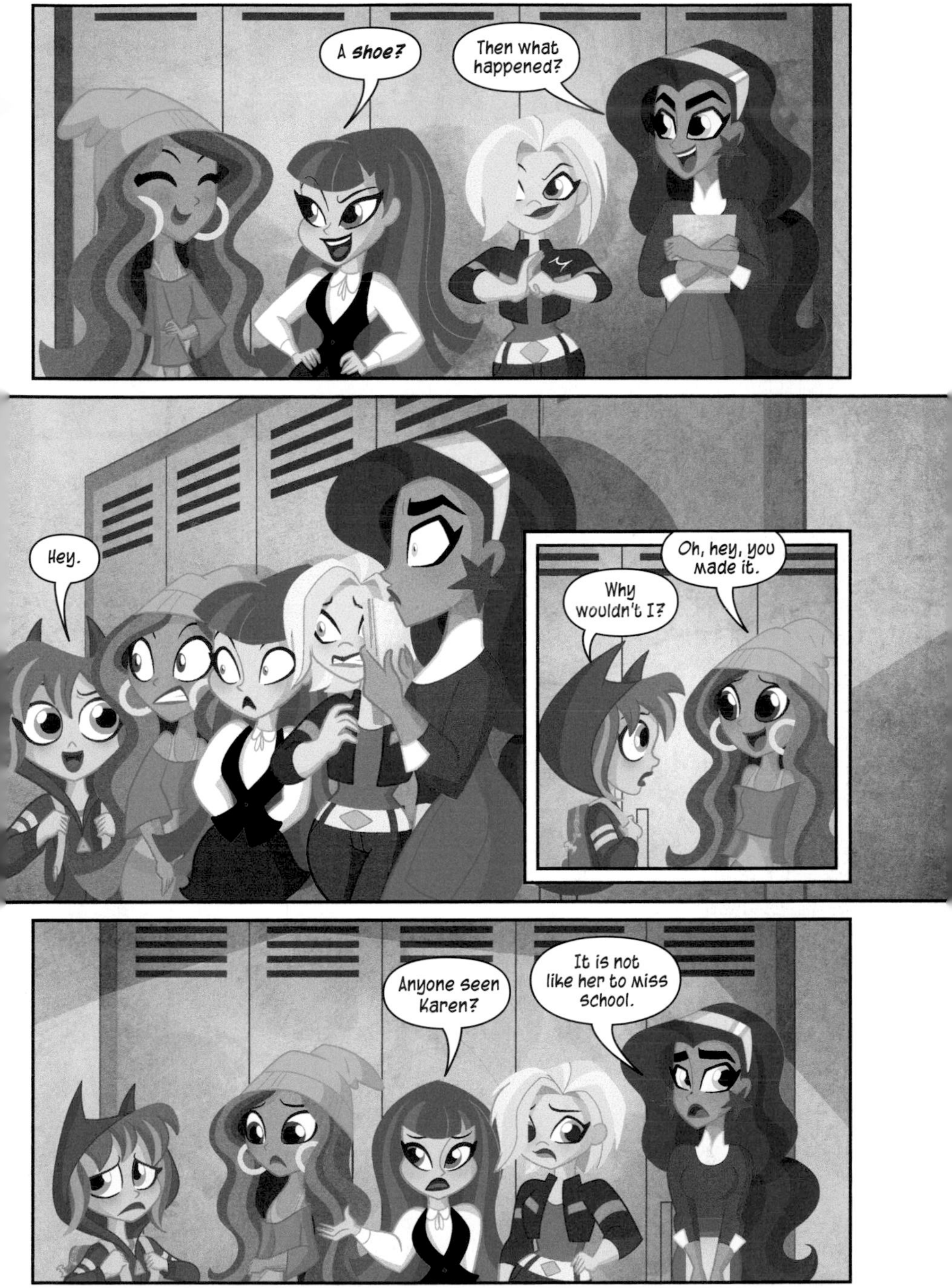
A *shoe?*
Then what happened?
Hey.
Oh, hey, you made it.
Why wouldn't I?
Anyone seen Karen?
It is not like her to miss school.

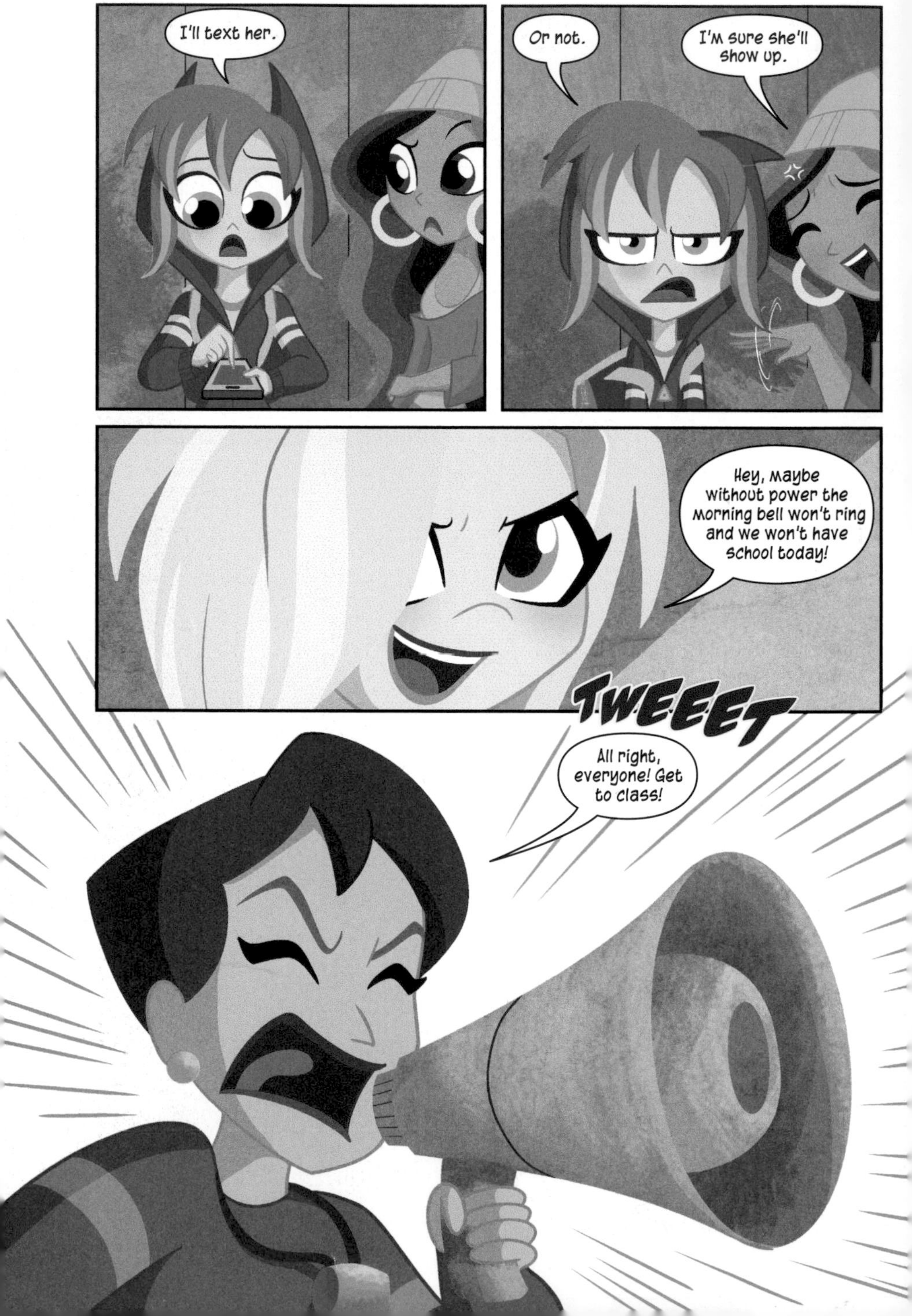
I'll text her.
Or not.
I'm sure she'll show up.
Hey, maybe without power the morning bell won't ring and we won't have school today!
TWEEET
All right, everyone! Get to class!

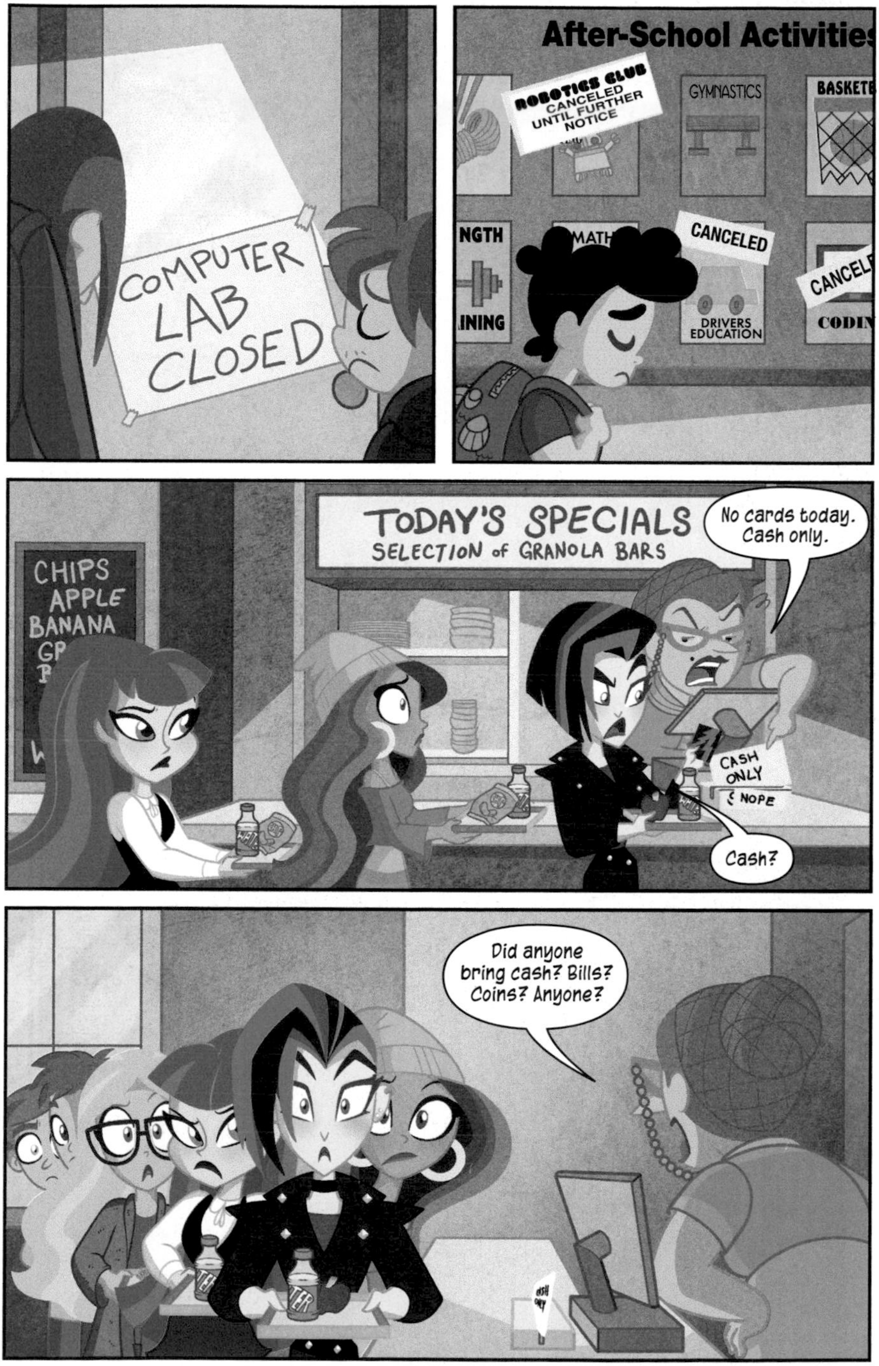
COMPUTER LAB CLOSED
After-School Activities
ROBOTICS CLUB CANCELED UNTIL FURTHER NOTICE
GYMNASTICS
CANCELED
DRIVERS EDUCATION
TODAY'S SPECIALS
SELECTION of GRANOLA BARS
CHIPS
APPLE
BANANA
No cards today. Cash only.
CASH ONLY
NOPE
Cash?
Did anyone bring cash? Bills? Coins? Anyone?

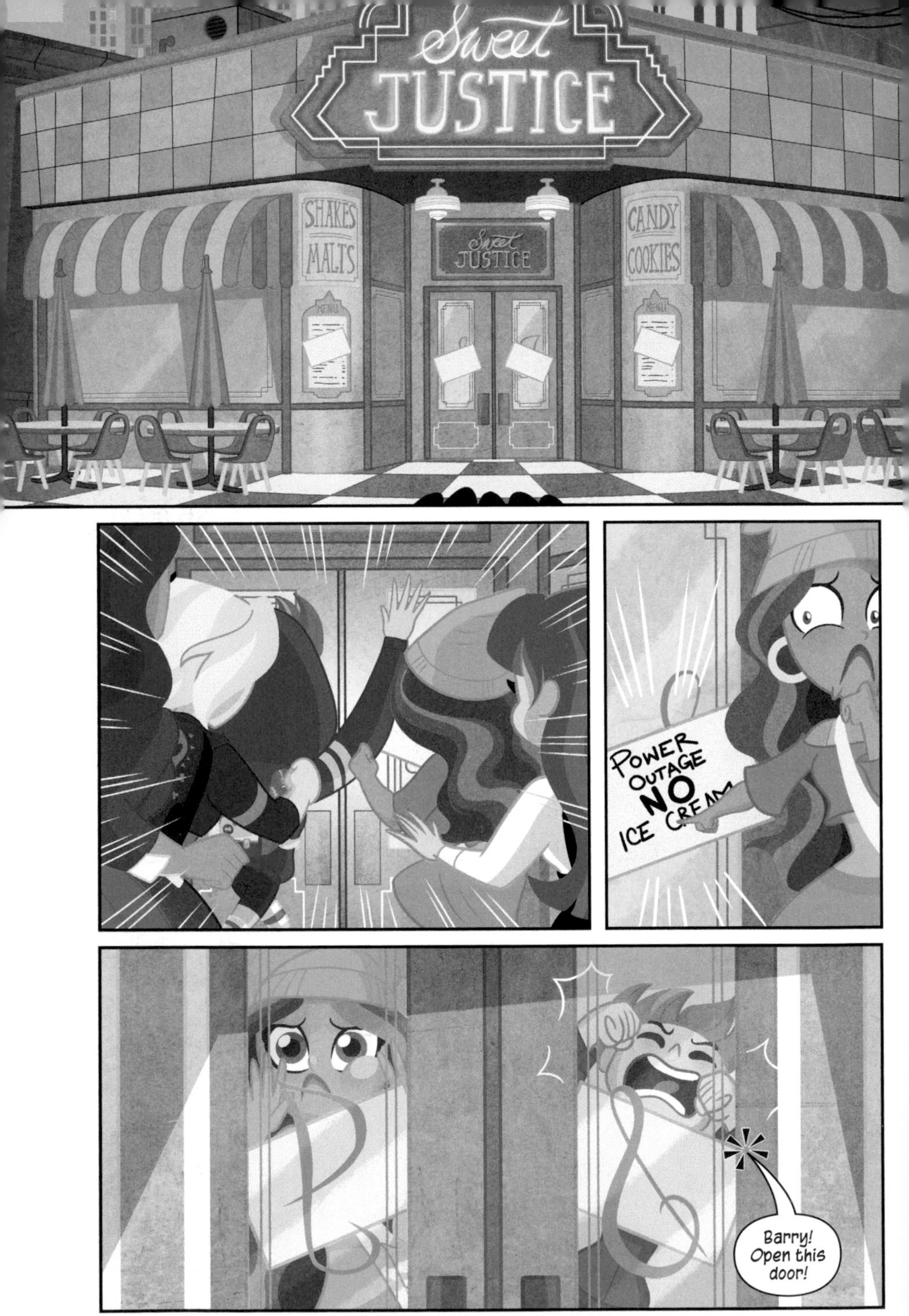
Sweet JUSTICE
SHAKES MALTS
CANDY COOKIES
MENU
MENU
Sweet JUSTICE
POWER OUTAGE NO ICE CREAM
Barry! Open this door!

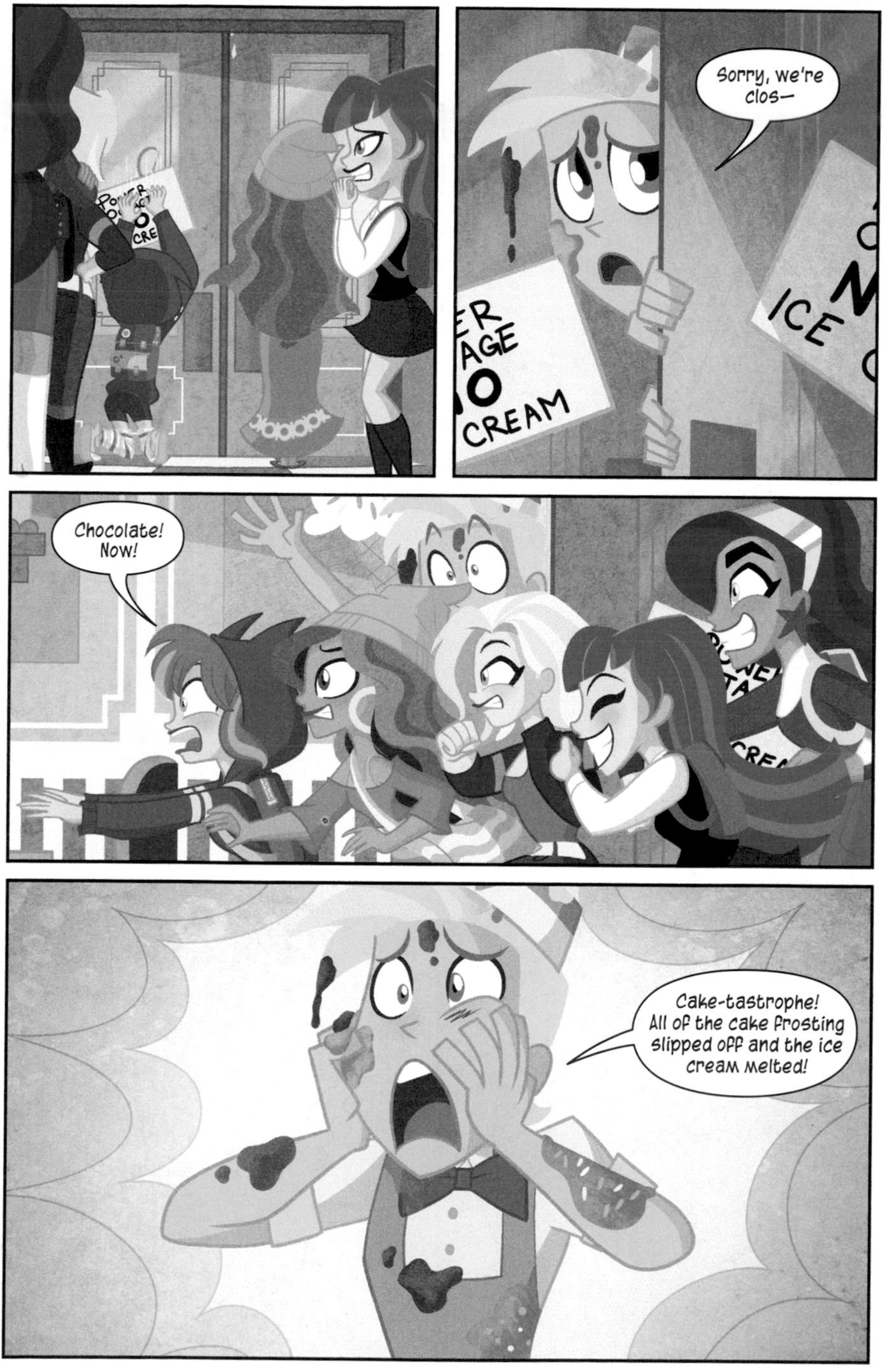
Sorry, we're clos—
Chocolate! Now!
Cake-tastrophe! All of the cake frosting slipped off and the ice cream melted!

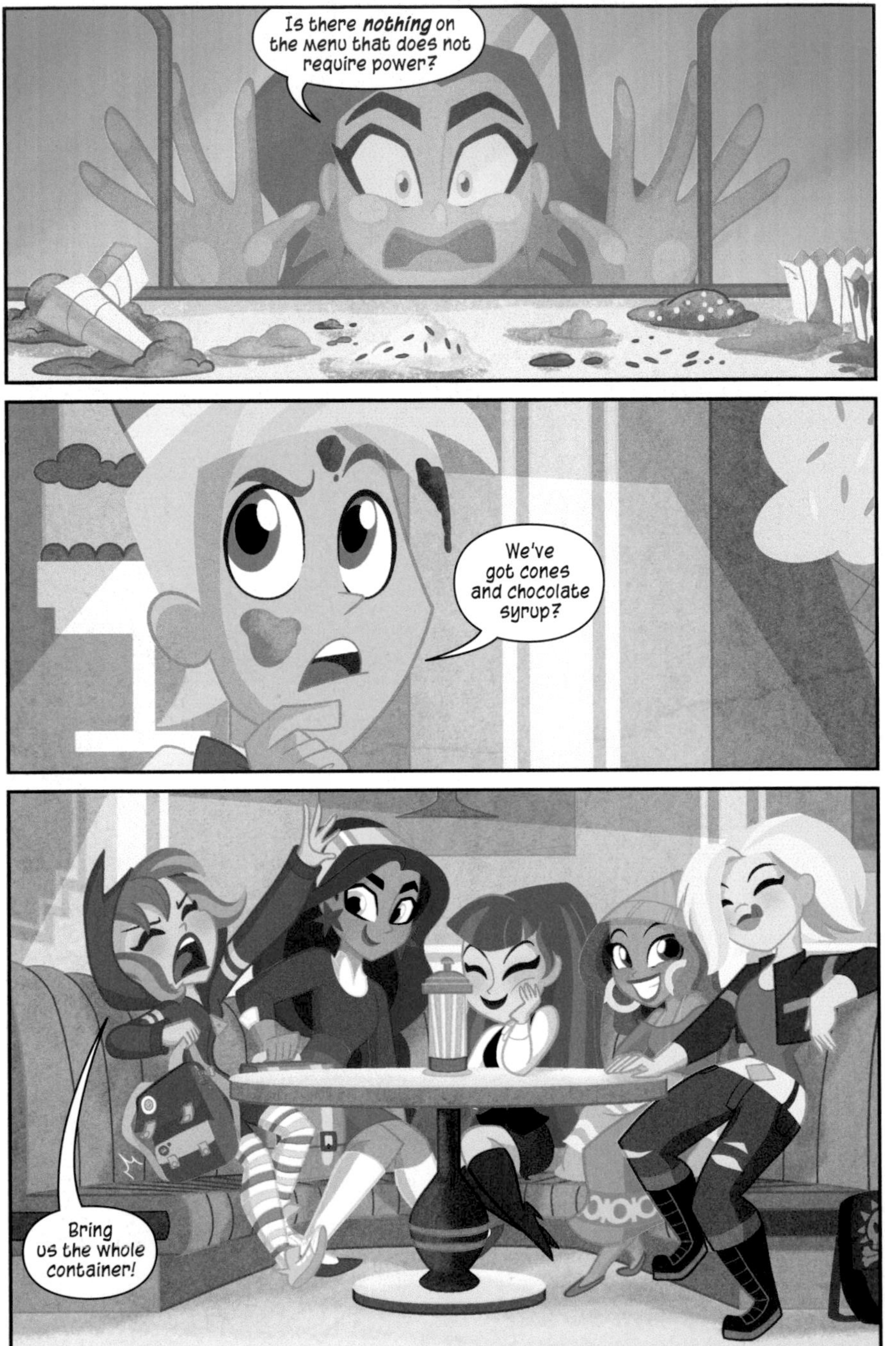
Is there *nothing* on the menu that does not require power?
We've got cones and chocolate syrup?
Bring us the whole container!

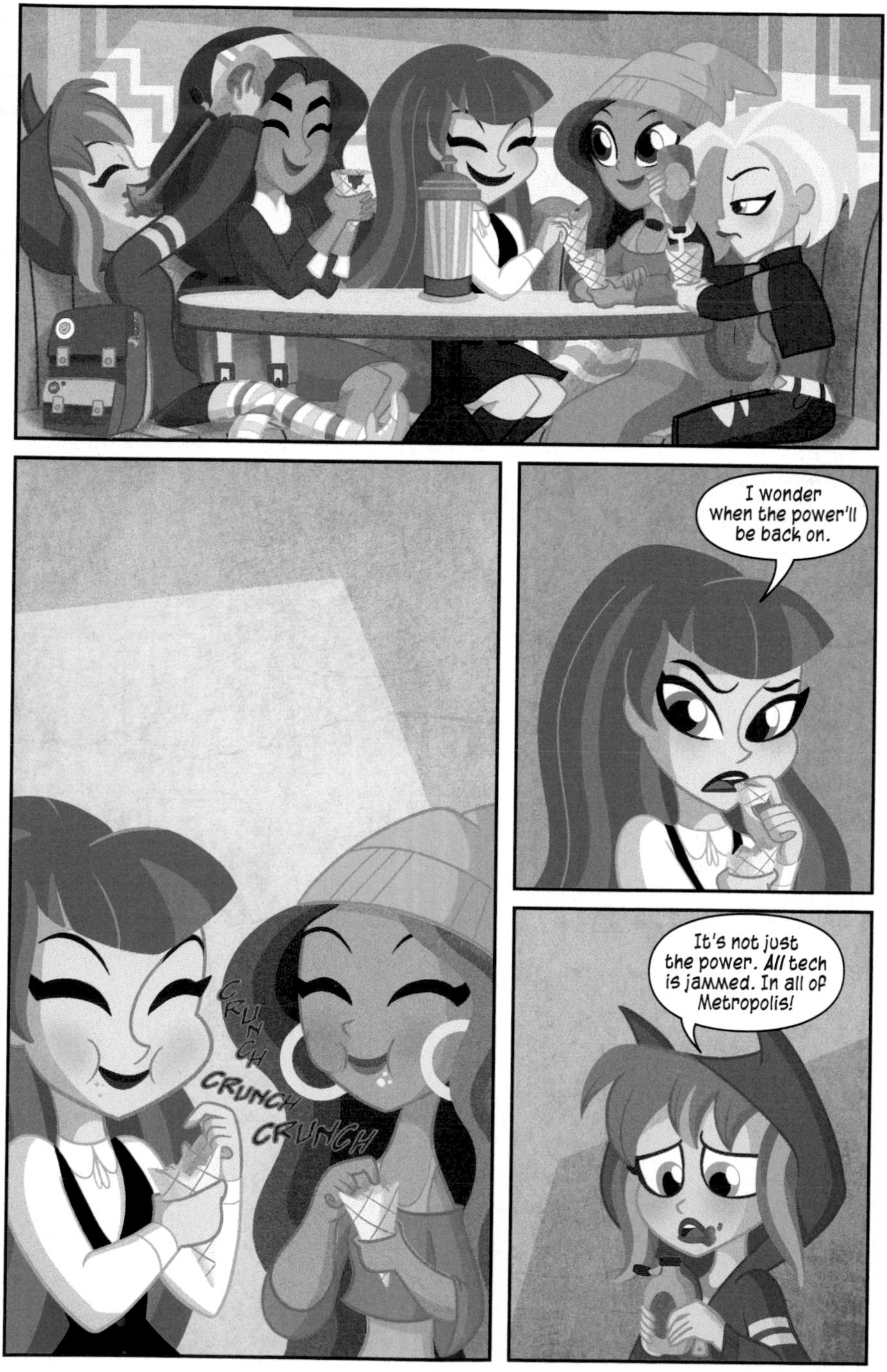
CRUNCH
CRUNCH
CRUNCH
I wonder when the power'll be back on.
It's not just the power. *All* tech is jammed. In all of Metropolis!

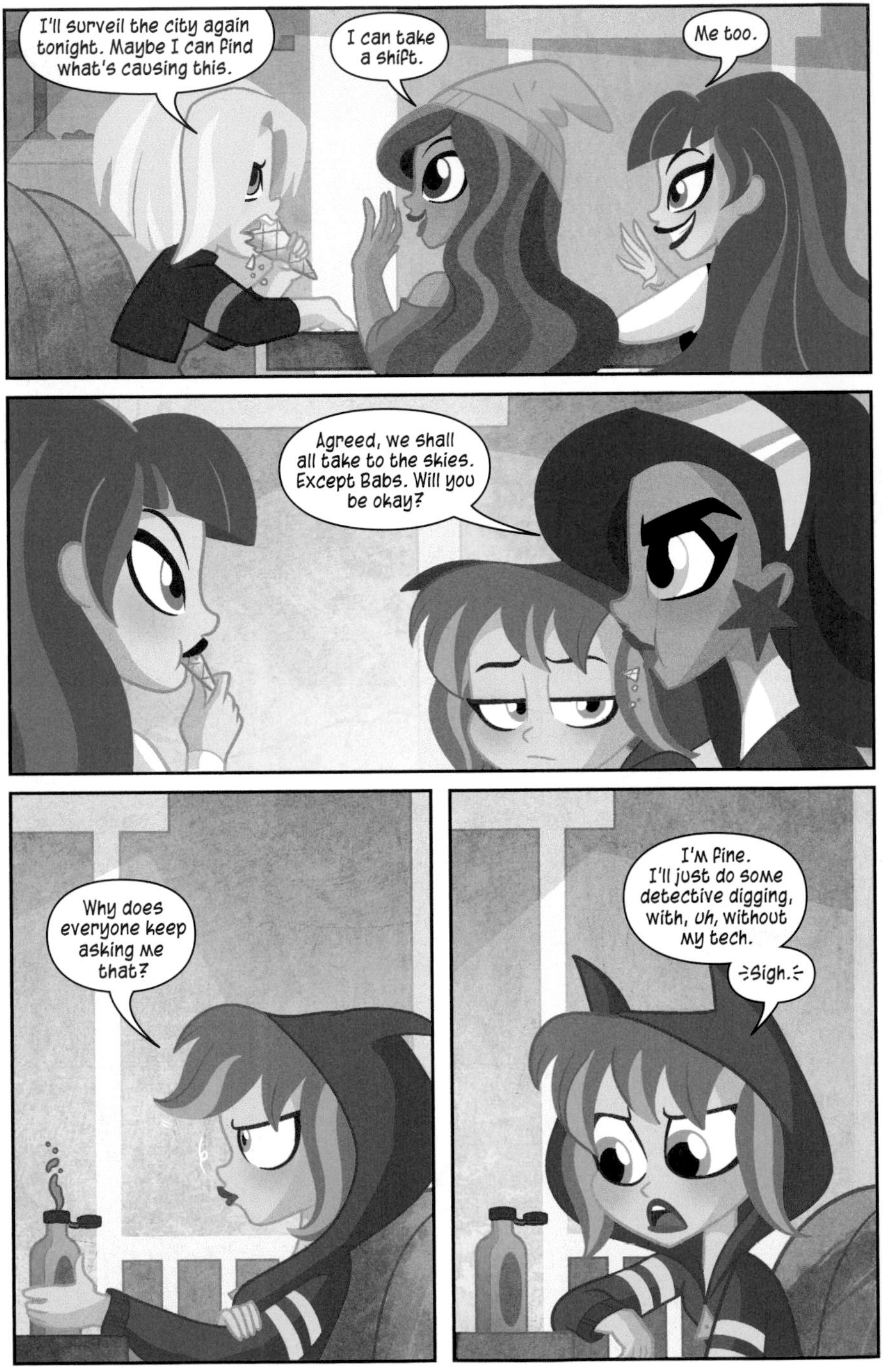

I'll surveil the city again tonight. Maybe I can find what's causing this.
I can take a shift.
Me too.
Agreed, we shall all take to the skies. Except Babs. Will you be okay?
Why does everyone keep asking me that?
I'm fine. I'll just do some detective digging, with, *uh*, without my tech.
Sigh.

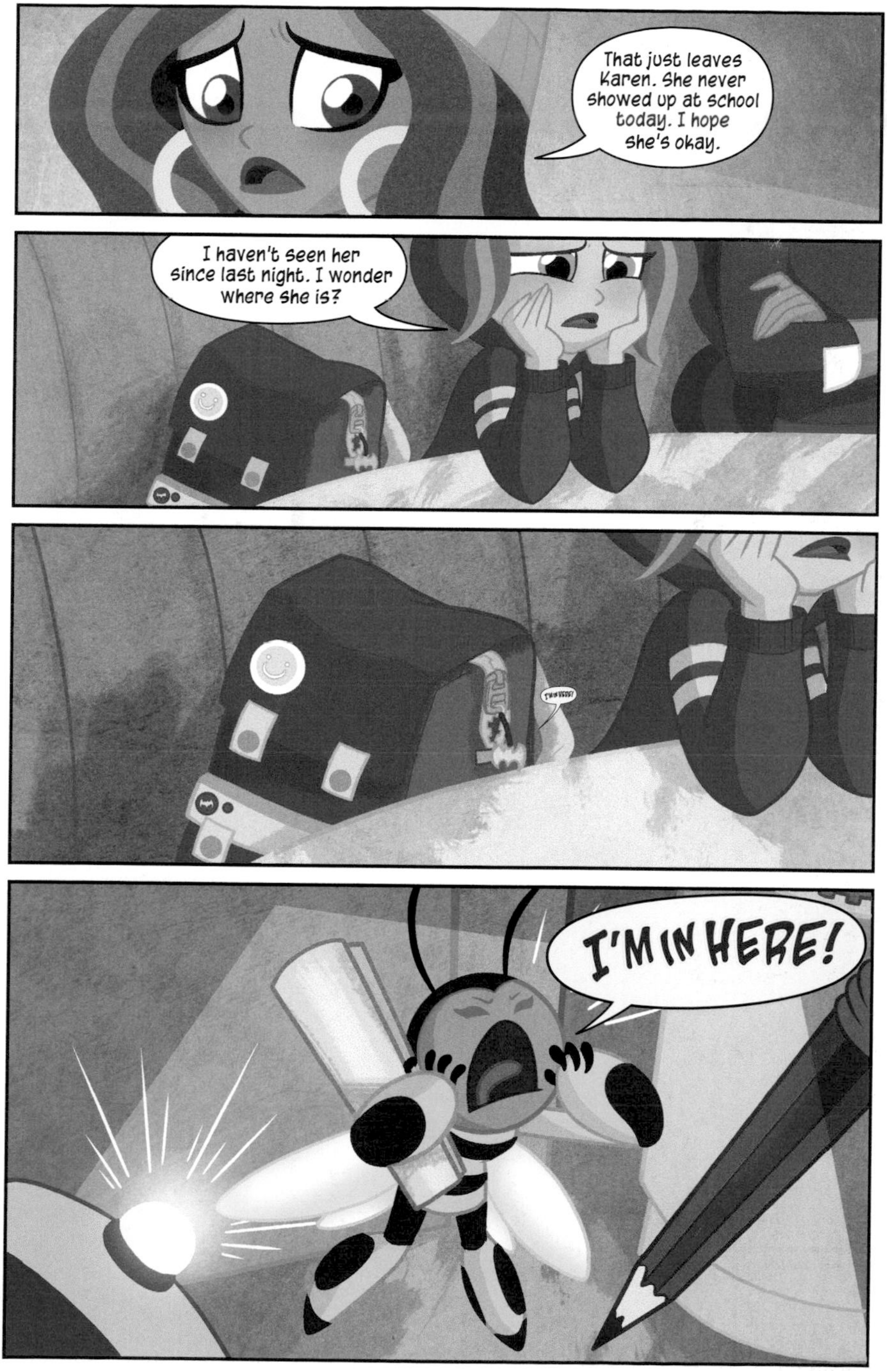
That just leaves Karen. She never showed up at school today. I hope she's okay.
I haven't seen her since last night. I wonder where she is?
I'M IN HERE!

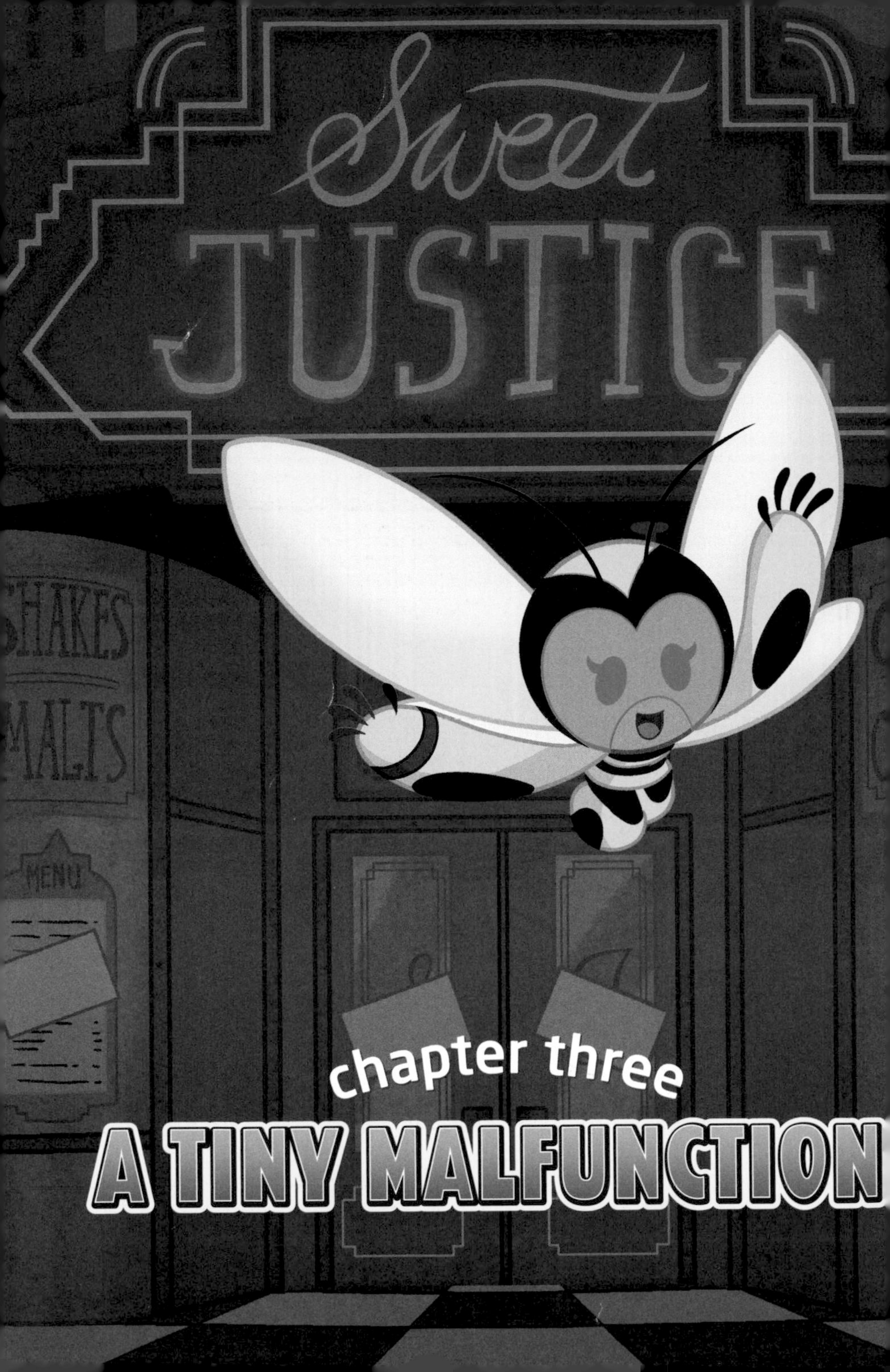
Sweet
JUSTICE
SHAKES
MALTS
MENU

chapter three
A TINY MALFUNCTION

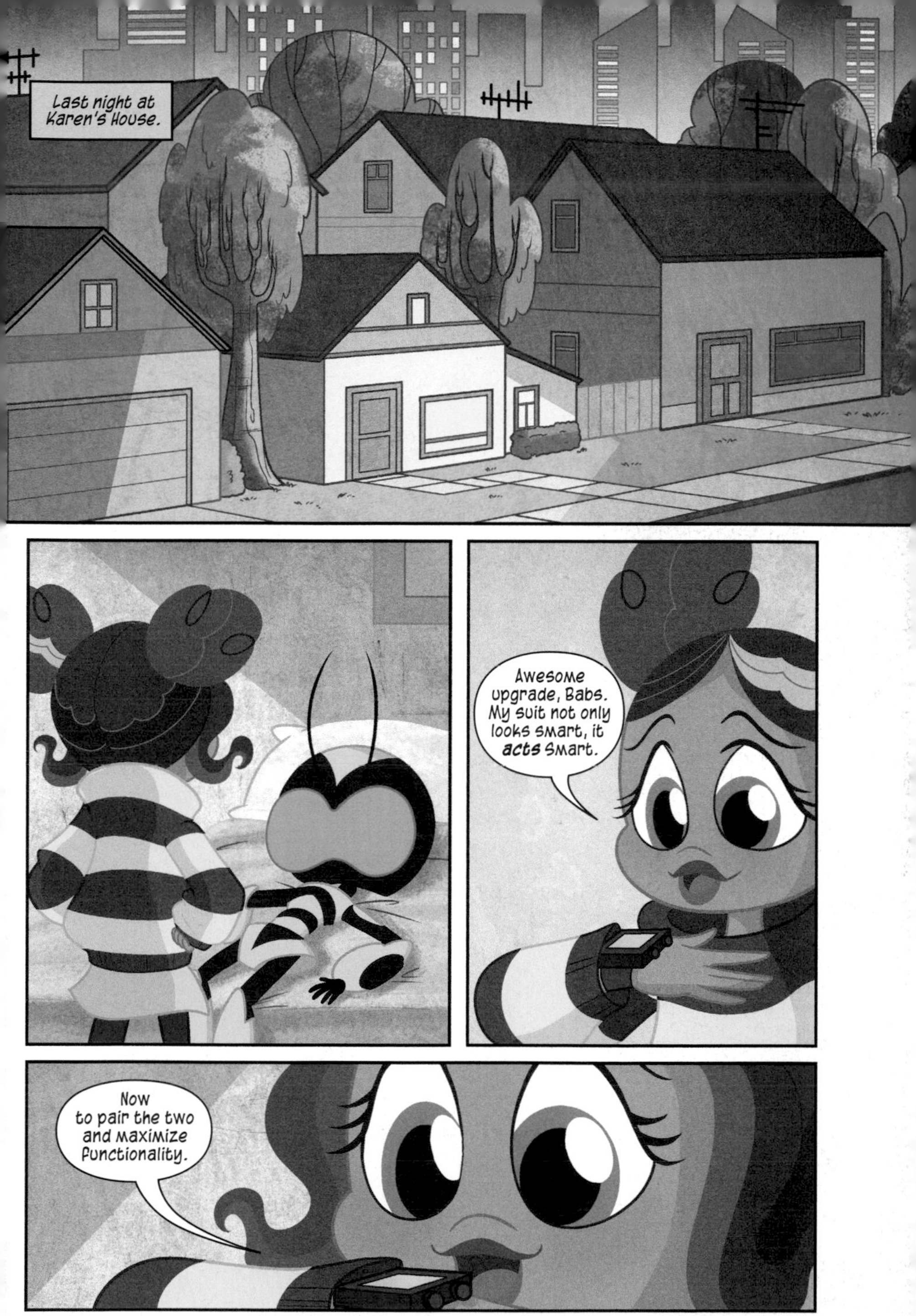
Last night at Karen's House.
Awesome upgrade, Babs. My suit not only looks smart, it **acts** smart.
Now to pair the two and maximize functionality.

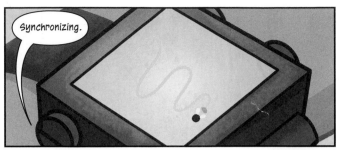

Synchronizing.

Whoa, don't go without me!

Looks like we're good to go.

Crime alert, Jewelers Row.

Just in time for a trial run!

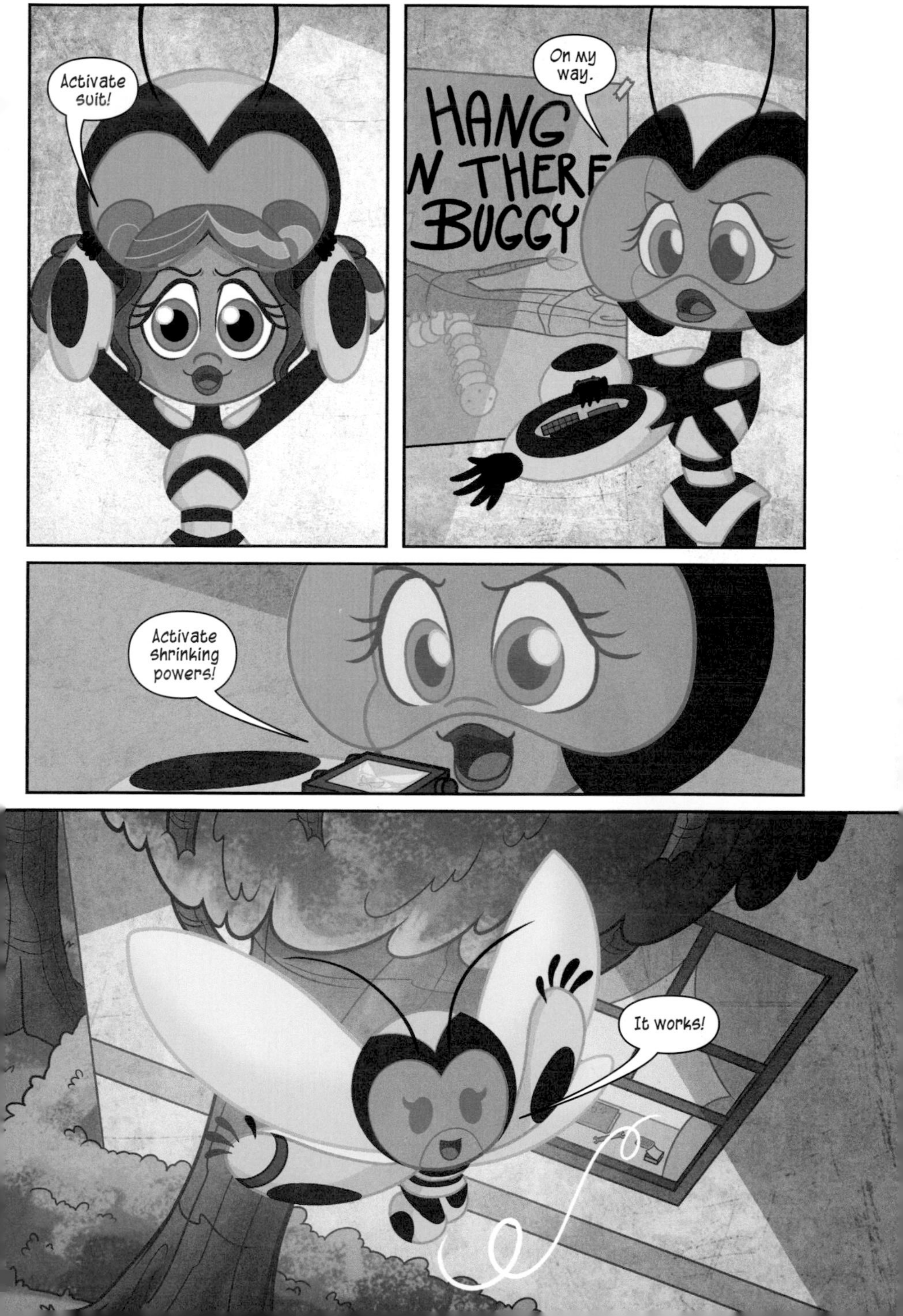
Activate suit!
On my way.
HANG IN THERE BUGGY
Activate shrinking powers!
It works!

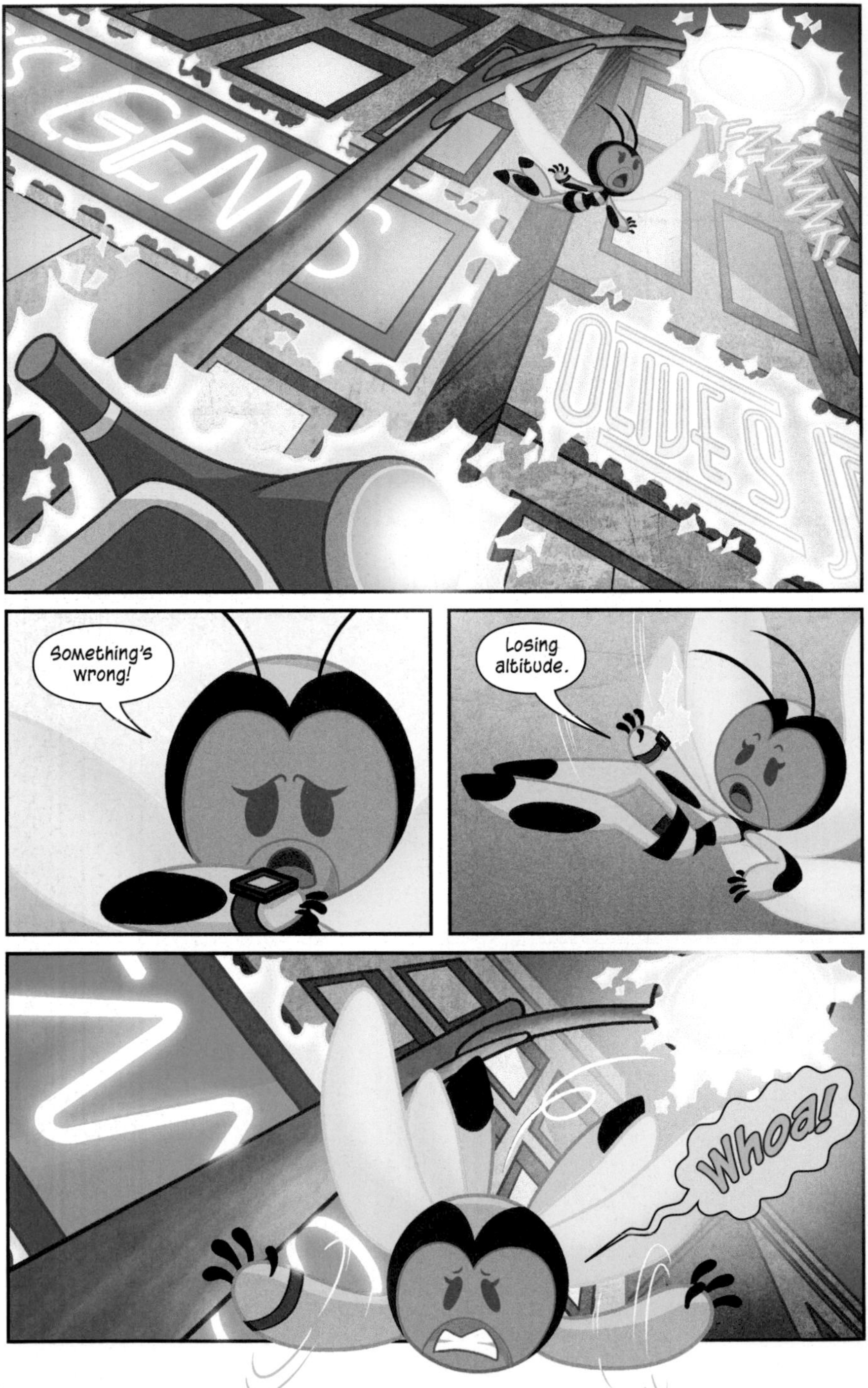
FZZZZZT!
Something's wrong!
Losing altitude.
Whoa!

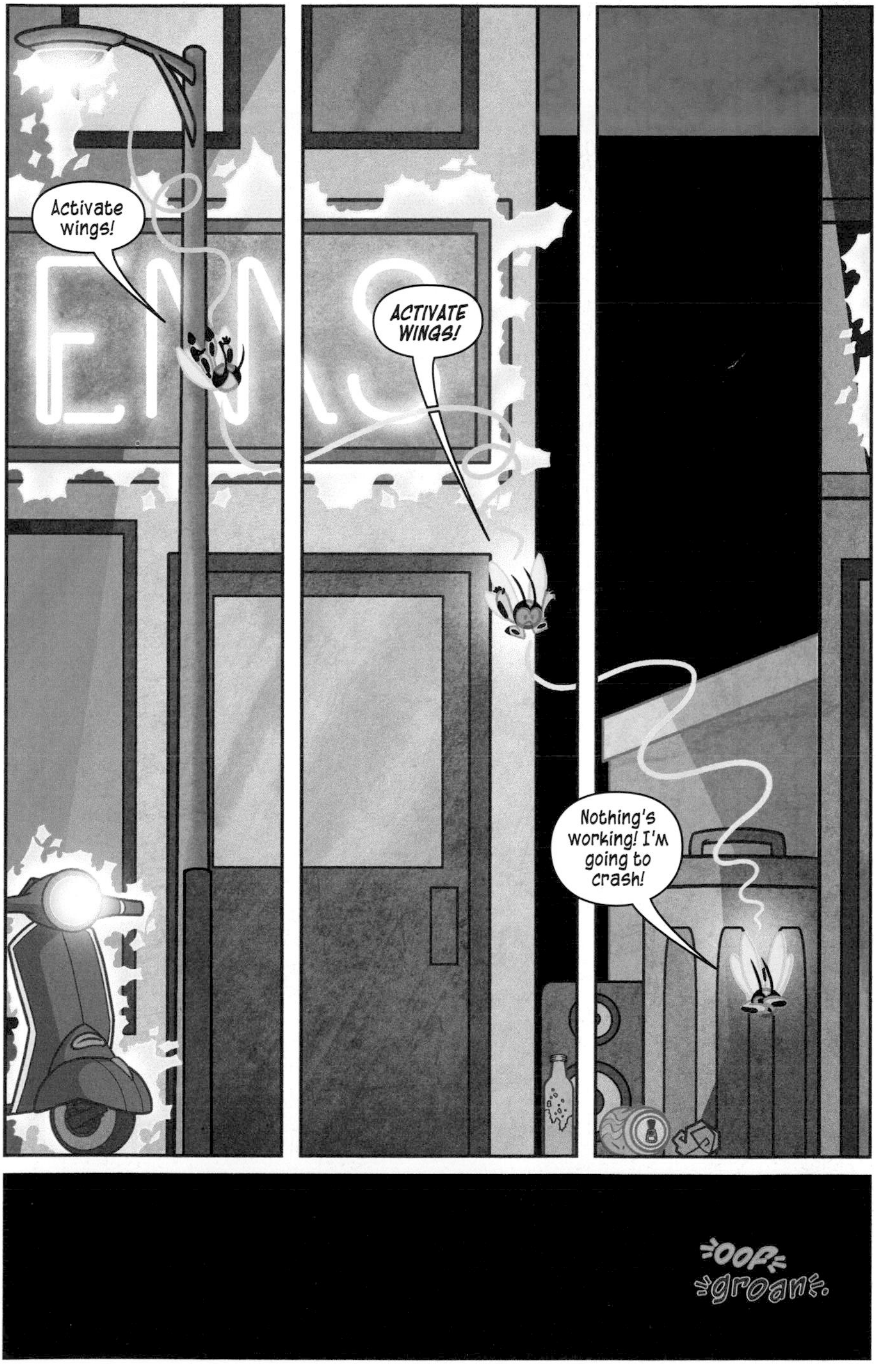
Activate wings!
ACTIVATE WINGS!
Nothing's working! I'M going to crash!
OOF
groan

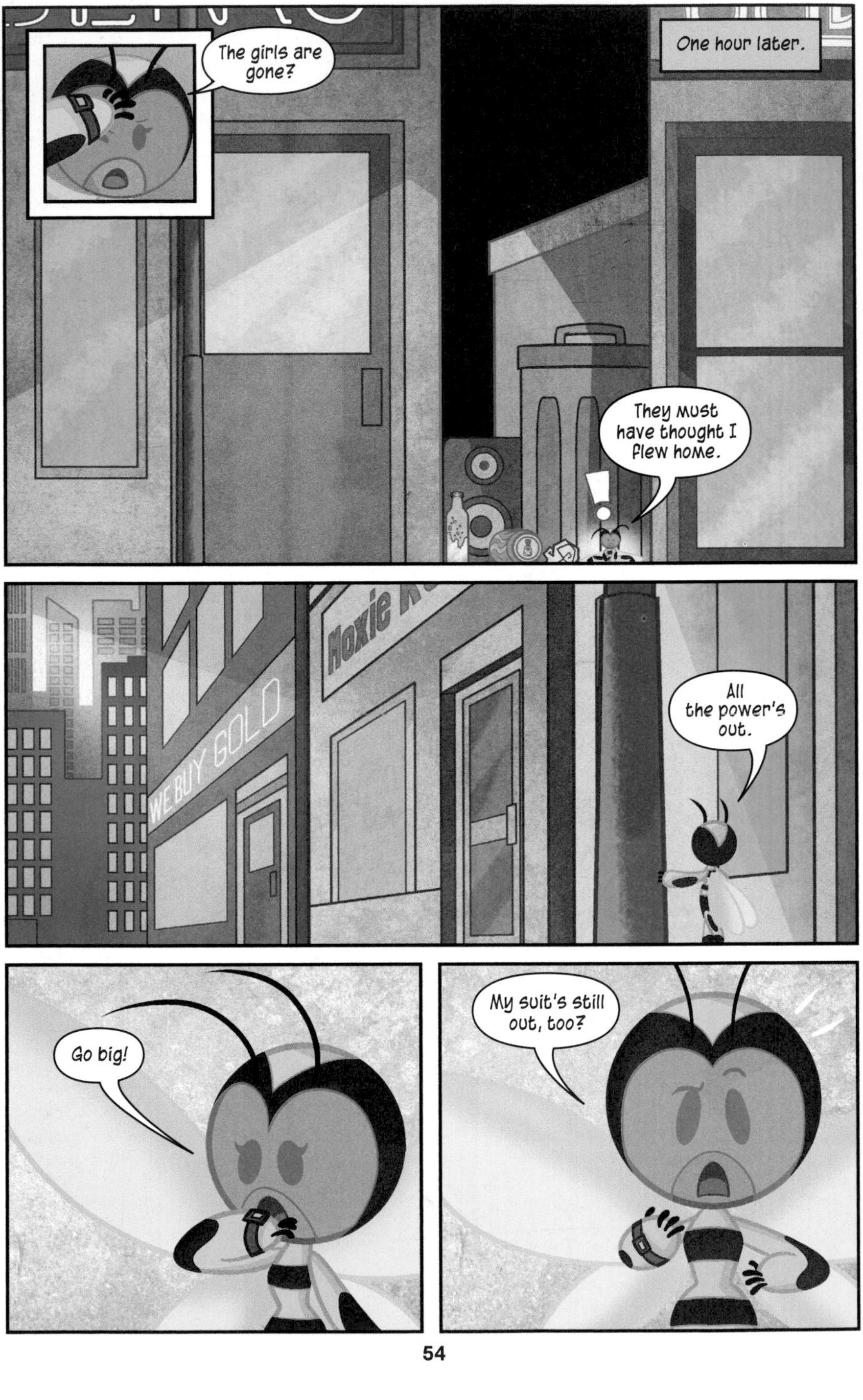
The girls are gone?
One hour later.
They must have thought I flew home.
Moxie
WE BUY GOLD
All the power's out.
Go big!
My suit's still out, too?

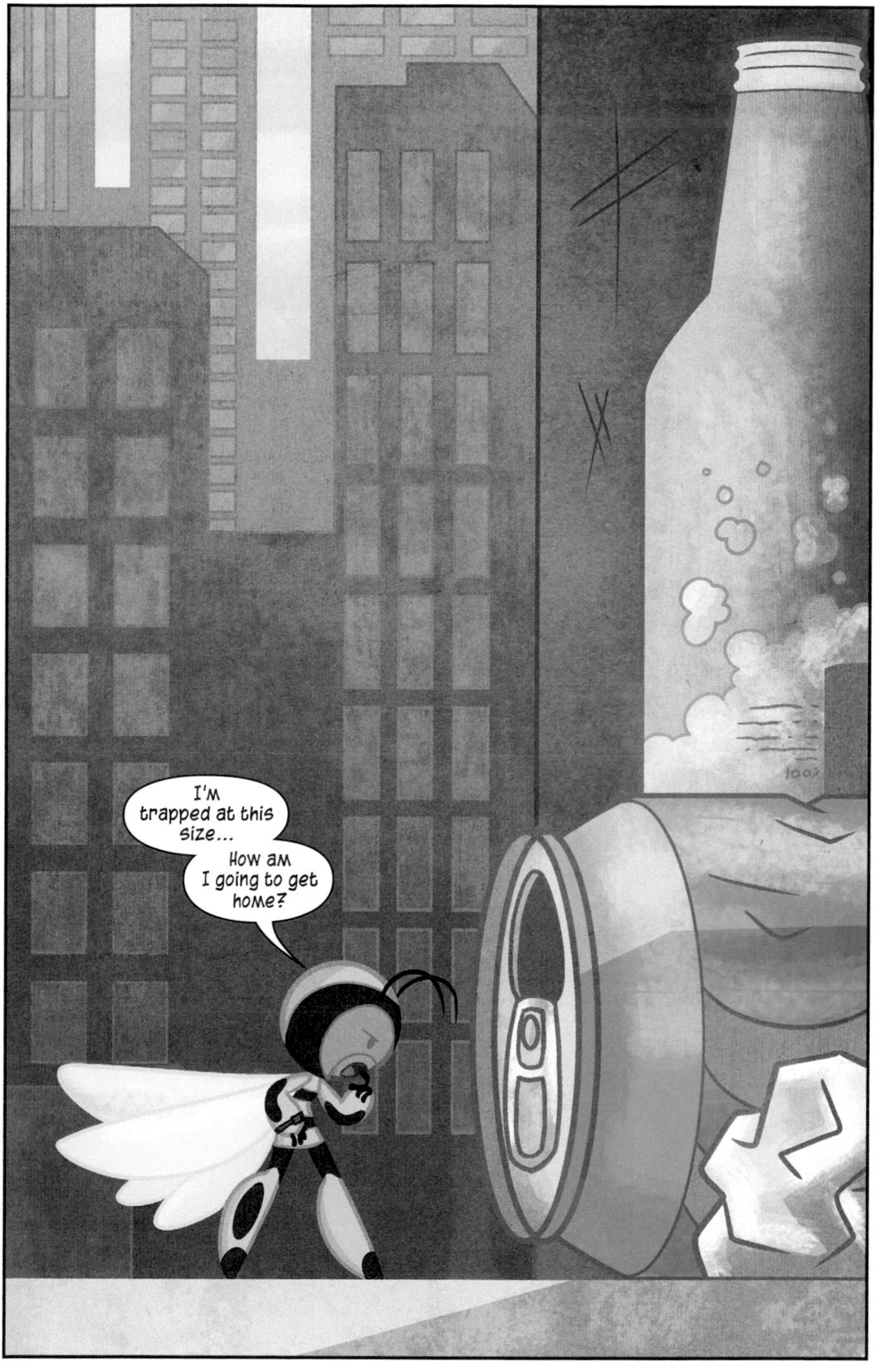
I'M trapped at this size...
HOW AM I going to get home?

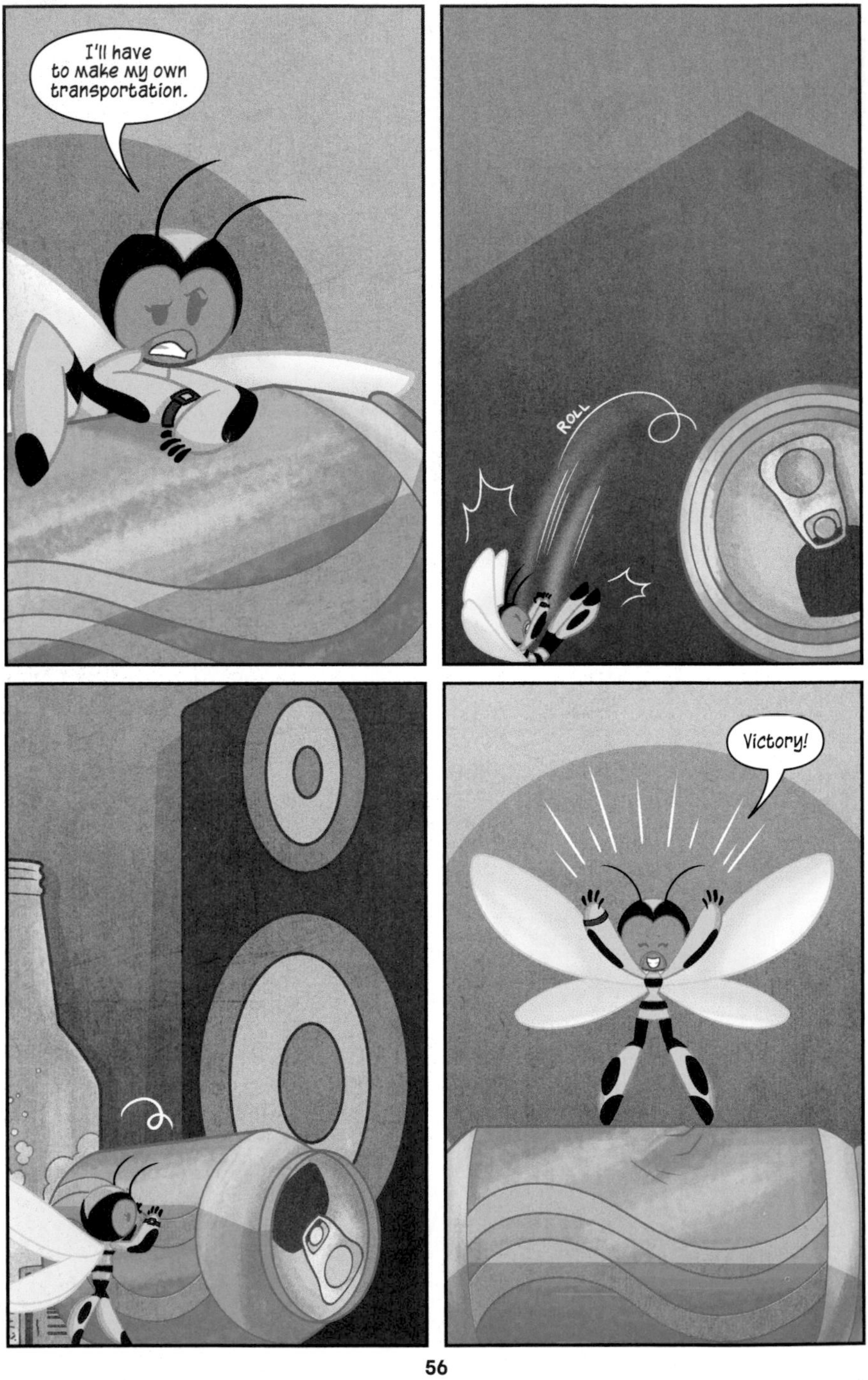
I'll have to make my own transportation.
ROLL
Victory!

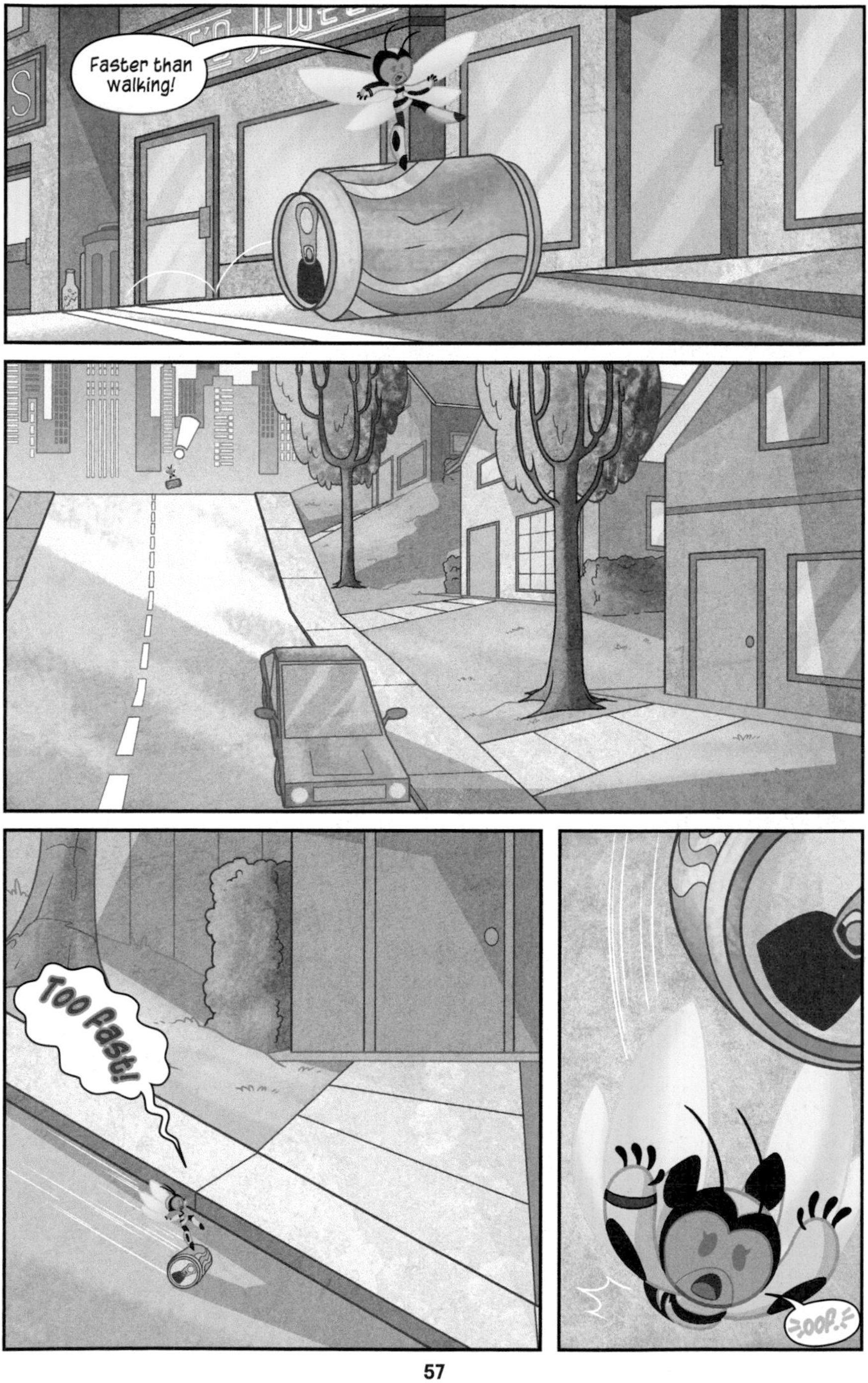
Faster than walking!
Too Fast!
OOP.

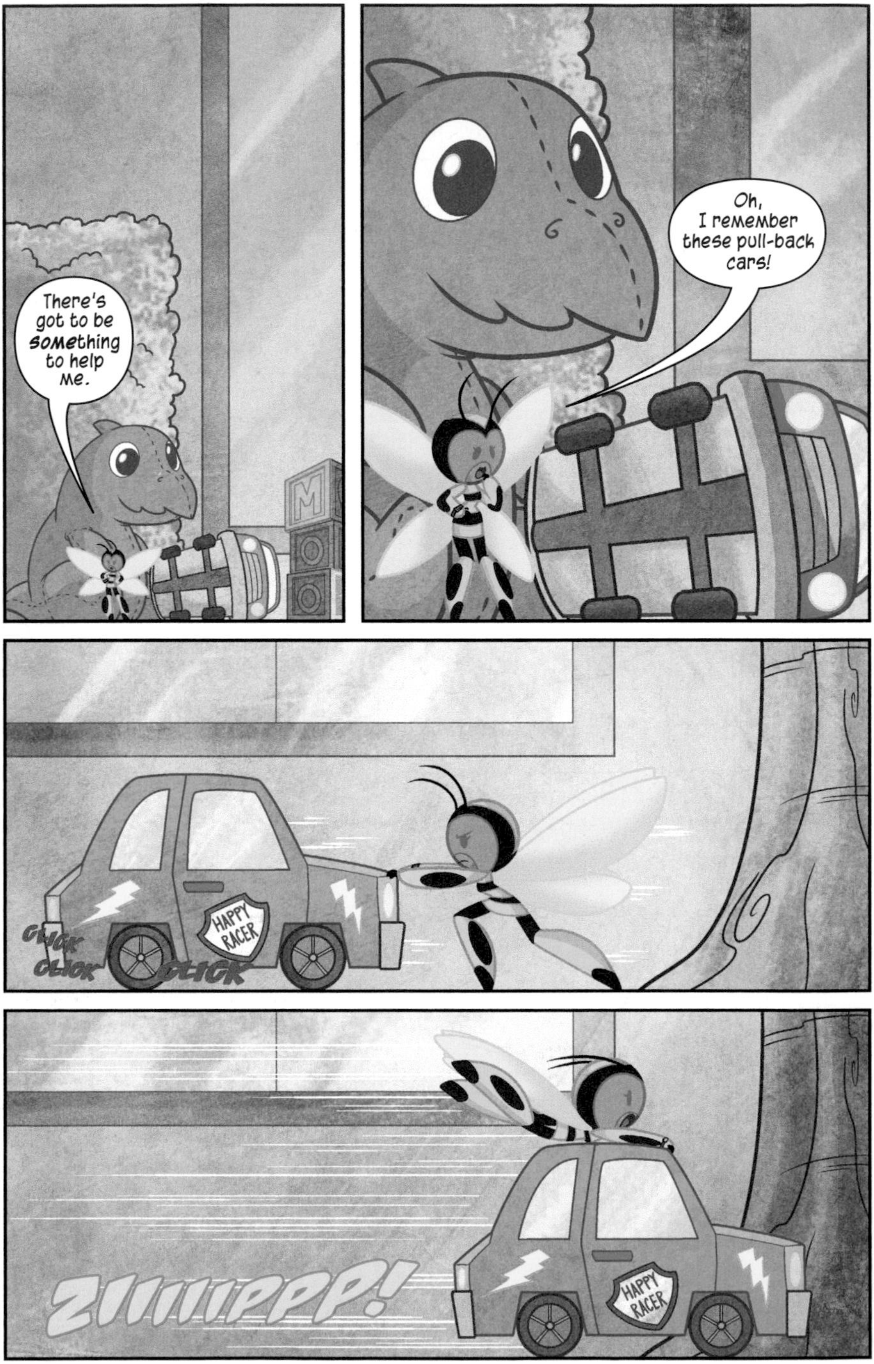
There's got to be SOMEthing to help me.
Oh, I remember these pull-back cars!
CLICK
CLICK
CLICK
HAPPY RACER
ZIIIIPPP!
HAPPY RACER

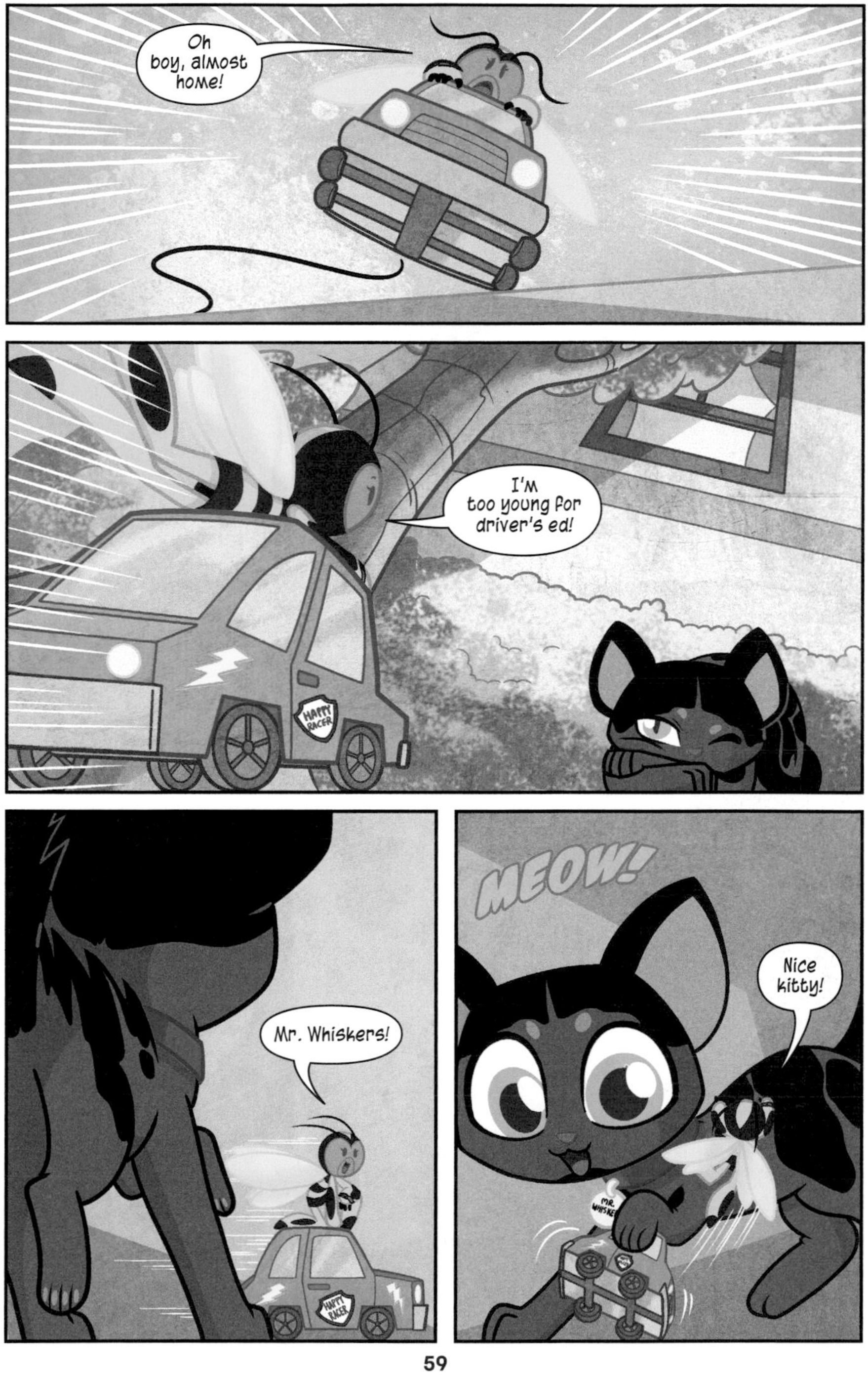
Oh boy, almost home!
I'm too young for driver's ed!
HAPPY RACER
Mr. Whiskers!
HAPPY RACER
MEOW!
Nice kitty!

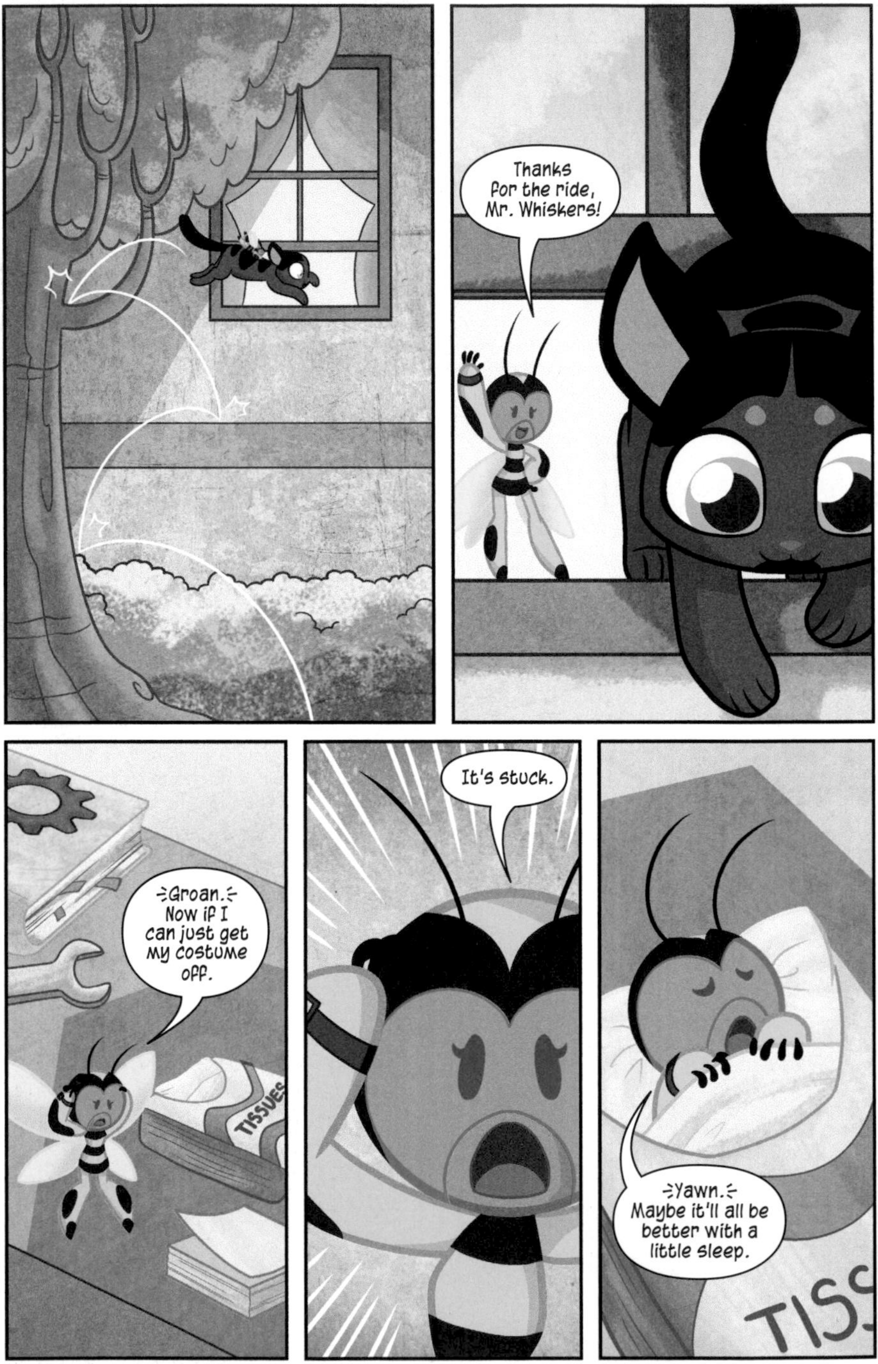
Thanks for the ride, Mr. Whiskers!
Groan. Now if I can just get my costume off.
TISSUES
It's stuck.
Yawn. Maybe it'll all be better with a little sleep.
TISS

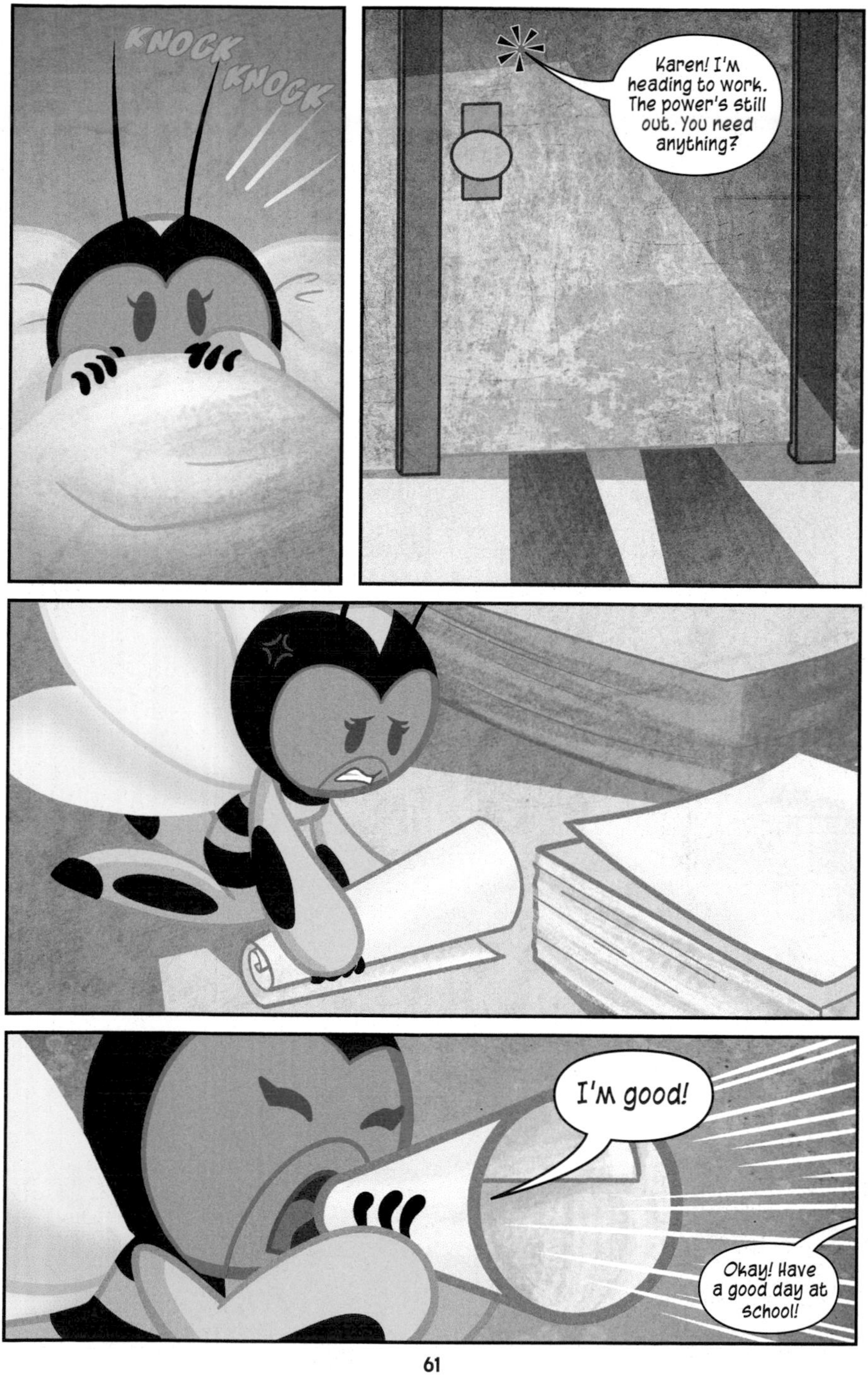
KNOCK
KNOCK
Karen! I'M heading to work. The power's still out. You need anything?
I'M good!
Okay! Have a good day at school!

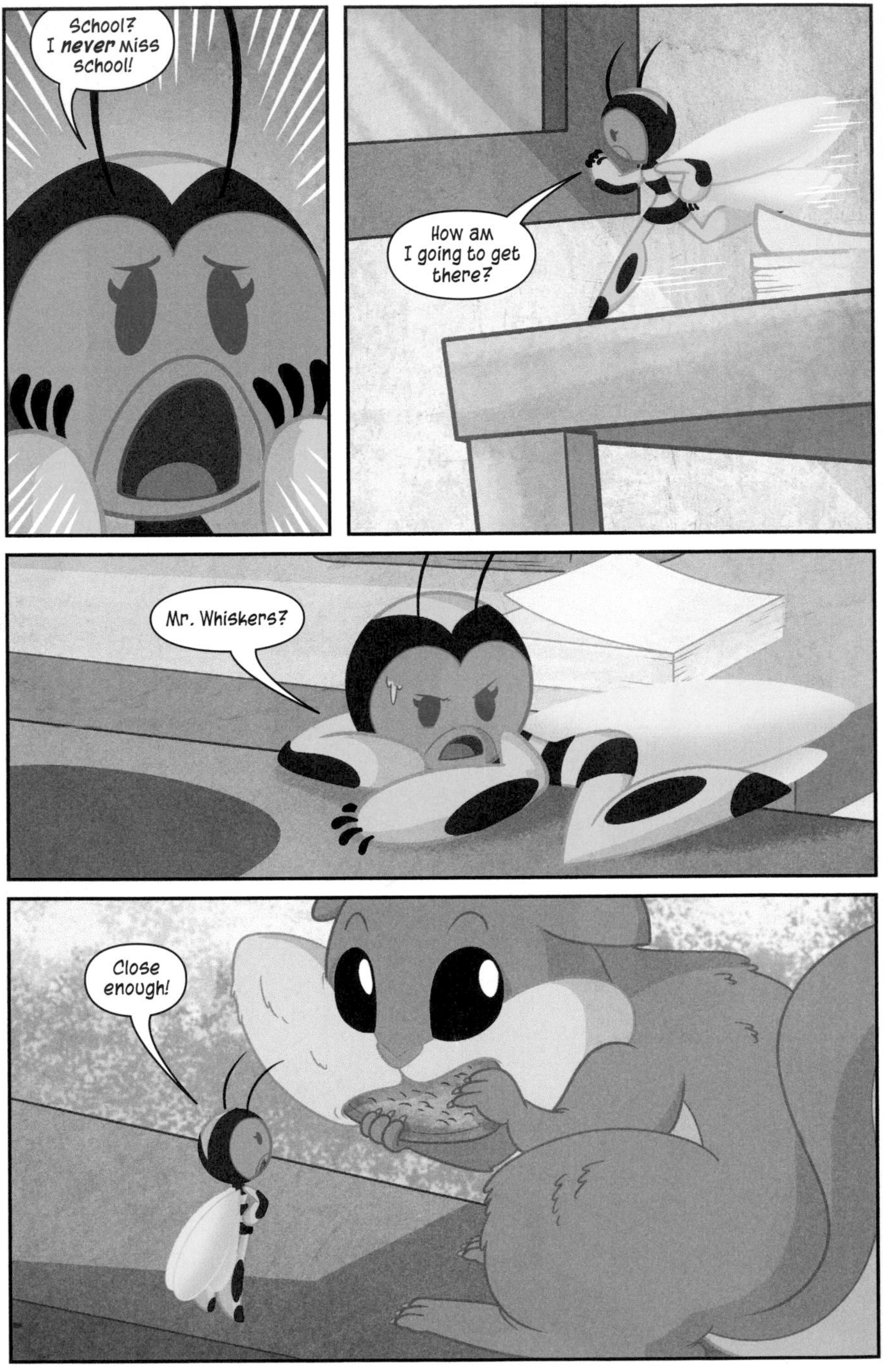
School? I **never** miss school!
How am I going to get there?
Mr. Whiskers?
Close enough!

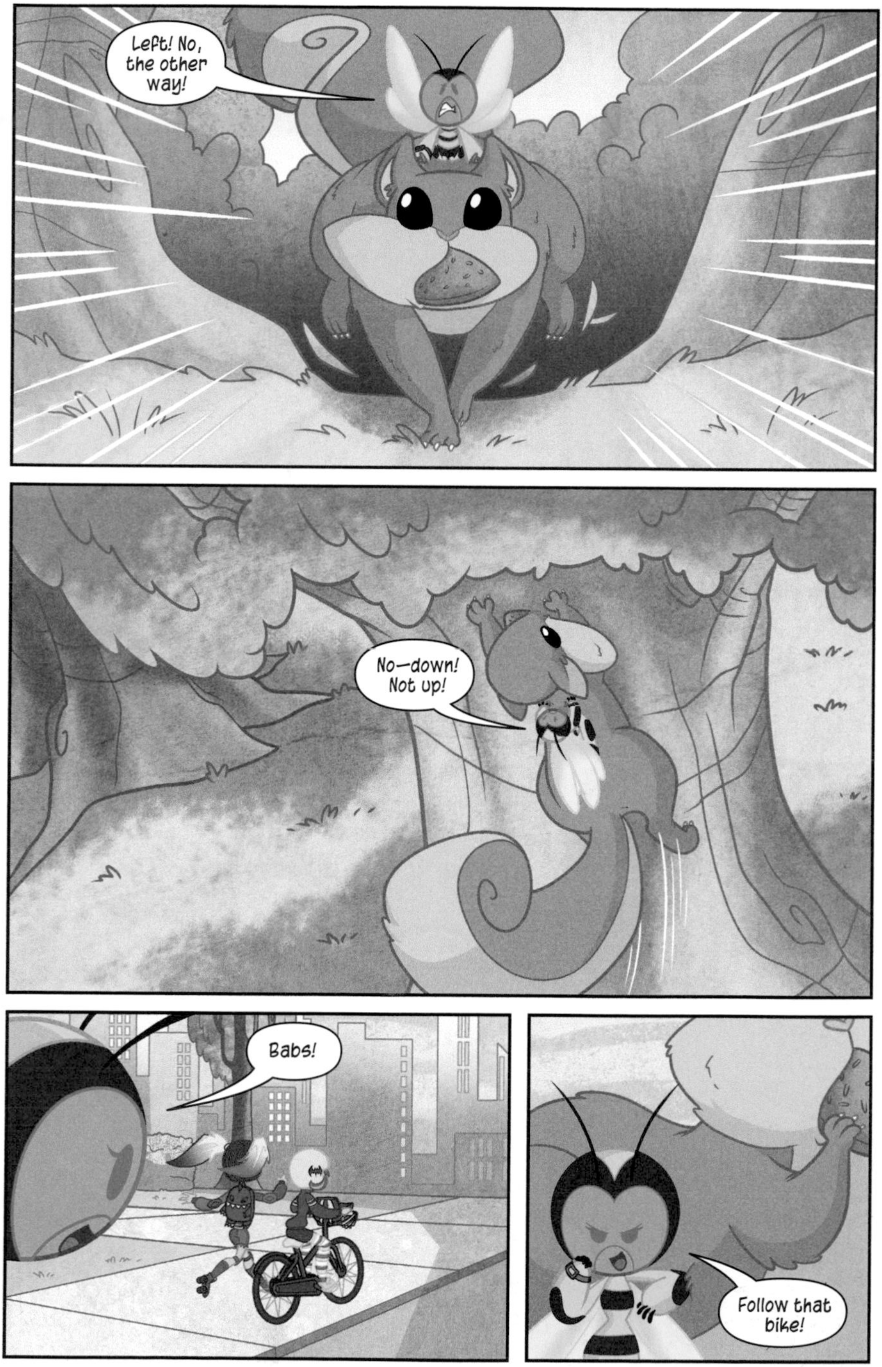
Left! No, the other way!
No—down! Not up!
Babs!
Follow that bike!

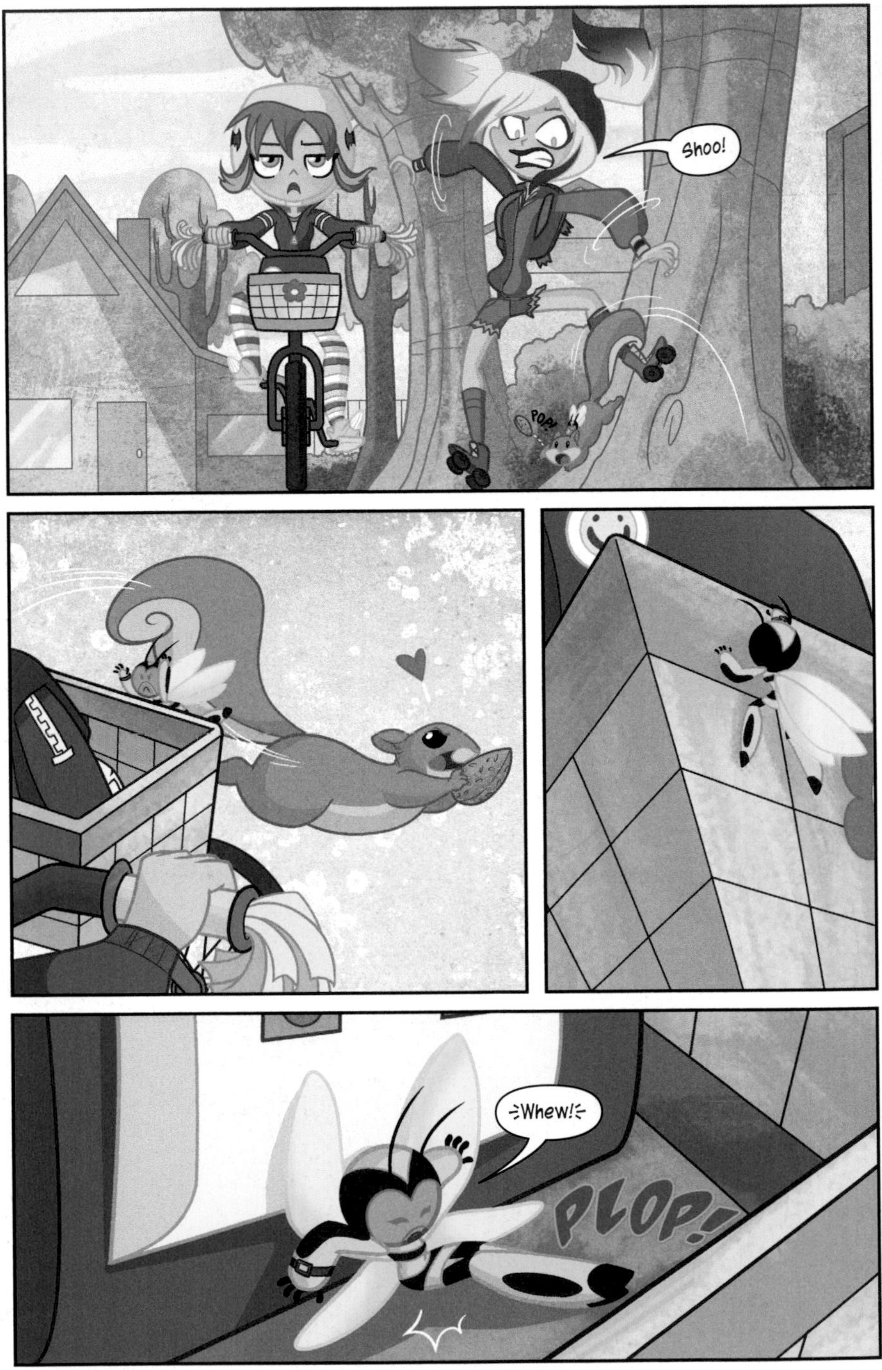
Shoo!
POP!
Whew!
PLOP!

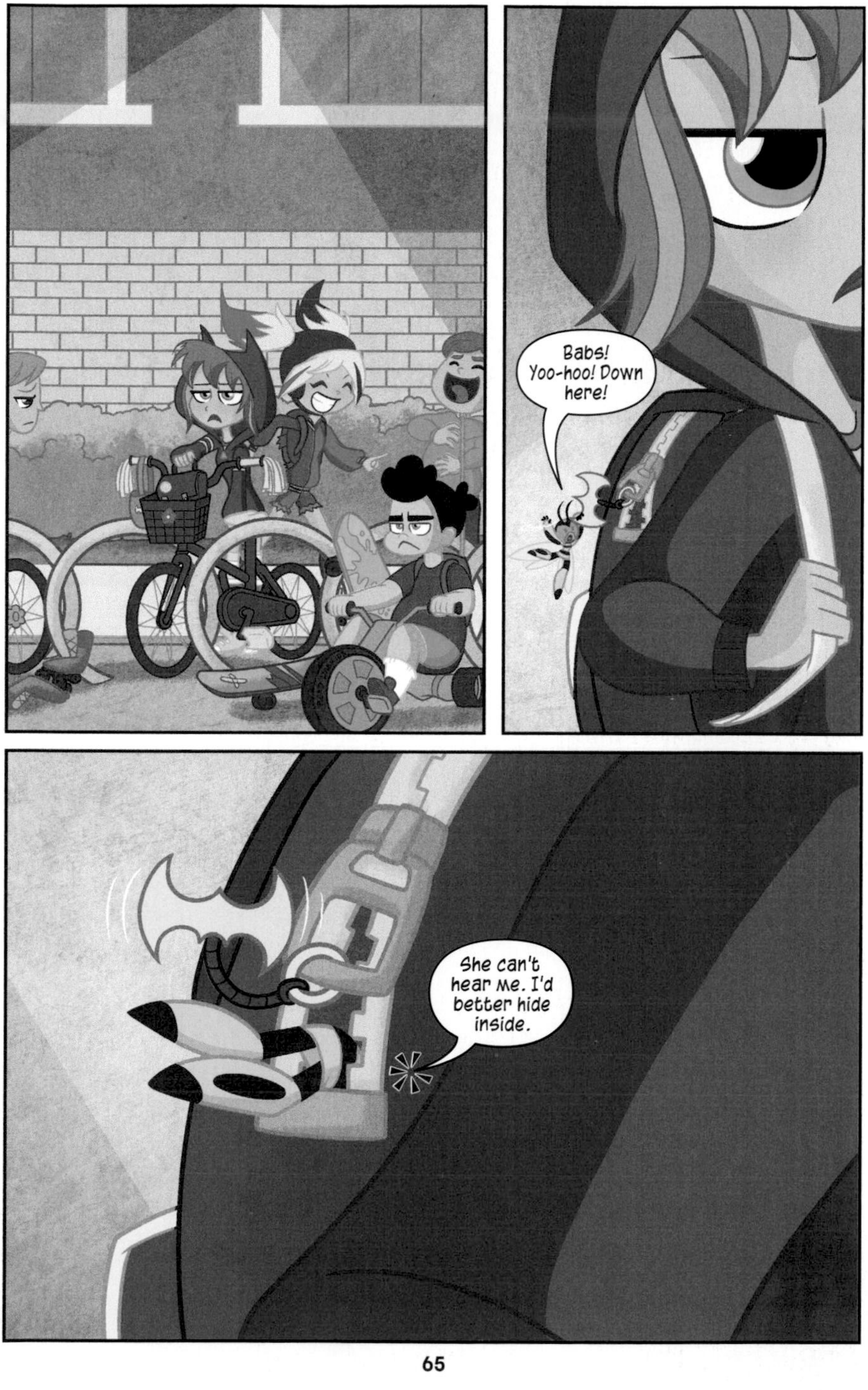
Babs! Yoo-hoo! Down here!
She can't hear me. I'd better hide inside.

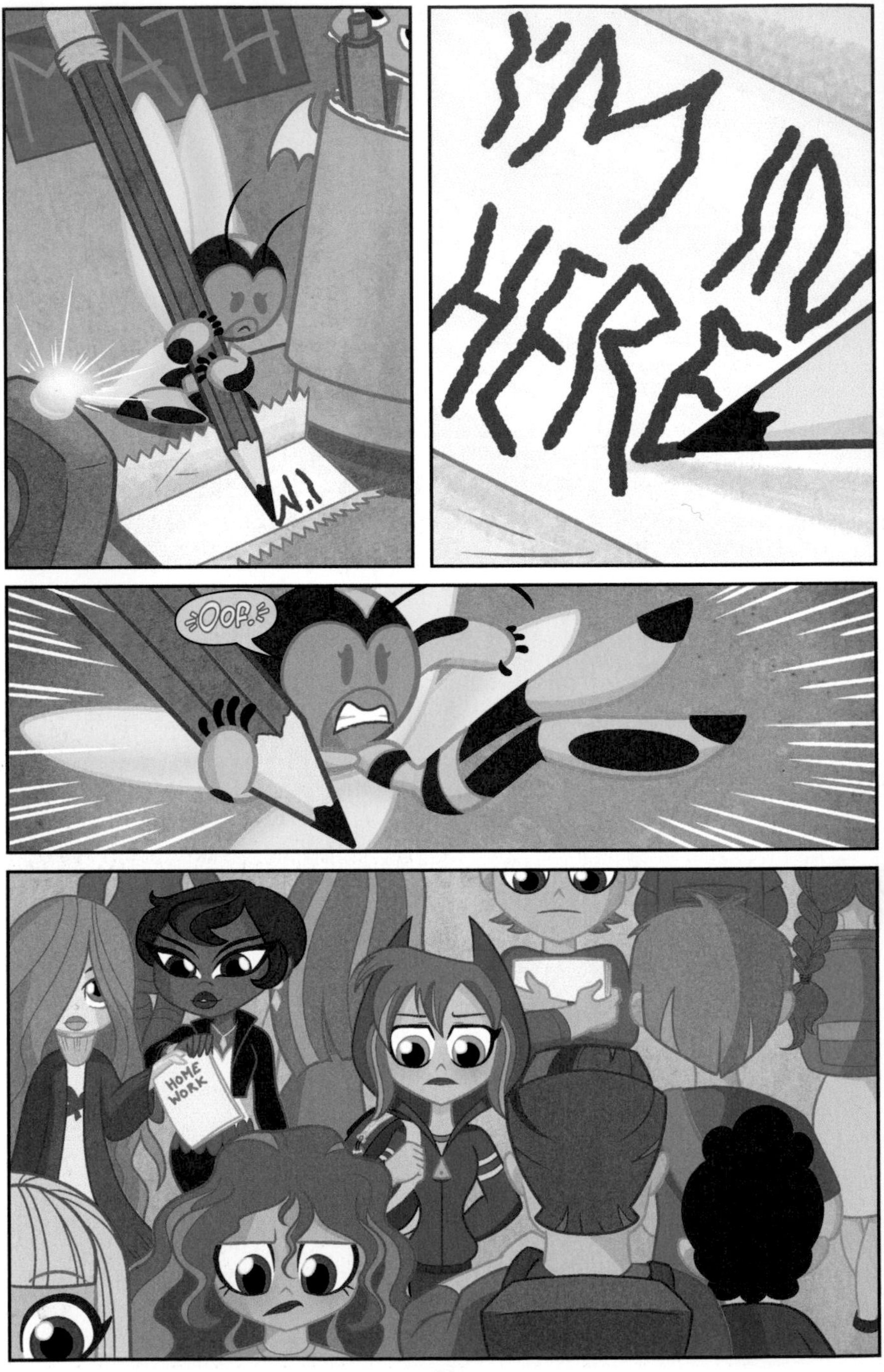
MATH
I'M IN HERE!!
OOF.
HOME WORK

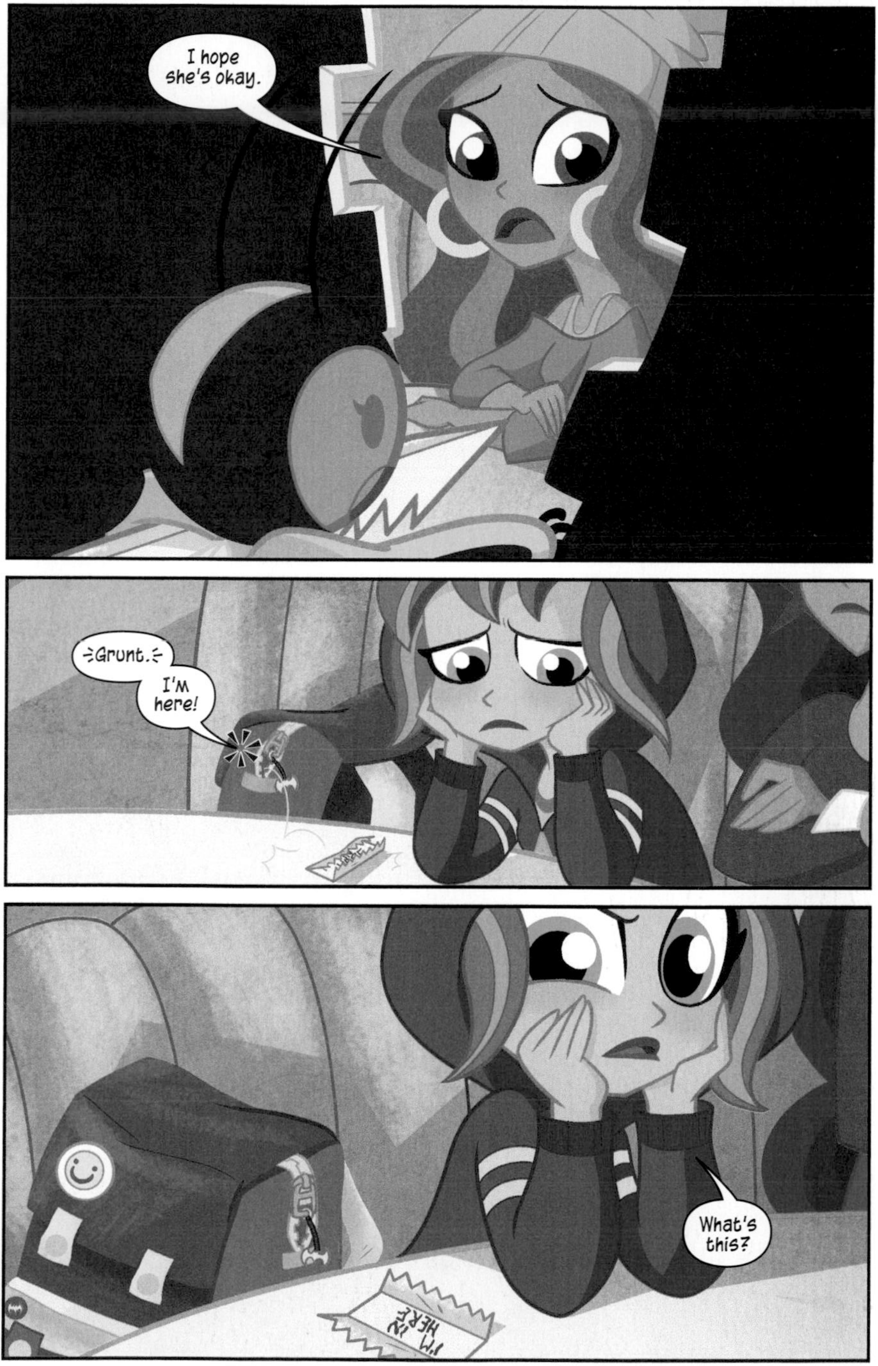
I hope she's okay.
Grunt.
I'M here!
What's this?
I'M IN HERE

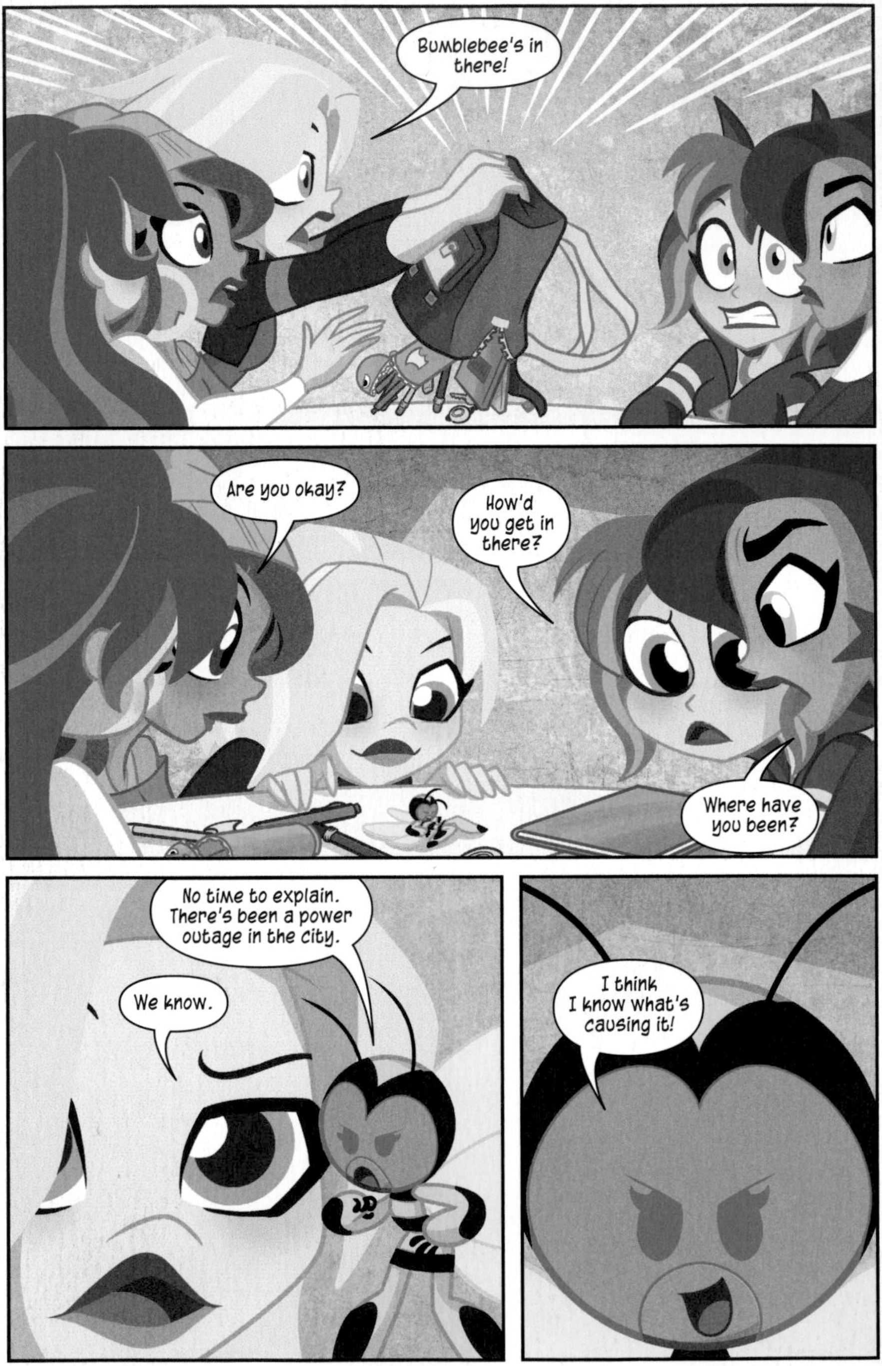
Bumblebee's in there!
Are you okay?
How'd you get in there?
Where have you been?
No time to explain. There's been a power outage in the city.
We know.
I think I know what's causing it!

chapter four
DISCONNECTED

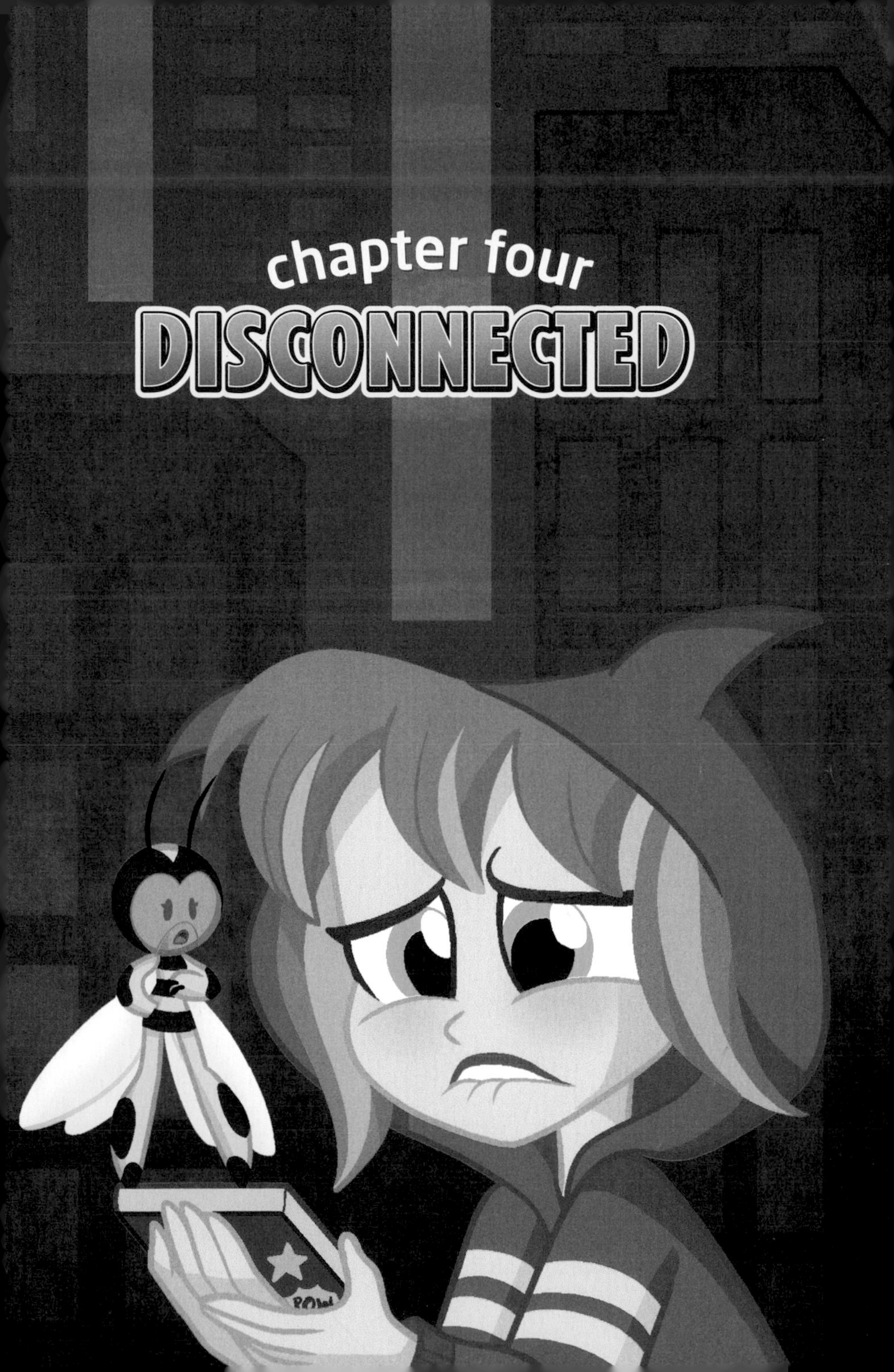

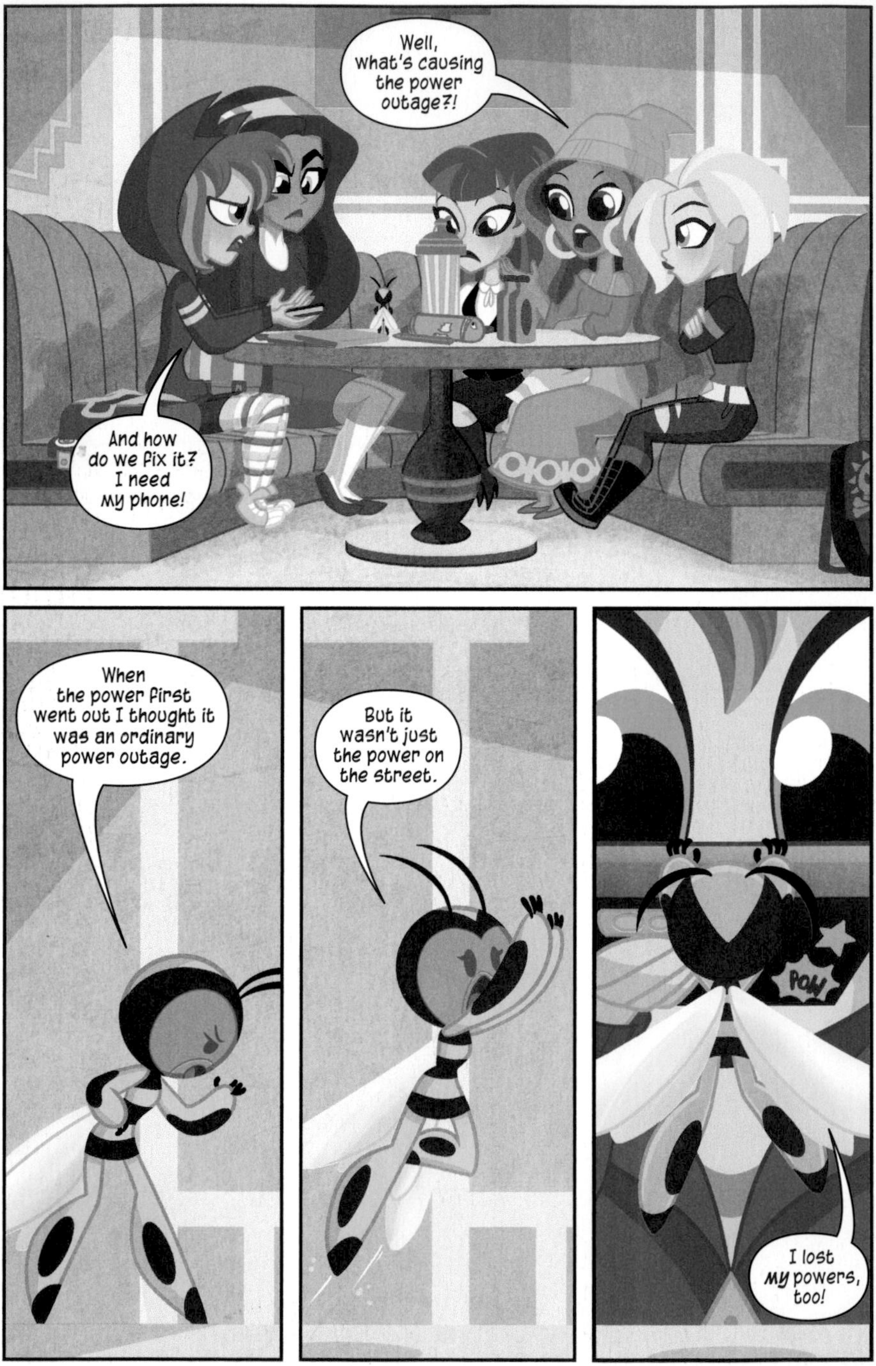
Well, what's causing the power outage?!
And how do we fix it? I need my phone!
When the power first went out I thought it was an ordinary power outage.
But it wasn't just the power on the street.
POW
I lost my powers, too!

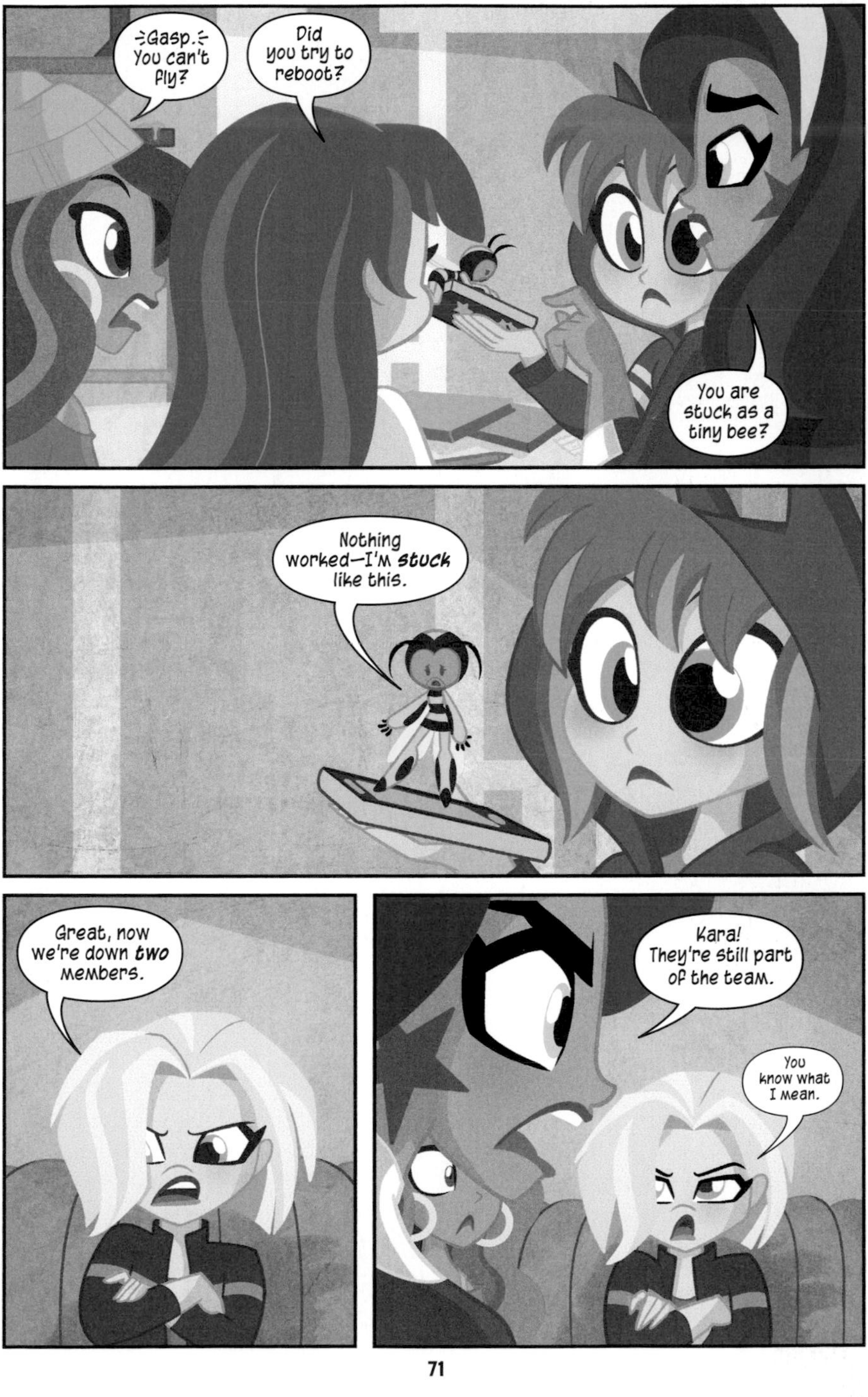

Gasp.
You can't fly?
Did you try to reboot?
You are stuck as a tiny bee?
Nothing worked—I'm **stuck** like this.
Great, now we're down **two** members.
Kara! They're still part of the team.
You know what I mean.

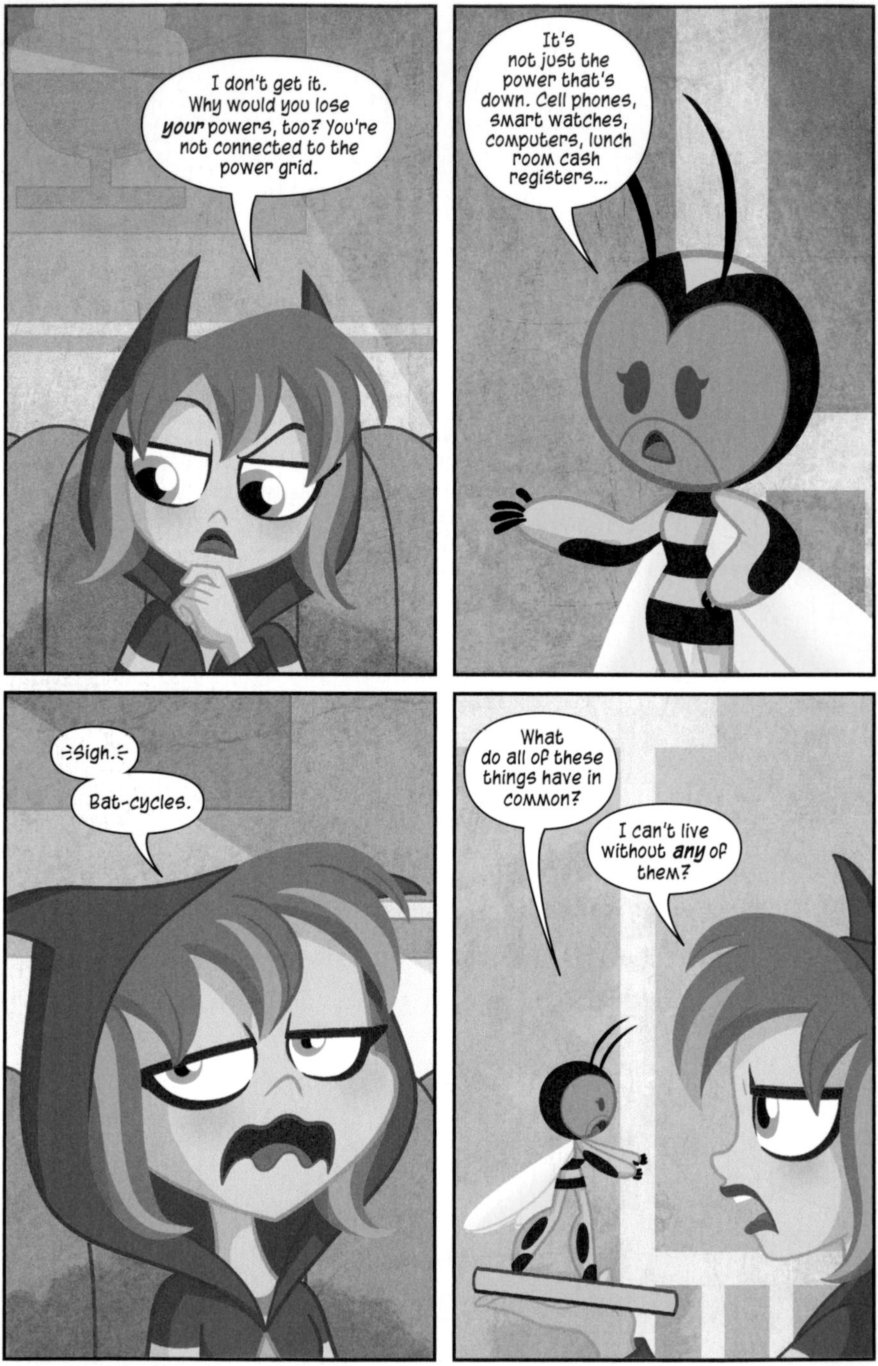
I don't get it. Why would you lose **your** powers, too? You're not connected to the power grid.
It's not just the power that's down. Cell phones, smart watches, computers, lunch room cash registers...
Sigh.
Bat-cycles.
What do all of these things have in common?
I can't live without **any** of them?

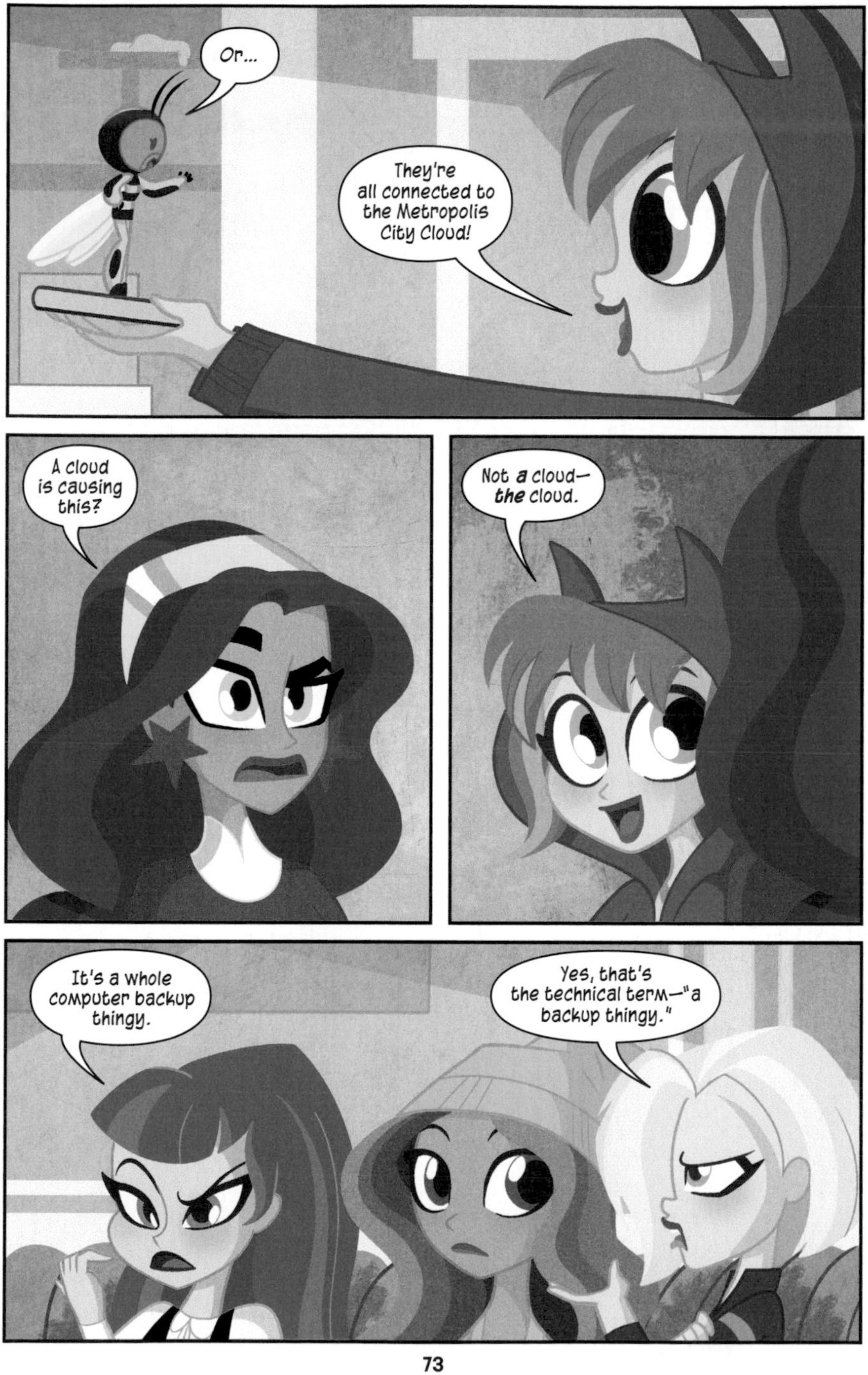
Or...
They're all connected to the Metropolis City Cloud!
A cloud is causing this?
Not *a* cloud—*the* cloud.
It's a whole computer backup thingy.
Yes, that's the technical term—"a backup thingy."

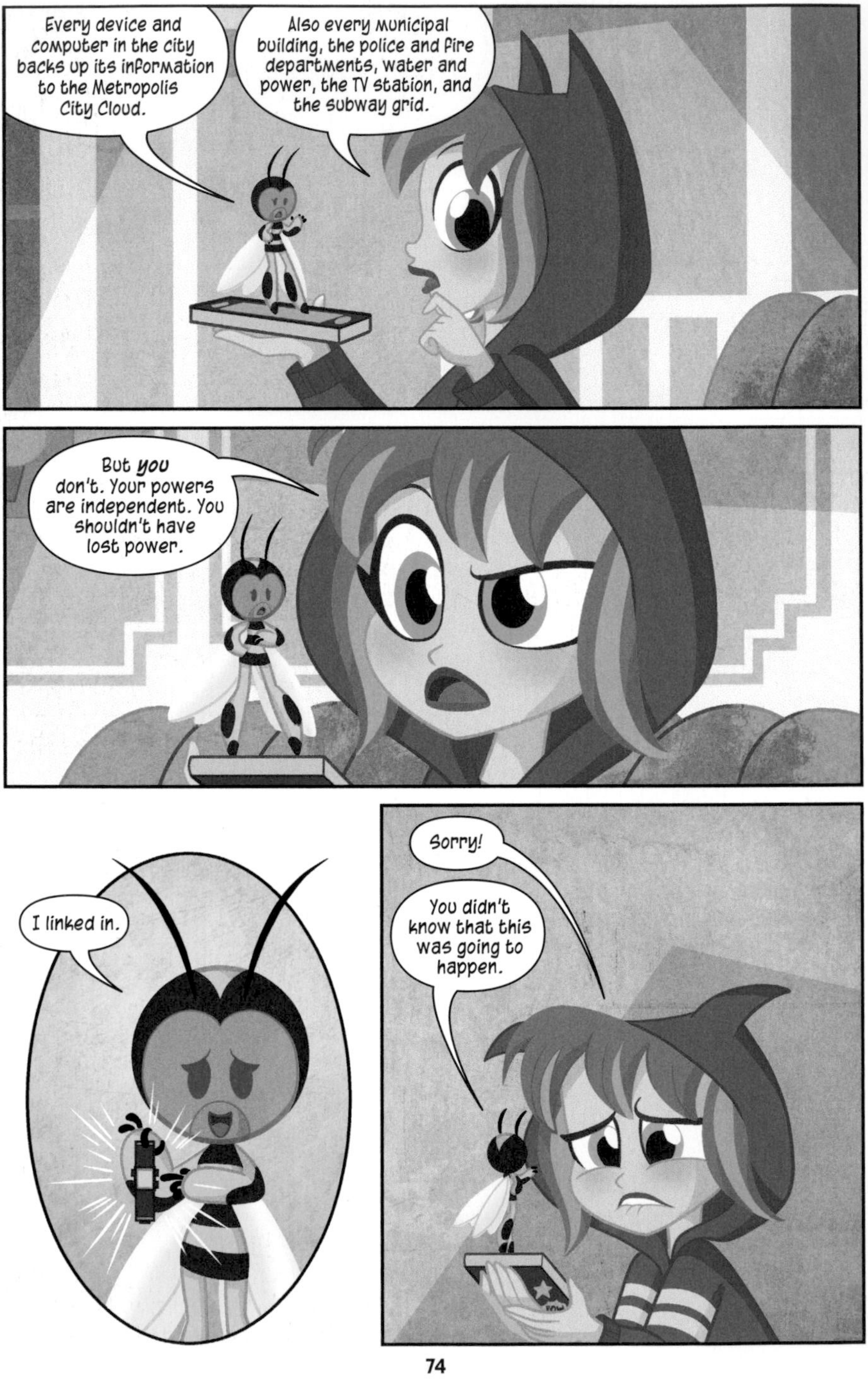

Every device and computer in the city backs up its information to the Metropolis City Cloud.
Also every municipal building, the police and fire departments, water and power, the TV station, and the subway grid.
But *you* don't. Your powers are independent. You shouldn't have lost power.
I linked in.
Sorry!
You didn't know that this was going to happen.

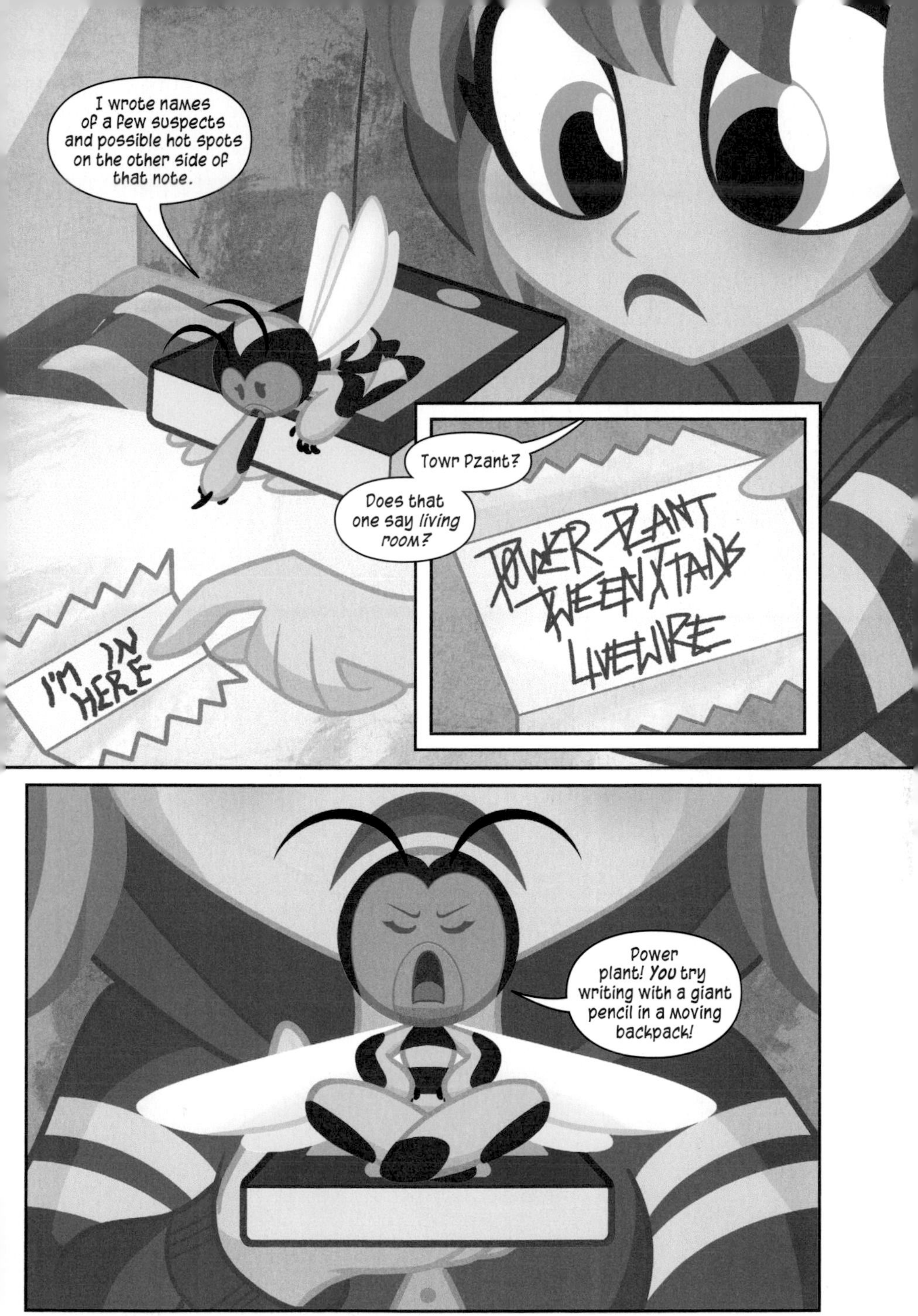
I wrote names of a few suspects and possible hot spots on the other side of that note.
I'M IN HERE
Towr Pzant?
Does that one say *living room?*
TOWER PLANT
TWEEN TTANS
LIVEWIRE
Power plant! *You* try writing with a giant pencil in a moving backpack!

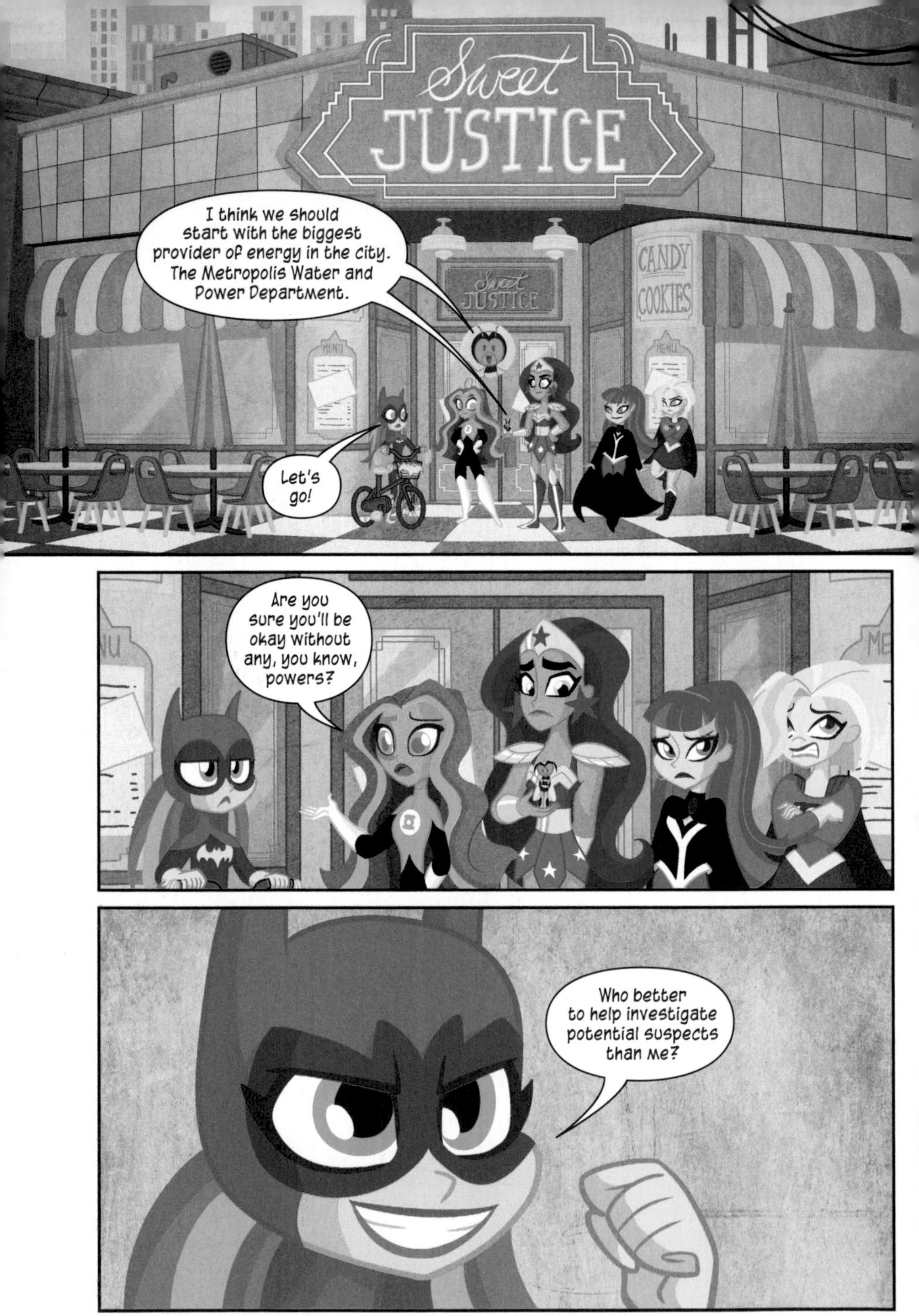
Sweet JUSTICE
I think we should start with the biggest provider of energy in the city. The Metropolis Water and Power Department.
CANDY COOKIES
Let's go!
Are you sure you'll be okay without any, you know, powers?
Who better to help investigate potential suspects than me?

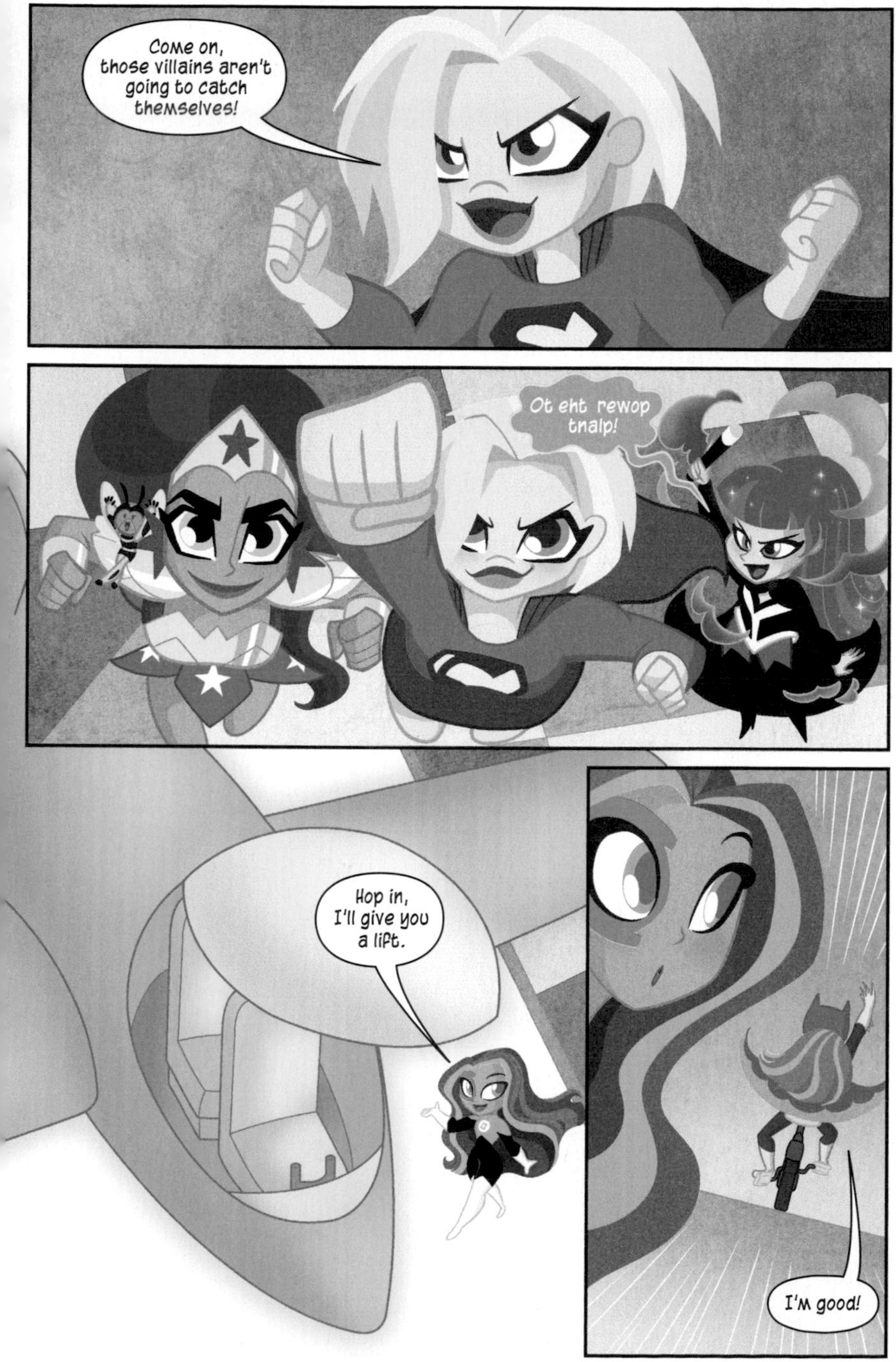

Come on, those villains aren't going to catch themselves!
Ot eht rewop tnalp!
Hop in, I'll give you a lift.
I'M good!

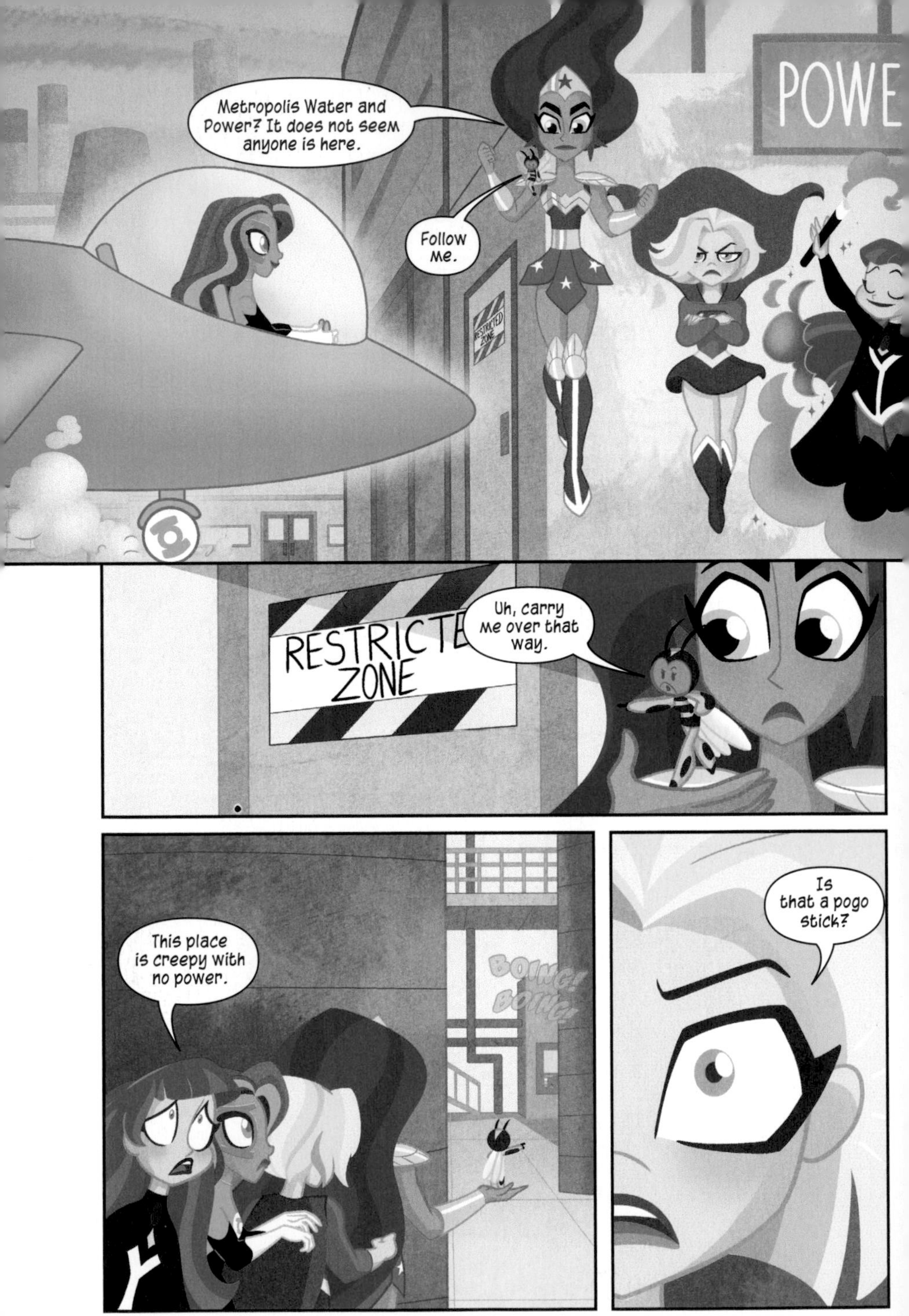
POWE
Metropolis Water and Power? It does not seem anyone is here.
Follow me.
RESTRICTED ZONE
RESTRICTE ZONE
Uh, carry me over that way.
This place is creepy with no power.
BOING! BOING!
Is that a pogo stick?

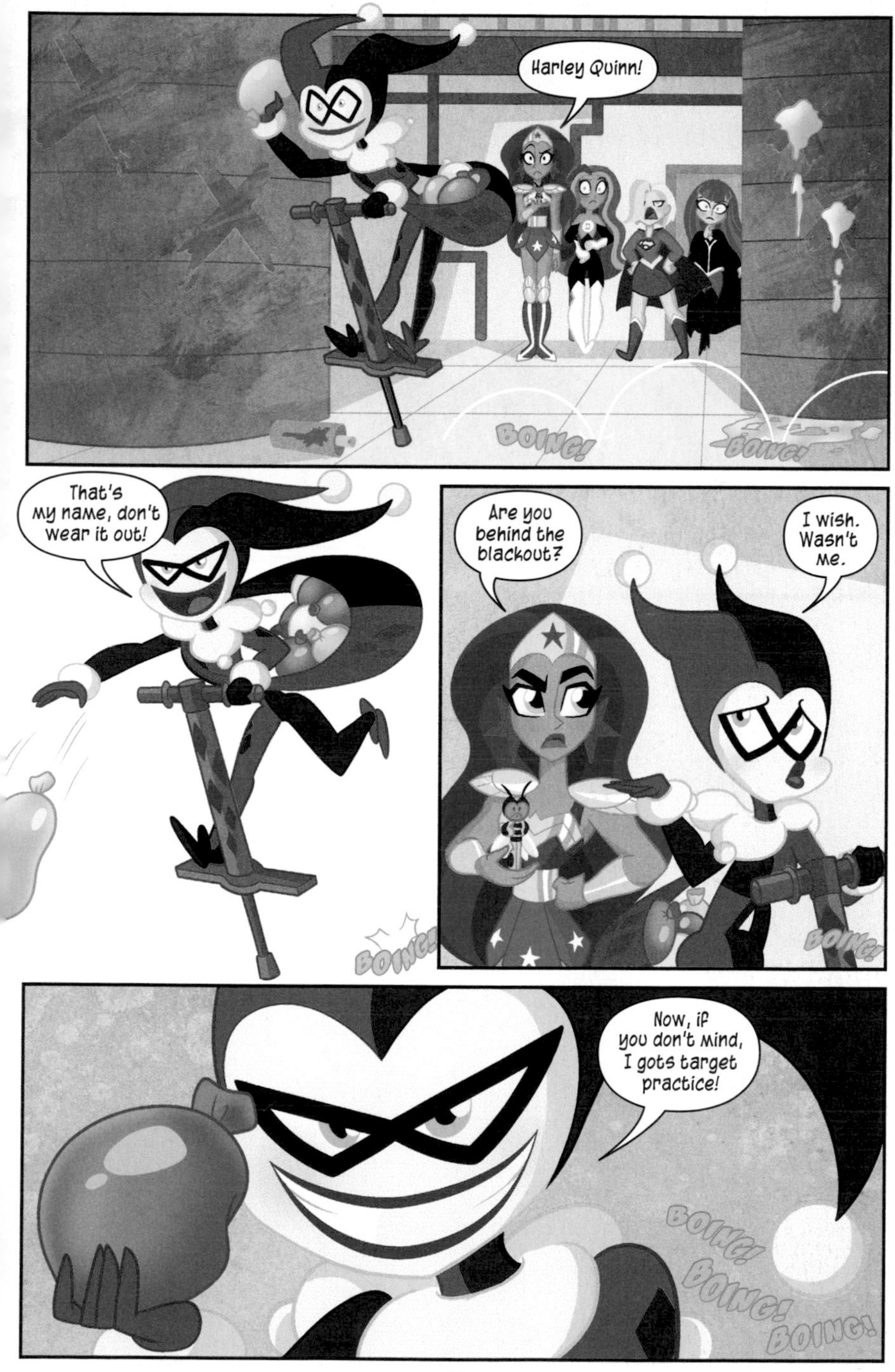
Harley Quinn!
BOING!
BOING!
That's my name, don't wear it out!
BOING!
Are you behind the blackout?
I wish. Wasn't me.
BOING!
Now, if you don't mind, I gots target practice!
BOING!
BOING!
BOING!

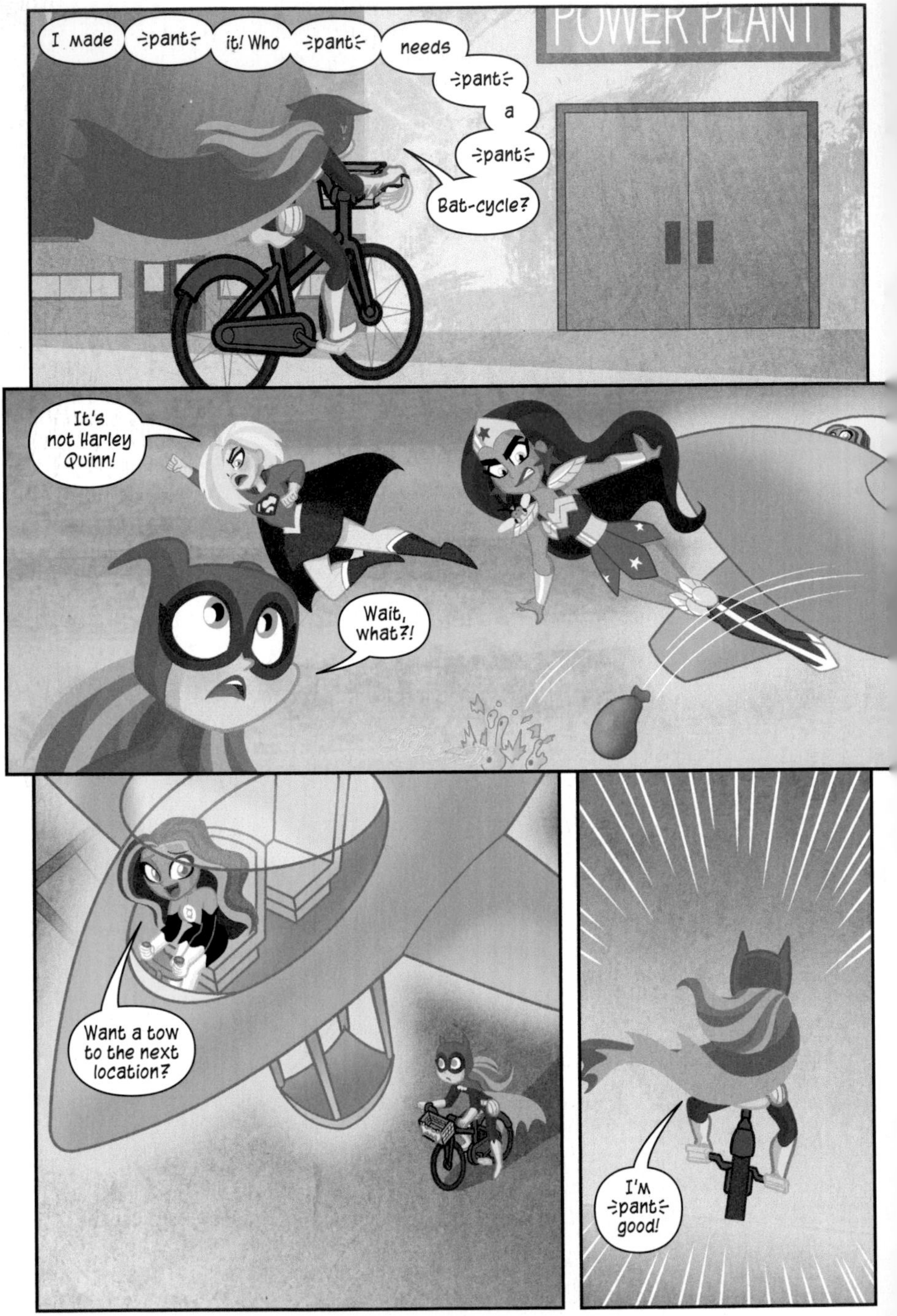
POWER PLANT
I made
=pant=
it! Who
=pant=
needs
=pant=
a
=pant=
Bat-cycle?
It's not Harley Quinn!
Wait, what?!
Want a tow to the next location?
I'M =pant= good!

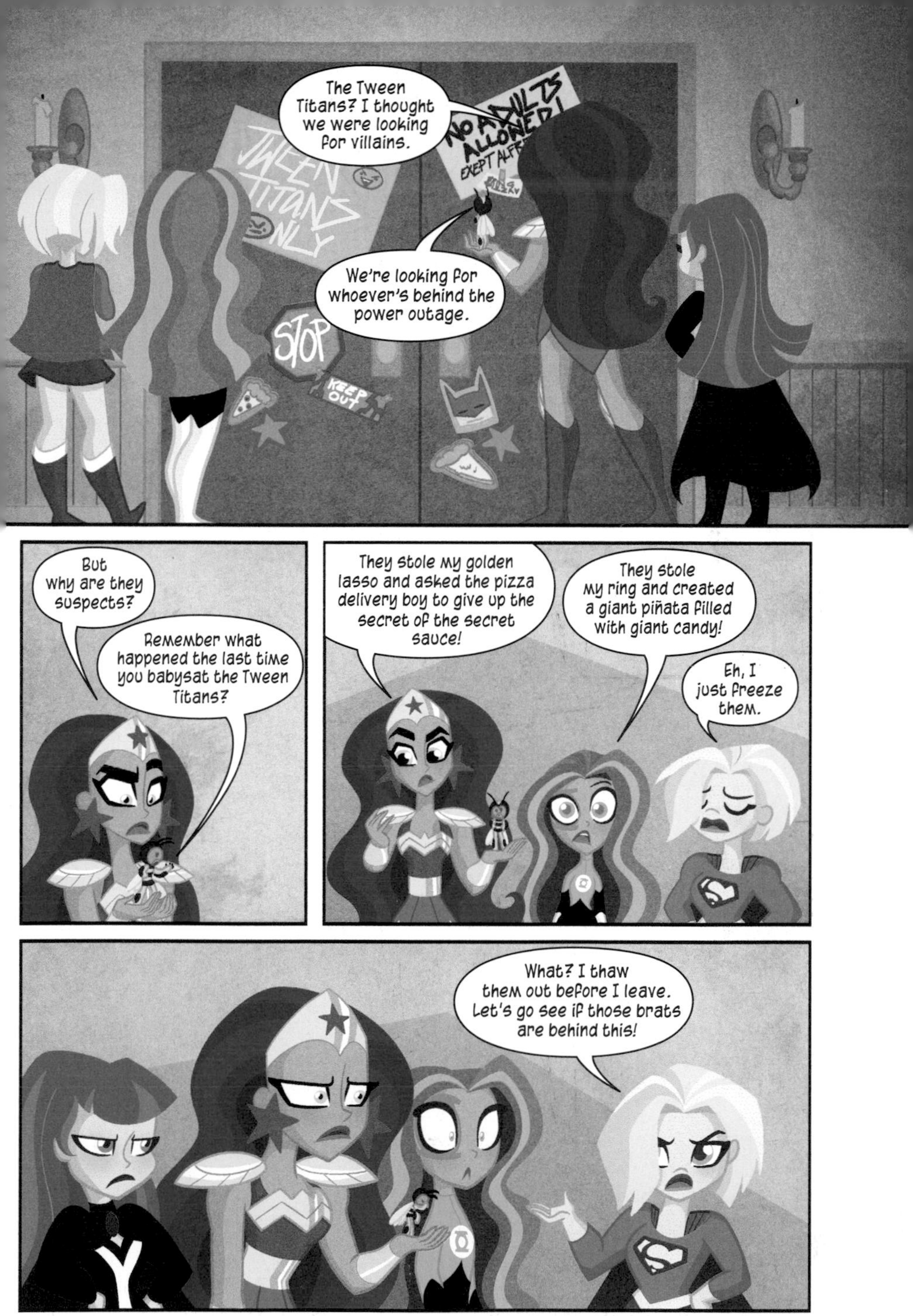

The Tween Titans? I thought we were looking for villains.
TWEEN TITANS ONLY
We're looking for whoever's behind the power outage.
STOP
KEEP OUT
But why are they suspects?
Remember what happened the last time you babysat the Tween Titans?
They stole my golden lasso and asked the pizza delivery boy to give up the secret of the secret sauce!
They stole my ring and created a giant piñata filled with giant candy!
Eh, I just freeze them.
What? I thaw them out before I leave. Let's go see if those brats are behind this!

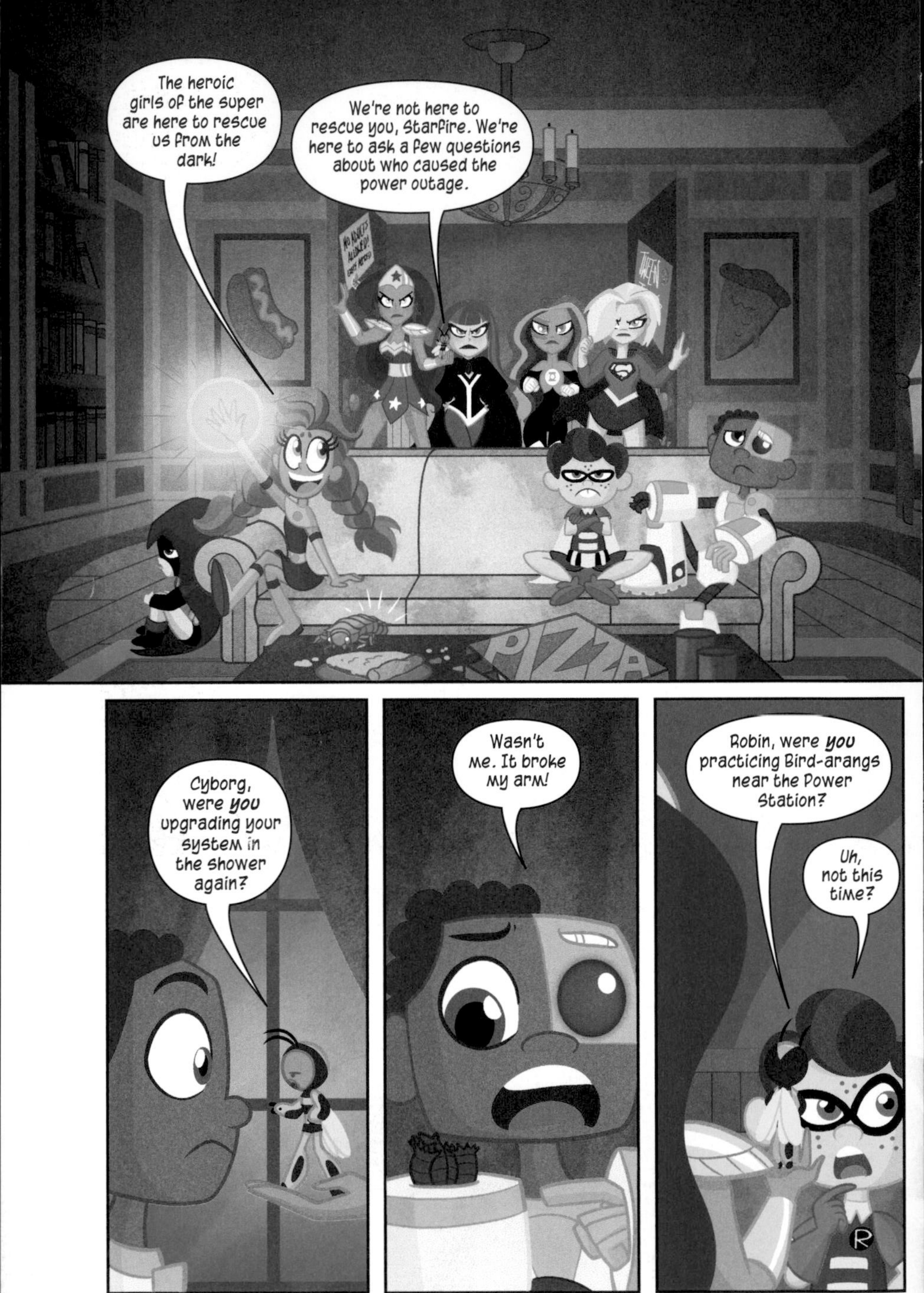
The heroic girls of the super are here to rescue us from the dark!
We're not here to rescue you, Starfire. We're here to ask a few questions about who caused the power outage.
PIZZA
Cyborg, were *you* upgrading your system in the shower again?
Wasn't me. It broke my arm!
Robin, were *you* practicing Bird-arangs near the Power Station?
Uh, not this time?

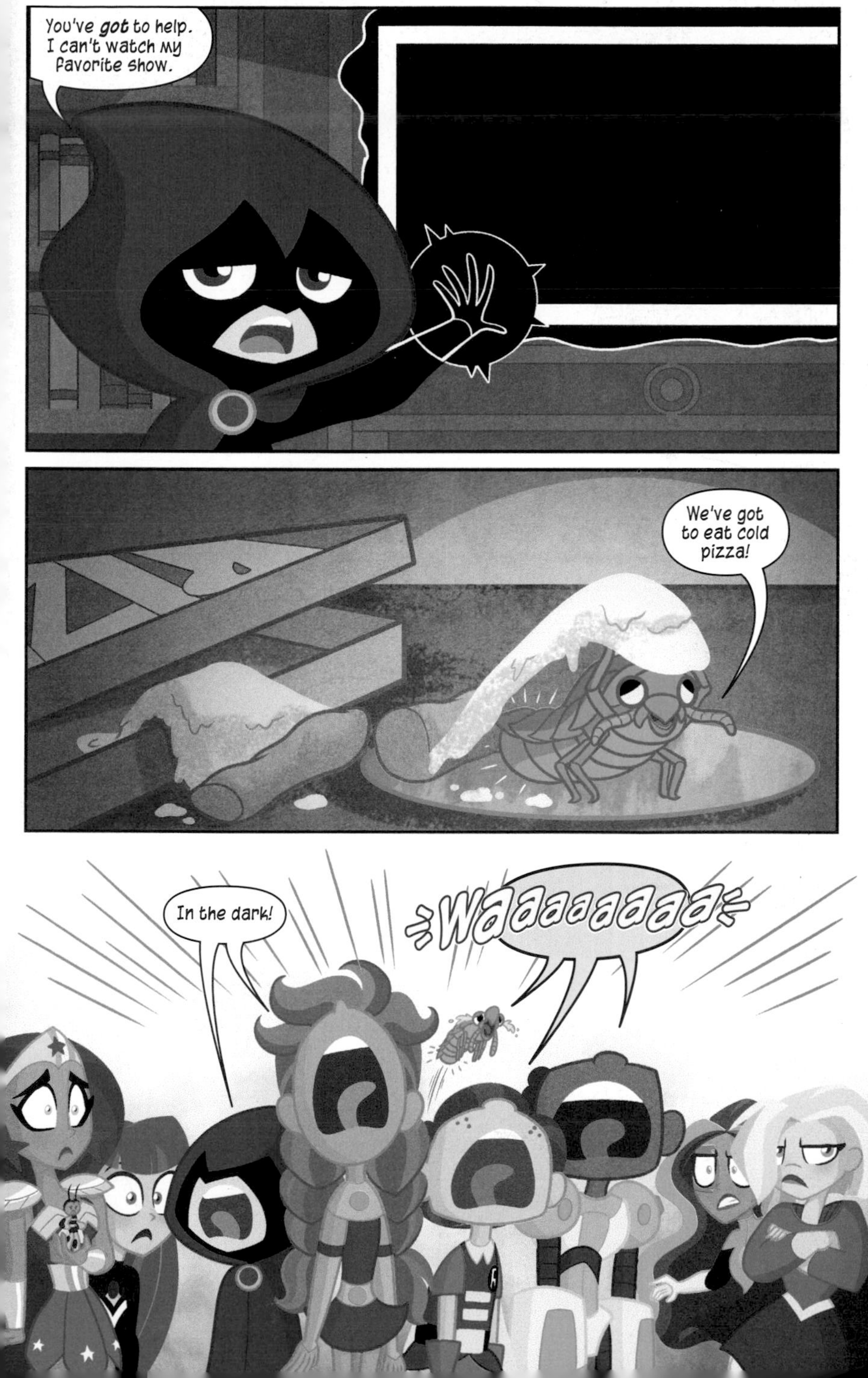
You've **got** to help. I can't watch my favorite show.
We've got to eat cold pizza!
In the dark!
WAAAAAAAAA

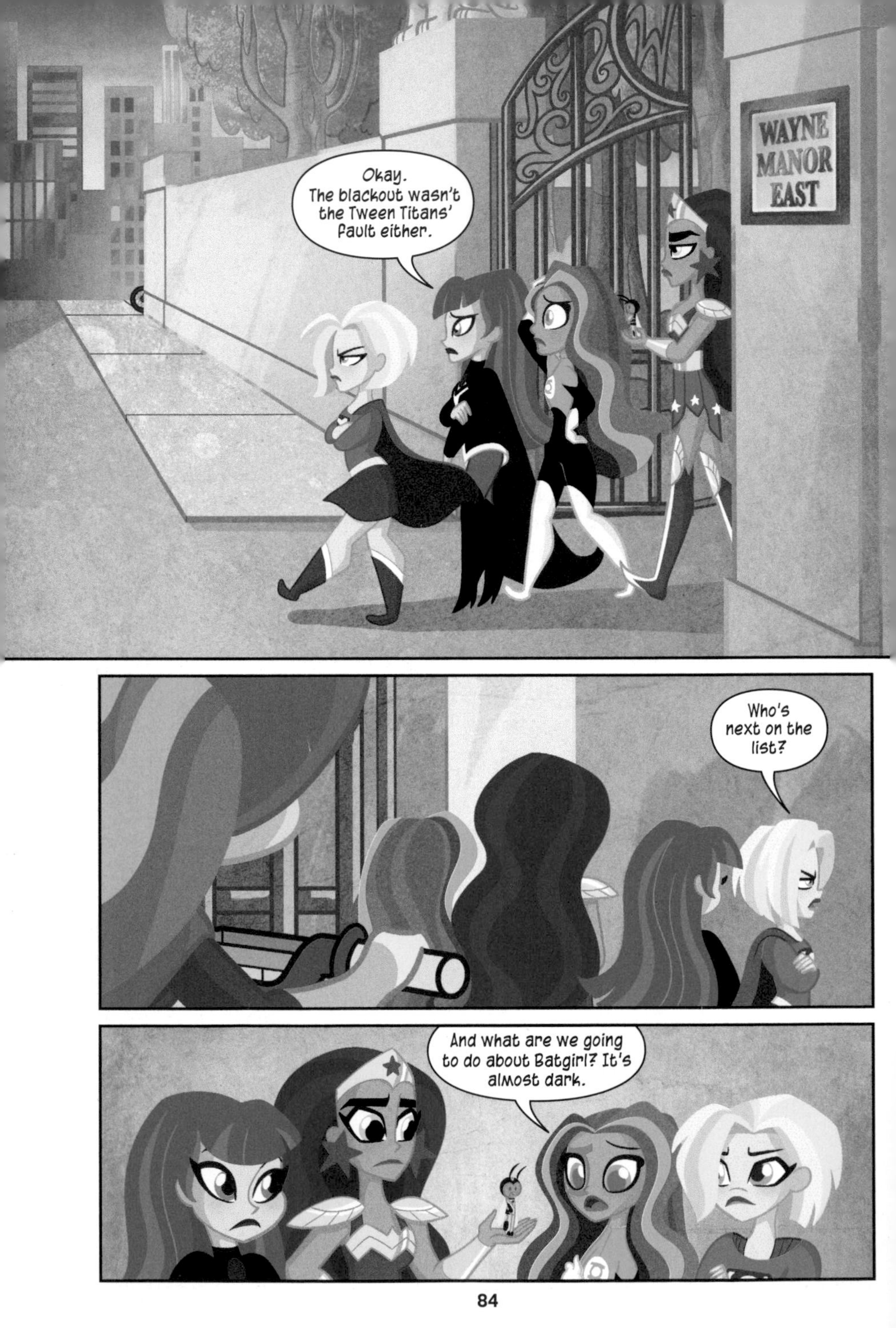
WAYNE MANOR EAST
Okay. The blackout wasn't the Tween Titans' fault either.
Who's next on the list?
And what are we going to do about Batgirl? It's almost dark.

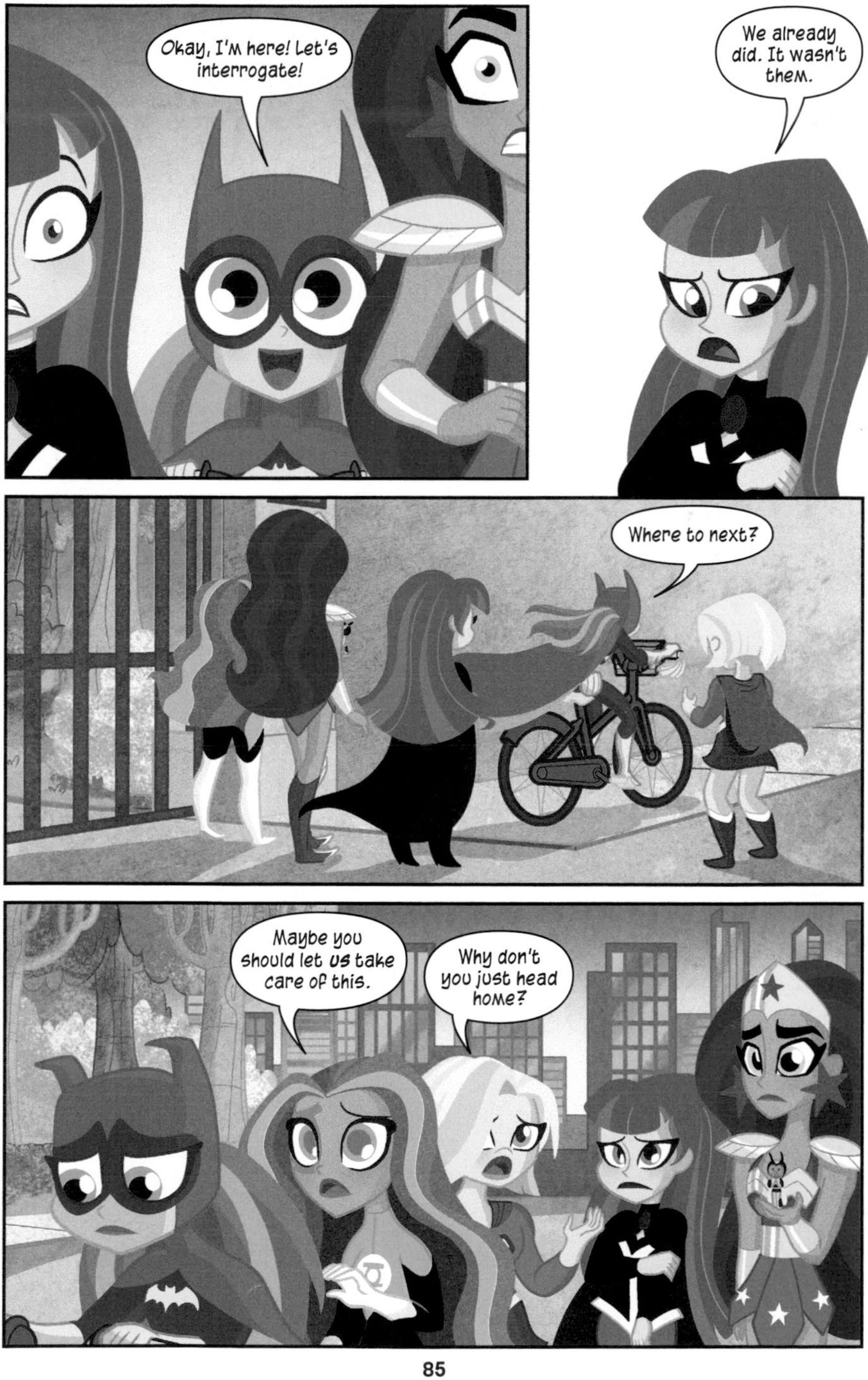
Okay, I'm here! Let's interrogate!
We already did. It wasn't them.
Where to next?
Maybe you should let us take care of this.
Why don't you just head home?

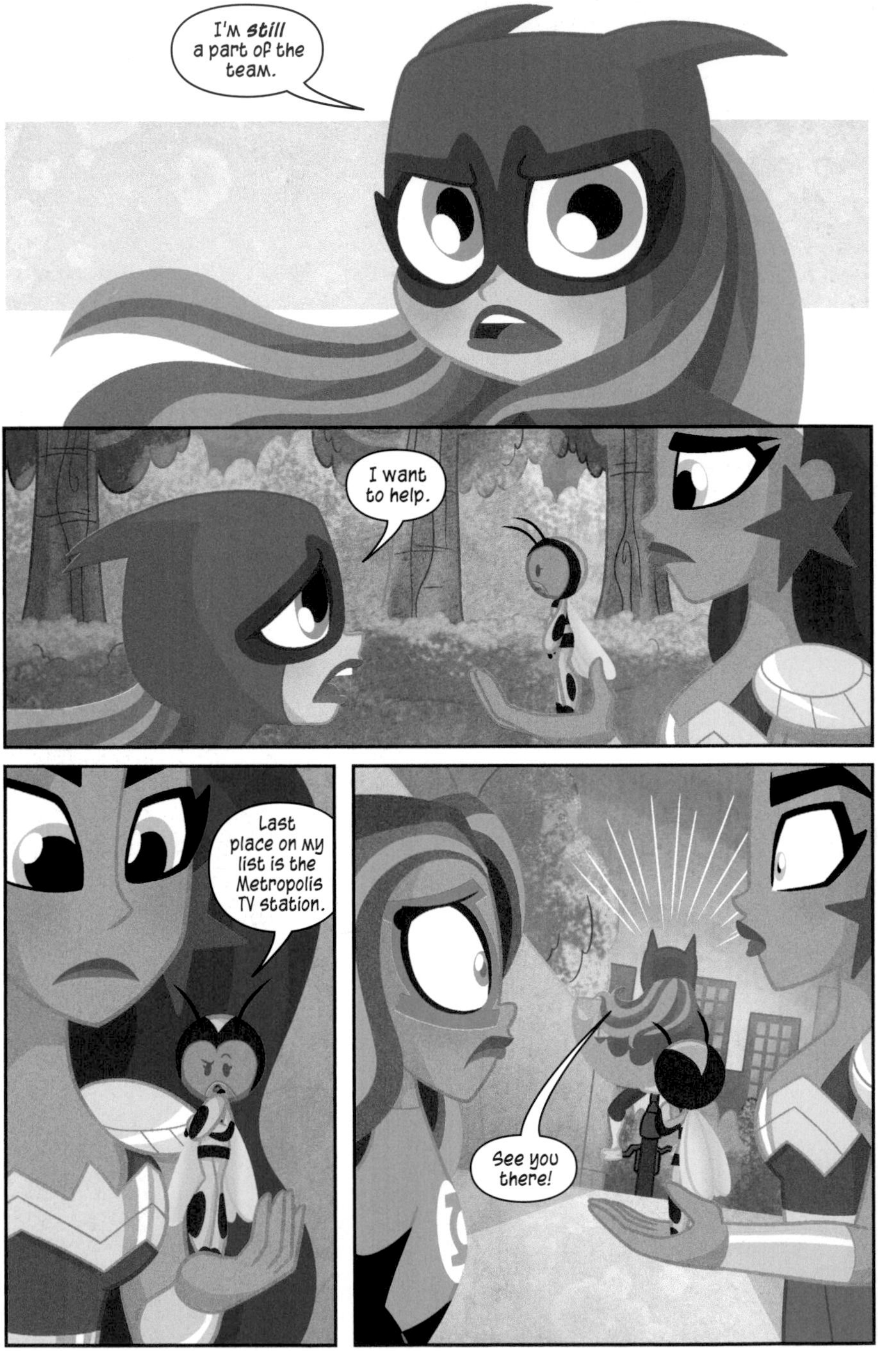
I'm still a part of the team.
I want to help.
Last place on my list is the Metropolis TV station.
See you there!

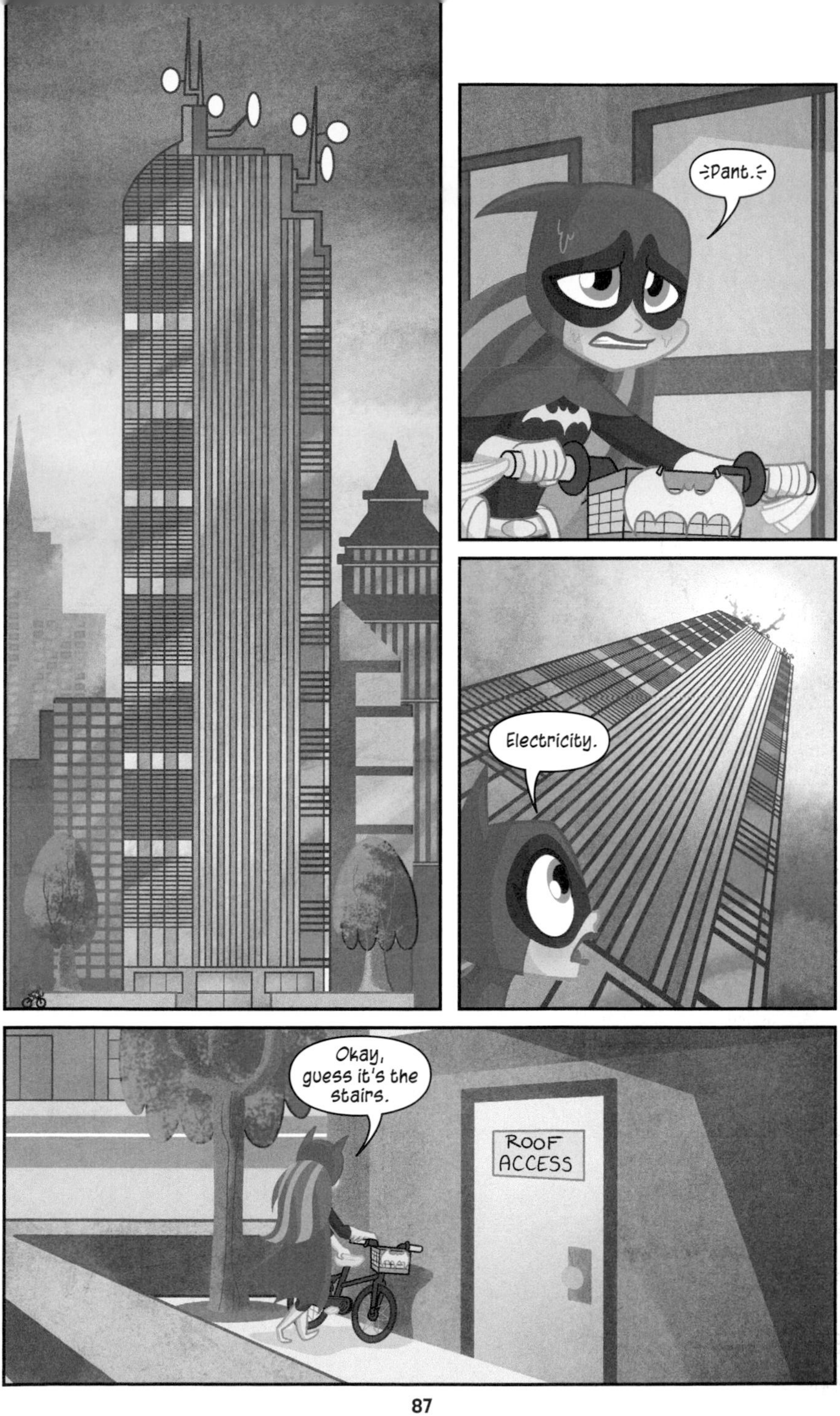
Pant.
Electricity.
Okay, guess it's the stairs.
ROOF ACCESS

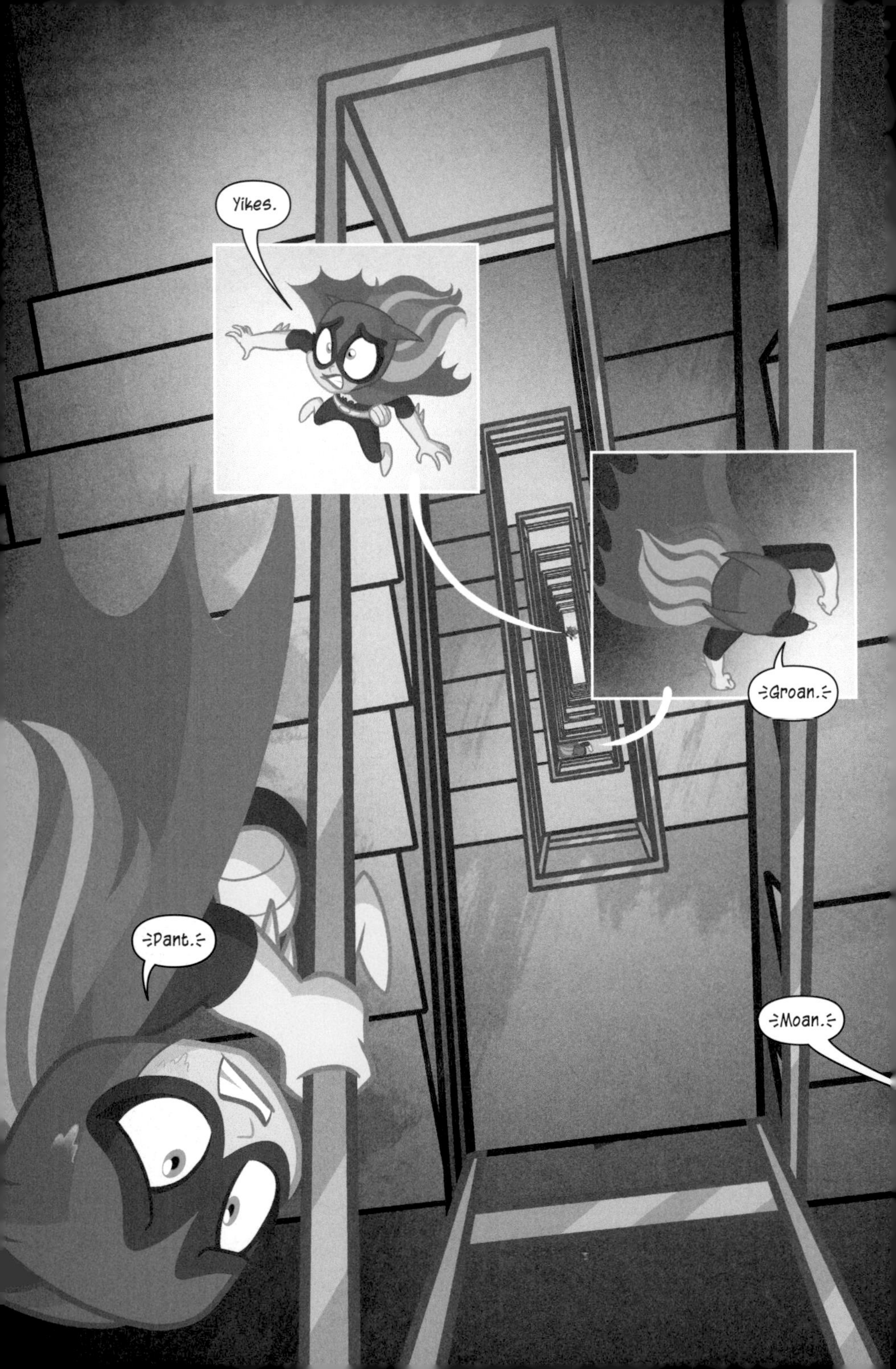
Yikes.
Groan.
Pant.
Moan.

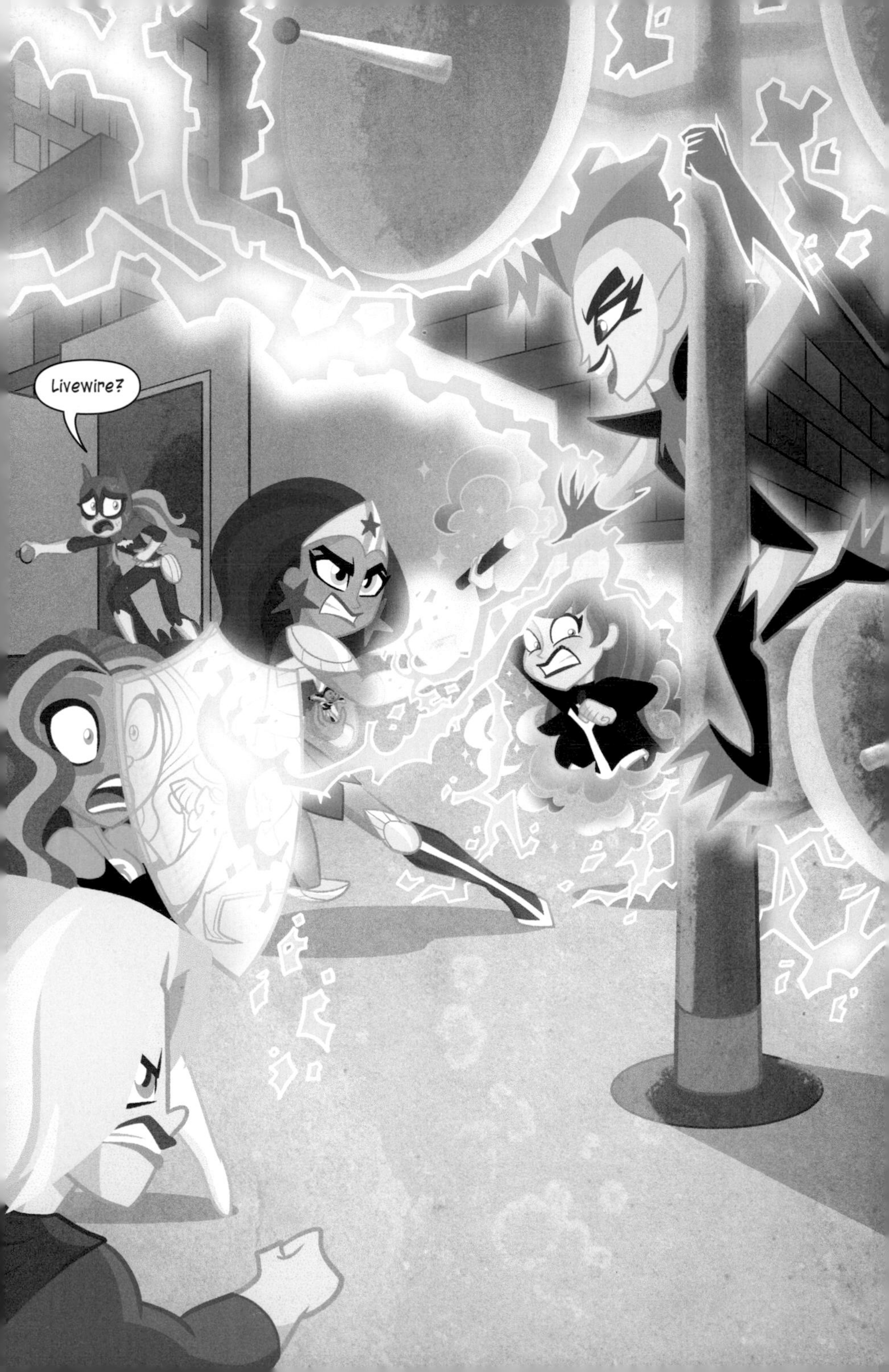
Livewire?

chapter five

DANGER! HIGH VOLTAGE

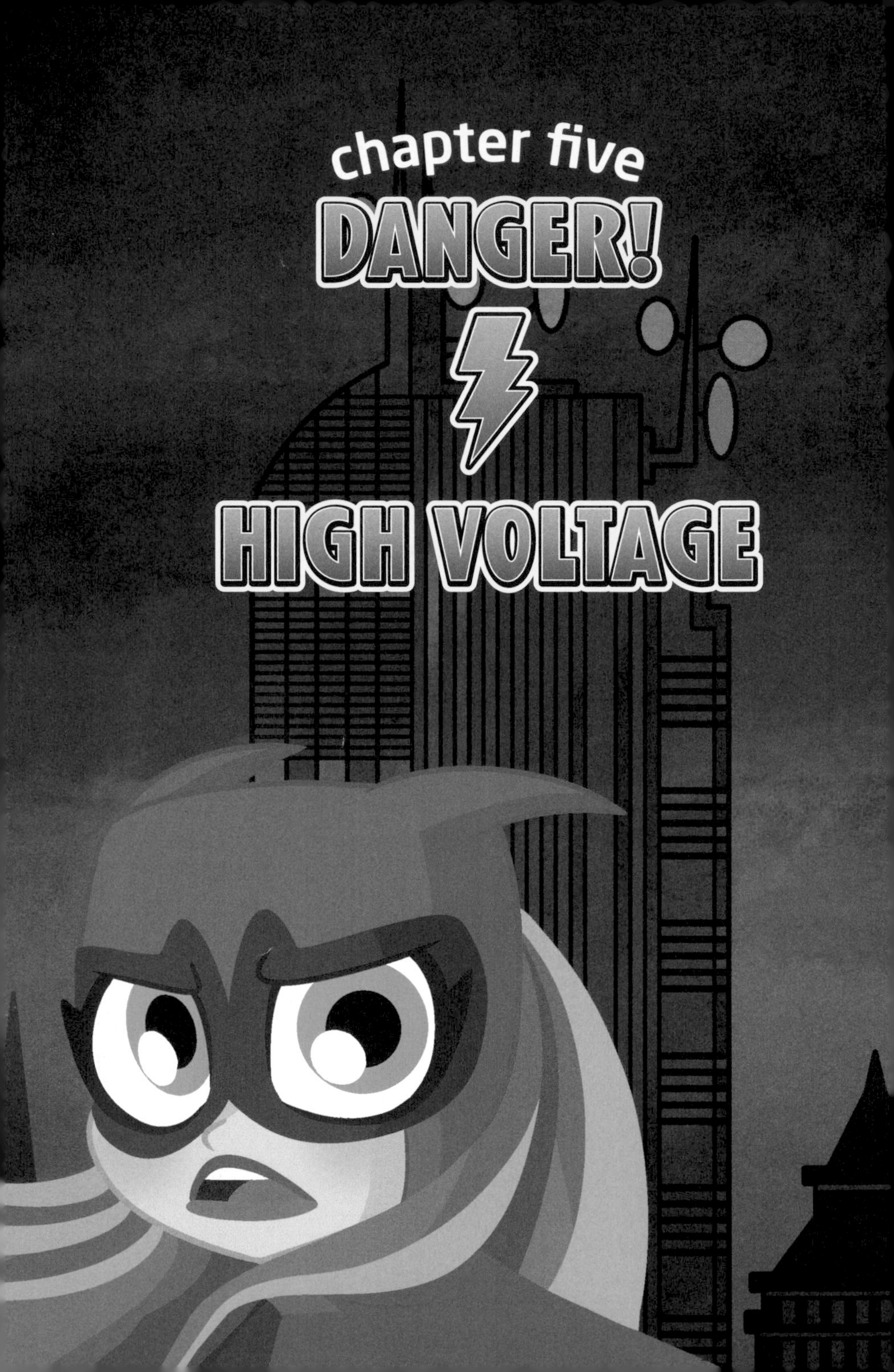

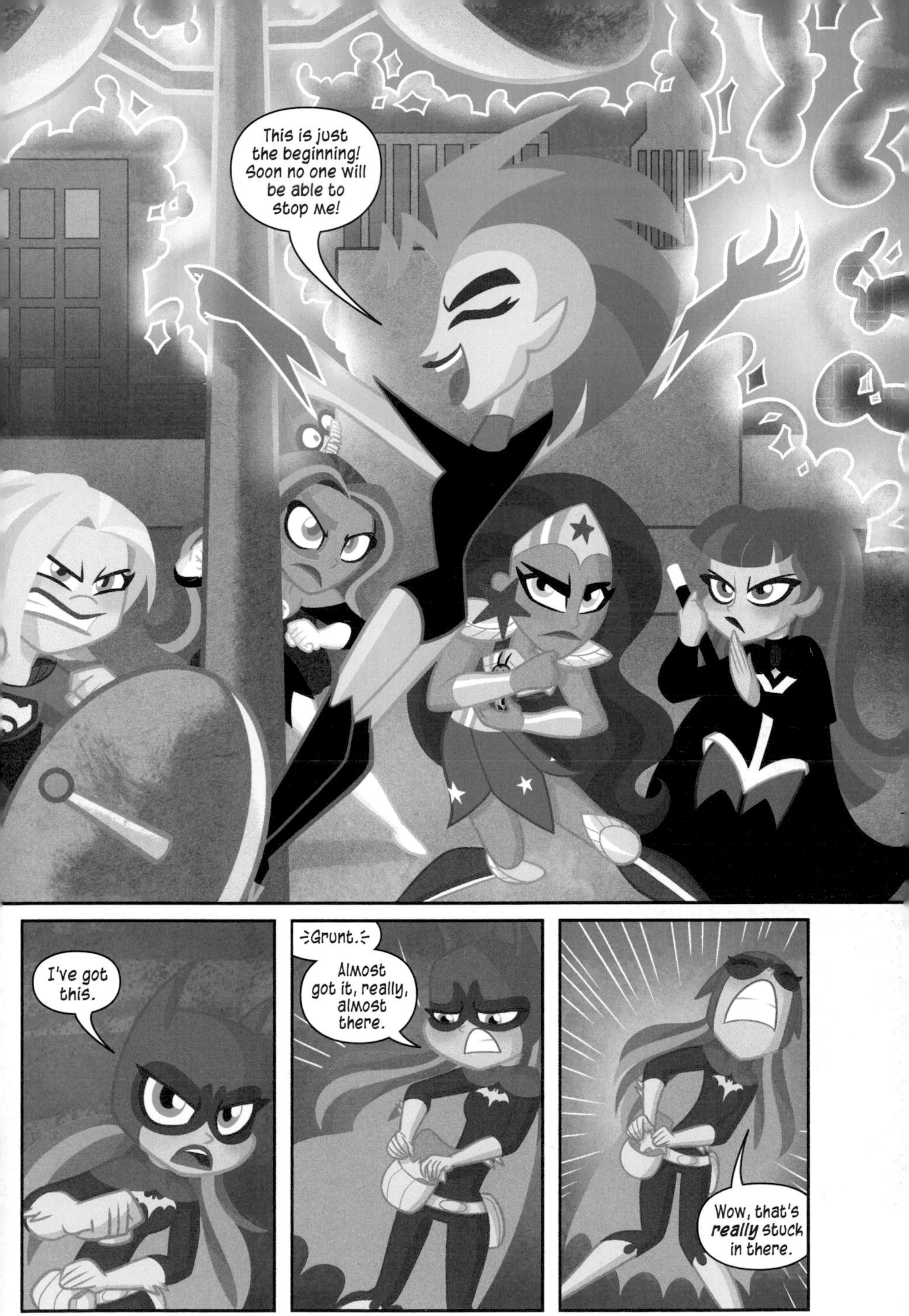

This is just the beginning! Soon no one will be able to stop me!
I've got this.
Grunt.
Almost got it, really, almost there.
Wow, that's *really* stuck in there.

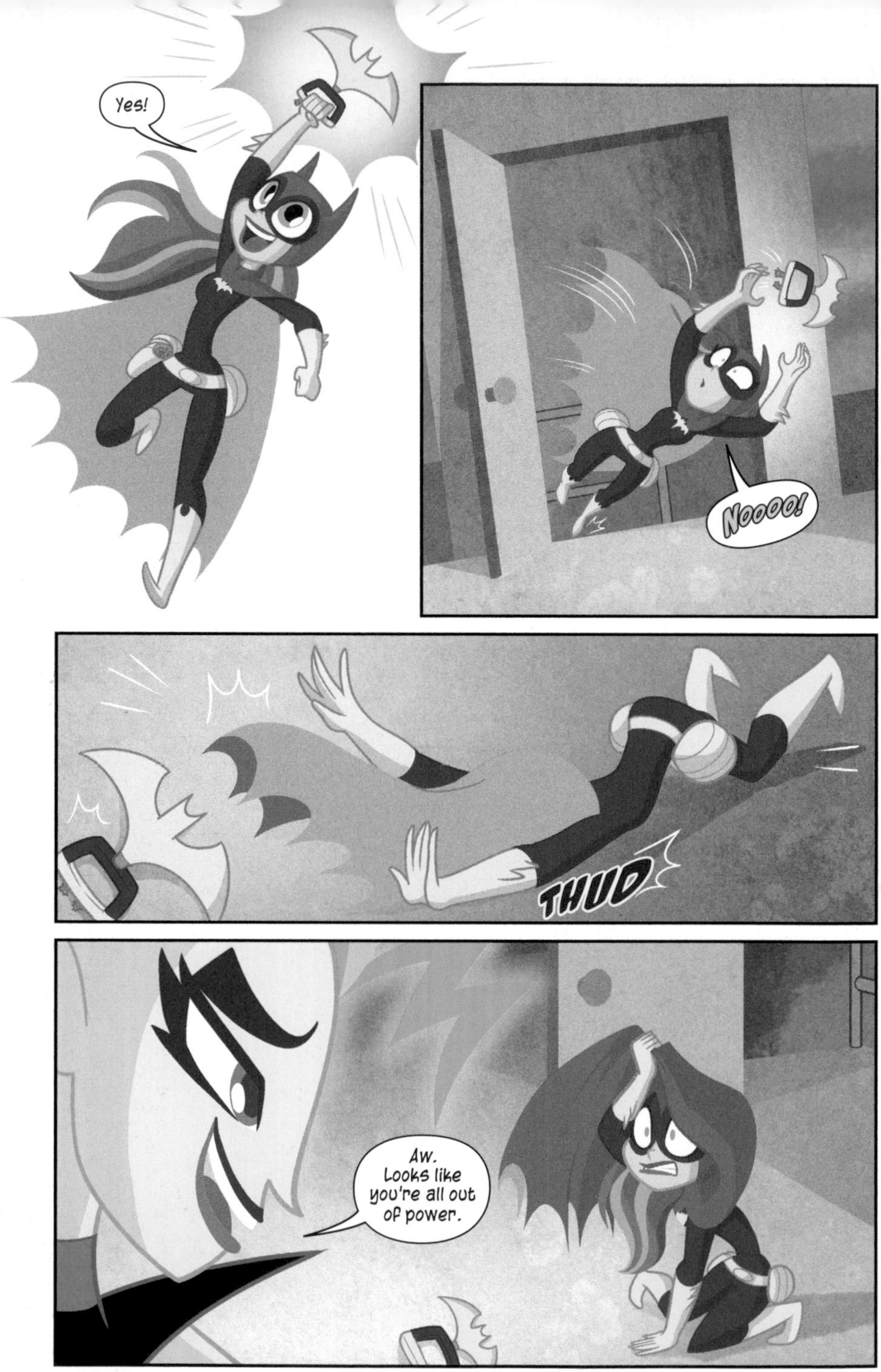
Yes!
NOOOO!
THUD
Aw. Looks like you're all out of power.

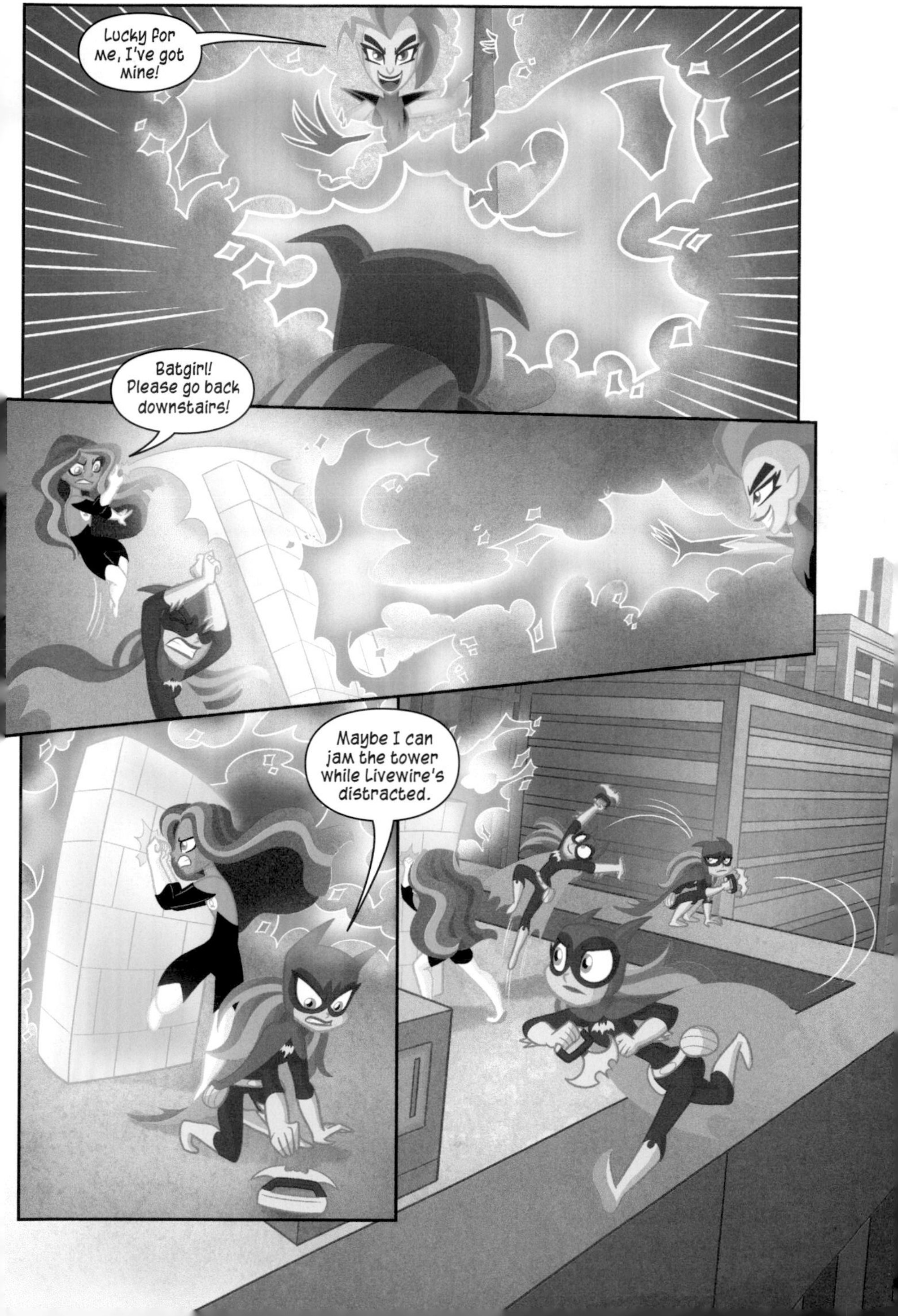
Lucky for me, I've got mine!
Batgirl! Please go back downstairs!
Maybe I can jam the tower while Livewire's distracted.

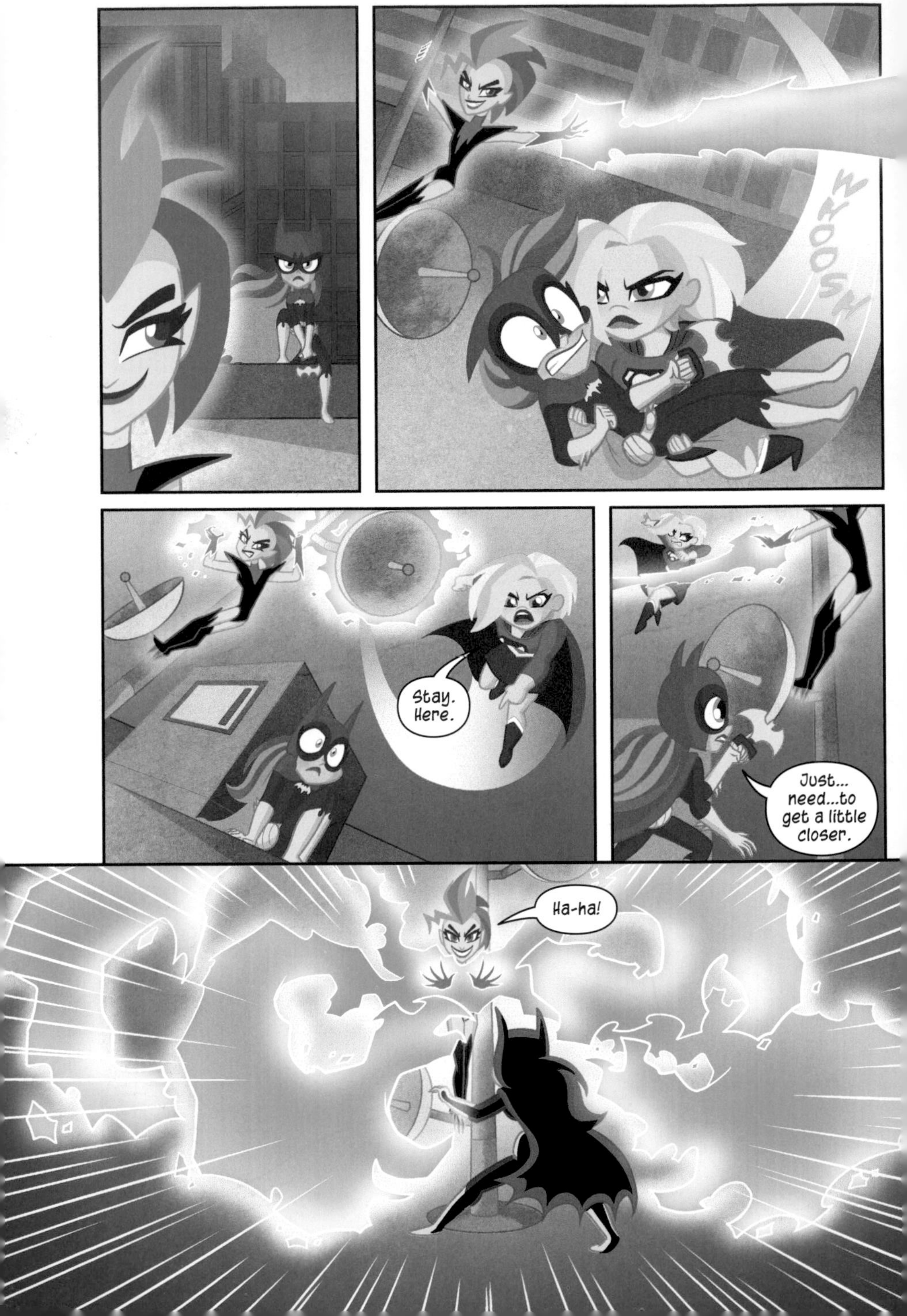
WHOOSH
Stay. Here.
Just... need...to get a little closer.
Ha-ha!

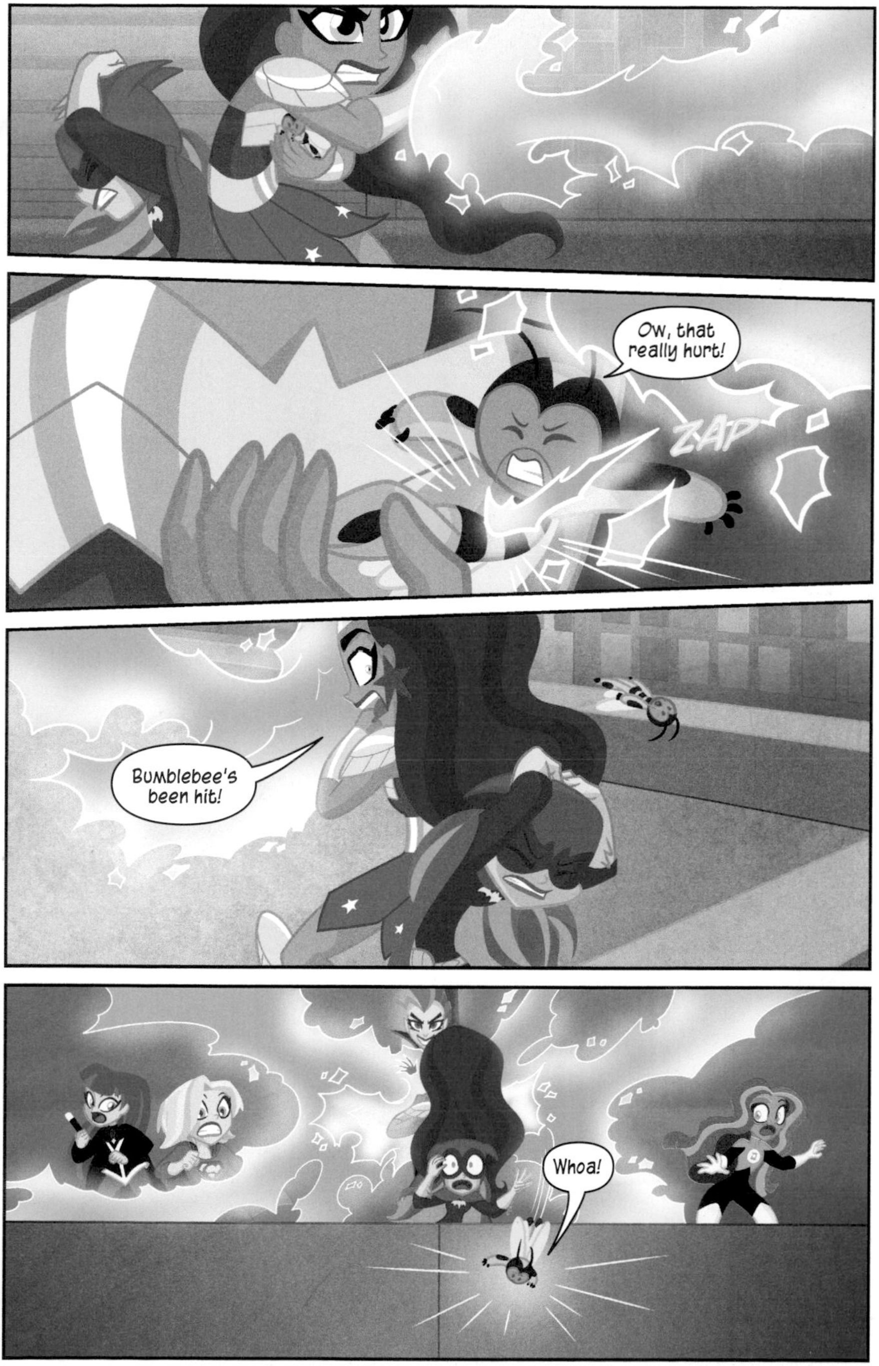
Ow, that really hurt!
ZAP
Bumblebee's been hit!
Whoa!

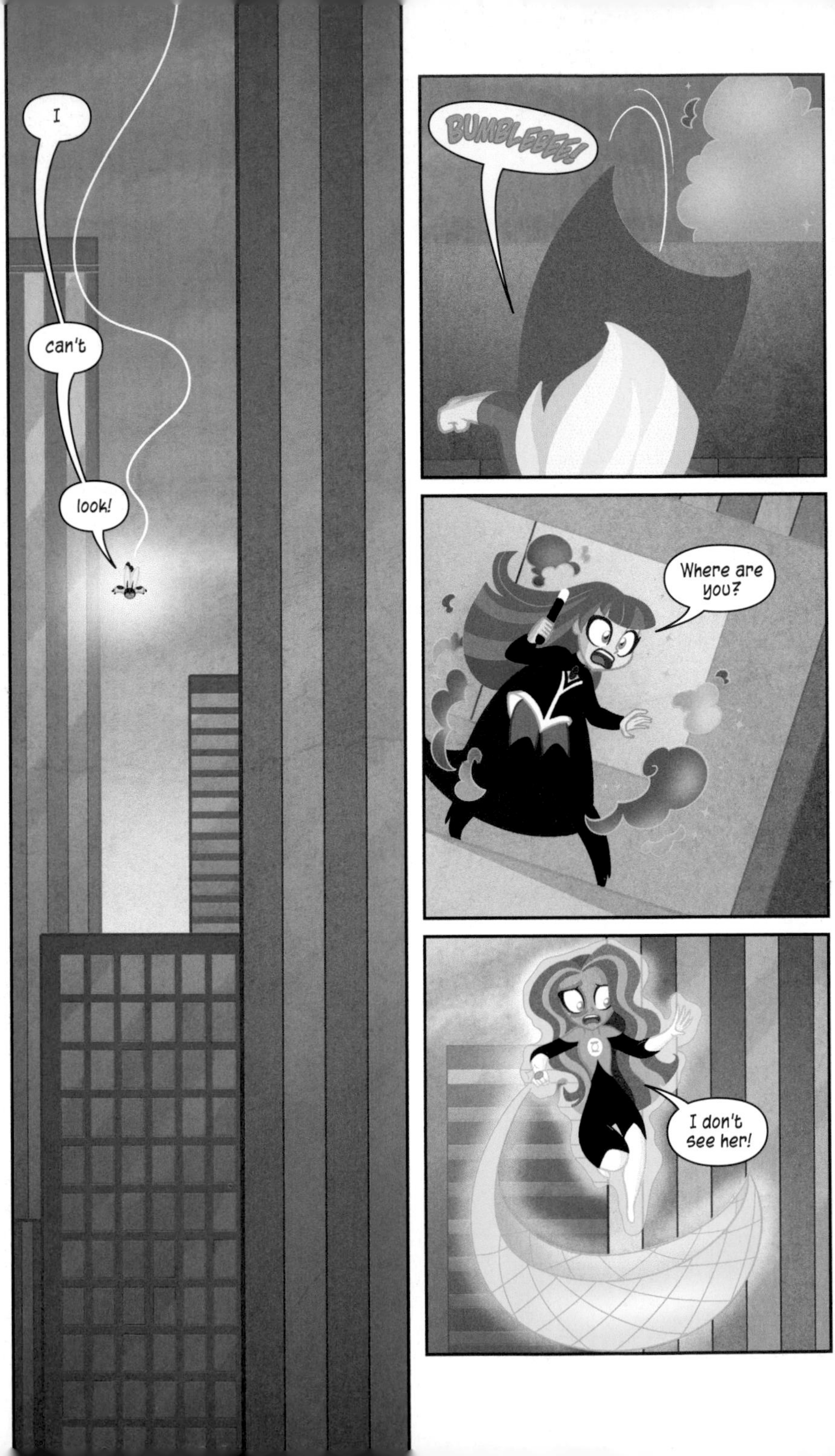
I
can't
look!
BUMBLEBEE!
Where are you?
I don't see her!

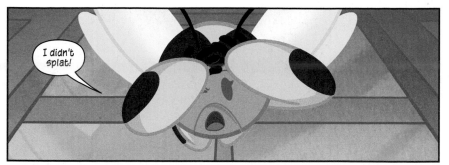

I didn't splat!

Wings are working! I can fly!

Stingers, too!

The jolt must have recharged my suit.

CRACKLE

Sixty percent. Not enough power to grow big, but I'm mostly back!

97

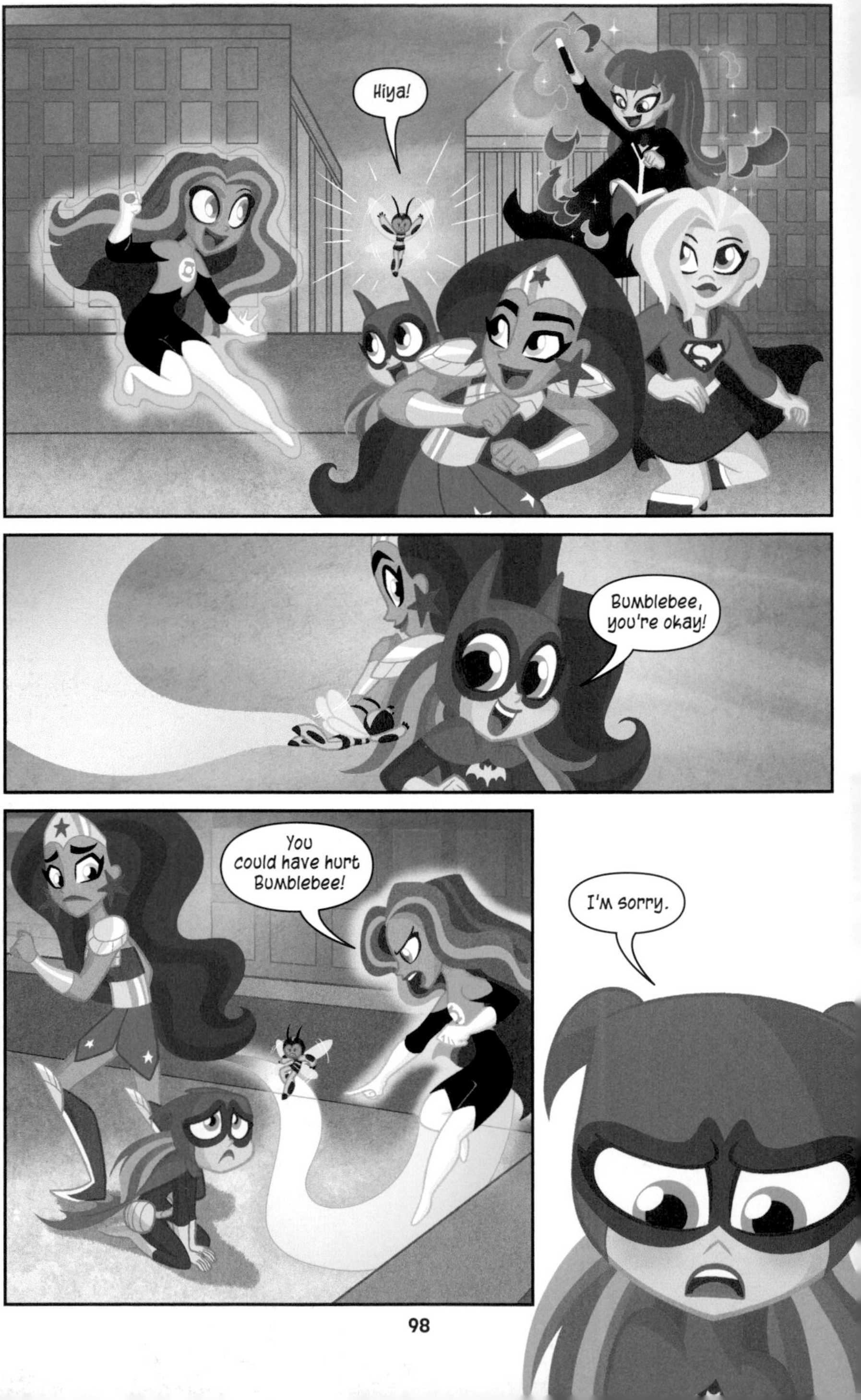
Hiya!
Bumblebee, you're okay!
You could have hurt Bumblebee!
I'm sorry.

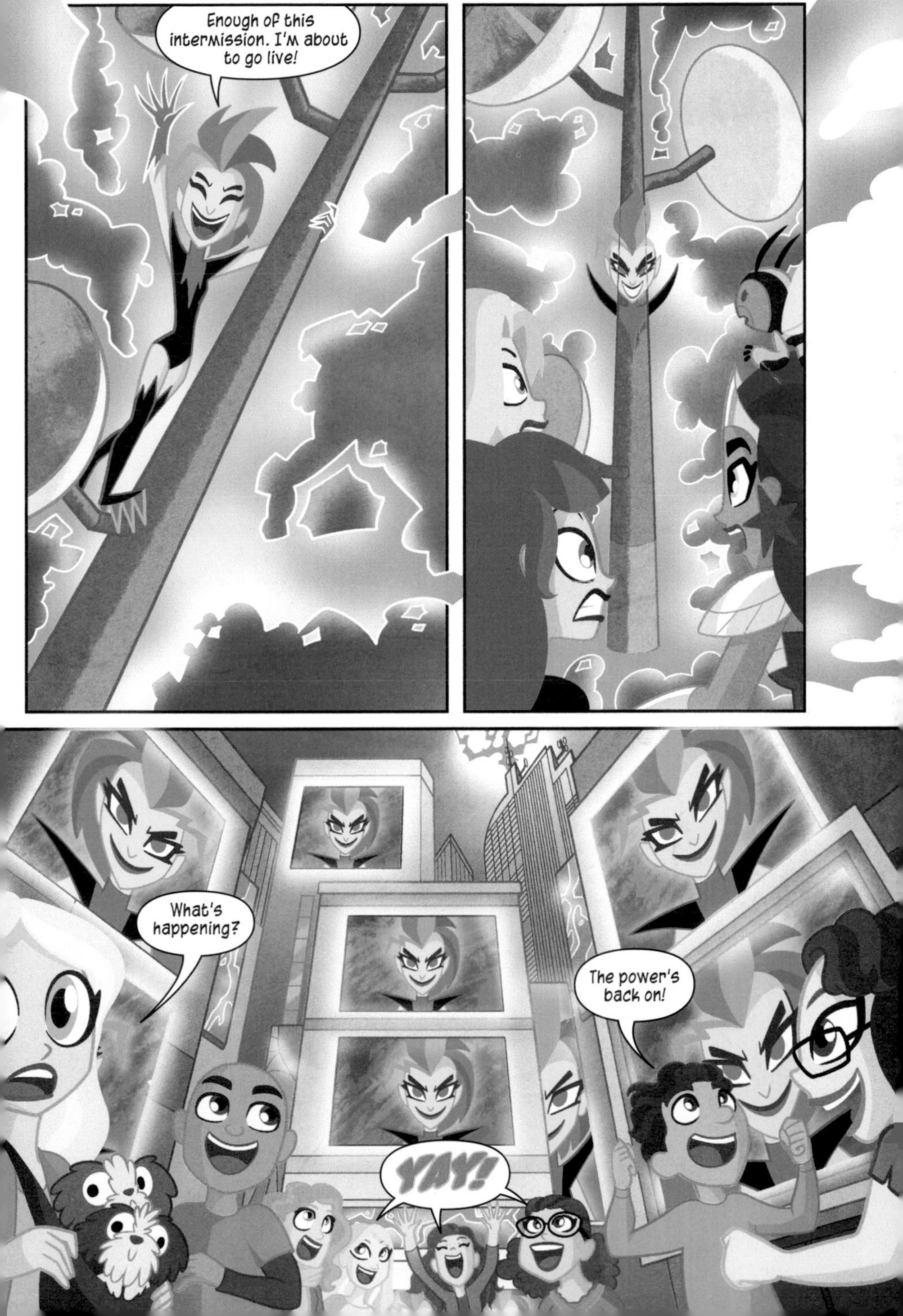
Enough of this intermission. I'm about to go live!
What's happening?
The power's back on!
YAY!

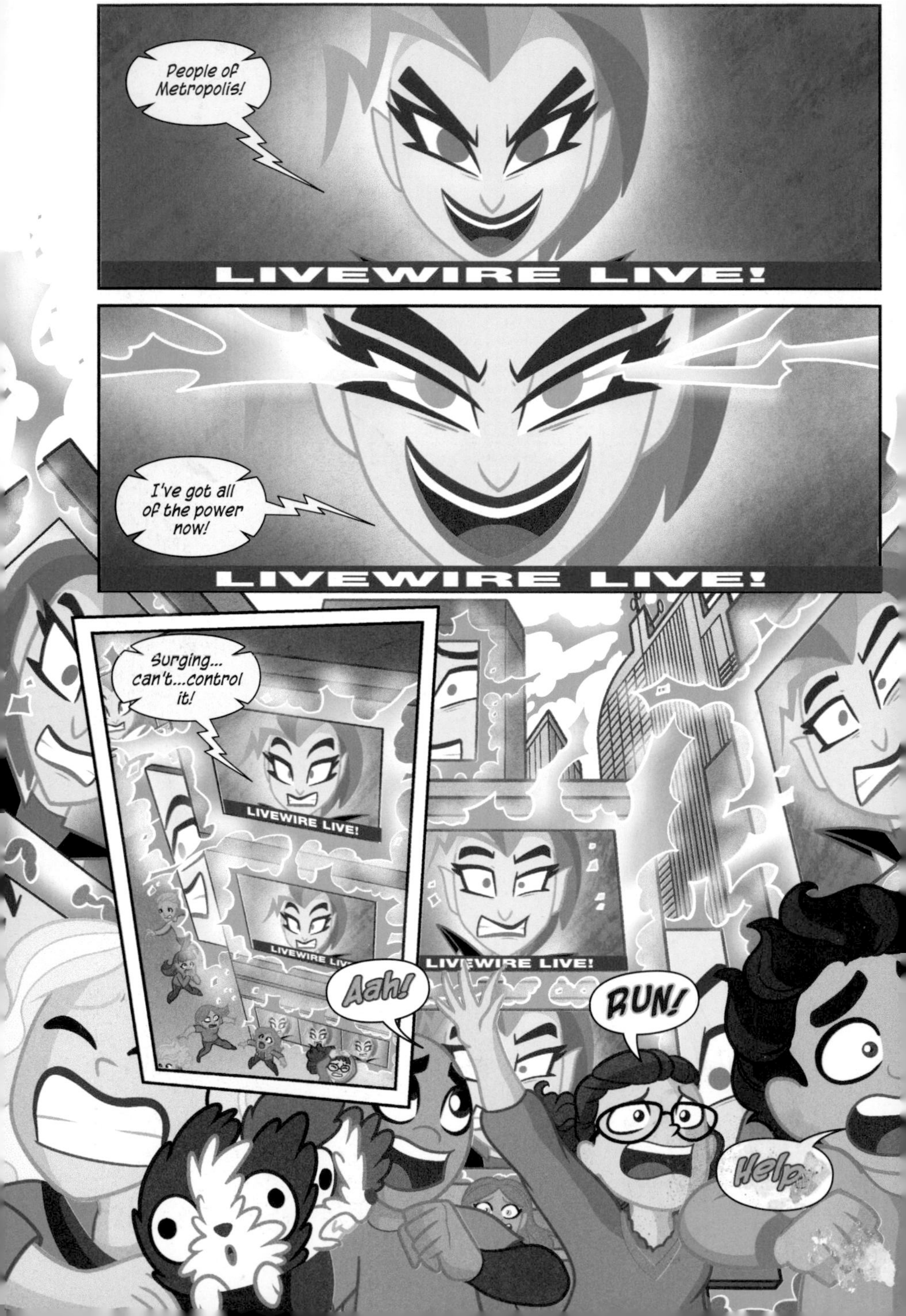

People of Metropolis!
LIVEWIRE LIVE!
I've got all of the power now!
LIVEWIRE LIVE!
Surging... can't...control it!
LIVEWIRE LIVE!
LIVEWIRE LIVE!
Aah!
RUN!
Help

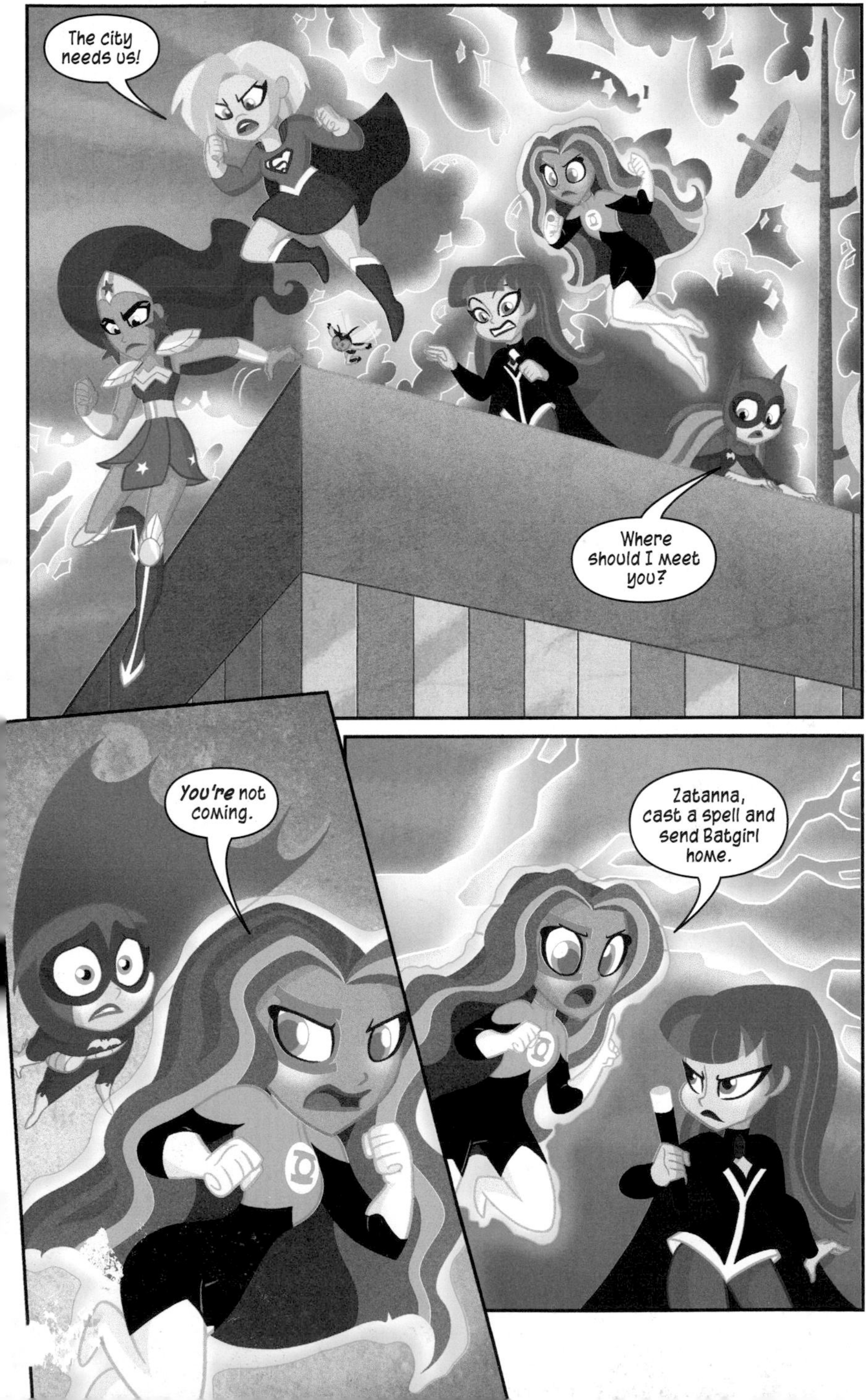
The city needs us!
Where should I meet you?
You're not coming.
Zatanna, cast a spell and send Batgirl home.

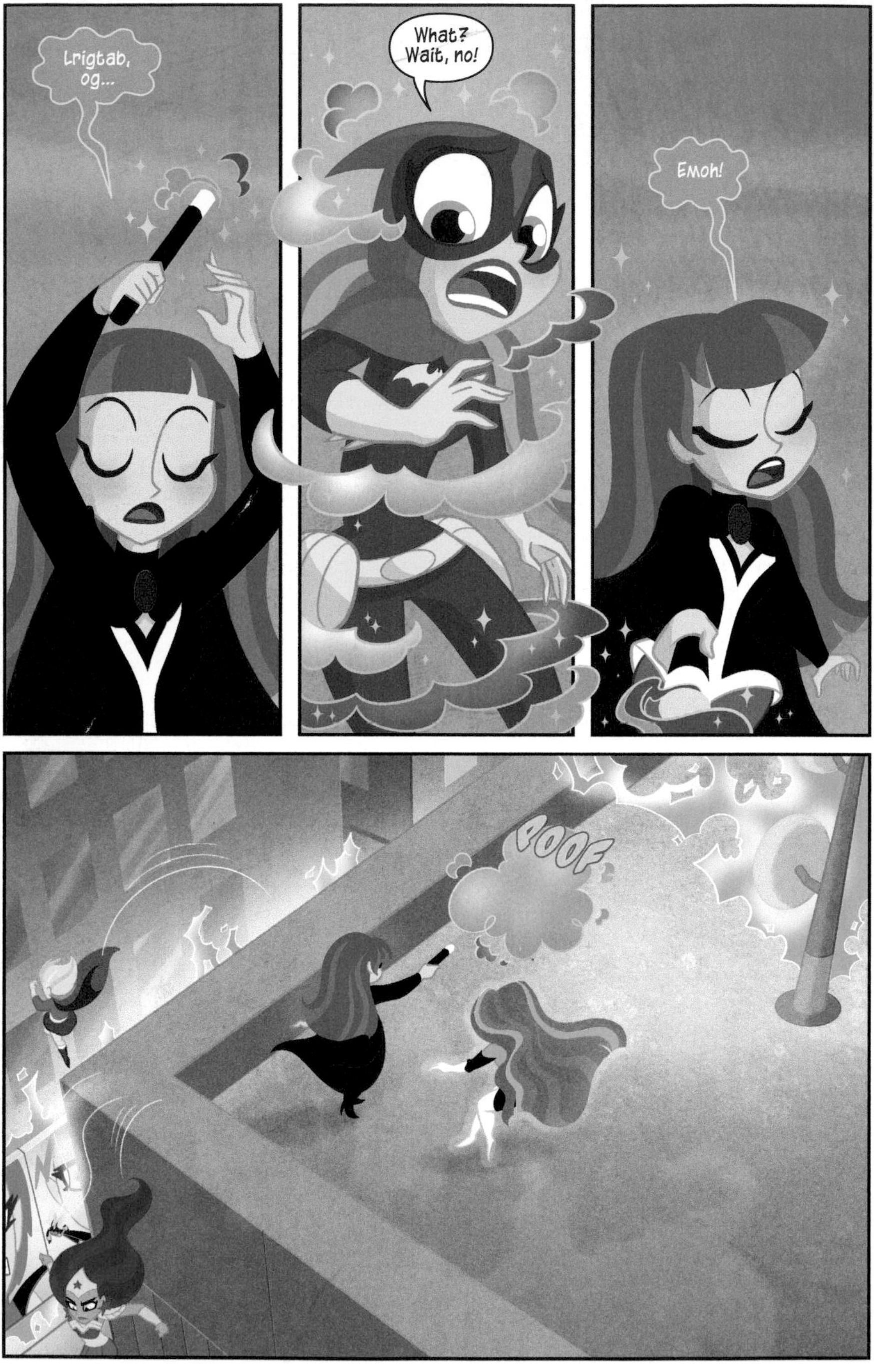
Lrigtab, og...
What? Wait, no!
Emoh!
POOF

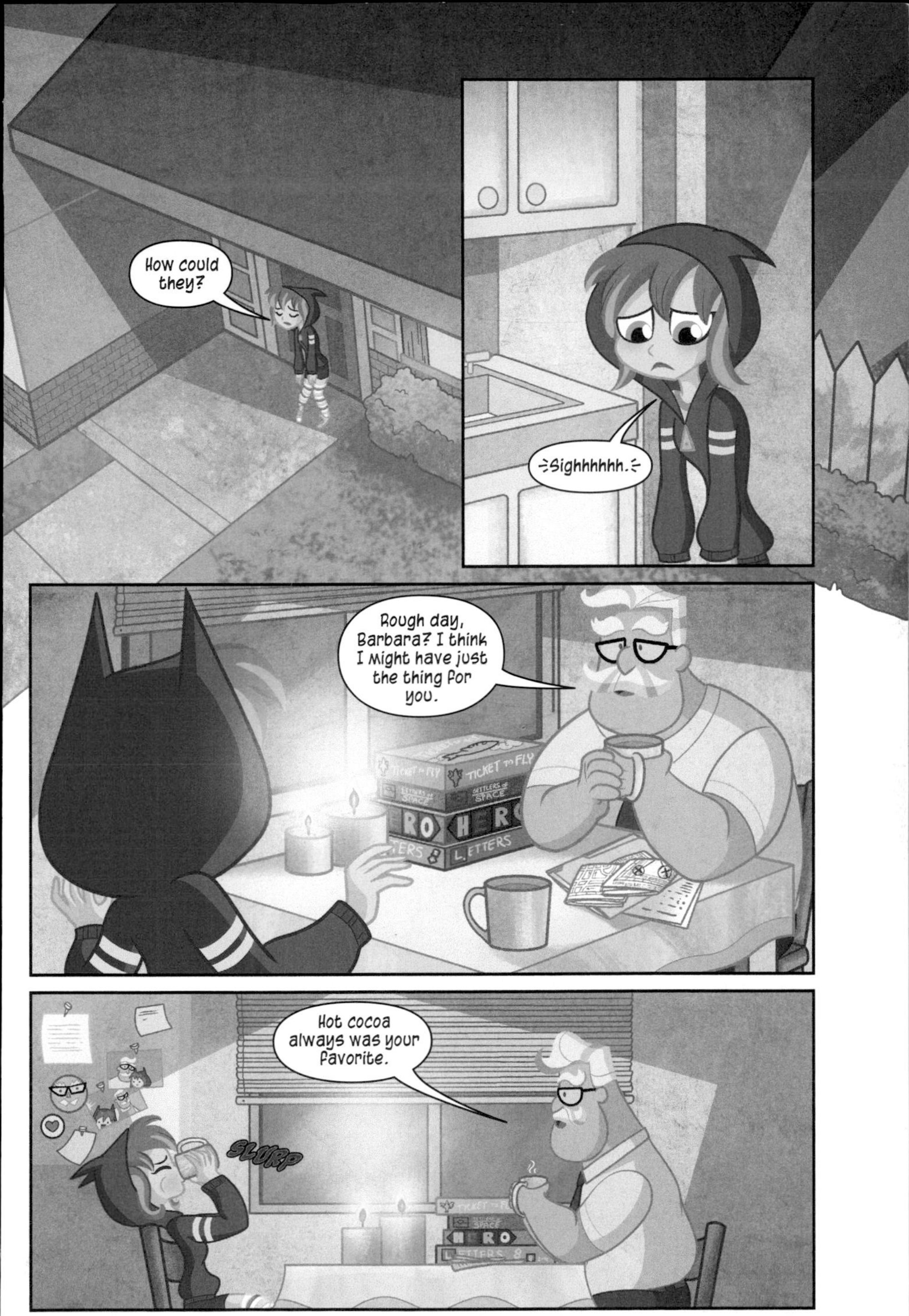
How could they?
Sighhhhhh.
Rough day, Barbara? I think I might have just the thing for you.
TICKET TO FLY
SETTLERS of SPACE
HERO
LETTERS
Hot cocoa always was your favorite.
SLURP

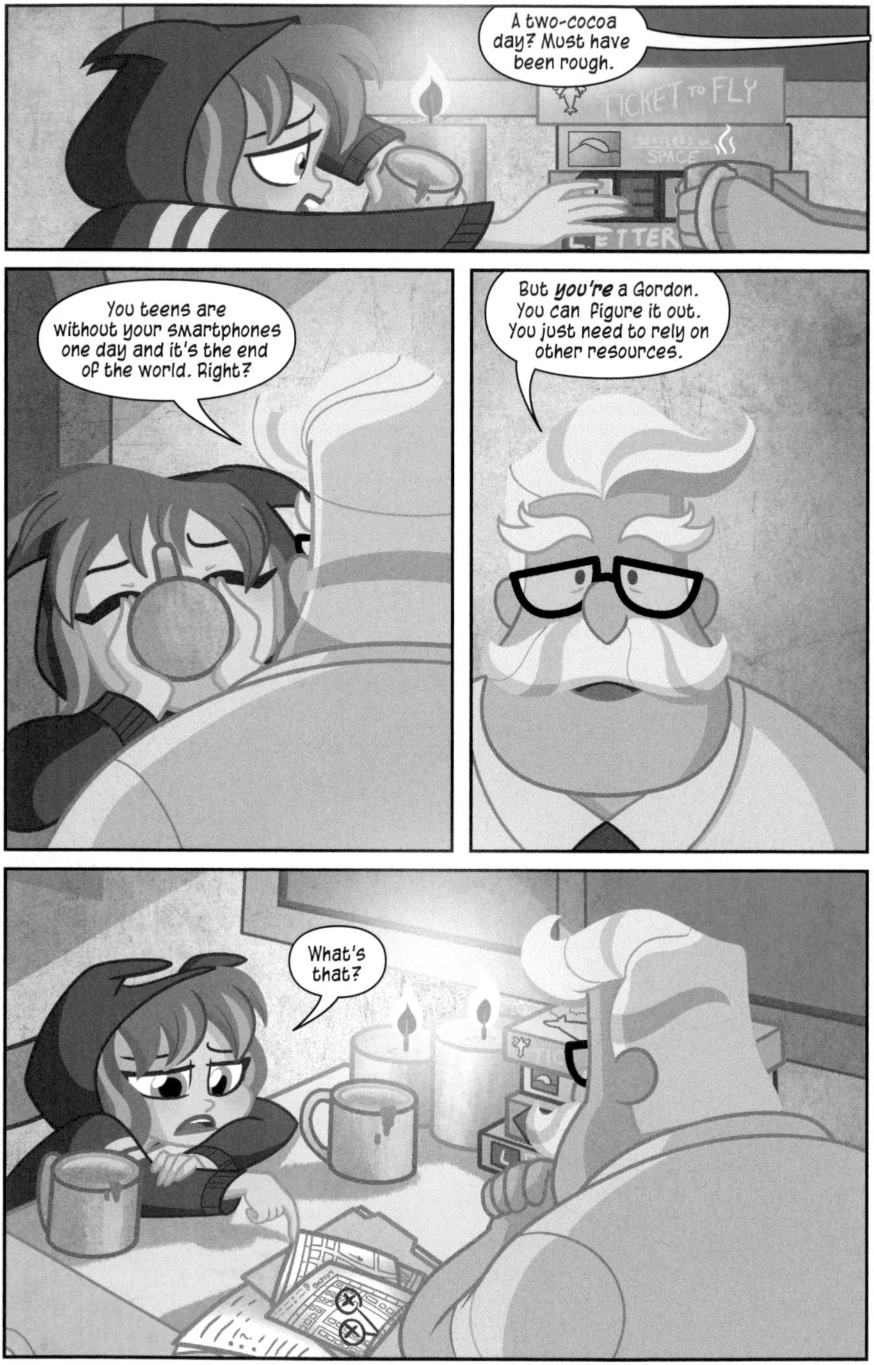
A two-cocoa day? Must have been rough.
TICKET TO FLY
SETTLERS of SPACE
LETTER
You teens are without your smartphones one day and it's the end of the world. Right?
But ***you're*** a Gordon. You can figure it out. You just need to rely on other resources.
What's that?

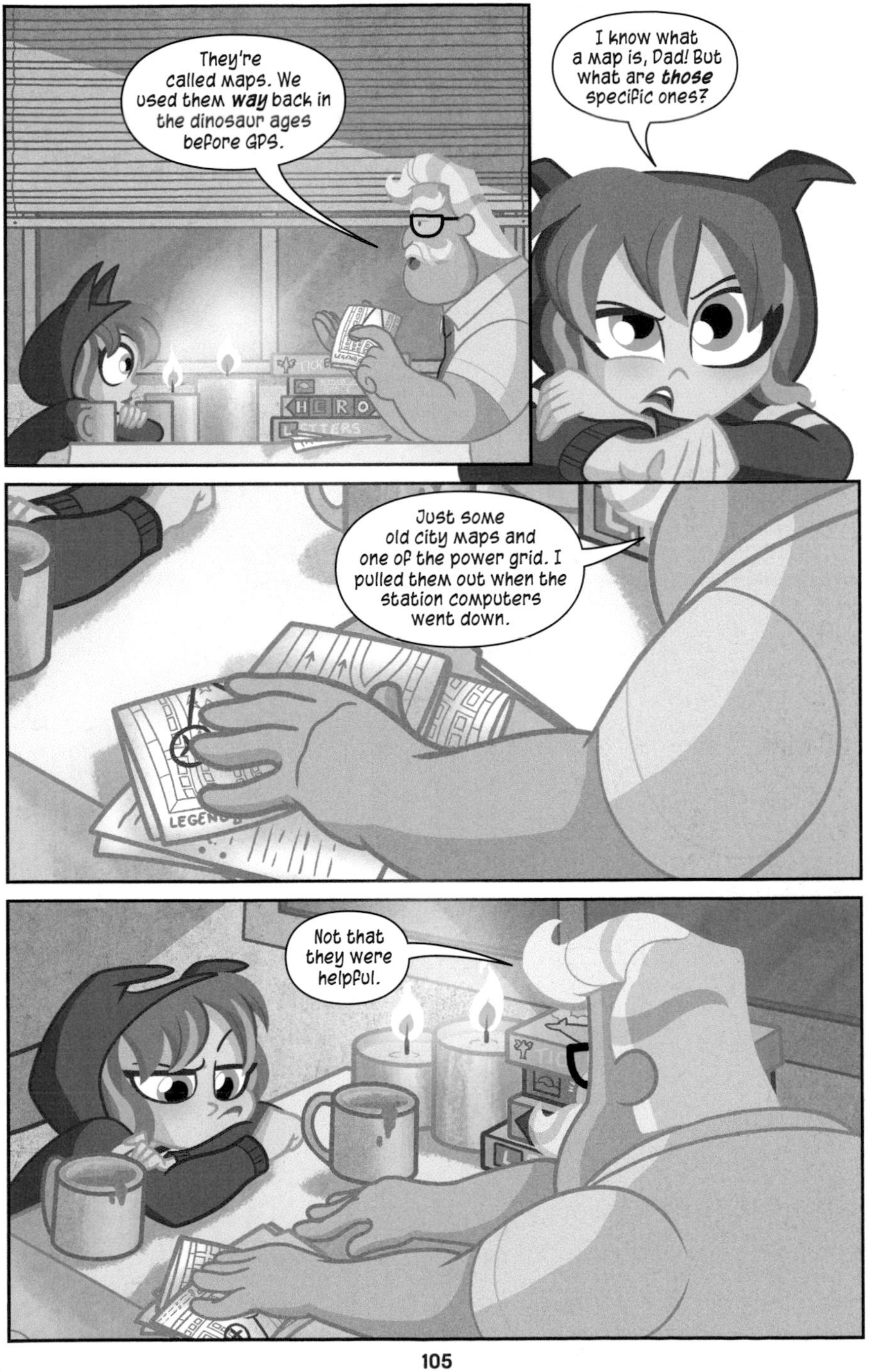
They're called maps. We used them **way** back in the dinosaur ages before GPS.
I know what a map is, Dad! But what are **those** specific ones?
HERO
LETTERS
Just some old city maps and one of the power grid. I pulled them out when the station computers went down.
Not that they were helpful.

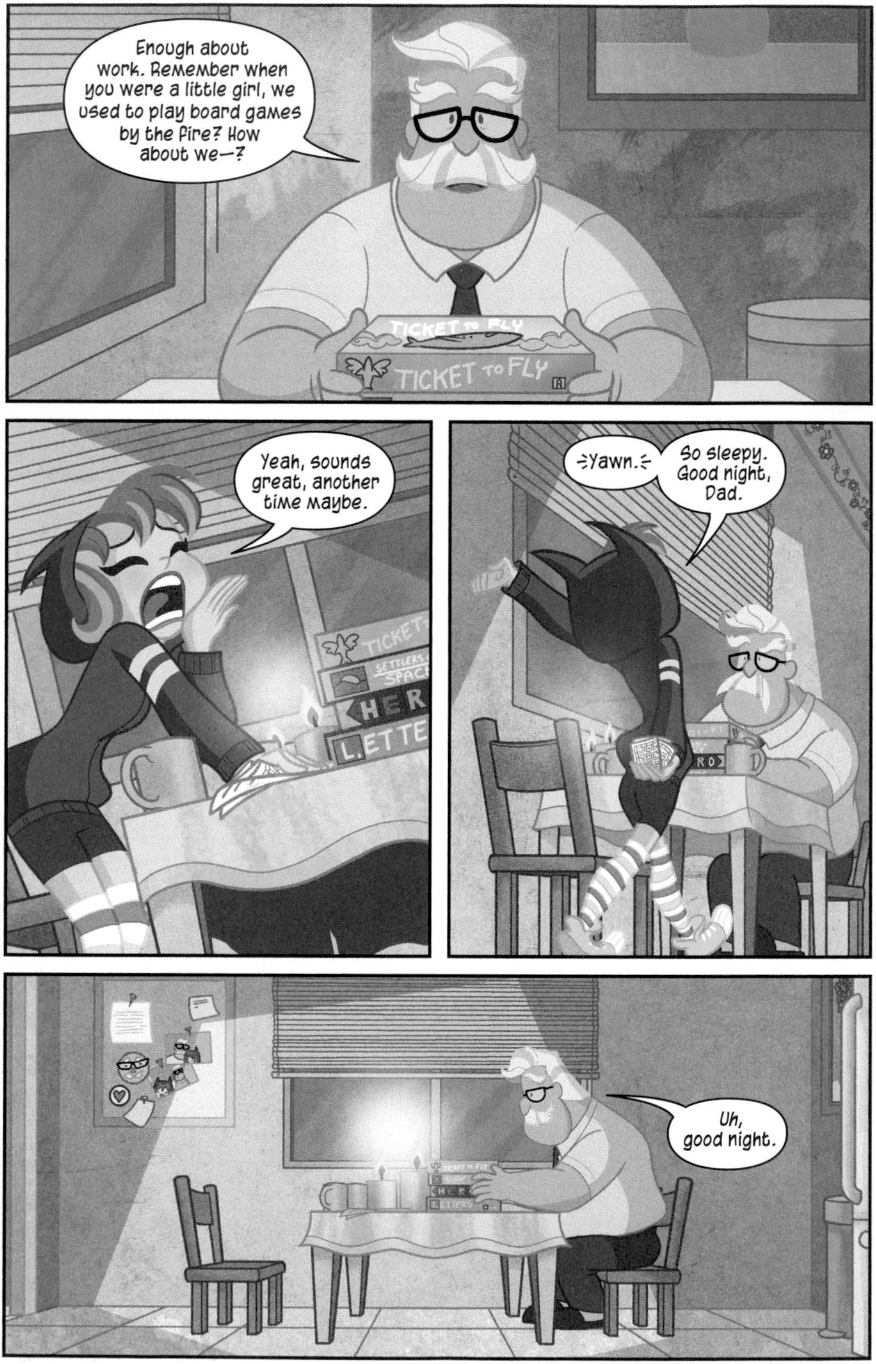
Enough about work. Remember when you were a little girl, we used to play board games by the fire? How about we—?
TICKET TO FLY
TICKET TO FLY
Yeah, sounds great, another time maybe.
-Yawn.-
So sleepy. Good night, Dad.
Uh, good night.

Dad's right. I'm a Gordon. I can figure this out!

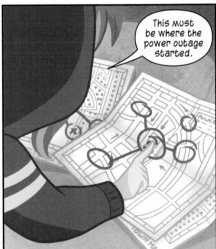

This must be where the power outage started.

That can't be right. There's nothing on the map.

I've *got* to find out what's there.

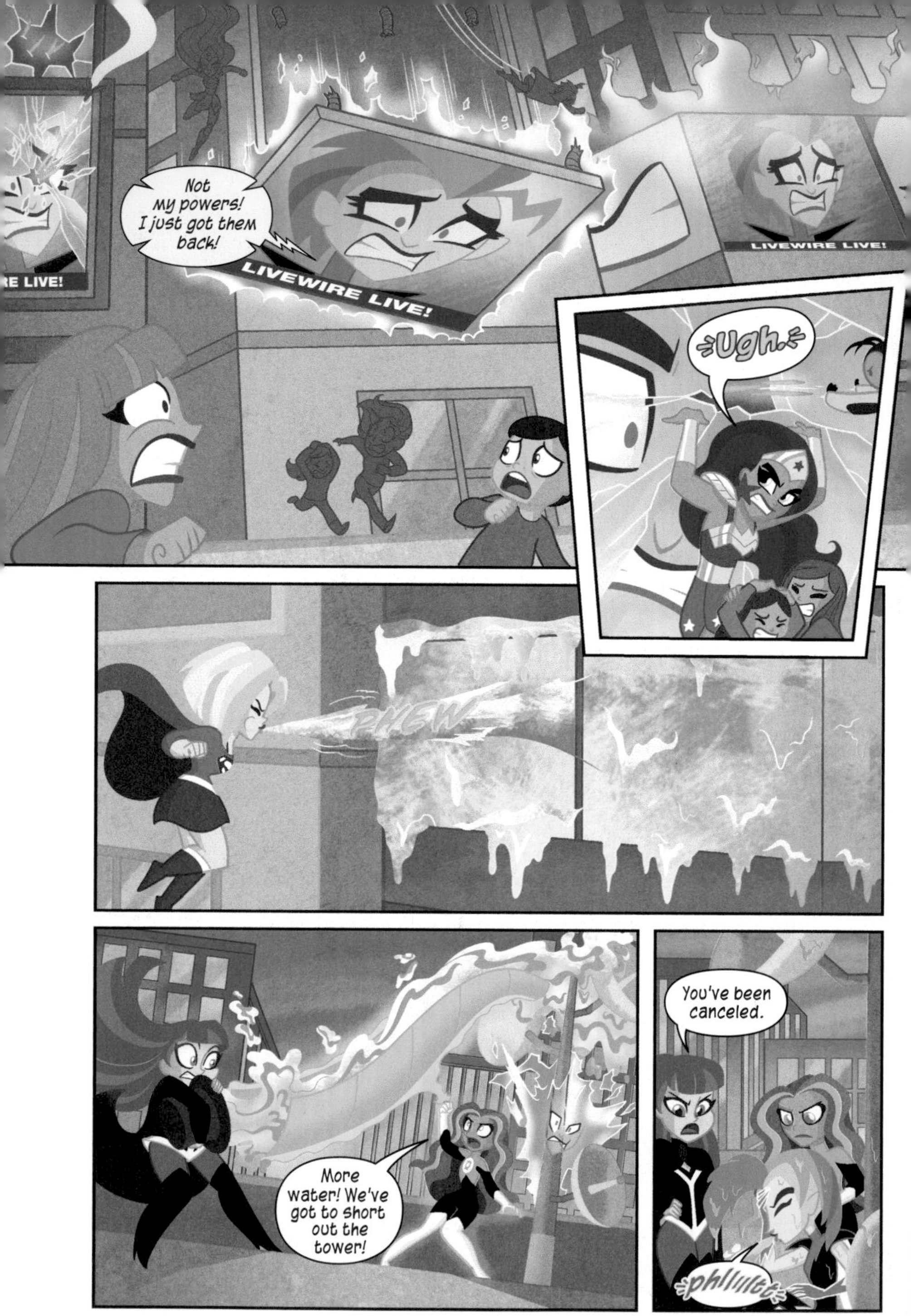
RE LIVE!
Not my powers! I just got them back!
LIVEWIRE LIVE!
LIVEWIRE LIVE!
Ugh.
PHEW
More water! We've got to short out the tower!
You've been canceled.
phllllltt

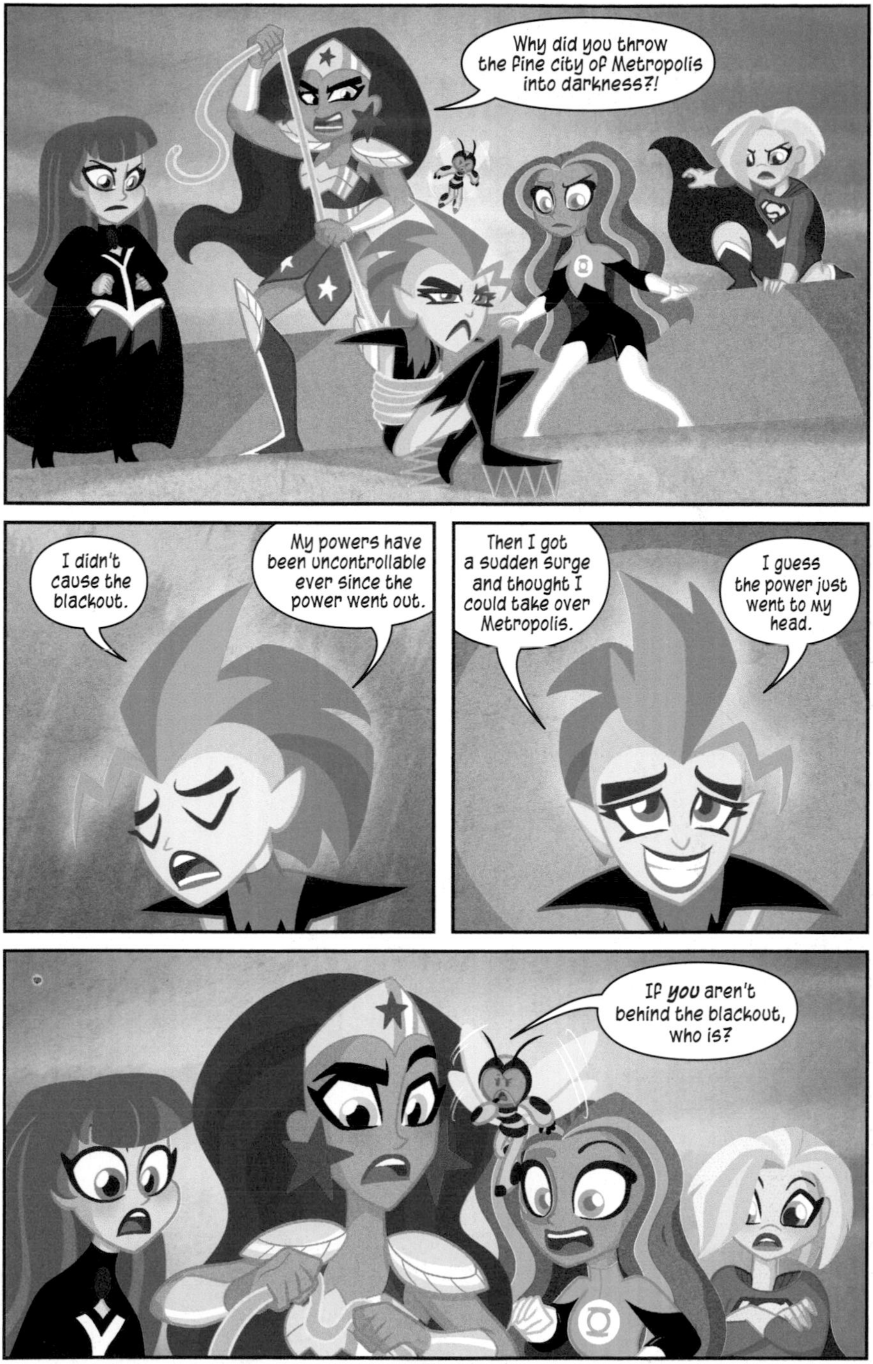

Why did you throw the fine city of Metropolis into darkness?!
I didn't cause the blackout.
My powers have been uncontrollable ever since the power went out.
Then I got a sudden surge and thought I could take over Metropolis.
I guess the power just went to my head.
If *you* aren't behind the blackout, who is?

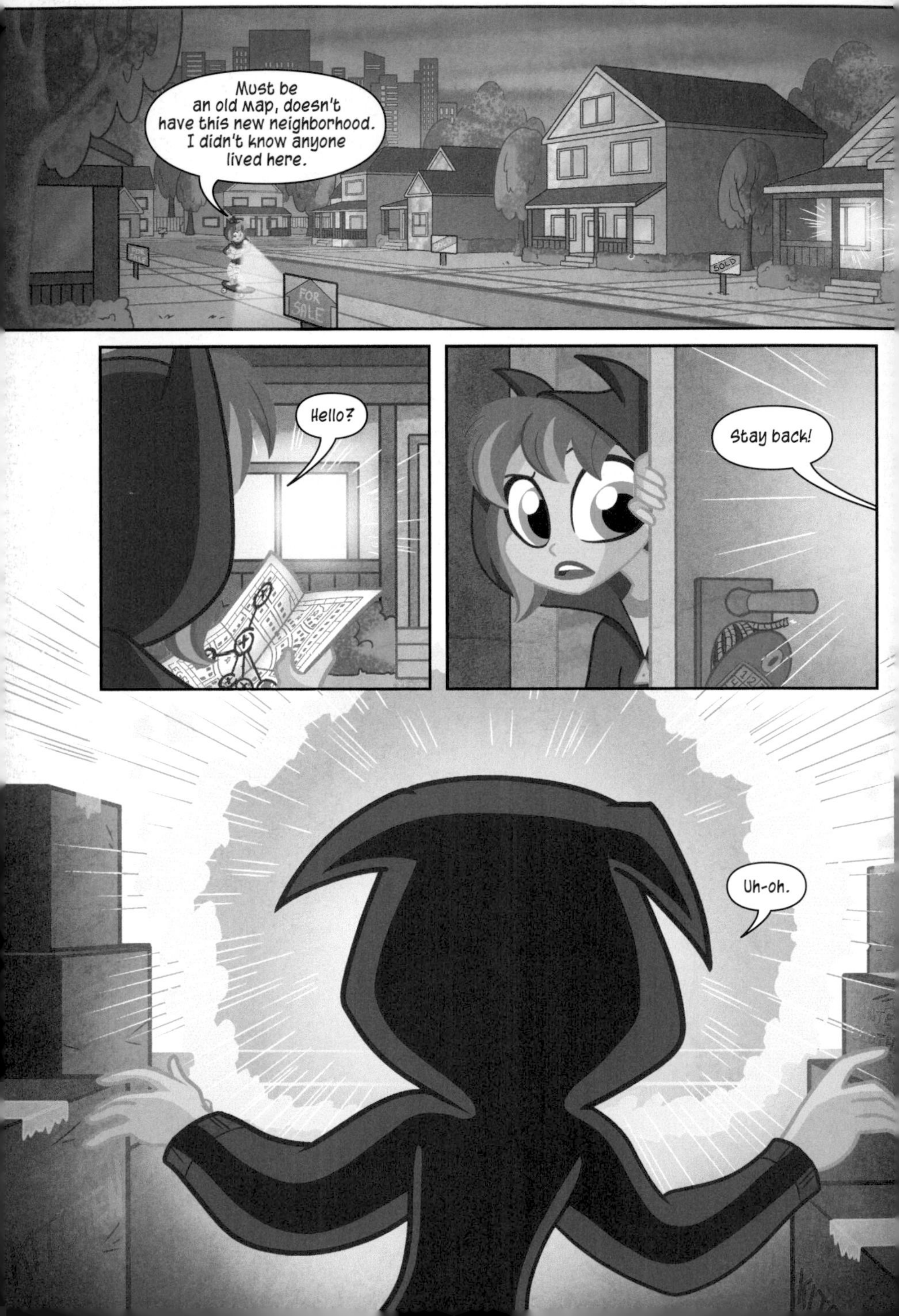
Must be an old map, doesn't have this new neighborhood. I didn't know anyone lived here.
FOR SALE
SOLD
SOLD
FOR SALE
Hello?
Stay back!
Uh-oh.

chapter six

RECONNECTED

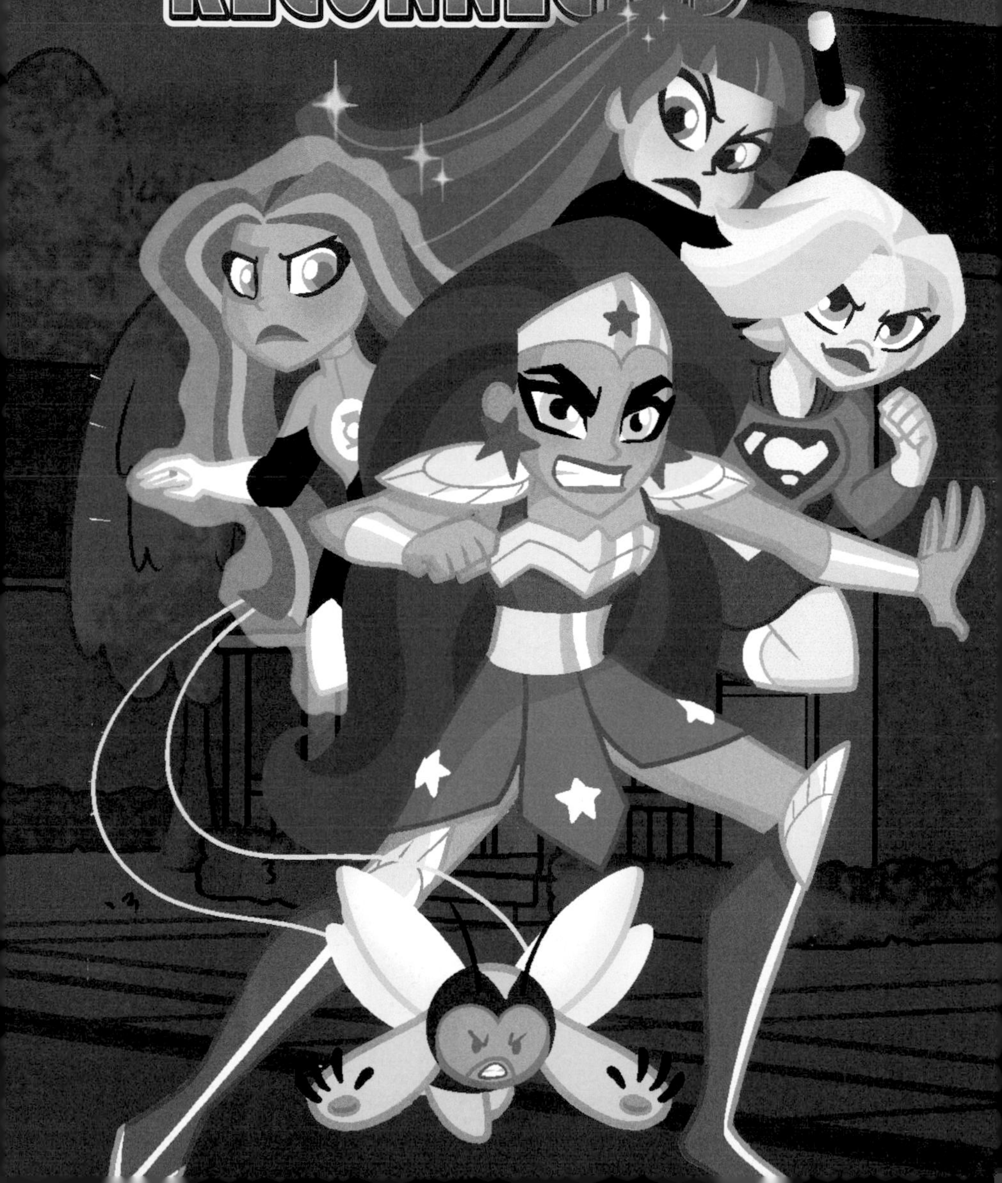

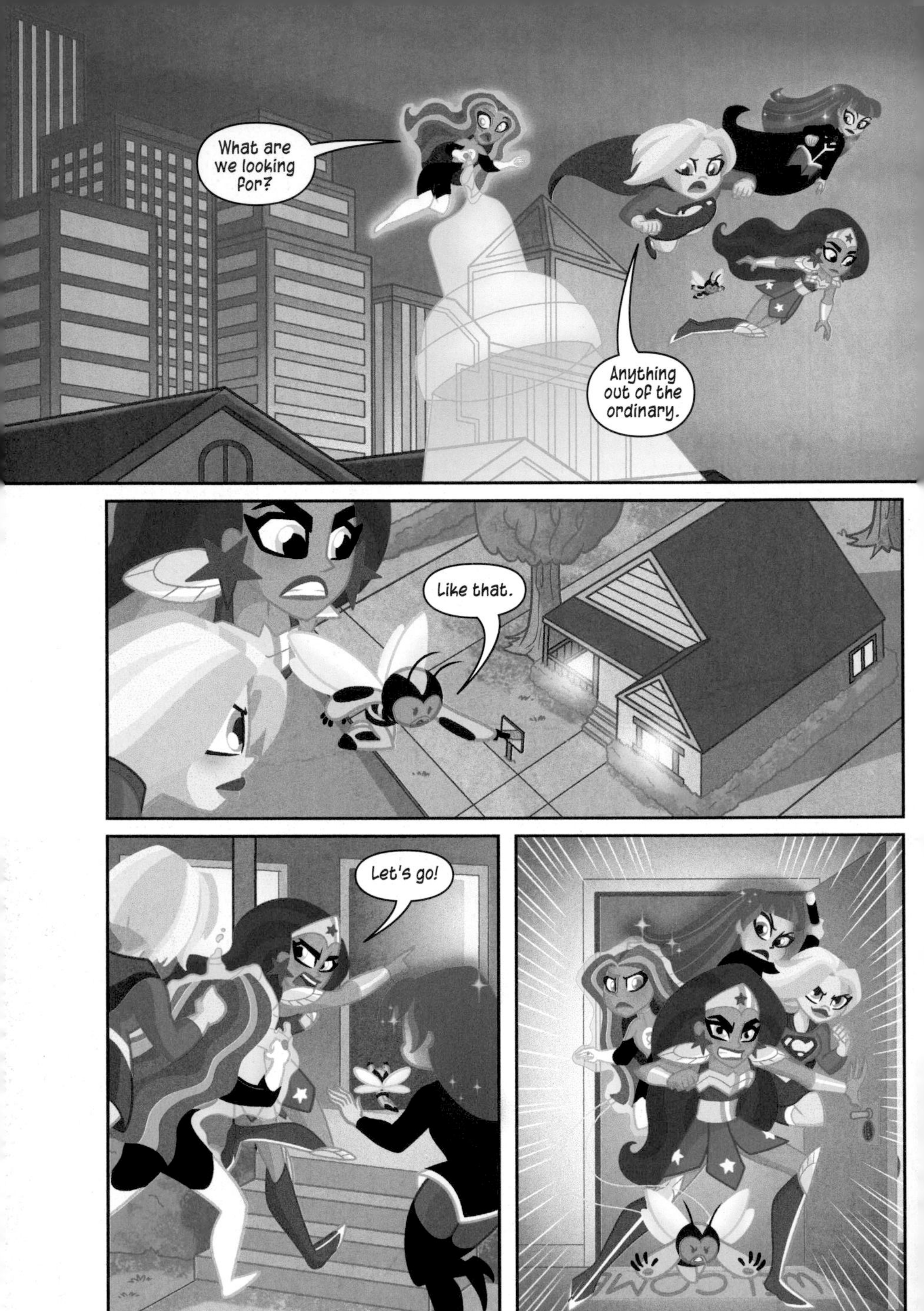
What are we looking for?
Anything out of the ordinary.
Like that.
Let's go!

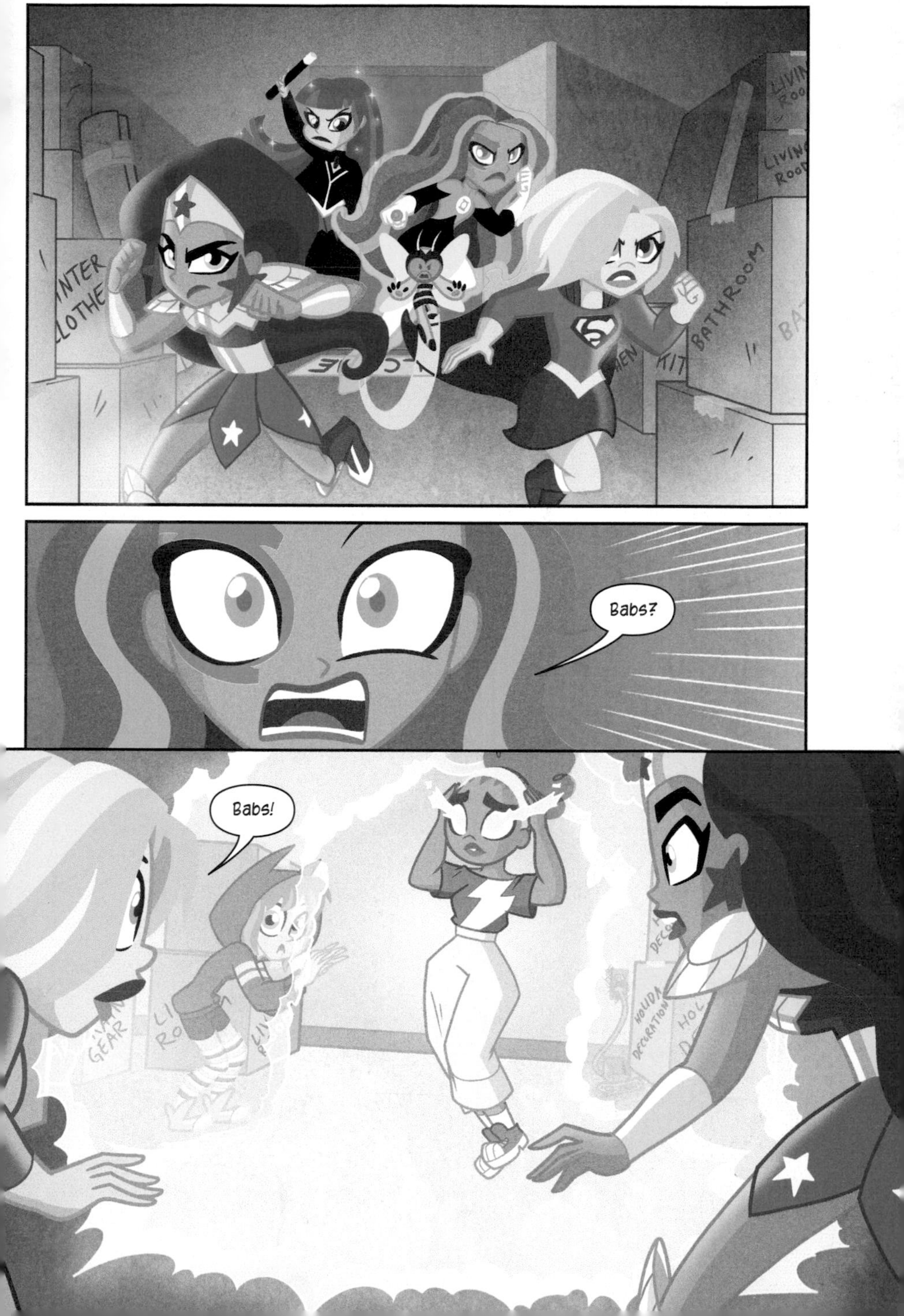
Babs?
Babs!

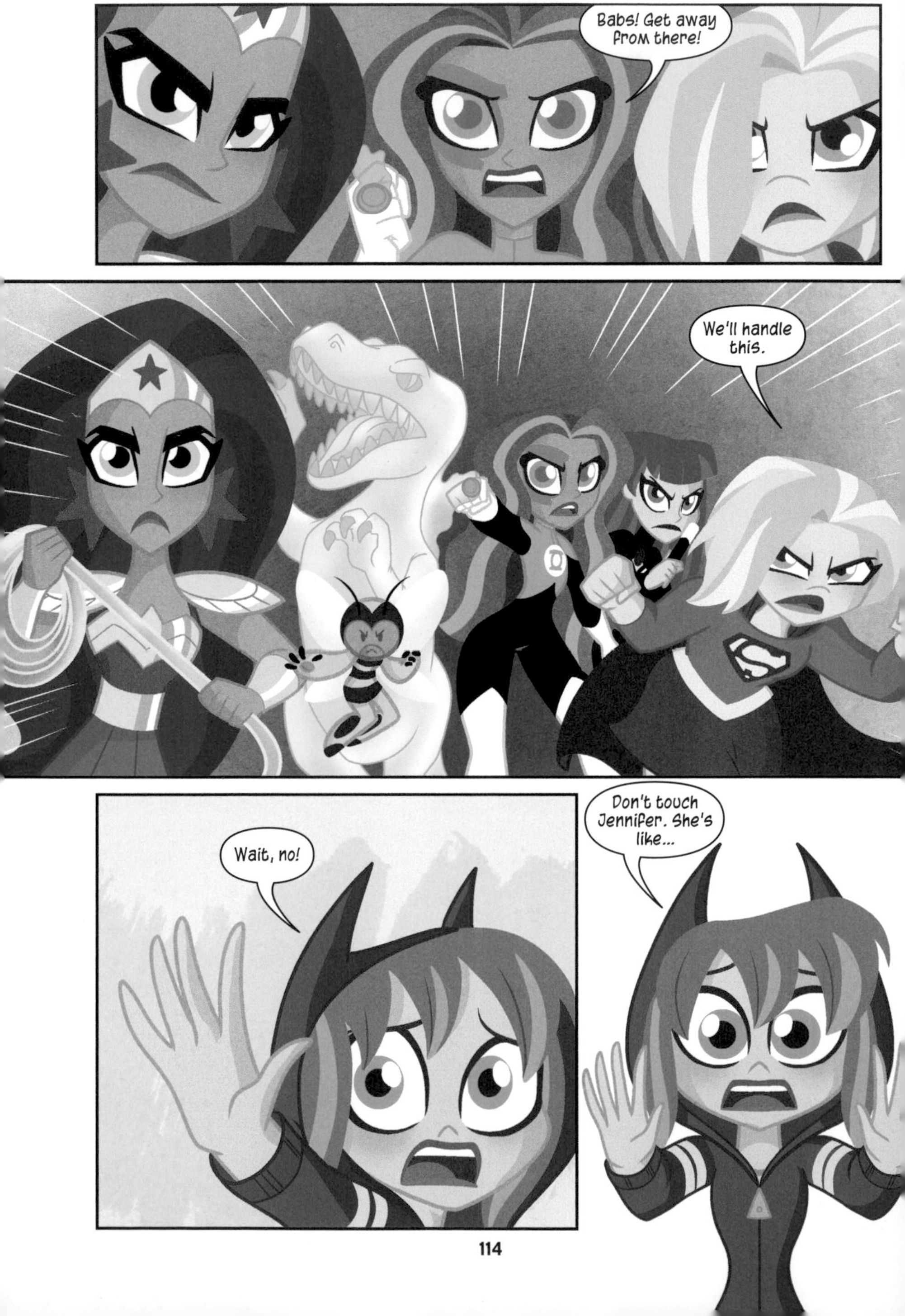
Babs! Get away from there!
We'll handle this.
Wait, no!
Don't touch Jennifer. She's like...

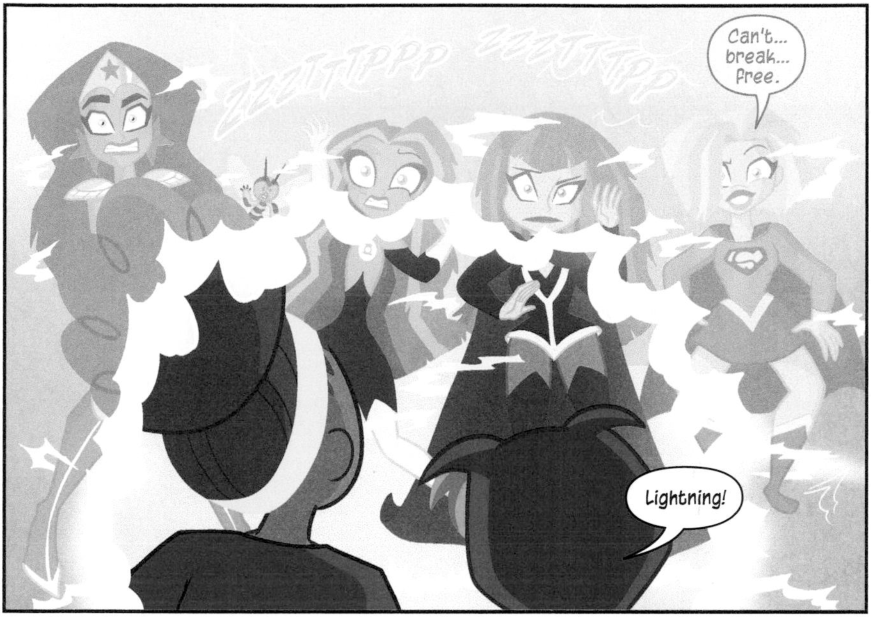
ZZZZTTTPPP
ZZZZTTTPPP
Can't... break... free.
Lightning!

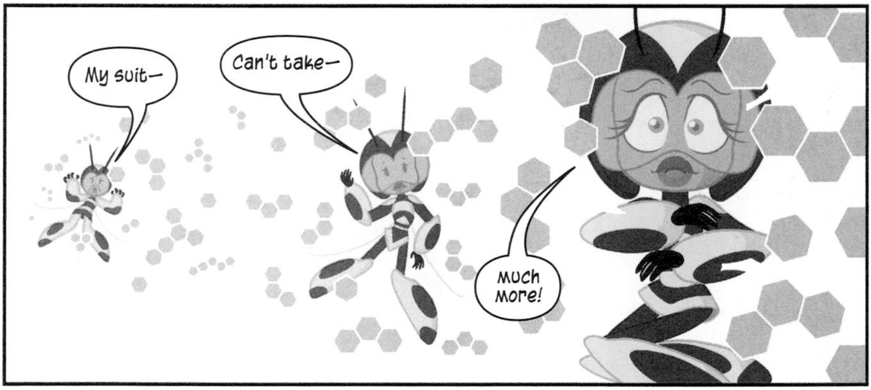
My suit—
Can't take—
Much more!

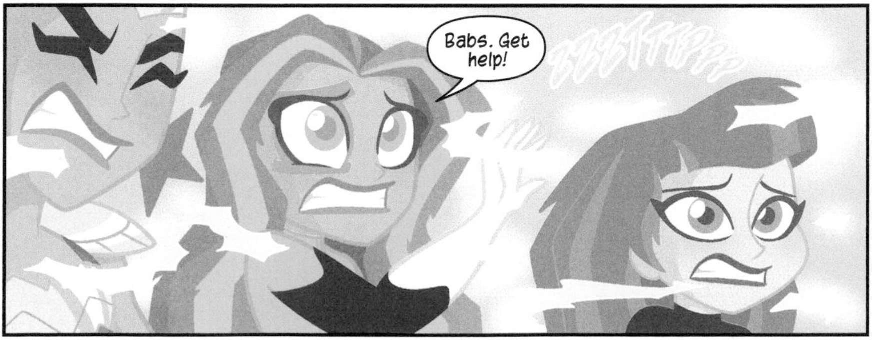
Babs. Get help!

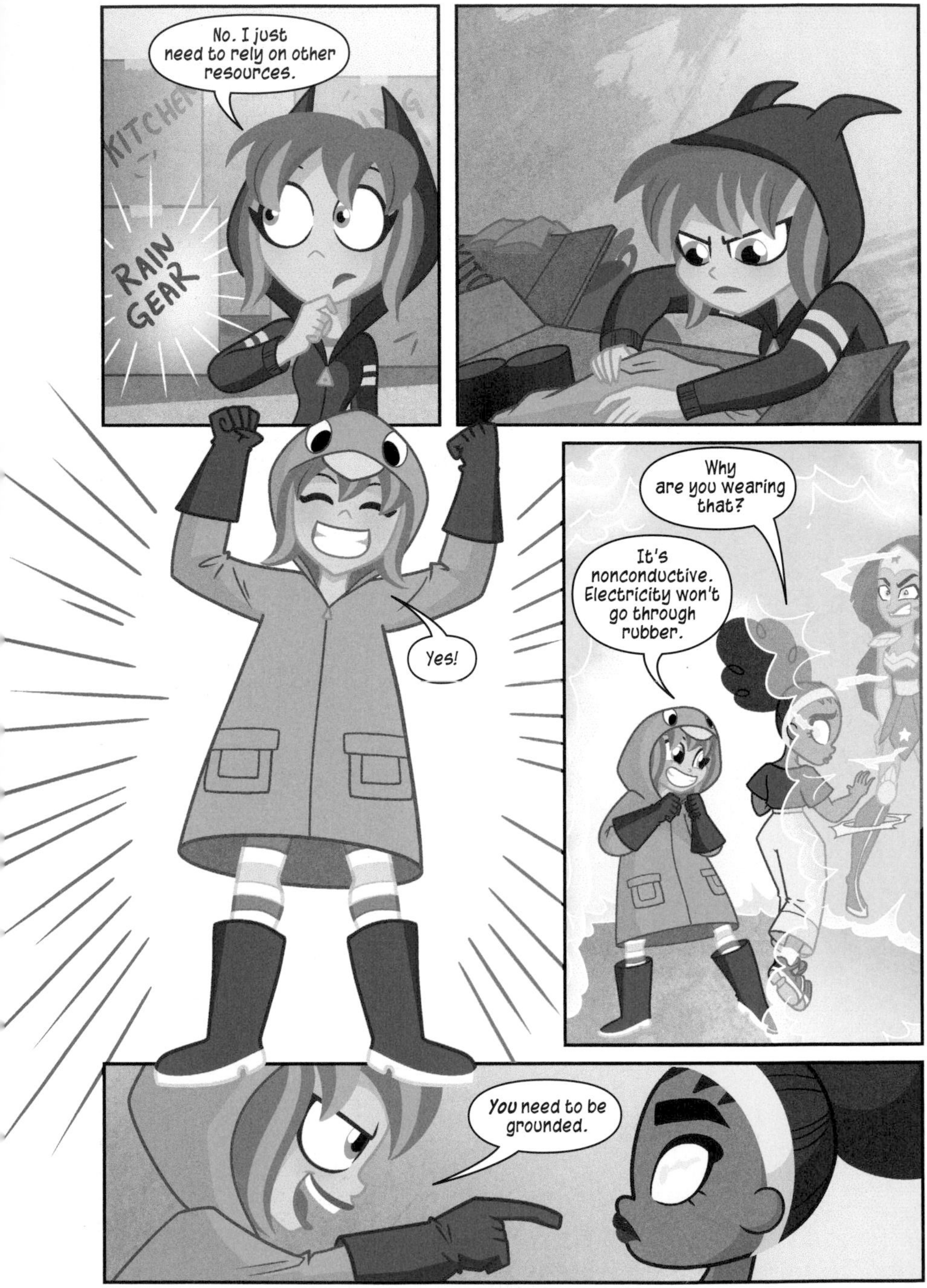
No. I just need to rely on other resources.
KITCHEN
RAIN GEAR
Yes!
Why are you wearing that?
It's nonconductive. Electricity won't go through rubber.
You need to be grounded.

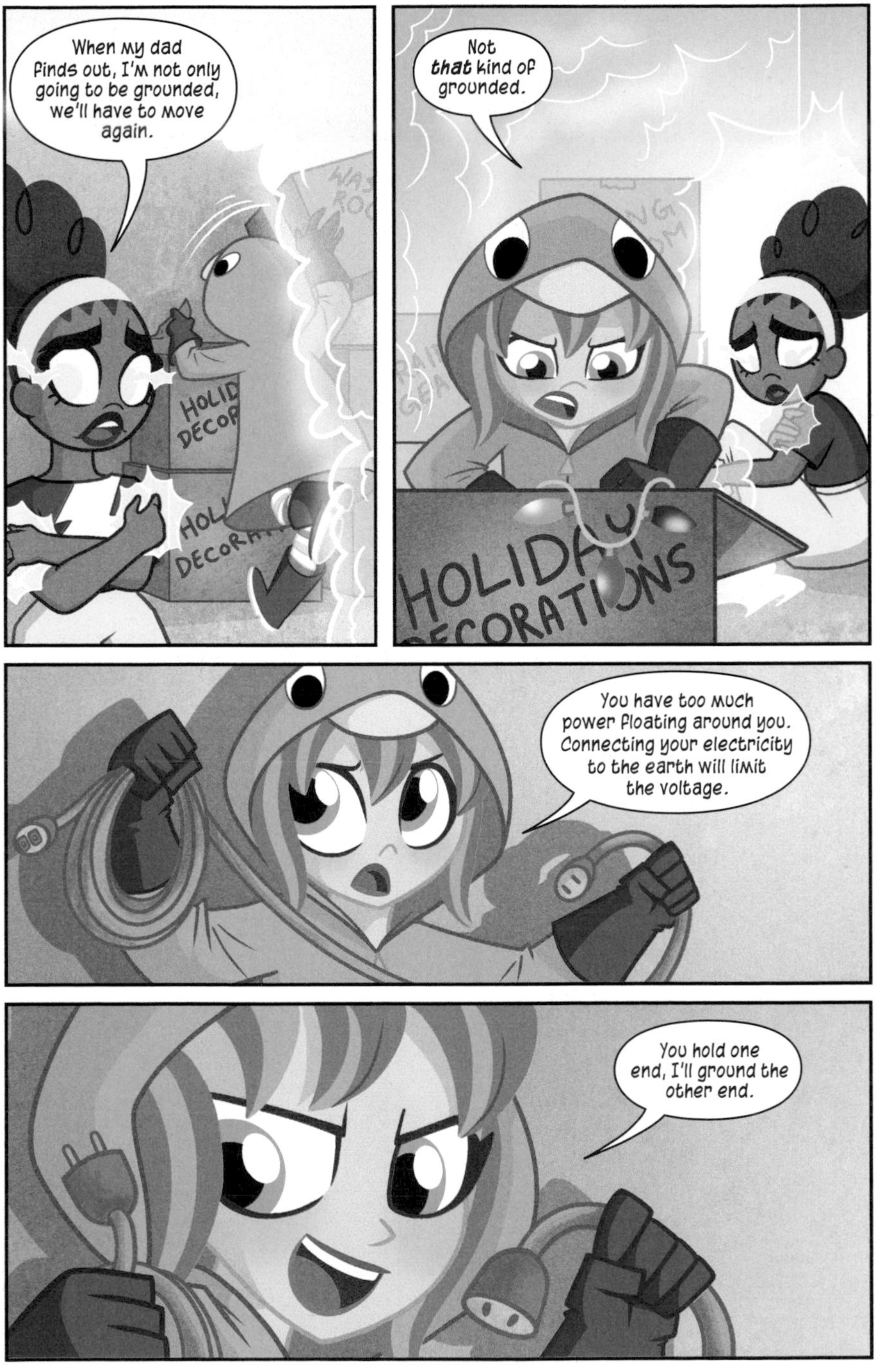
When my dad finds out, I'm not only going to be grounded, we'll have to move again.
HOLIDAY DECORATIONS
Not *that* kind of grounded.
HOLIDAY DECORATIONS
You have too much power floating around you. Connecting your electricity to the earth will limit the voltage.
You hold one end, I'll ground the other end.

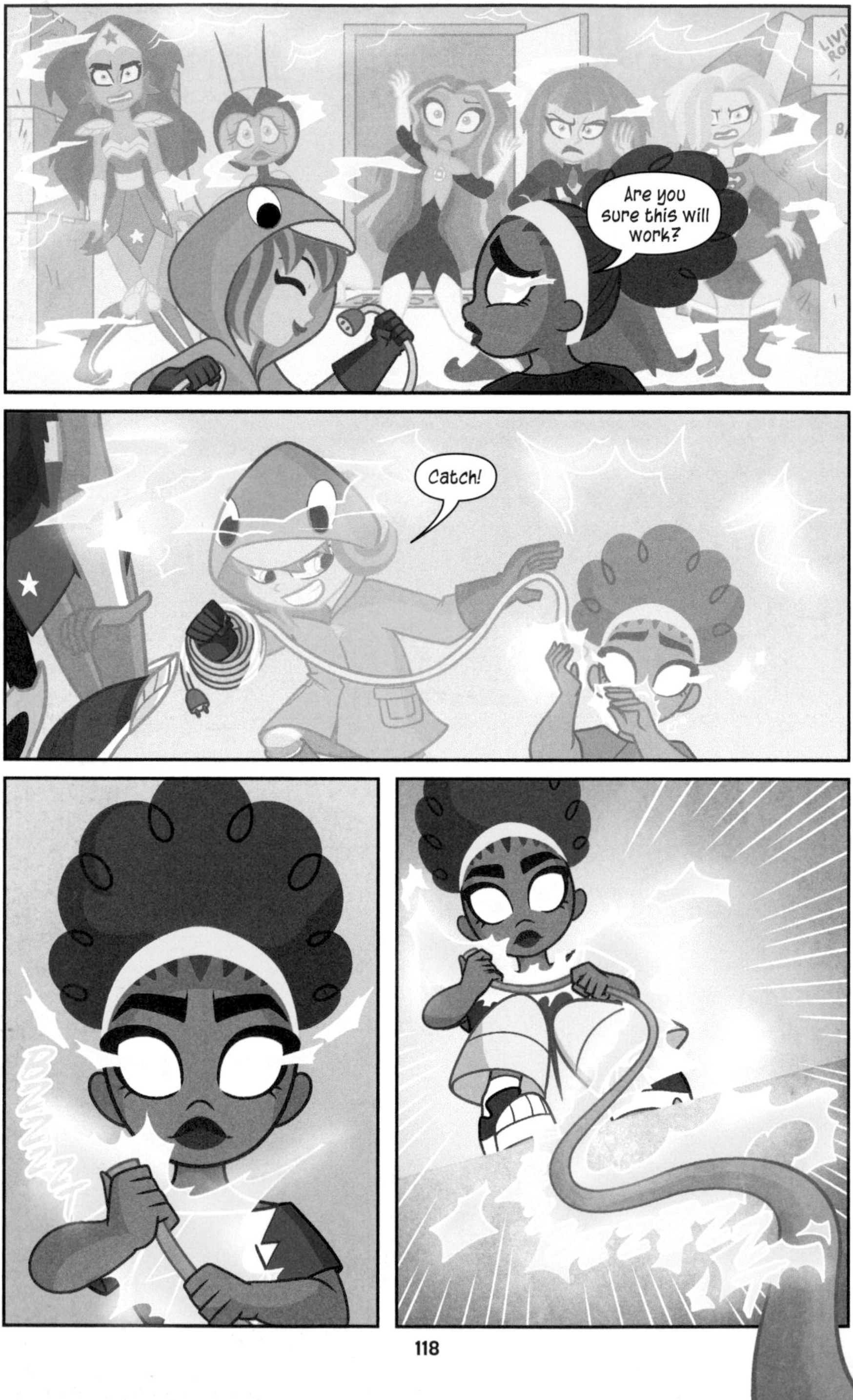
Are you sure this will work?
Catch!

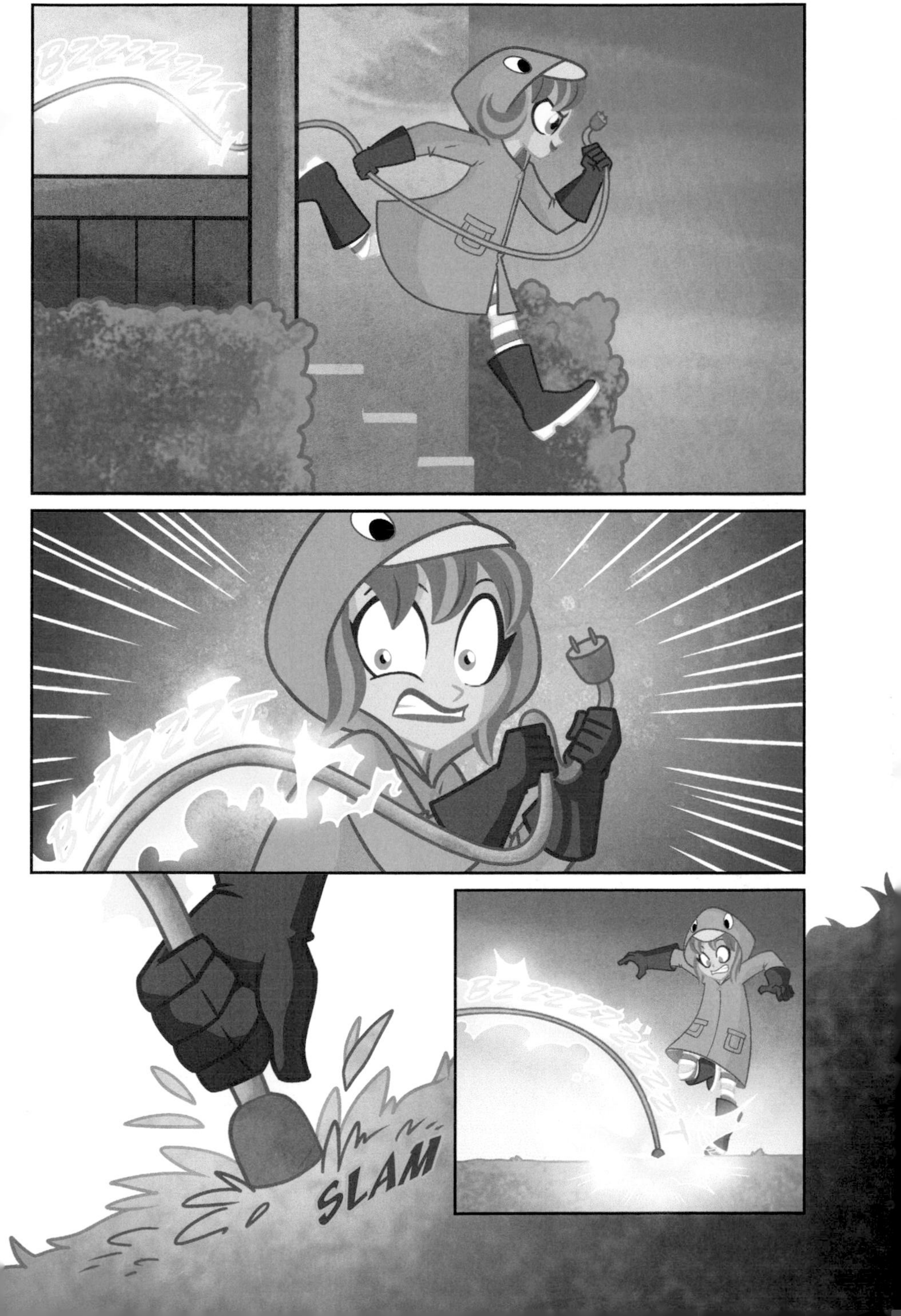
BZZZZZZZT
BZZZZZZT
SLAM
BZZZZZZZZZZZT

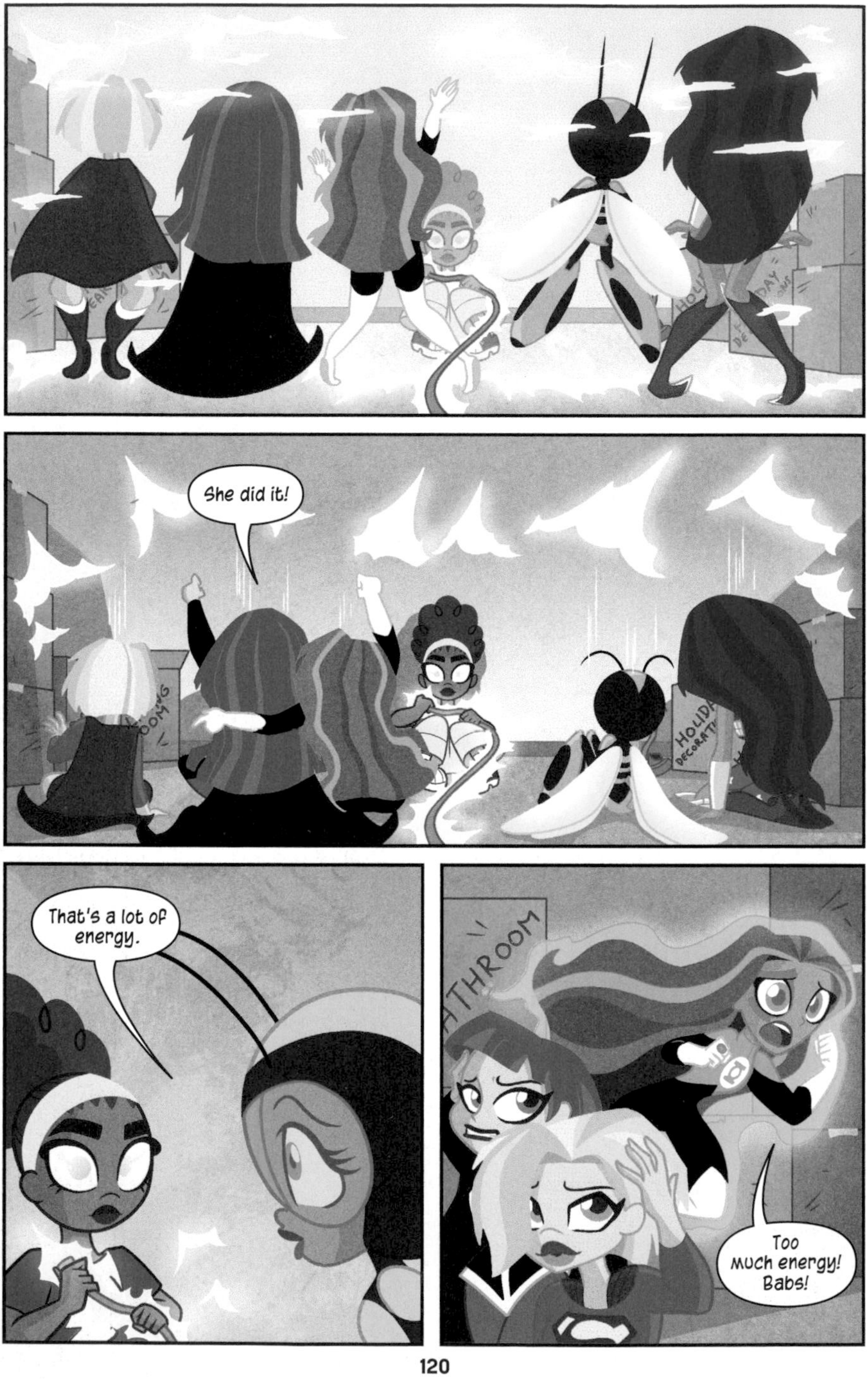
She did it!
That's a lot of energy.
Too much energy! Babs!

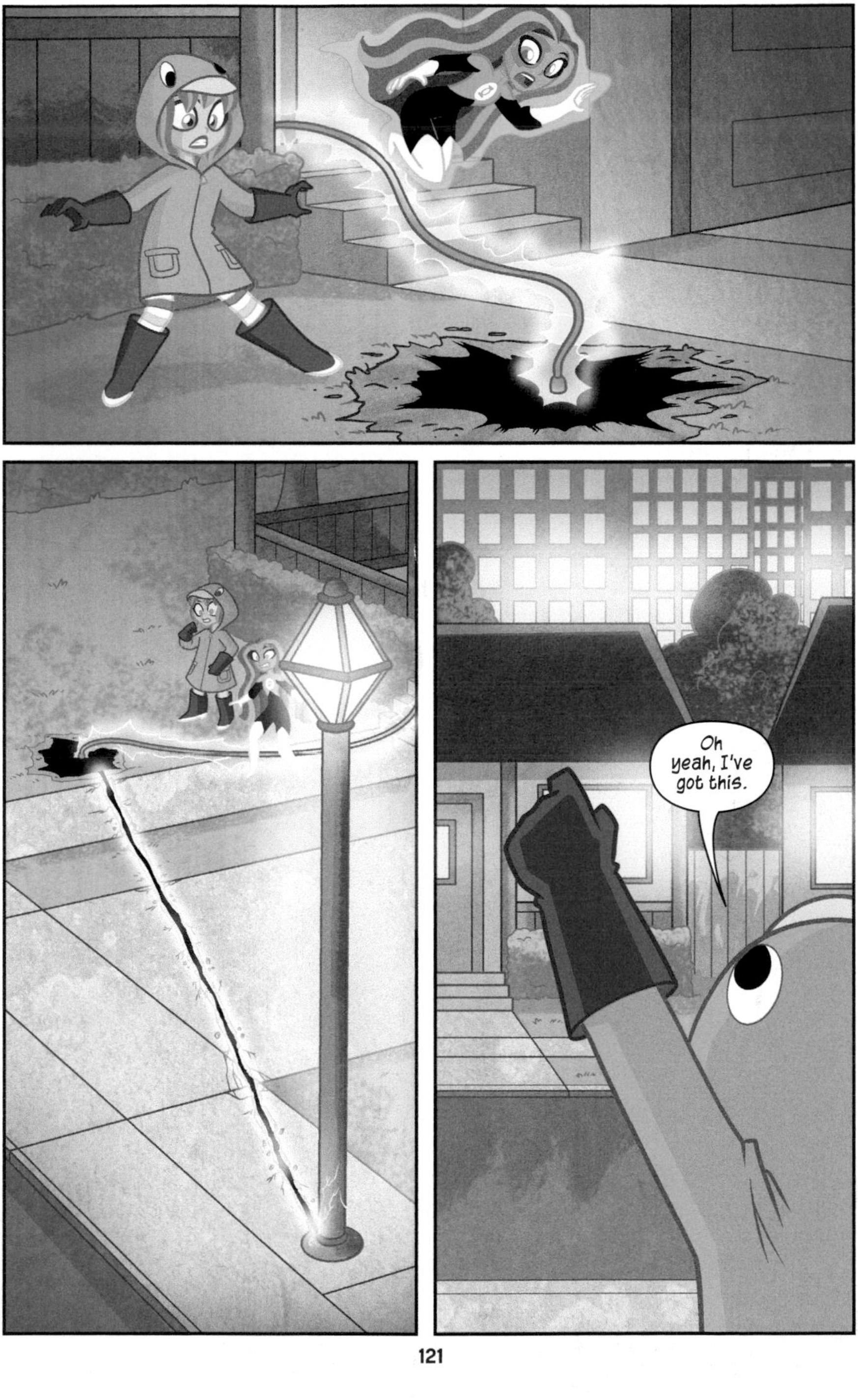
Oh yeah, I've got this.

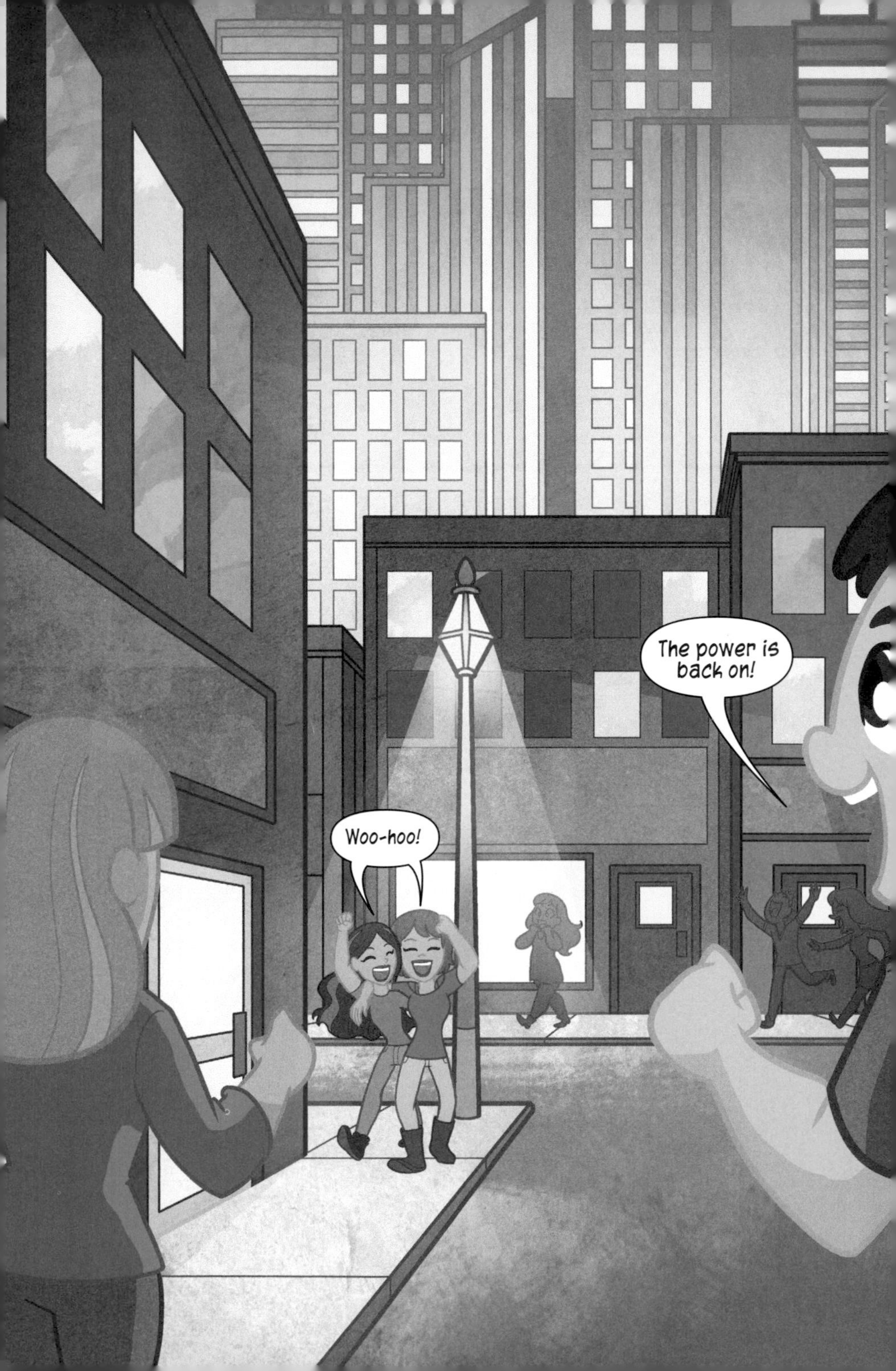
Woo-hoo!
The power is back on!

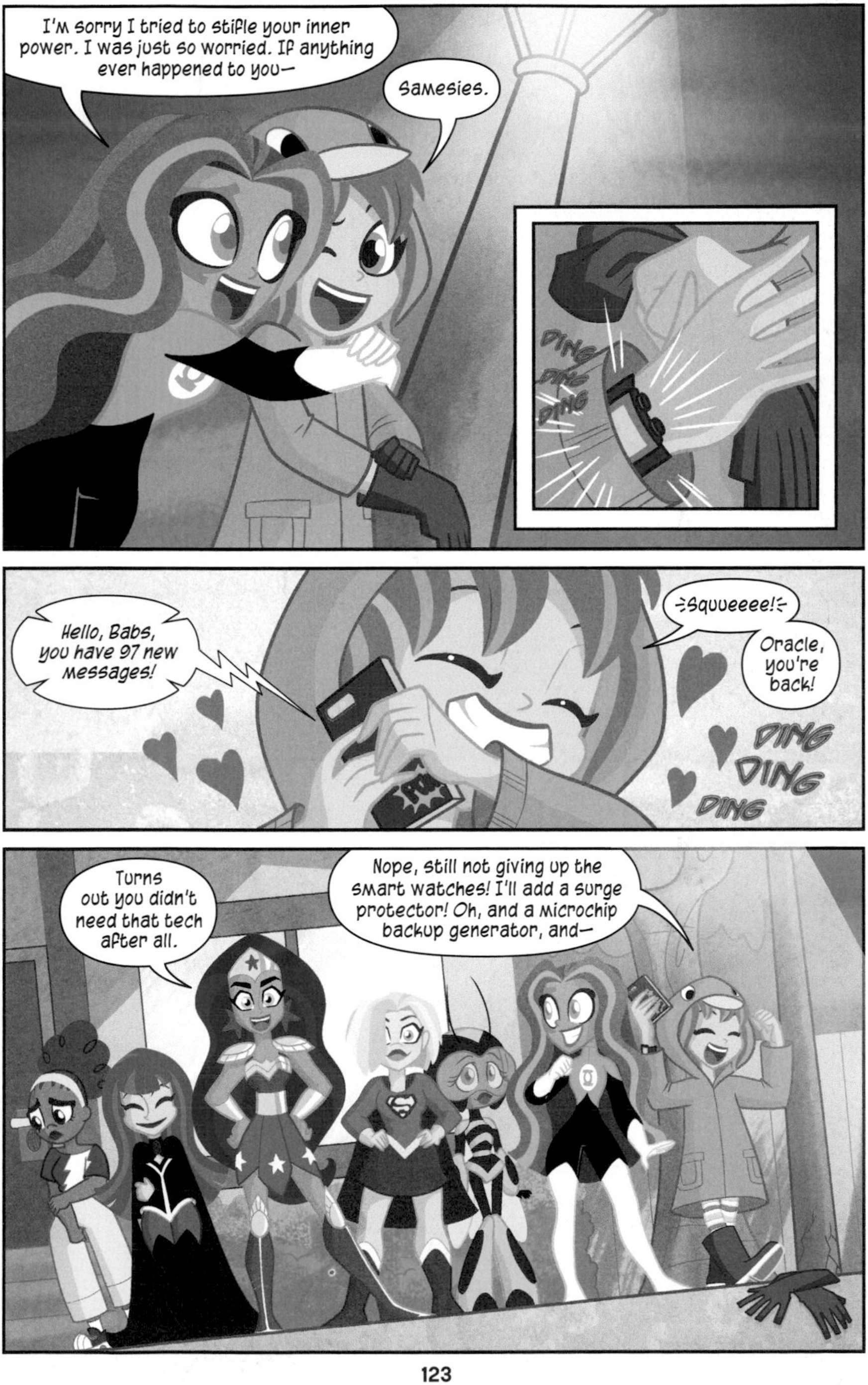

I'm sorry I tried to stifle your inner power. I was just so worried. If anything ever happened to you—
Samesies.
DING DING DING
Hello, Babs, you have 97 new messages!
-Squueeee!-
Oracle, you're back!
DING DING DING
Turns out you didn't need that tech after all.
Nope, still not giving up the smart watches! I'll add a surge protector! Oh, and a microchip backup generator, and—

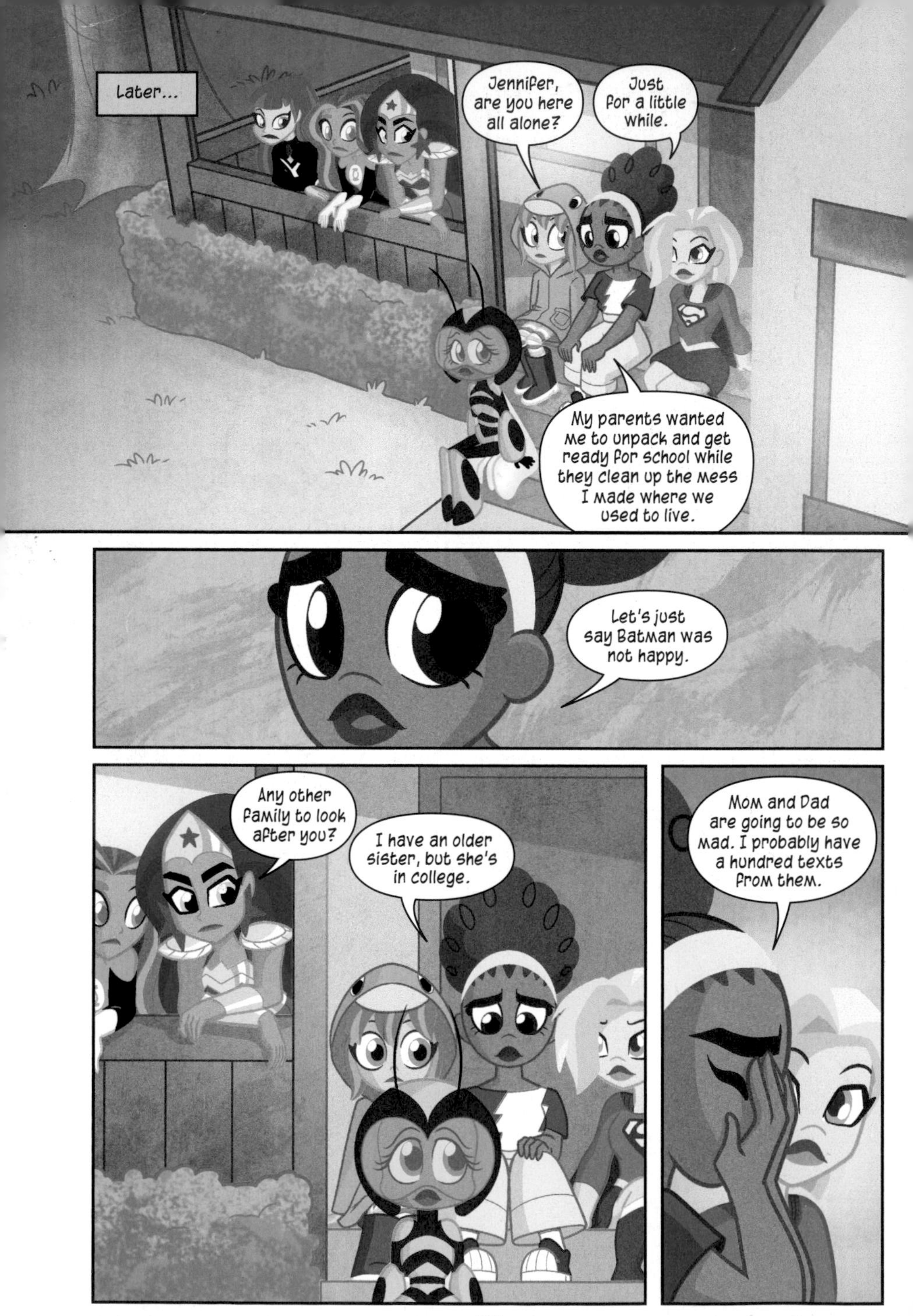
Later...
Jennifer, are you here all alone?
Just for a little while.
My parents wanted me to unpack and get ready for school while they clean up the mess I made where we used to live.
Let's just say Batman was not happy.
Any other family to look after you?
I have an older sister, but she's in college.
Mom and Dad are going to be so mad. I probably have a hundred texts from them.

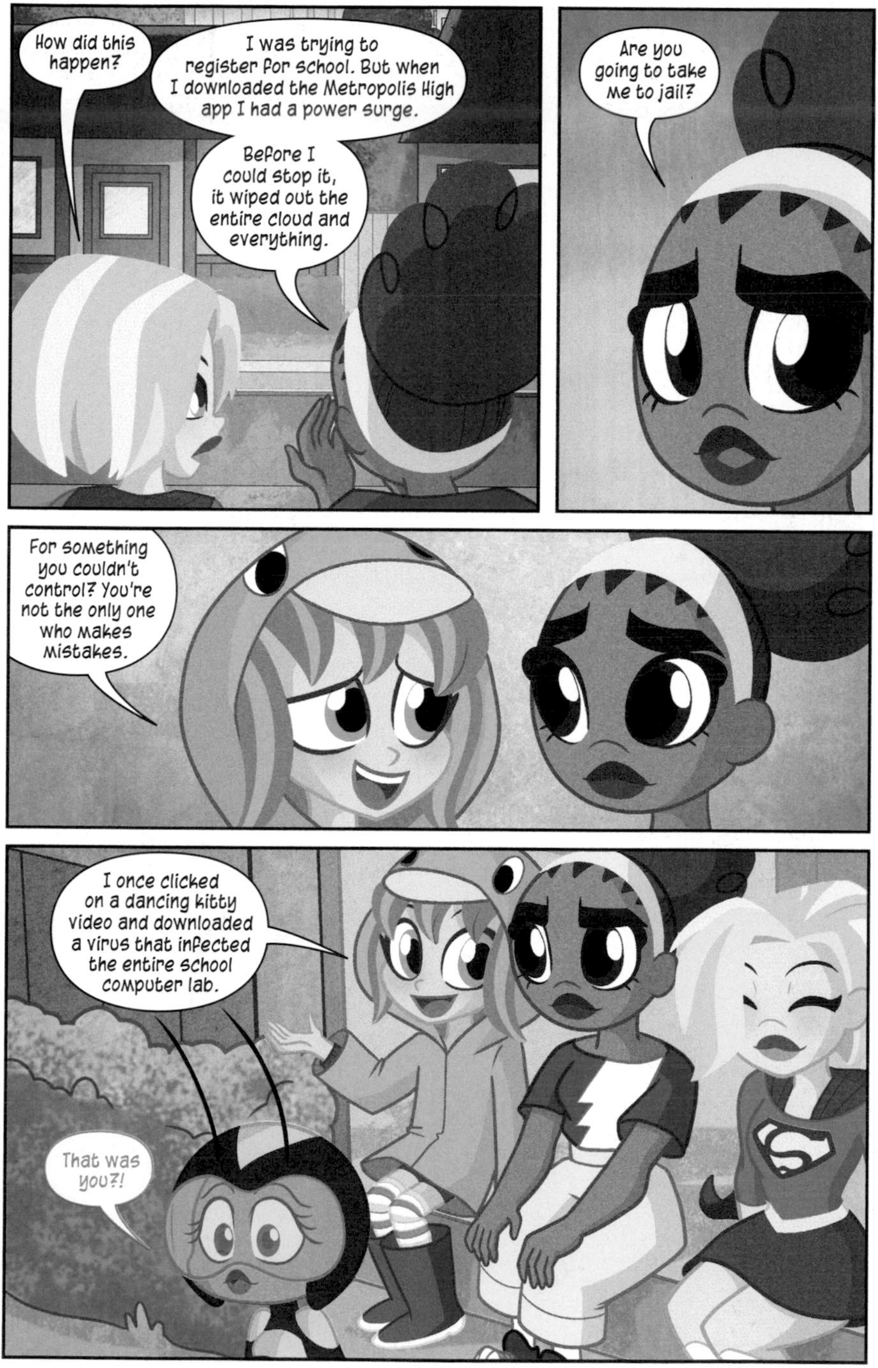
How did this happen?
I was trying to register for school. But when I downloaded the Metropolis High app I had a power surge.
Before I could stop it, it wiped out the entire cloud and everything.
Are you going to take me to jail?
For something you couldn't control? You're not the only one who makes mistakes.
I once clicked on a dancing kitty video and downloaded a virus that infected the entire school computer lab.
That was you?!

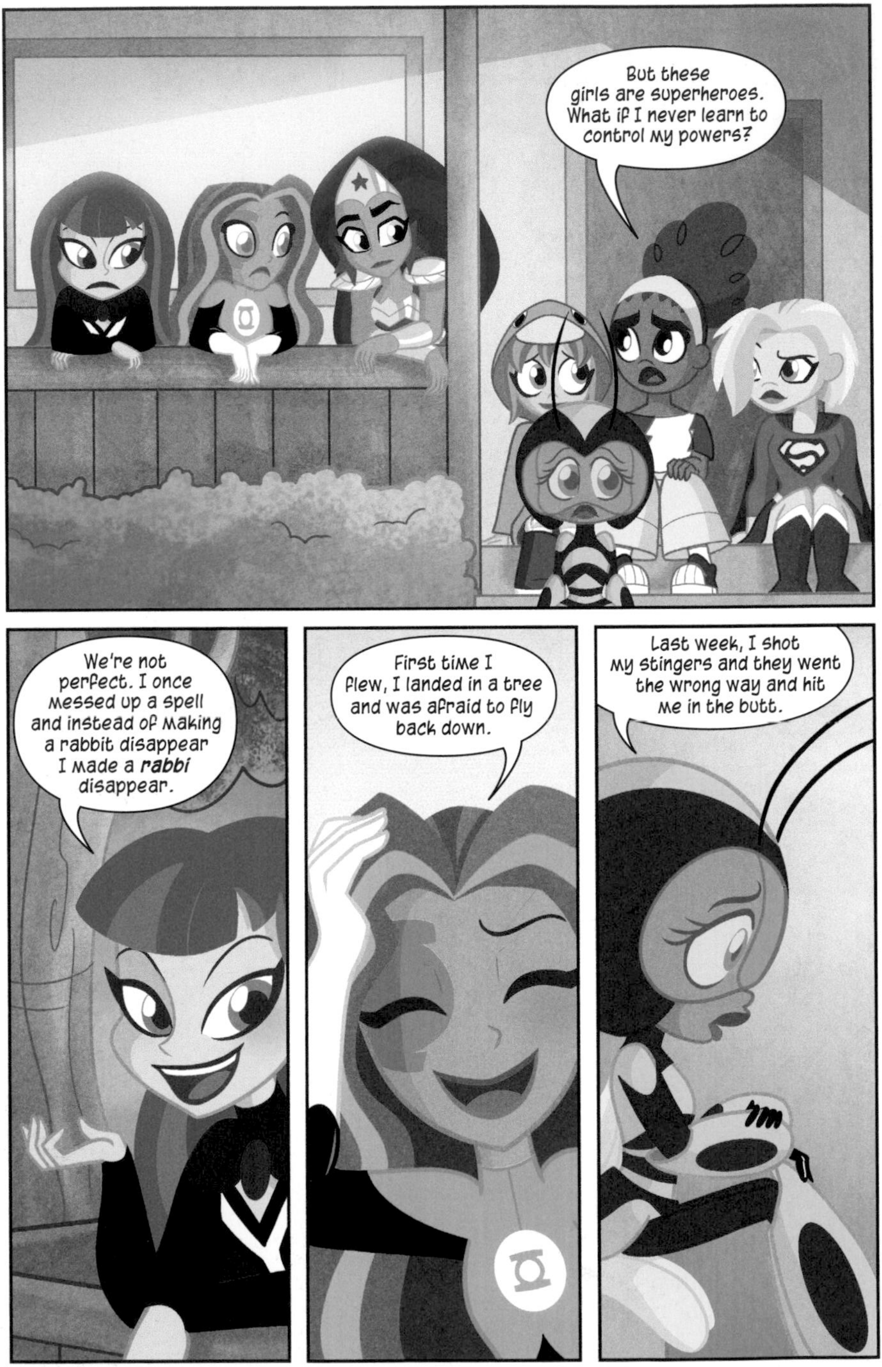
But these girls are superheroes. What if I never learn to control my powers?
We're not perfect. I once messed up a spell and instead of making a rabbit disappear I made a *rabbi* disappear.
First time I flew, I landed in a tree and was afraid to fly back down.
Last week, I shot my stingers and they went the wrong way and hit me in the butt.

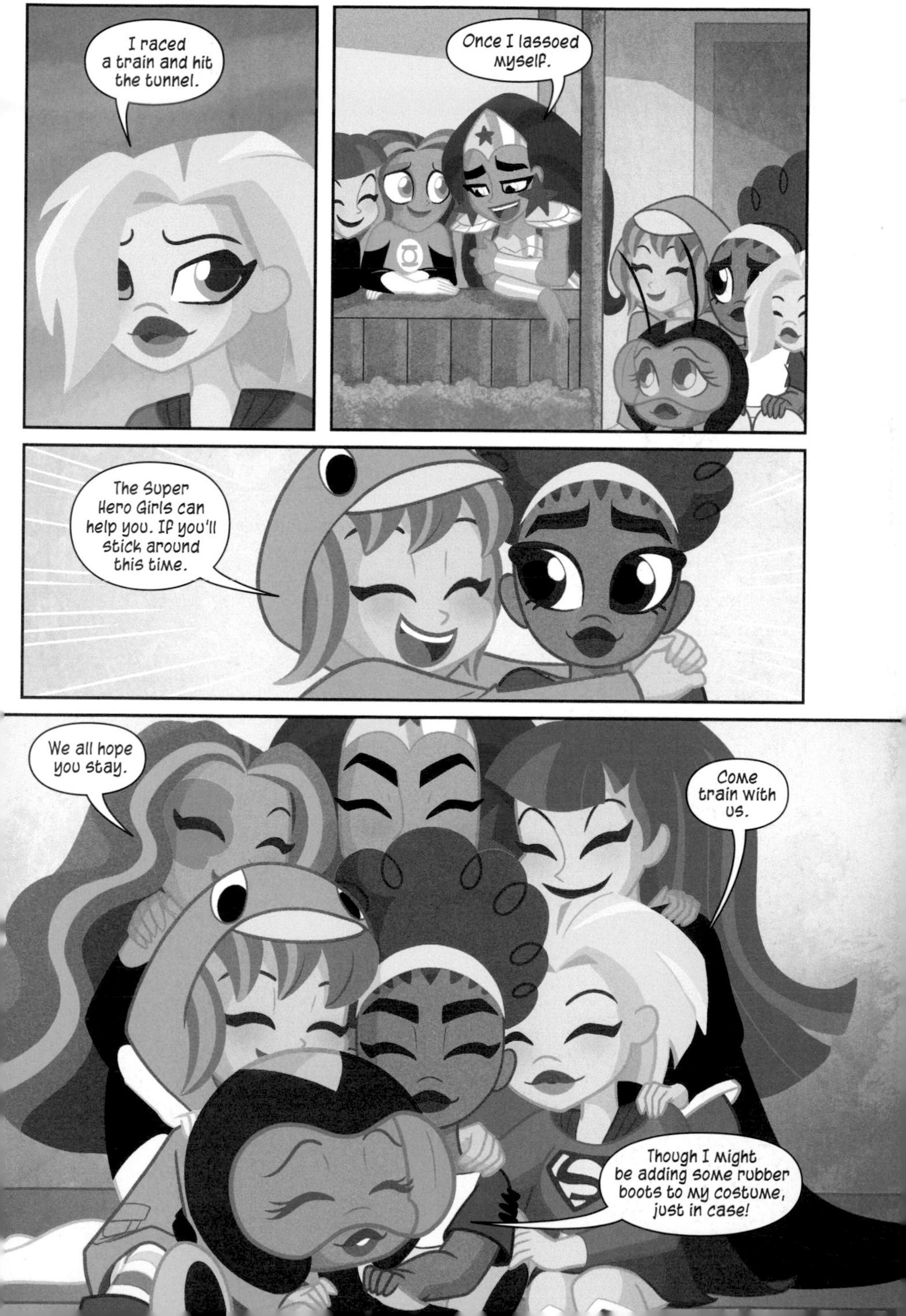
I raced a train and hit the tunnel.
Once I lassoed myself.
The Super Hero Girls can help you. If you'll stick around this time.
We all hope you stay.
Come train with us.
Though I might be adding some rubber boots to my costume, just in case!

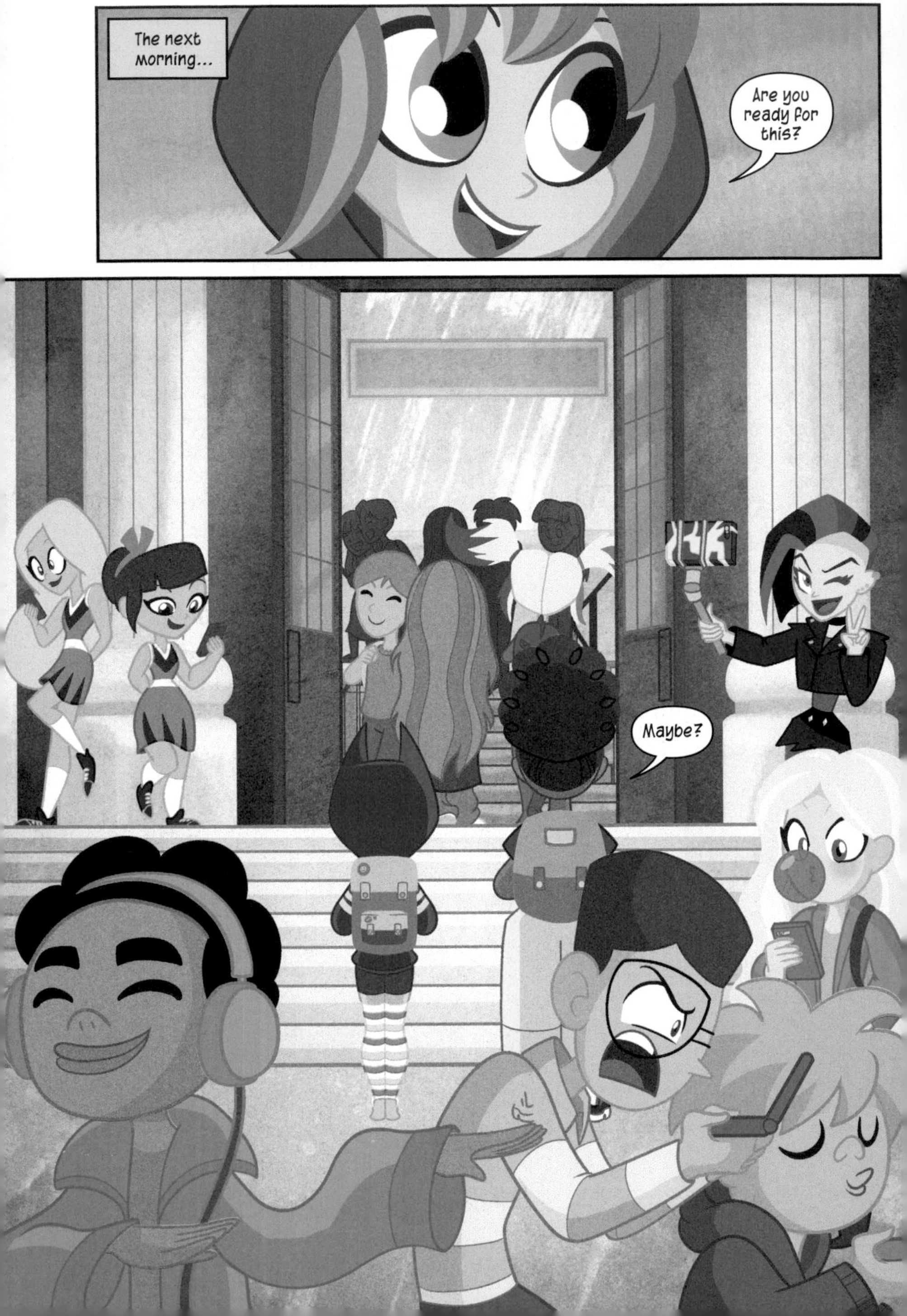
The next morning...
Are you ready for this?
Maybe?

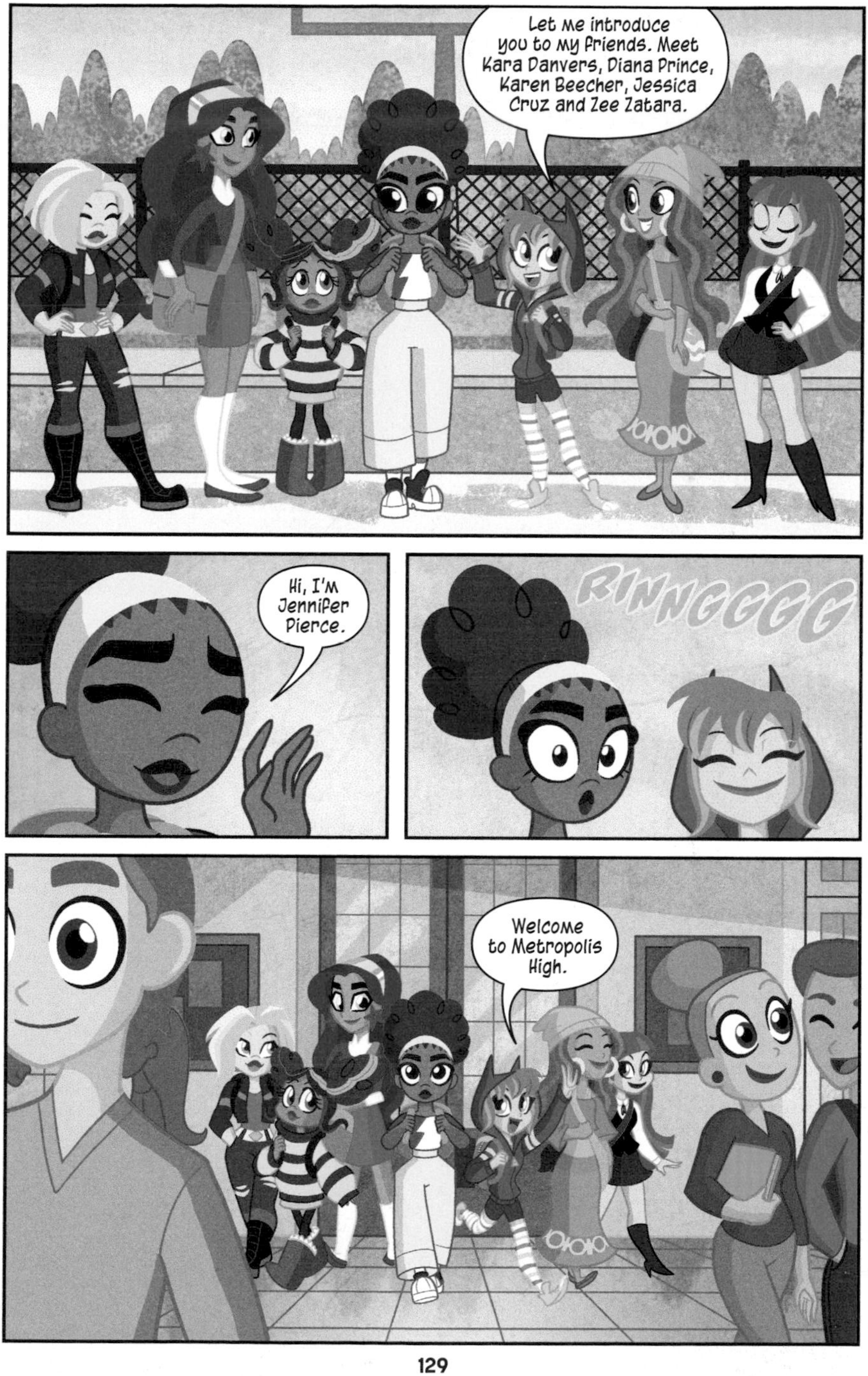
Let me introduce you to my friends. Meet Kara Danvers, Diana Prince, Karen Beecher, Jessica Cruz and Zee Zatara.
Hi, I'm Jennifer Pierce.
RINNGGGG
Welcome to Metropolis High.

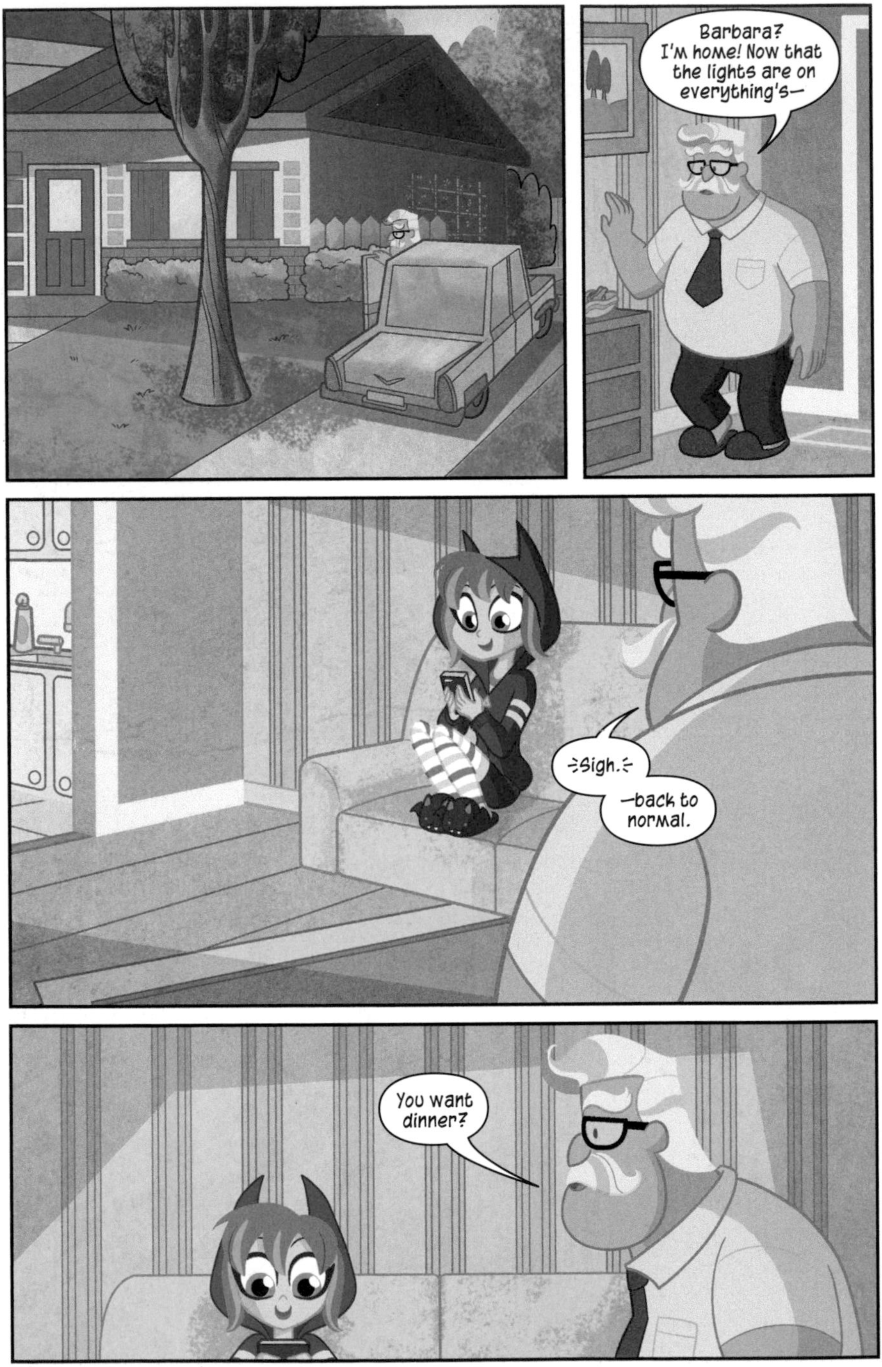
Barbara? I'm home! Now that the lights are on everything's—
Sigh.
—back to normal.
You want dinner?

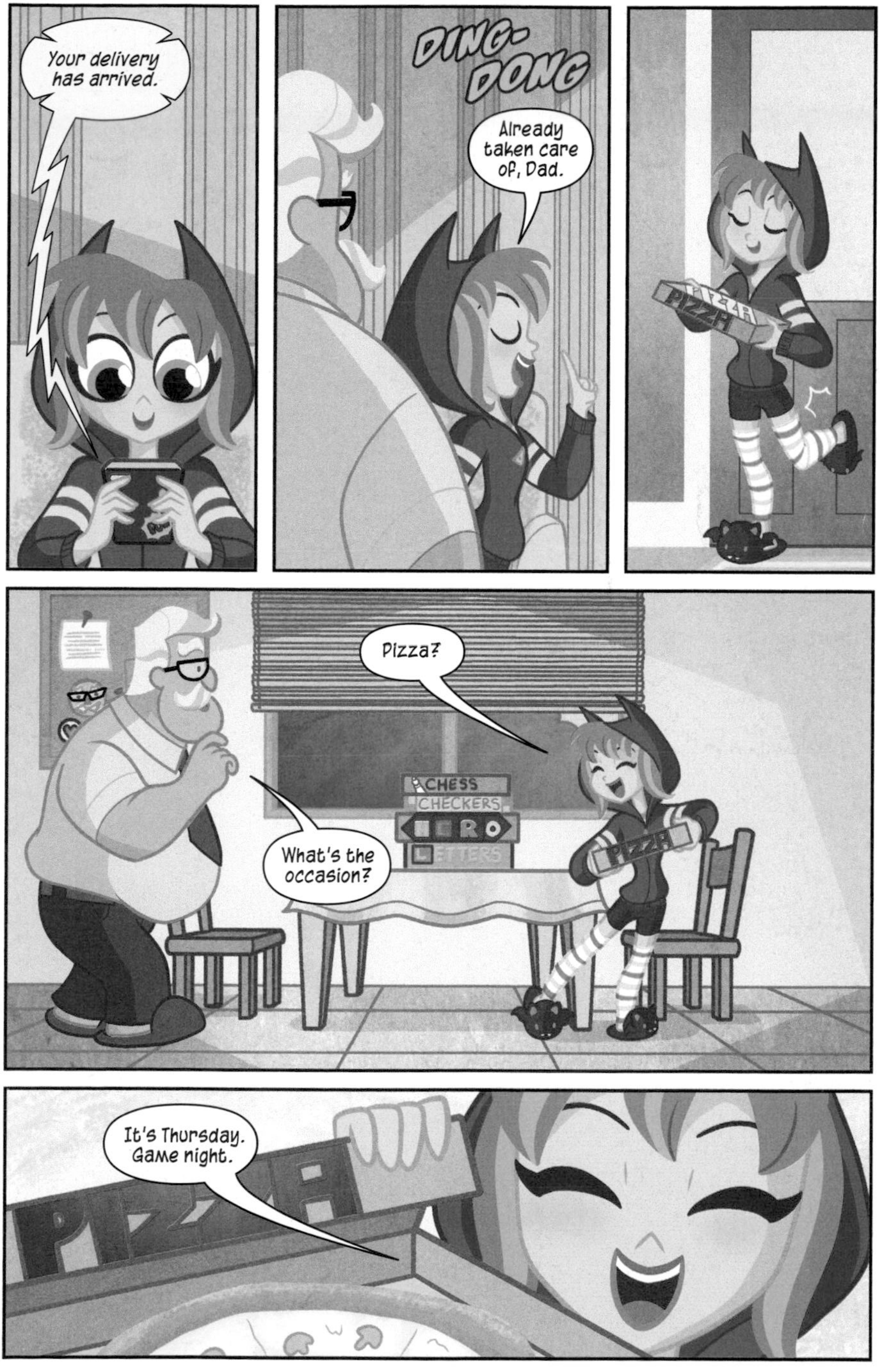
Your delivery has arrived.
DING-DONG
Already taken care of, Dad.
PIZZA
Pizza?
CHESS
CHECKERS
LETTERS
What's the occasion?
It's Thursday. Game night.
PIZZA

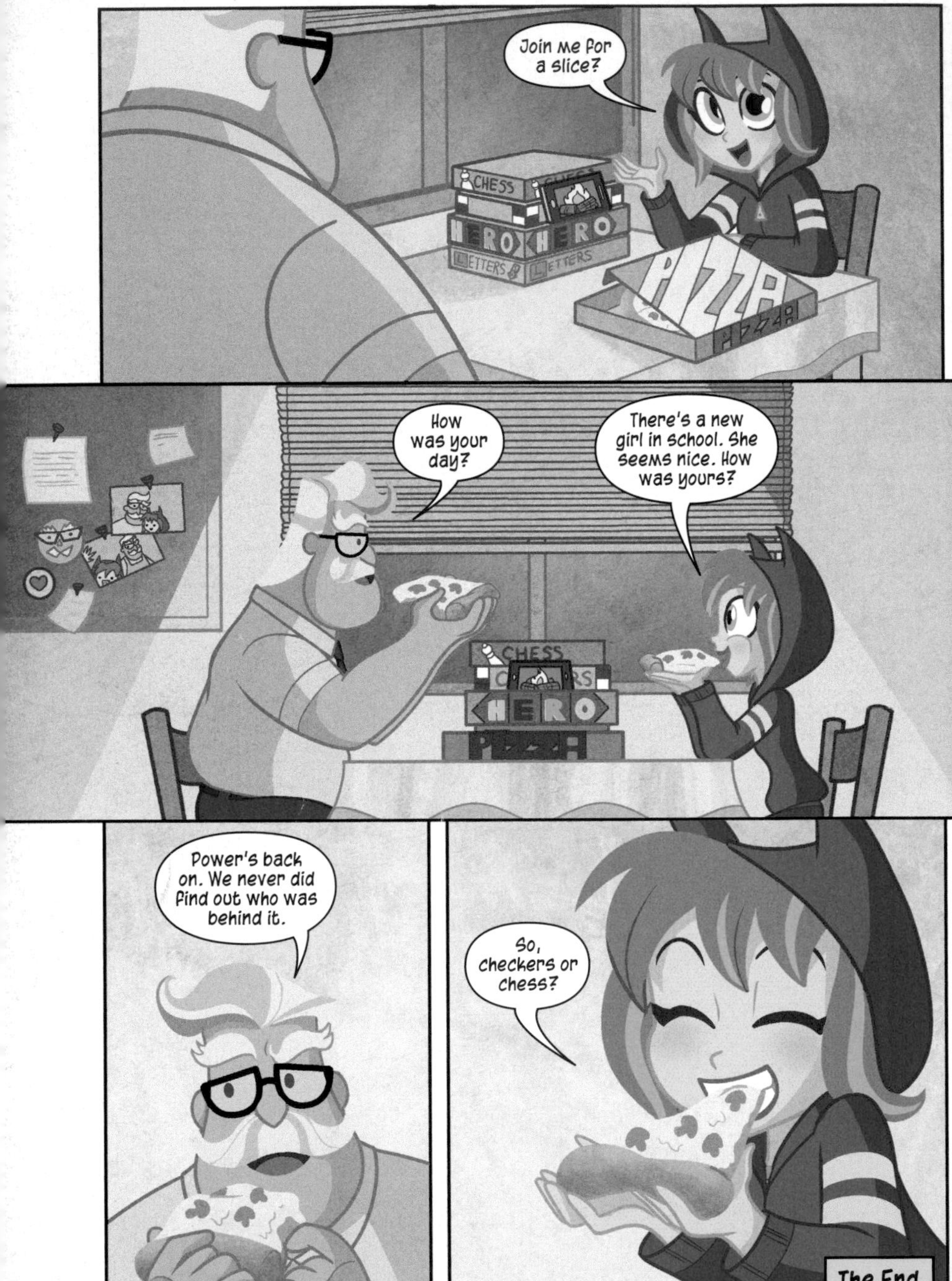
Join me for a slice?
CHESS
HERO HERO
LETTERS LETTERS
PIZZA
How was your day?
There's a new girl in school. She seems nice. How was yours?
CHESS
HERO
Power's back on. We never did find out who was behind it.
So, checkers or chess?
The End

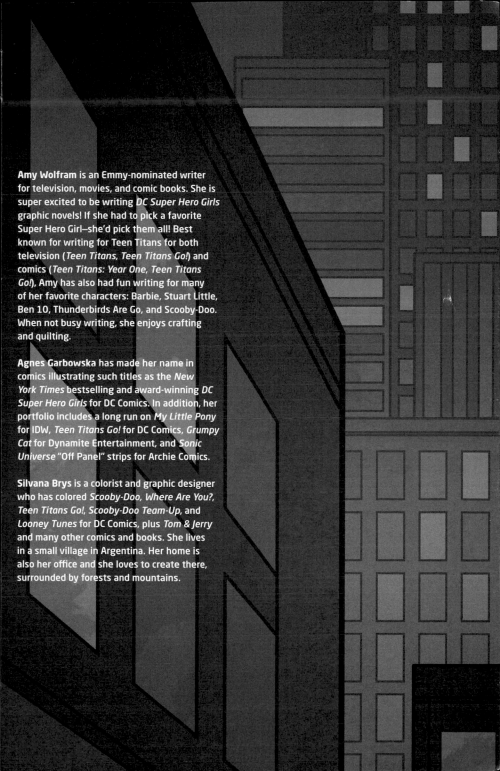

Amy Wolfram is an Emmy-nominated writer for television, movies, and comic books. She is super excited to be writing *DC Super Hero Girls* graphic novels! If she had to pick a favorite Super Hero Girl—she'd pick them all! Best known for writing for Teen Titans for both television (*Teen Titans, Teen Titans Go!*) and comics (*Teen Titans: Year One, Teen Titans Go!*), Amy has also had fun writing for many of her favorite characters: Barbie, Stuart Little, Ben 10, Thunderbirds Are Go, and Scooby-Doo. When not busy writing, she enjoys crafting and quilting.

Agnes Garbowska has made her name in comics illustrating such titles as the *New York Times* bestselling and award-winning *DC Super Hero Girls* for DC Comics. In addition, her portfolio includes a long run on *My Little Pony* for IDW, *Teen Titans Go!* for DC Comics, *Grumpy Cat* for Dynamite Entertainment, and *Sonic Universe* "Off Panel" strips for Archie Comics.

Silvana Brys is a colorist and graphic designer who has colored *Scooby-Doo, Where Are You?*, *Teen Titans Go!*, *Scooby-Doo Team-Up*, and *Looney Tunes* for DC Comics, plus *Tom & Jerry* and many other comics and books. She lives in a small village in Argentina. Her home is also her office and she loves to create there, surrounded by forests and mountains.

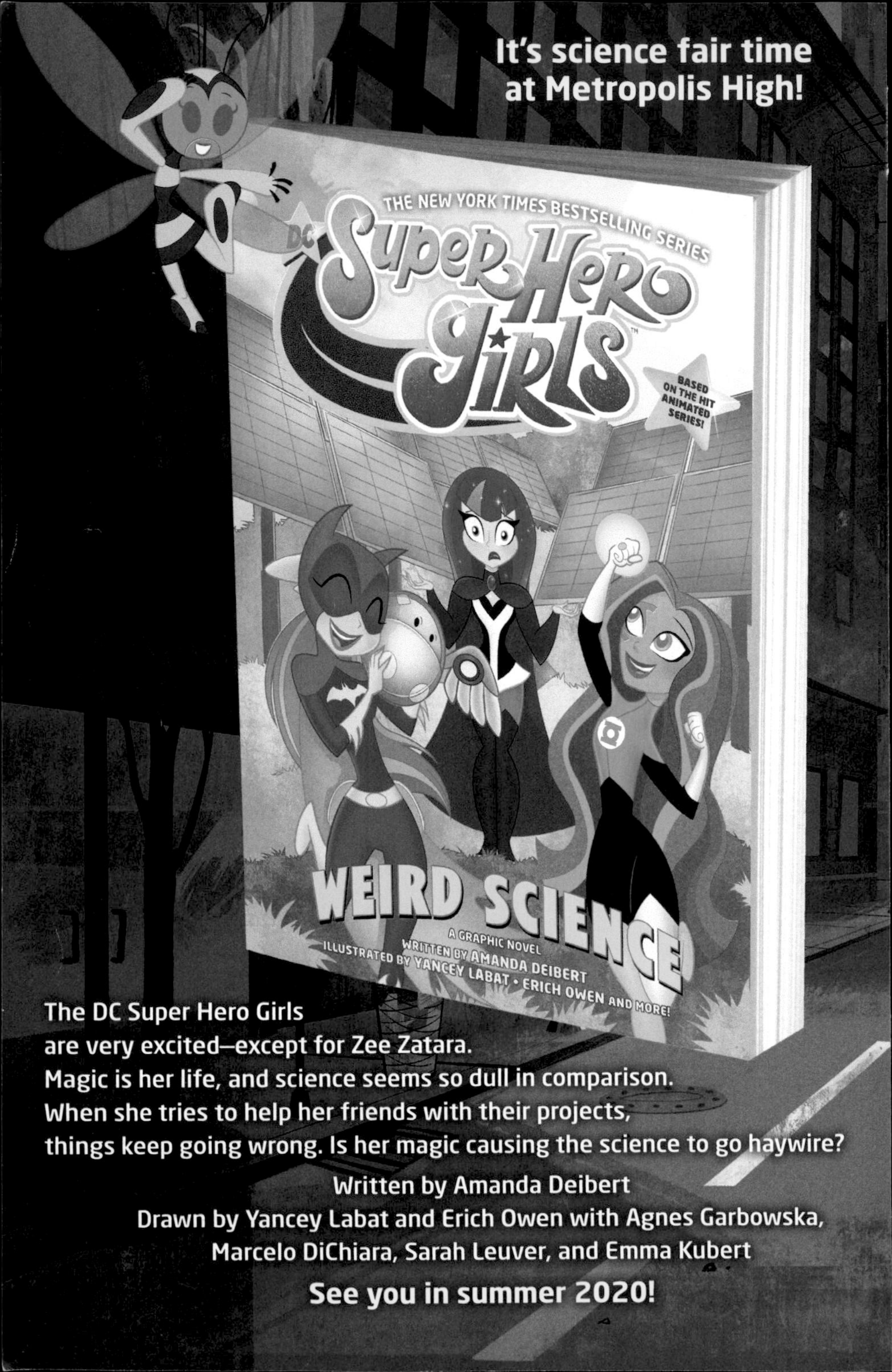
It's science fair time
at Metropolis High!
THE NEW YORK TIMES BESTSELLING SERIES
DC
Super Hero Girls
BASED ON THE HIT ANIMATED SERIES!
WEIRD SCIENCE
A GRAPHIC NOVEL
WRITTEN BY AMANDA DEIBERT
ILLUSTRATED BY YANCEY LABAT • ERICH OWEN AND MORE!
The DC Super Hero Girls
are very excited—except for Zee Zatara.
Magic is her life, and science seems so dull in comparison.
When she tries to help her friends with their projects,
things keep going wrong. Is her magic causing the science to go haywire?
Written by Amanda Deibert
Drawn by Yancey Labat and Erich Owen with Agnes Garbowska,
Marcelo DiChiara, Sarah Leuver, and Emma Kubert
See you in summer 2020!

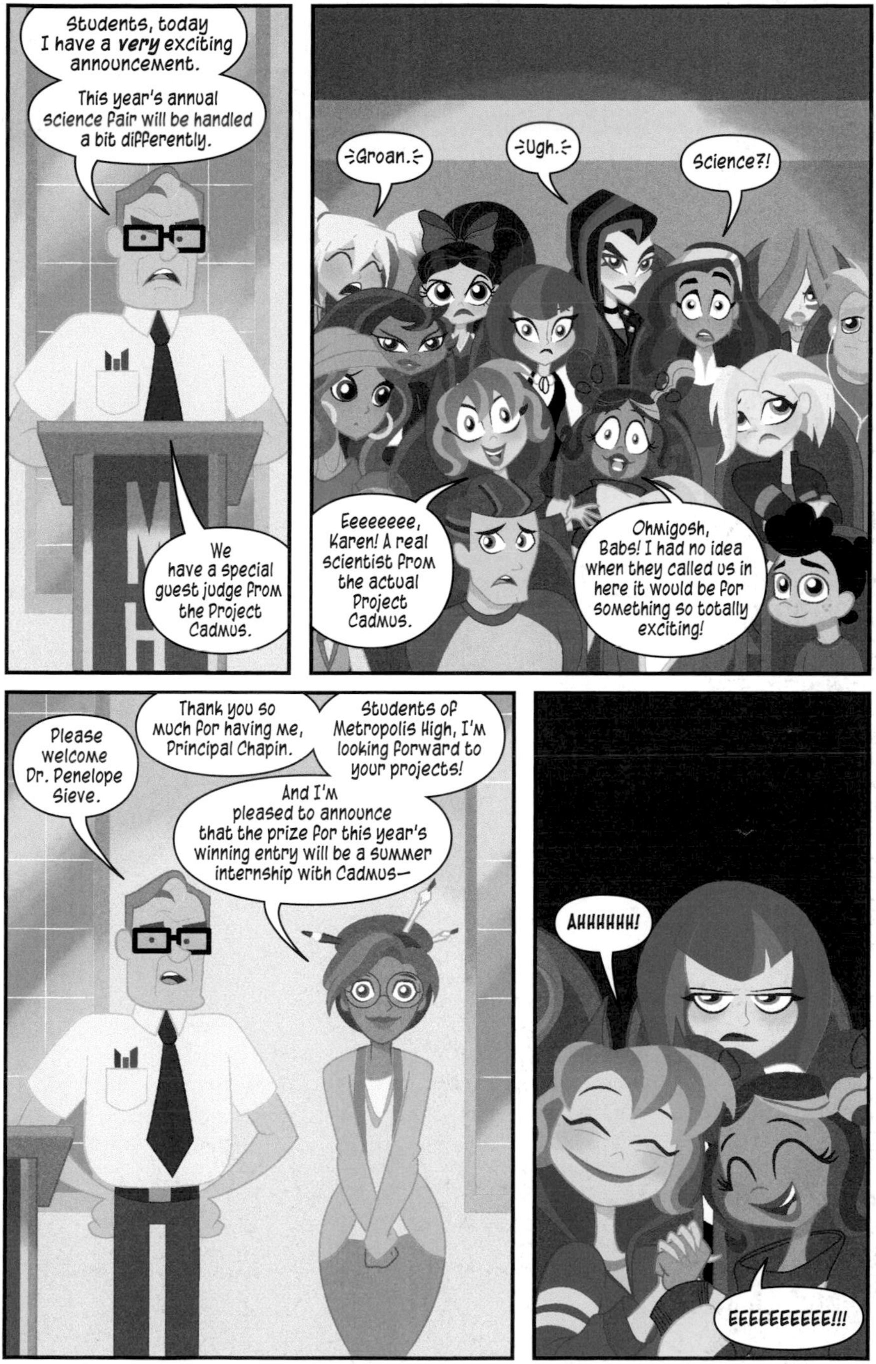
Students, today I have a very exciting announcement.
This year's annual science fair will be handled a bit differently.
We have a special guest judge from the Project Cadmus.
Groan.
Ugh.
Science?!
Eeeeeeee, Karen! A real scientist from the actual Project Cadmus.
Ohmigosh, Babs! I had no idea when they called us in here it would be for something so totally exciting!
Please welcome Dr. Penelope Sieve.
Thank you so much for having me, Principal Chapin.
Students of Metropolis High, I'm looking forward to your projects!
And I'm pleased to announce that the prize for this year's winning entry will be a summer internship with Cadmus—
AHHHHHH!
EEEEEEEEEE!!!

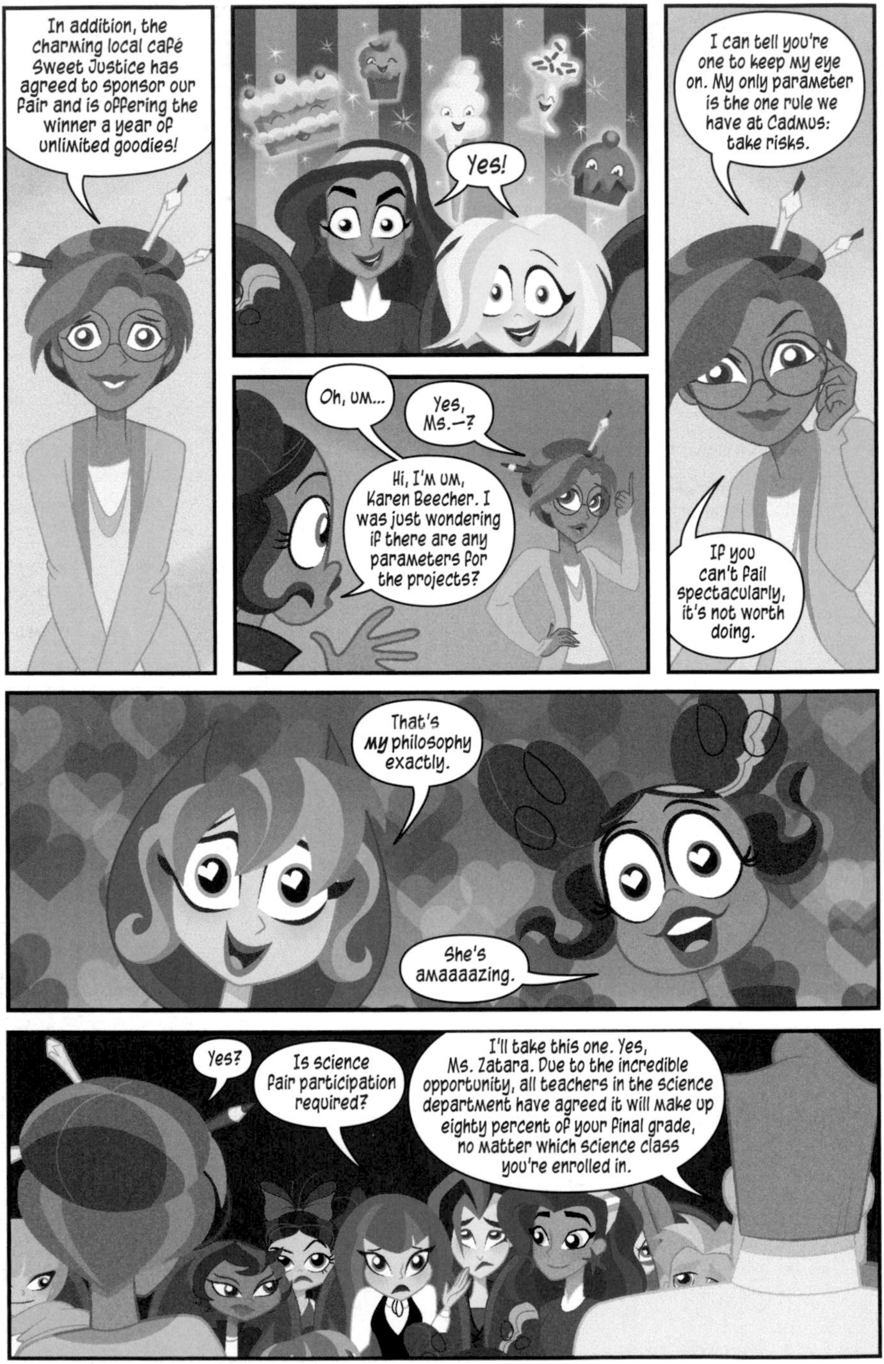
In addition, the charming local café Sweet Justice has agreed to sponsor our fair and is offering the winner a year of unlimited goodies!
Yes!
I can tell you're one to keep my eye on. My only parameter is the one rule we have at Cadmus: take risks.
Oh, um...
Yes, Ms.—?
Hi, I'm um, Karen Beecher. I was just wondering if there are any parameters for the projects?
If you can't fail spectacularly, it's not worth doing.
That's *my* philosophy exactly.
She's amaaaazing.
Yes?
Is science fair participation required?
I'll take this one. Yes, Ms. Zatara. Due to the incredible opportunity, all teachers in the science department have agreed it will make up eighty percent of your final grade, no matter which science class you're enrolled in.

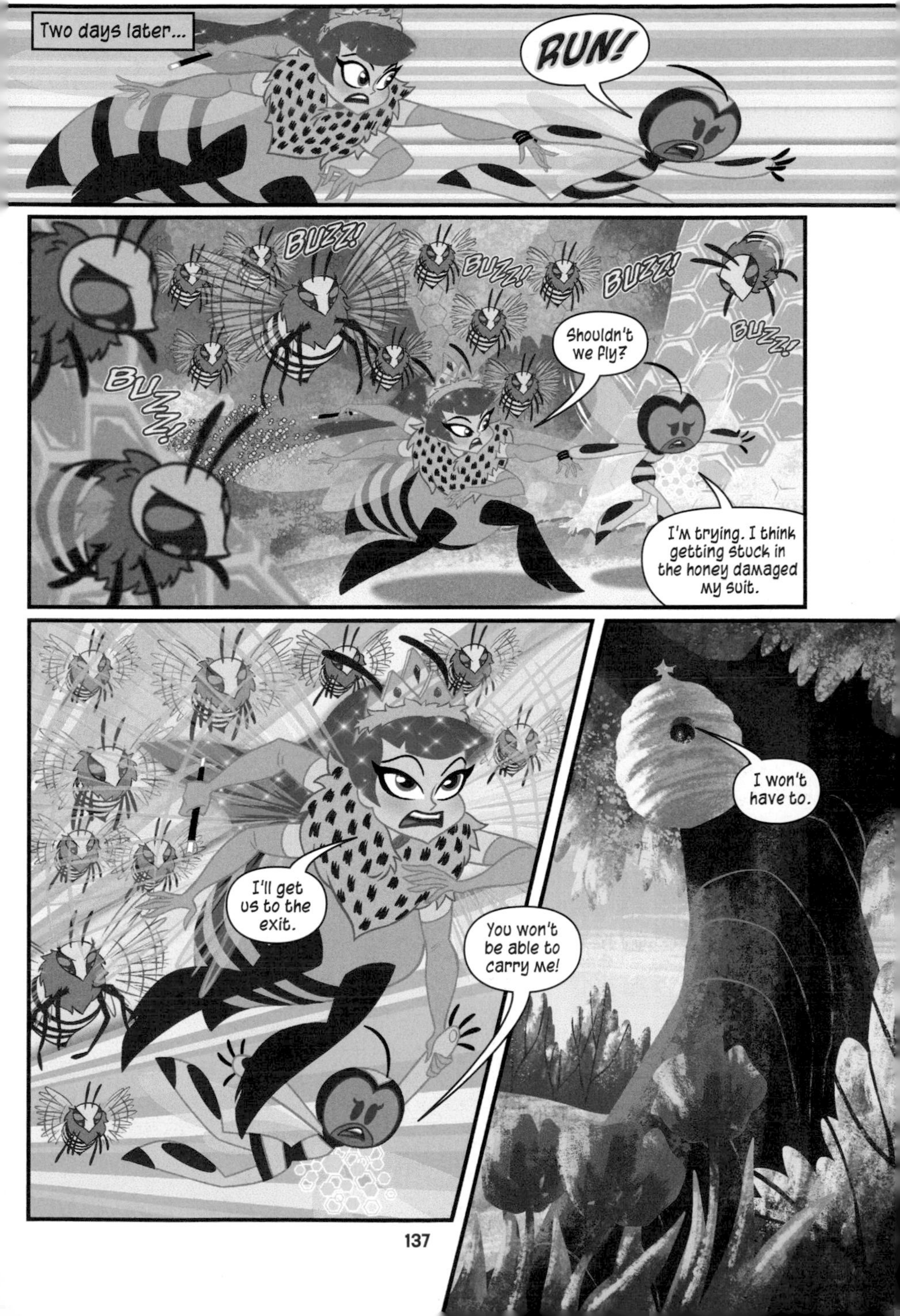
Two days later...
RUN!
BUZZ!
BUZZ!
BUZZ!
BUZZ!
BUZZ!
Shouldn't we fly?
I'm trying. I think getting stuck in the honey damaged my suit.
I'll get us to the exit.
You won't be able to carry me!
I won't have to.

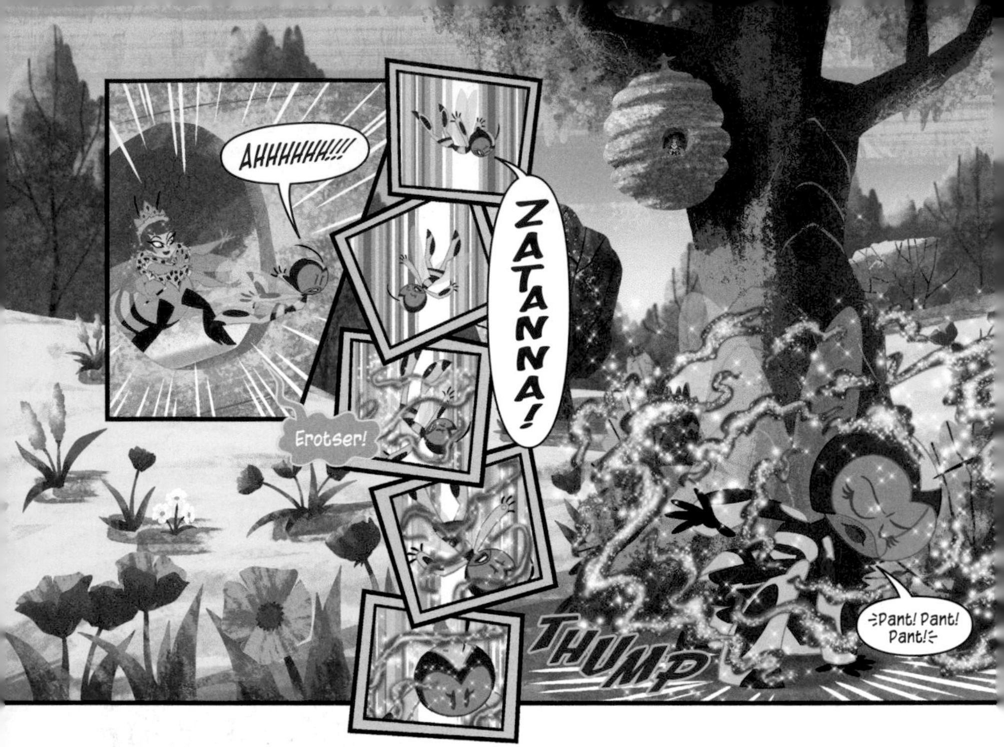
AHHHHHH!!!
ZATANNA!
Erotser!
THUMP
Pant! Pant! Pant!

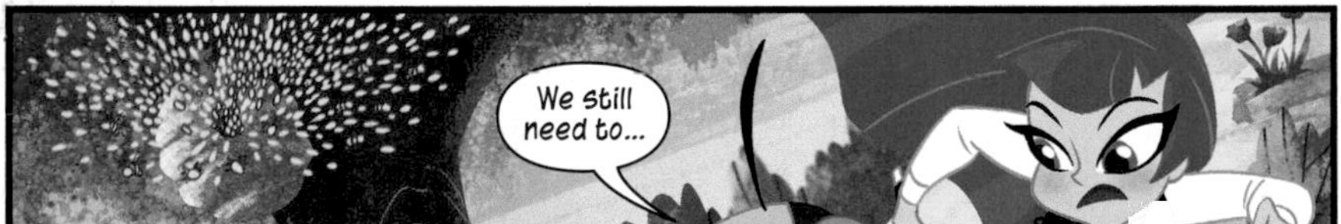
We still need to...

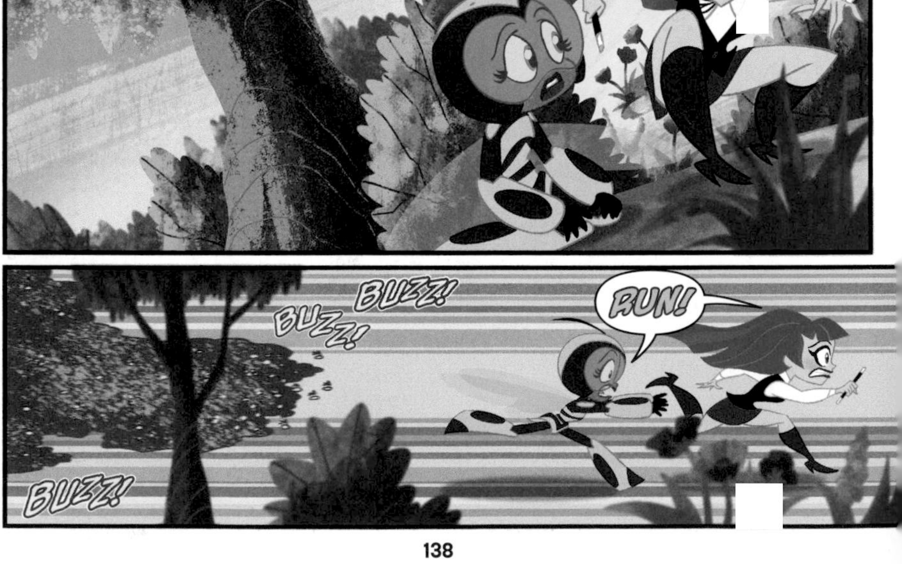
BUZZ!
BUZZ!
RUN!
BUZZ!

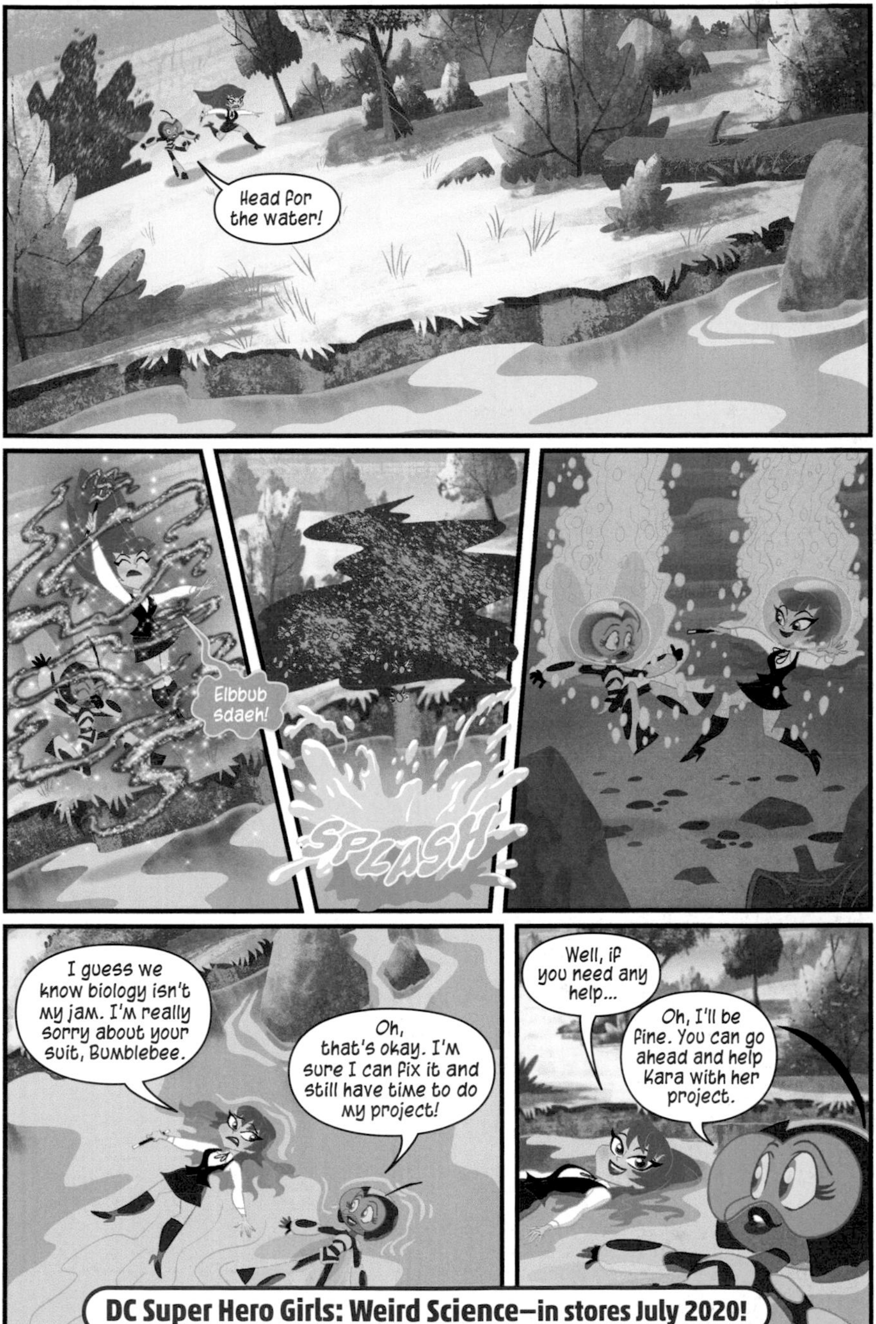
Head for the water!
Elbbub sdaeh!
SPLASH
I guess we know biology isn't my jam. I'm really sorry about your suit, Bumblebee.
Oh, that's okay. I'm sure I can fix it and still have time to do my project!
Well, if you need any help...
Oh, I'll be fine. You can go ahead and help Kara with her project.
DC Super Hero Girls: Weird Science—in stores July 2020!

A super-strong (and super-clumsy) teen meets her match in a (possibly) villainous genius— and neither girl is prepared for the havoc that switching lives will wreak on Gotham!

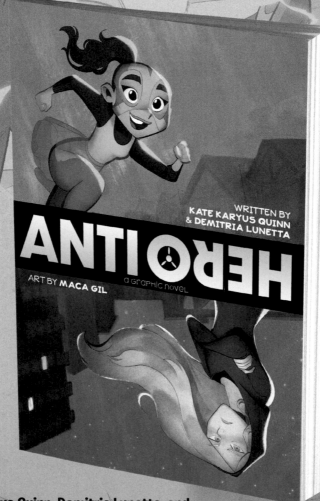

WRITTEN BY
KATE KARYUS QUINN
& DEMITRIA LUNETTA

ANTI HERO
a graphic novel

ART BY MACA GIL

Kate Karyus Quinn, Demitria Lunetta, and Maca Gil introduce new heroes to the DC Universe!

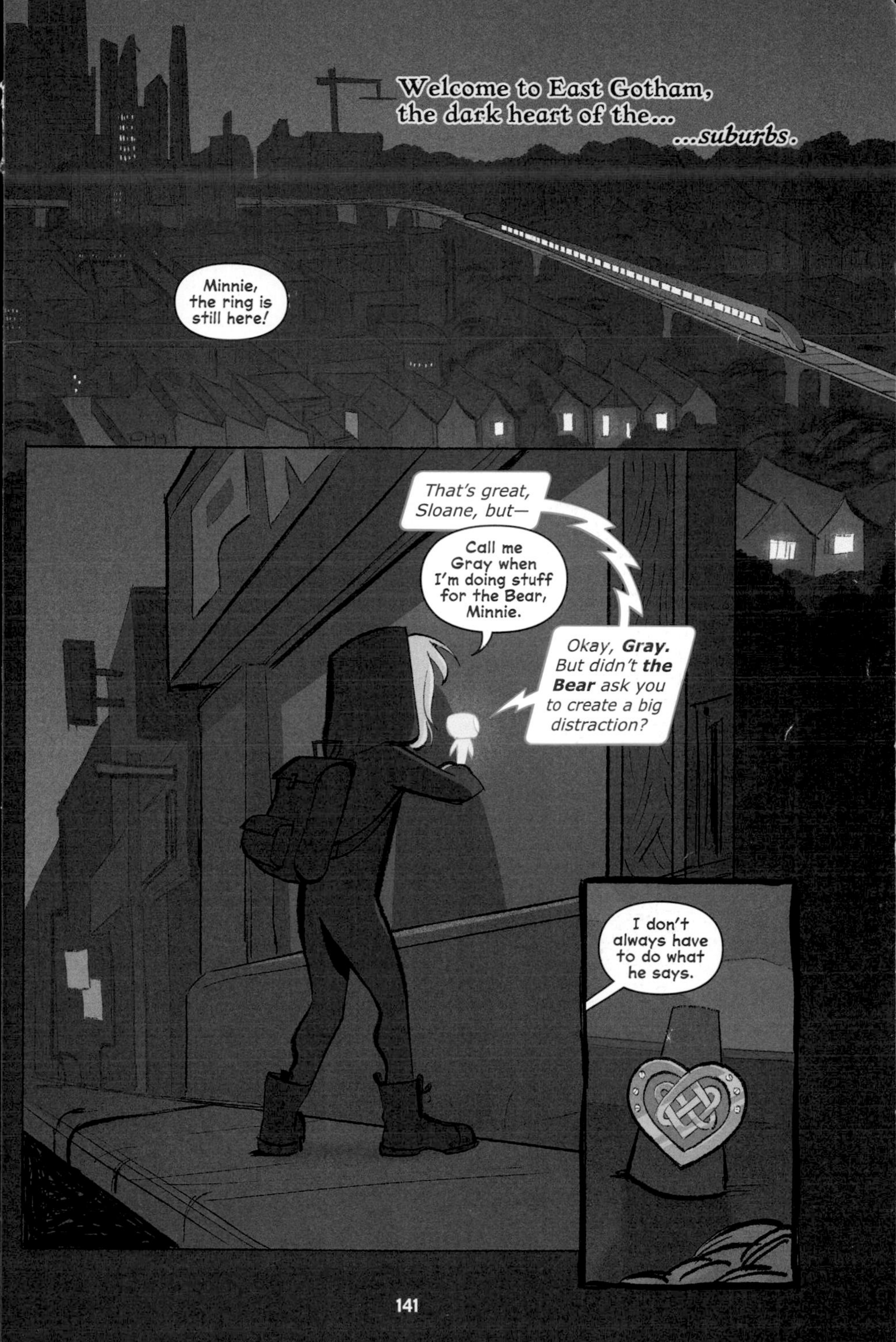
Welcome to East Gotham, the dark heart of the... ...suburbs.
Minnie, the ring is still here!
That's great, Sloane, but—
Call me Gray when I'm doing stuff for the Bear, Minnie.
Okay, **Gray.** But didn't **the Bear** ask you to create a big distraction?
I don't always have to do what he says.

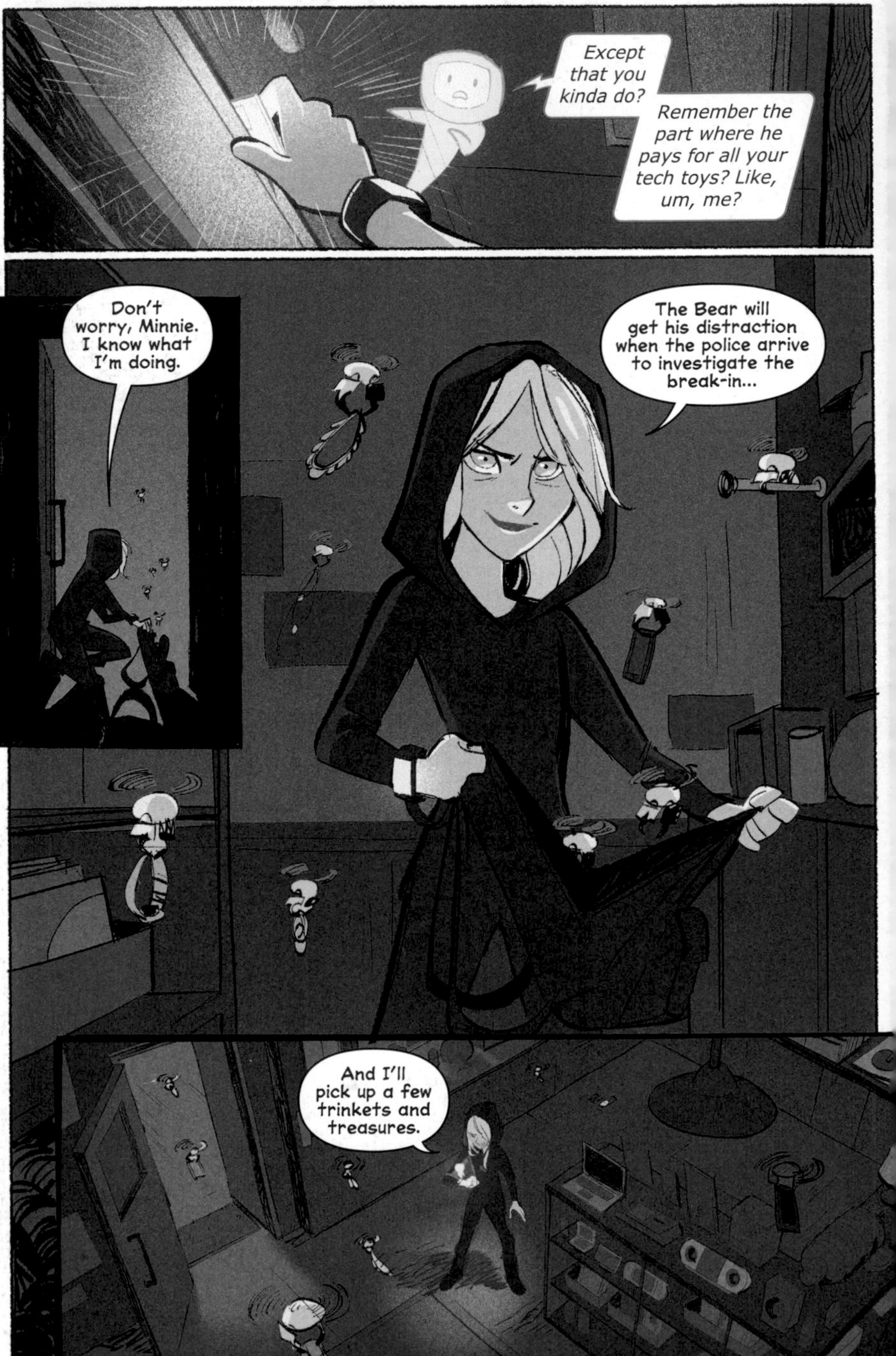
Except that you kinda do?
Remember the part where he pays for all your tech toys? Like, um, me?
Don't worry, Minnie. I know what I'm doing.
The Bear will get his distraction when the police arrive to investigate the break-in...
And I'll pick up a few trinkets and treasures.

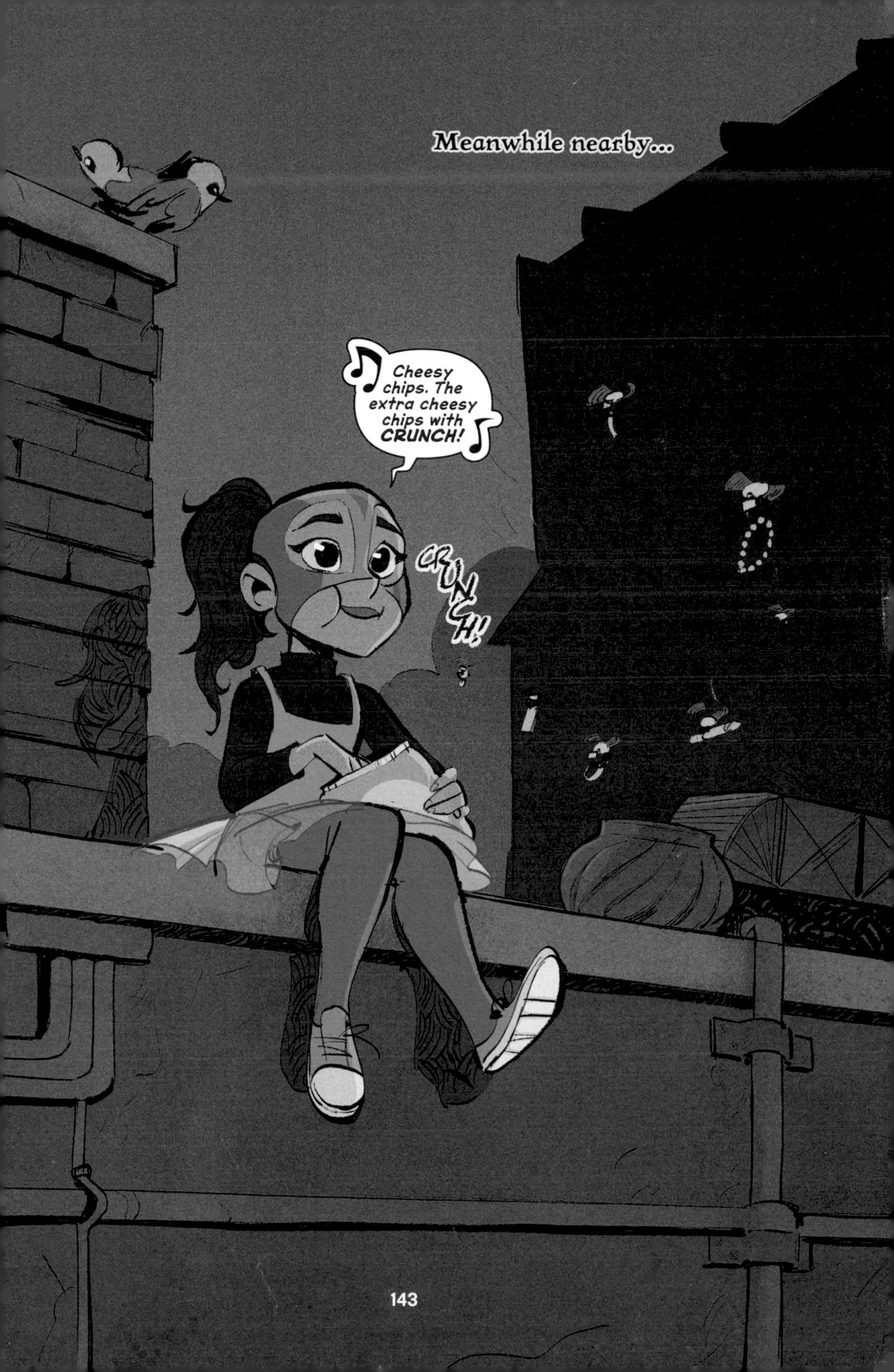
Meanwhile nearby...
Cheesy chips. The extra cheesy chips with CRUNCH!
CRUNCH!

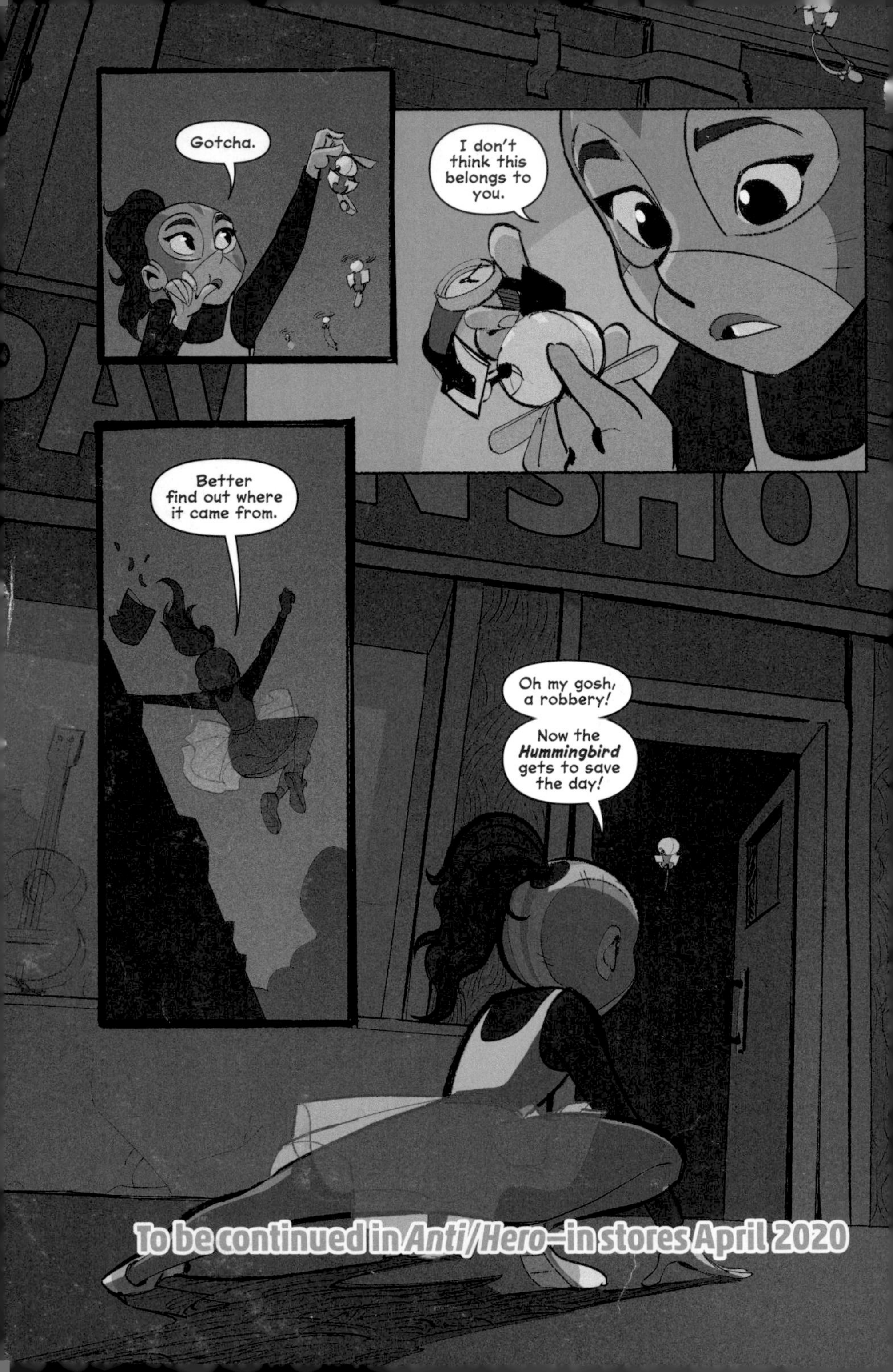
Gotcha.
I don't think this belongs to you.
Better find out where it came from.
Oh my gosh, a robbery!
Now the *Hummingbird* gets to save the day!
To be continued in *Anti/Hero*—in stores April 2020